CRITICAL ACCLAIM FOR THE NOVELS OF STEVEN PRESSFIELD

THE VIRTUES OF WAR

"The story of Alexander the Great is perhaps the greatest tale of battle and glory in human history, and Steven Pressfield tells it in brilliant, thrilling fashion. I turned the pages so fast I didn't realize how much I was learning."
—Vince Flynn, author of *Memorial Day*

"If you want to know what it might have felt like to ride into battle with Alexander, read this striking book. From the mad rush of the cavalry to the trumpet of the war elephants, and from the solid bronze wall of the phalanx to the melee around the royal chariot, Pressfield has it all. *The Virtues of War* blends a scholar's accuracy and a novelist's eye."
—Barry Strauss, author of *The Battle of Salamis* and Professor of History and Classics, Cornell University

"Steven Pressfield has created a cracking, fast-paced contemporary retelling of the legend that is Alexander. This man was the greatest warrior of his time, possibly of all time, and Pressfield brings him alive for the modern audience with the verve and skill with which he conjured the heroes of Thermopylae in *Gates of Fire*. His first-person Alexander is a man who lives with the heart-blood of war flowing in every vein; he's a hero, a general, a diplomat, and a scholar, but first and always, he is a warrior, a man who strives to hold his own integrity in the hardest of fields. Now more than ever, we need to remember what it is to live with integrity in the face of adversity. Steven Pressfield reminds us in style."
—Manda Scott, author of *Boudica: Dreaming the Eagle*

"In *The Virtues of War* Pressfield has tackled a subject worthy of his enormous talent . . . and triumphed again."
—Stephen Coonts, author of *Liars & Thieves*

"Pressfield continues with his top-quality historicals about classic antiquity. Pressfield, deft and graceful as always in his historical authenticity, creates an Alexander so understandable, personable, and psychologically modern that, for the only very occasionally doubting reader, the pleasure of sitting back and letting the tale go by is as great as usual in the company of this author . . . historical drama from Pressfield again ranks among the best and finest."
—*Kirkus Reviews*

"Acclaimed historical novelist Pressfield turns his attention to the ever-fascinating life of Alexander the Great. The rapidly paced first-person narrative is distinguished by Alexander's own matter-of-fact voice. . . . This splendid fictional biography is calculated to appeal to antiquarians, Grecophiles, and fans of a darn good read."
—*Booklist*

LAST OF THE AMAZONS

"[A] splendid tale of valor, honor and comradeship memorializes those women whose lives and deeds have faded into the mists of legend. Highly recommended."
—*Library Journal*

"Pressfield presents a love story so grand it pits nations against one another. Pressfield's javelin is his pen and he wields it well in this gruesome tale of ancient bloodlust in an age when there is no word for mercy."
—*Publishers Weekly*

"The best book of the summer, fascinating in its detail, precise in its logic, well-paced, sad, and, another Pressfield trademark, gory."
—*Detroit Free Press*

"The battles are as gripping, realistic, vivid, and detailed as ever; the extremities that lives are driven to are just as unflinchingly portrayed as in the earlier books; and the complex panorama of culture, alliances, betrayals, calamity, and despair is as perfectly realized as before."
—*Kirkus Reviews*

STEVEN PRESSFIELD

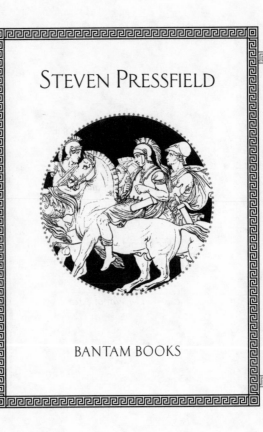

BANTAM BOOKS

The Virtues of
WAR

A Novel of
Alexander
the Great

THE VIRTUES OF WAR
A Bantam Book

PUBLISHING HISTORY
Doubleday hardcover edition published November 2004
Bantam trade paperback edition / October 2005

Published by
Bantam Dell
A Division of Random House, Inc.
New York, New York

Cover illustration: *The Sabine Women Halting the Battle Between Romans and Sabines*
by Jacques-Louis David, 1799. Erich Lessing/Art Resource
Maps by David Cain
Book design by Terry Karydes

Library of Congress Catalog Card Number: 2004050038

ISBN-13: 978-0-553-38205-1
ISBN-10: 0-553-38205-5

Printed in the United States of America
Published simultaneously in Canada

www.bantamdell.com

BVG 10 9 8 7 6 5 4 3 2

For Mike and Chrissy

Black Sea

THRACE

Bosporus

Perinthus • Byzantium

• Chalcedon

Propontis

• Dascylium

• Abydos

Granicus River

• Troy

Hellespont

MYSIA

Gordium •→

LESBOS

• Mytilene

LYDIA

GREATER

PHRYGIA

CHIOS

IONIA

• Sardis

• Ephesus

PISIDIA

Miletus •

CARIA

Halicarnassus •

LYCIA

• Phaselis

RHODES

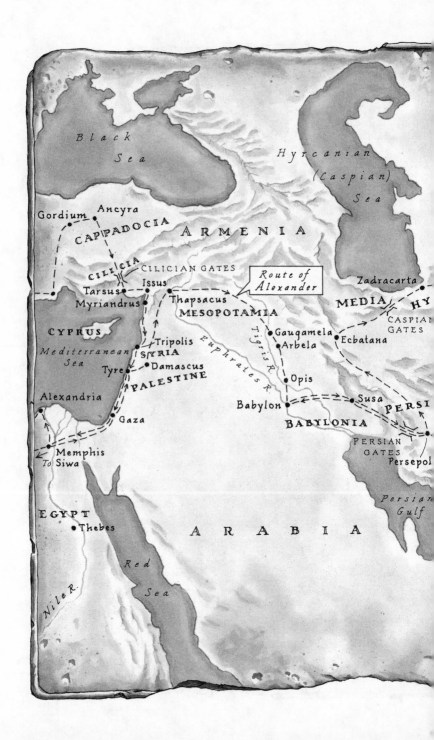

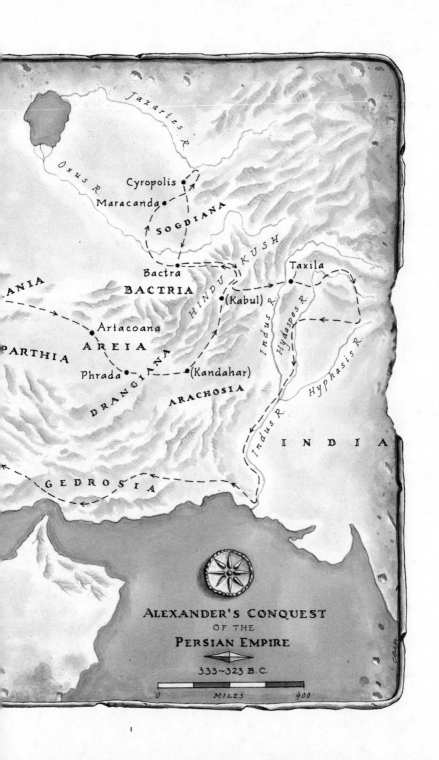

ALEXANDER'S CONQUEST
OF THE
PERSIAN EMPIRE

333~323 B.C.

0   MILES   400

DRAMATIS PERSONAE

Alexander, son of Philip	King of Macedon, conqueror of Persian empire
Philip of Macedon	Alexander's father, extraordinary general in his own right
Olympias	Philip's wife, Alexander's mother
Cyrus the Great	Founder of Persian empire, circa 547 B.C.
Darius III	Great King of Persia, defeated by Alexander
Epaminondas	General of Thebes, inventor of the "oblique order"
Parmenio	Philip and Alexander's senior general
Antipater	Senior Macedonian general, garrisoned Greece
Antigonus One-Eye	"Monophthalmos," senior general
Aristotle	Philosopher, tutor of Alexander
Hephaestion	Alexander's general and dearest friend
Telamon	Arcadian mercenary, friend and mentor to Alexander
Craterus	Alexander's general
Perdiccas	Alexander's general
Ptolemy	Alexander's general; later dynast of Egypt
Seleucus	Alexander's general
Coenus	Alexander's general
Eumenes	Alexander's Counselor-at-War
Leonnatus	Alexander's friend and bodyguard

Philotas — Parmenio's son; Commander of
Companion Cavalry

Nicanor — Parmenio's son; Commander of
Royal Guards brigades

Black Cleitus — Commander of Royal Squadron of Companion
Cavalry; murdered by Alexander in Maracanda

Roxanne — Alexander's Bactrian bride, "Little Star"

Itanes — Roxanne's brother; later a Royal Page in
Alexander's service and, later still,
a companion

Oxyartes — Bactrian warlord, father of Roxanne

Memnon of Rhodes — Greek mercenary general, commander
under Darius

Barsine — Alexander's mistress, daughter of Artabazus,
widow of Memnon

Artabazus — Persian noble, father of Barsine;
Alexander's satrap of Bactria

Bessus — Darius's satrap of Bactria, commander of the
Persian left at Gaugamela; murderer of Darius
and pretender to the throne

Mazaeus — Satrap of Mesopotamia, commander of the
Persian right at Gaugamela; later Alexander's
governor of Babylonia

Spitamenes — Rebel commander in Bactria and Sogdiana

Bucephalus — Alexander's horse

Porus — King of Punjab in India; defeated by Alexander at
Battle of Hydaspes River

Tigranes — Persian cavalry commander, later friend
of Alexander

A NOTE TO THE READER

What follows is fiction, not history. Scenes and characters have been invented; license has been taken. Words have been put into the mouths of historical figures, which are entirely the product of the author's imagination.

Although nothing in this telling is untrue to the spirit of Alexander's life as I understand it, still I have transposed certain historical events in the interest of the theme and the storytelling. The speech that Arrian tells us Alexander gave at Opis, I have made his eulogy for Philip. I have Parmenio in Ecbatana, when Curtius tells us he was still at Persepolis. The harangue that I have Alexander delivering at the Hydaspes, he actually made at the Hyphasis, while the plea of his men, which Arrian tells us Coenus voiced at the latter, I have him offering at the former. I note this so that the knowledgeable reader will not believe that events are migrating perversely of their own will.

I have taken the liberty of using, on occasion, contemporary place names, such as Afghanistan, the Danube, and words such as miles, yards, acres, which obviously did not exist in Alexander's time, as well as such latter-day concepts as chivalry, mutiny, knight, guerrilla, and others, which technically have no equivalent in Greco-Macedonian thought but which, in my judgment, communicate to the modern reader so vividly and so closely in spirit to the ancient import that their employment may be by the purist, perhaps, forgiven.

He ruled over these nations, even though they did not speak the same language as he, nor one nation the same as another; for all that, he was able to cover so vast a region with the fear which he inspired, that he struck all men with terror and no one tried to withstand him; and he was able to awaken in all so lively a desire to please him, that they always wished to be guided by his will.

—XENOPHON, "THE EDUCATION OF CYRUS"

Book One

THE WILL TO FIGHT

One

A SOLDIER

I HAVE ALWAYS BEEN A SOLDIER. I HAVE KNOWN NO OTHER LIFE. The calling of arms, I have followed from boyhood. I have never sought another.

I have known lovers, sired offspring, competed in games, and committed outrages when drunk. I have vanquished empires, yoked continents, been crowned as an immortal before gods and men. But always I have been a soldier.

From the time I was a boy, I fled my tutor to seek the company of the men in the barracks. The drill field and the stable, the smell of leather and sweat, these are congenial to me. The scrape of the whetstone on iron is to me what music is to poets. It has always been this way. I can remember no time when it was otherwise.

One such as myself must have learned much, a fellow might think, from campaign and experience. Yet I may state in candor: All that I know, I knew at thirteen and, truth to tell, at ten and younger. Nothing has come to me as a grown commander that I did not apprehend as a child.

As a boy I instinctively understood the ground, the march, the occasion, and the elements. I comprehended the crossing of rivers and the exploitation of terrain; how many units of what composition may traverse such and such a distance, how swiftly, bearing how much kit, arriving in what condition to fight. The drawing up of troops came as second nature to me: I simply looked; all showed itself clear. My father was the greatest soldier of his day, perhaps the greatest ever. Yet when I was ten I informed him that I would excel him. By twenty-three I had done so.

As a lad I was jealous of my father, fearing that he would achieve glory on such a scale as would leave none for me. I have never feared anything, save that mischance that would prevent me from fulfilling my destiny.

The army it has been my privilege to lead has been invincible across Europe and Asia. It has united the states of Greece and the islands of the Aegean; liberated from the Persian yoke the Greek cities of Ionia and Aeolia. It has brought into subjection Armenia, Cappadocia, both Lesser and Greater Phrygia, Paphlagonia, Caria, Lydia, Pisidia, Lycia, Pamphylia, both Hollow and Mesopotamian Syria, and Cilicia. The great strongholds of Phoenicia—Byblus, Sidon, Tyre, and the Philistine city of Gaza—have fallen before it. It has vanquished the central empire of Persia—Egypt and nearer Arabia, Mesopotamia, Babylonia, Media, Susiana, the rugged land of Persia herself—and the eastern provinces of Hyrcania, Areia, Parthia, Bactria, Tapuria, Drangiana, Arachosia, and Sogdiana. It has crossed the Hindu Kush into India. It has never been beaten.

This force has been insuperable not for its numbers, for in every campaign it has entered the field outmounted and outmanned; nor for the brilliance of its generalship or tactics, though these have not been inconsiderable; nor for the proficiency of its supply train and logistical corps, without which no force in the field can survive, let alone prevail. Rather, this army has succeeded because of qualities of warriorship in its individual soldiers, specifically that property expressed by the Greek word *dynamis*, "the will to fight." No general of this or any age has been so favored by fortune as I, to lead such men, possessed of such warlike spirit, imbued with such resources of self-enterprise, committed so to their commanders and to their call.

Yet now what I have feared most has come to pass. The men themselves have grown weary of conquest. They draw up on the bank of this river of India, and they fail of passion to cross it. They have come too far, they believe. It is enough. They want to go home.

For the first time since I acceded to command, I have found it necessary to constitute a unit of the army as *Atactoi*—"Malcontents"—and to segregate them from the central divisions of the corps. Nor are these fellows renegades or habitual delinquents, but crack troops, decorated veterans—many of whom trained under my father and his great general Parmenio—who have become so disaffected, from actions and words taken or omitted by me, that I can station them in the battle line only between units of unimpeachable loyalty, lest they prove false in the fatal hour. This day I have been compelled to execute five of their officers, homegrown Macedonians all, whose families are dear to me, for failure to promptly carry out an order. I hate this, not only for the barbarity of the measure but also for the deficiency of imagination it signalizes in me. Must I lead now by terror and compulsion? Is this the state to which my genius has been reduced?

When I was sixteen and rode for the first time at the head of my own corps of cavalry, I was so overcome that I could not stay myself from weeping. My adjutant grew alarmed and begged to know what discomfited me. But the horsemen in their squadrons understood. I was moved by the sight of them in such brilliant order, by their scars and their silence, the weathered creasing of their faces. When the men saw my state, they returned my devotion, for they knew I would burst my heart for them. In strategy and tactics, even in valor, other commanders may be my equal. But in this, none surpasses me: the measure of my love for my comrades. I love even those who call themselves my enemies. Alone meanness and malice I despise. But the foe who stands with gallantry, him I draw to my breast, dear as a brother.

Those who do not understand war believe it contention between armies, friend against foe. No. Rather friend and foe duel as one against an unseen antagonist, whose name is Fear, and seek, even entwined in death, to mount to that promontory whose ensign is honor.

What drives the soldier is *cardia*, "heart," and *dynamis*, "the will to fight." Nothing else matters in war. Not weapons or tactics, philosophy or patriotism, not fear of the gods themselves. Only this love of glory, which is the seminal imperative of mortal blood, as ineradicable within man as in a wolf or a lion, and without which we are nothing.

Look out there, Itanes. Somewhere beyond that river lies the Shore of Ocean: the Ends of the Earth. How far? Past the Ganges? Across the Range of Perpetual Snows? I can feel it. It calls me. There I must stand, where no prince has stood before me. There I must plant the lion standard of Macedon. Not till then will I grant rest to my heart or release to this army.

That is why I have called you here, my young friend. Days, I can keep up a front, knowing the men's eyes are on me. But nights, the crisis of the army overwhelms me.

I must unburden myself. I must reorder my thoughts. I must find an answer to the corps's alienation.

I need someone I can talk to, someone who stands outside the chain of command, who can listen without judgment and keep his mouth shut. You are my bride Roxanne's younger brother and, as such, beneath my protection only. No other may be your mentor, to no other may you carry this tale. These are my motives of confidentiality. As well, I recognize in you (for I have watched you closely since you came into my service in Afghanistan) that instinct of command and gift for war that no amount of schooling may impart. You are eighteen and will soon receive your commission. When we cross this river, you will lead men in battle for the first time. It is my role to instruct you, for, though prince you be in your own country, here you are only a Page, a cadet in the academy of war which is my tent.

Will you stay and hear my tale? I shall not compel you, for such confidences as I must disclose in attempting to reorder my priorities may place you in peril, not now while I live, but later, for they who succeed me will seek to employ your testimony for their own ends.

Will you serve your king and kinsman? Say aye and you shall come to me each evening at this hour, or at such interval as may suit my convenience. You need not speak, only listen, though I may employ you as the occasion demands upon errands of trust or discretion. Say nay and I release you now, with no hard feelings.

You are honored to serve, you say?

Well, my young friend.

Sit then. Let us begin. . . .

Two

MY COUNTRY

M Y COUNTRY IS A RUGGED AND MOUNTAINOUS PLACE. I came out of it when I was twenty-one. I will never go back.

The great estates of Macedon's plains produce horsemen who call themselves Greeks, descendants of the sons of Heracles. The mountaineers are of Paeonian and Illyrian stock. Infantry comes from the mountains, cavalry from the plains.

Great clefts transect my country's uplands into natural cantons, spectacularly defensible, which themselves are divided into mountain valleys called "creases" or "runs." A run is a watershed; what "runs" is the rill or wash. One vale may contain a dozen runs; each has its clan and each clan hates every other.

The law of my country is *phratreris*. This means "feud warfare." Custom forbids a man to marry within his crease; he must court a maiden from another. If her father will not give his consent, the suitor steals the maid. Now the bride's kin mount a raid to take her back. No end of bloodshed is produced by this, and of saga and ballad. I have heard melodies all over the world, yet none more haunting than those of the mountains of my home. The songs are of feuds and lovers' quarrels, of loss and heartbreak and revenge.

The love a highlander bears for his crease is irrational and ineffaceable. I have officers whose fortunes exceed those of rajahs; yet each dreams of nothing grander than to return to his crease and tell his tales around the fire. Look there, to those three soldiers beside the stacked arms. They are from the same crease. Two are brothers; the third is their uncle. See the four beyond? They are from a rival crease. If they were home now, these fellows could not sleep, hatching schemes to split one another's skulls. Yet here in this far country they are the best of mates.

The Greek of the south grows to manhood in a *polis*, a city-state with a marketplace, an assembly, and walls of stone to keep out the foe. He is a good talker but a poor fighter. The plainsman of Scythia lives on horseback, trailing his stock and the seasonal grass. He is savage but not strong.

Ah, but the hill clansman. Tough as dirt, mean as a snake, here is a man whose belly you can split with a pike of iron and he'll still crawl back to carve out your heart and eat it raw before your face. The mountain man is proud; he will rend your liver over a trifle. Yet he knows how to obey. His father has schooled him by the oxhide of his belt.

Here is the stock of which great soldiers are made. My father understood this. Once in the high country when I offered a smart remark of some clay-eating creaseman, Philip snatched me short. "My son has fallen under the spell of Homer's Achilles," he remarked to Parmenio and Telamon at his side (both of whom served my father before they served me). "He cites his descent from the hero—by his mother's blood, not mine—and dreams of assembling his own corps of Myrmidons, the invincible 'ant men' who followed 'the best of the Achaeans' to Troy." Philip laughed and swatted me gaily across the thigh. "Who do you imagine Achilles' men were, my son, except raw bastards like these? Clansmen from the hinter creases of Thessaly, rude and unlettered, soaked in spirits, and hard as a centaur's hoof."

Men are hard in my country, and women harder. My father understood this too. He paid court to these lasses of the uplands, or, more accurately, to their fathers, whose friendship and fealty he secured by all means. Thirty-nine marriages he made, seven official, by my mother's count; the tally of his brats may only be guessed at. There is an old jest of my army's loyalty: Of course they will not desert me; they are all my half brothers.

When I was twelve, my dear mate Hephaestion and I accompanied a recruiting party under my father to a crease called Triessa in the highlands above Hyperasopian Mara. Horses may not be ridden into such rugged country; their legs will break. One must use mules. My father had invited the clans from a number of contending runs. They all showed up, all drunk. Philip was born to rule such men. He boasted that he could "outdrink, outfight, and outfuck" the lot, and he could. The clansmen loved him. It was just after dark; a pig-riding contest was in progress. A sow the size of a small pony had broken loose; men and boys, mud-slathered, attempted to bring her down. Hephaestion and I looked on from the ring of the stone corral as one rogue with great mustaches flung himself upon the beast's neck. His mates began daring him to mount the sow and have intercourse with her. My father seconded this with exuberance, himself shit-faced and waist-deep in the slough. Cataracts of hilarity descended as the mustached fellow wrestled the sow in the slop. When the act had been accomplished, the luckless beast was butchered. The banquet of its flesh went on all night.

As we rode home next day, I asked my father how he could countenance such brutishness in men he would soon lead into battle. "War," he replied, "is a brutish business."

This response struck me as outrageous. "I would sooner have the sow," I declared, "than the man."

Philip laughed. "You will not win battles, my son, leading an army of sows."

It was my father's genius to forge these carlish highlanders into a disciplined modern army. He perceived the utility of recruiting such clansmen, who had been enslaved for centuries by their own vices and vendettas, to a new conception of soldiering, in which station and birth counted for nothing, but where a man might make his career on guts alone, and within whose order the very qualities that had held the hillman in chains—his own clannishness, brutishness, ignorance, and implacability—would be transformed into the warrior virtues of loyalty, obedience, dedication, and the ruthless application of force and terror.

From the time I was a child, it was acknowledged that Philip's Macedonians were the fiercest fighters on earth. Not only because they were individually tough, reared in this harsh and flinty land, or that my father and his great generals Parmenio and Antipater had drilled them to thoroughgoing professionalism, so that in discipline and cohesion, speed and mobility, tactics and weaponry, they surpassed all the militia armies of Greece and the royal and conscript levies of Asia, but also because they were possessed of such *dynamis*, such will to fight, born of their poverty and their hatred of the contempt with which their rivals had held them before Philip came, that it could be said truly of this force, as of none save the Spartans before them, that in action they never asked how many were the enemy but only where were they.

My father never schooled me in warfare as such. Rather he plunged me into it. I first fought beneath his command at twelve, led infantry at fourteen, cavalry at sixteen. I never saw him so proud as when I showed him my first wound, a lance thrust through my left shoulder, got on Mount Rhodope against the Thracians of the Nestus valley. "Does it hurt?" he bawled, spurring up in the flush of victory, and when I answered yes, he roared, "Good, it's supposed to!" Then turning to the officers and soldiers round about: "My son's wound is in front, where it should be."

My father loved me, I believe, far more than he knew or cared to show. I loved him too and was as guilty as he of failing to display it. He drew a blade on me once, when I was seventeen, and would have spitted me through had he not been so soused he pitched flat on his cheesehole. My own dagger held poised in my fist, and I would have used it. For a time after that, my mother had to retire to her kinsmen's court at Epirus and I take refuge among the Illyrians. For it was known to all that my ambition, even as a boy, exceeded my father's and that I understood (or my mother did) that there may be, as the proverb declares,

Only one lion on a hill.

I was twenty when Philip was assassinated and the nation in arms called me forward as its king. I rarely, then, gave my father a thought. Lately, however, he has been much on my mind. I miss him. I would call upon his counsel. What would he do about mutiny on the plains of the Punjab? How would he reinspirit a corps gone sour?

And how, by the track to hell, may I get across this river?

Three

INDIA

HEPHAESTION ARRIVES FROM THE INDUS in time to witness the executions. Two captains and three warrant officers of the company of Malcontents have been put to the sword. Hephaestion comes straight to my side, in formation, without stopping even to relieve his thirst. He holds himself expressionless throughout the proceeding, but afterward, in my tent, he trembles and has to sit. He is thirty years old, nine months older than I; we have been the best of mates since childhood.

He speaks of this unit of Malcontents. Their numbers are only three hundred, seemingly insignificant among a force whose total exceeds fifty thousand. Yet such is their prestige among the corps, from past performance of valor, that I can neither detain them in camp under arrest (where they would only spread the contagion of their disgruntlement) nor cashier them and post them home (where their appearance would foment yet further disaffection). I can't break up the company and distribute its men among other units; it was to remedy this that I segregated them in the first place. What can I do with them? My skull aches just thinking of it. Worse, I need their prowess—and their courage—to cross this river.

In India there is no such thing as a staked tent. It's too hot. My pavilion is fly-rigged, open on all sides to catch the breeze. Papers blow; every scrap must be weighted. "Even my charts are trying to fly home."

Hephaestion glances about, noting the composition of the corps of Royal Pages. "No more Persians?"

"I got tired of them."

My mate says nothing. But I know he is relieved. That I have shown preference for homegrowns among my personal service is a good sign. It shows I am returning to my roots. My Macedonian roots. Hephaestion will not insult me by congratulation, but I see he is gratified.

After me, Hephaestion is the ranking general of the expeditionary force, which is to say of the army entire. Many envy him bitterly. Craterus, Perdiccas, Coenus, Ptolemy, Seleucus—all consider themselves better field commanders. They are. But Hephaestion is worth the pack to me. Him awake, I can sleep. Him on my flank, I need look neither right nor left. His worth exceeds warcraft. He has brought over a hundred cities without bloodshed, simply by the excellence of his forward envoyage. Tact and charity, which would be weaknesses in a lesser man, are with him so innate that they disarm even the haughtiest and most ill-disposed of enemy chieftains. It is his gift to represent to these princes the reality of their position in such a way that accommodation (I resist the word *submission*) appears not at his instance, but at theirs, and with such generosity that we wind up straining to contain its excesses. Five score capitals have our forces entered, thanks to him, to find the populace lining the streets, hoarse with jubilation. He has saved the army deaths and casualties ten times its number. Nor have his feats of individual valor been less spectacular. He carries nine great wounds, all in the front. He is taller and better-looking than I, as good a speaker, with as keen an eye for country. Only one thing keeps him from being my equal. He lacks the element of the monstrous.

For this I love him.

I contain the monstrous. All my field commanders do. Hephaestion is a philosopher; they are warriors. He is a knight and a gentleman; they are murderers. Don't mistake me; Hephaestion has depopulated districts. He has presided over massacres. Yet these don't touch him. He remains a good man. The monstrous does not exist within him, and even the commission of monstrous acts cannot cede it purchase upon him. He suffers as I do not. He will not give voice to it, but the executions today appalled him. They appalled me too, but for different reasons. I despise the inutility of such measures; he hates their cruelty. I scourge myself for failure of attention and imagination. He looks in the eyes of the condemned and dies with them.

"Whom will you set in command now?" he asks. He means over the Malcontents.

I don't know. "Telamon's bringing the two youngest lieutenants. Stay and we'll see what they look like."

Craterus enters; the mood lightens at once. He is my toughest and most resourceful general. The executions haven't bothered him a bit. He has an appetite. He farts. He curses the heat. He launches into a tirade of this crust-sucking river and how, by the steam off a whore's dish, can we get this salt-licking army across? He stalks to the water pitcher. "So," he says, splashing his face and neck, "which marshals are plotting our ruin today?"

Soldiers, the proverb says, are like children. Generals are worse. To the private soldier's fecklessness and ungovernability, the general officer adds pride and petulance, impatience, intransigence, avarice, arrogance, and duplicity. I have generals who will stand unflinching before the battalions of hell, yet who cannot meet my eye to tell me they are broke, or played out, or need my assistance. My marshals will obey me but not one another. They duel like women. Do I fear their insurrection? Never, for they are so jealous of one another, they cannot abide beneath the same roof long enough to contrive my overthrow.

My generals won't stick their toes in this river. Each has his eye on the empire behind. Perdiccas wants Syria; Seleucus schemes for Babylon; I'm already calling Ptolemy "Egypt." The last thing each marshal needs, he believes, is a spear in the guts, chasing some fresh adventure. Who can blame them? They've made their kill; they want to work their jaws on it. Of eleven corps commanders, I trust with my life only two, Hephaestion and Craterus. Do the others hate me? On the contrary. They adore me.

This is an aspect to the art of war, my young friend, that does not appear in the manuals. I mean the combat within one's own camp. The freshly commissioned officer imagines that the king rules his army. Not by far! The army rules him. He must feed its appetite for novelty and adventure, keep it fit and confident (but not too confident, lest it grow insolent), discipline it, coddle it, reward it with booty and bonuses but contrive to make sure it blows its loot on spirits and women, so that it's hungry to march and fight again. Leading an army is like wrestling a hundred-headed hydra; you quell one serpent, only to duel ninety-nine more. And the farther you march, the harder it gets. It has been near nine years for this corps; of its original complement, many have sons who have since come out to us, and a few grandsons. They have earned and lost fortunes; how can I keep them keen? They are incapable of it themselves. I must play to them, as an actor to his audience, and love and drive them as a father his wayward sons. The commander's options? In the end, he may lead his army only where it wants to go.

"Well," Craterus observes, "it didn't come off too badly."

He means the executions.

Not badly? "Yes, the show was a real crowd-pleaser!"

"Well, it's over. The pair you sent for are outside."

We step out. It is like entering an oven. The two lieutenants await on horseback. They are the most junior officers of the disaffected cohort, and the only ones unindicted. Telamon has brought them, as I instructed.

I regard them, hoping they have the belly to take over. The younger is from Pella in Old Macedonia; the elder from Anthemos in the new provinces. We ride out along the levee. I aim to make trial of these bucks.

The youth I know. His name is Arybbas; the men call him "Crow." His father and brother fell at Gaugamela, both officers of the Royal Guards; he has two more brothers and a cousin in my service, all decorated veterans. Crow himself served as a Page in my tent from fourteen to eighteen; he can read and write and is the best lightweight wrestler in the camp. The other lieutenant, Matthias, is older, near thirty, an up-through-the-ranks man, what the troops call a "mule," from a noble but poor family in the annexed Chersonese. He has a bride of Bactria, of extraordinary beauty, who left her people to follow him, and is, so I have been told, the engine of his ambition. Both officers are keen, and both in action stalwart, resourceful, and without fear.

I indicate the enemy fortifications across the river. To the Anthemiot, Matthias: "How would you attack?"

The river is eight hundred yards. Too deep to ford and too swift to swim; we must cross on boats and rafts. These will come under bowfire from enemy towers for the last hundred yards. The final fifty pass between further concentrations of archers, then terminate at an eight-foot mud bank, bristling with more bowmen and topped with ten feet of spiked and castellated dike. The length of this rampart is three miles. Behind it await Raj Porus and his war elephants, his corps of Indian *ksatriyas*—princes schooled from birth for war alone and renowned as the finest archers in the world—and an army of a hundred thousand.

The lieutenant turns back to meet my eye. "How would I attack, sire, if I were you, or if I were myself?"

Telamon laughs at such brass, and I too must bite my lip. I ask the lieutenant what the difference would be.

"If the army attacks with myself commanding, no scheme on earth could take that position. But if you lead, lord, it will fall with ease, though our troops be ill-armed, half-starved, and ragged as dirt."

I ask why.

"Knowing your eye is on them, sire, all men will compete furiously in valor, seeking to win your good opinion, which will mean more to them than their lives. Further, you, lord, by fighting at the fore, will inspire all to surpass themselves. Each will feel shame to call himself Alexander's man and not prove worthy of such fame."

Matthias finishes; Craterus snorts. Such flattery, he declares, is unseemly coming from officers in a company whose freshest repute is for mutiny!

The buck rejoins respectfully but with heat. No man may fault his comrades for want of spirit. "Indeed the king," he says, "has set us always the sternest chores, against the meat of the foe. If you condemn us, sir, cite the occasion and I shall refute it."

This is *dynamis*. I am encouraged.

I ask the second youngster his plan. This is Arybbas, Crow.

"First, lord," he replies, "I would try all else before risking battle. Raj Porus is canny, men say. Can we not treat with him? Offer him sovereignty beneath our rule, or simply request, or purchase, passage through his kingdom? Perhaps Porus has enemies he hates and fears more than ourselves. Will he accept us as allies to turn, united, upon these foes? Can we promise him rule over his rivals, vanquished by our mutual exertions, while our army passes eastward out of his realm, leaving it enlarged and enriched?"

It sounds so easy. Anything else?

"Sire, this river. Must we cross it here? Under fire? Against fixed fortifications? Why not ten miles north? Or twenty, or a hundred? Why even permit the river to remain?"

Why indeed?

"Divert her course, sire. Dig sluiceways and run her westward into the plain, as Cyrus the Great did at Babylon. Leave her high and dry and let our cavalry cross at the gallop!"

"Hear, hear," remarks Telamon. Craterus taps his breastplate in mock applause. I indicate the river, swollen by premonsoon rains. To turn it will take ten armies.

"Then let us raise ten armies, lord. I would sooner spend a barrel of my men's sweat than one thimble of their blood. Tyre took half a year to reduce. Let us spend two, if that's what it takes! And here is a further point, sire. The audacity of the stroke. Its temerity alone will awe the foe. He will believe the men who besiege his country are unlike any he has encountered, with resources of will and scale of imagination against which he cannot contend. He may delay, he will see, but not prevail. And this will render him more tractable to accommodation."

The elder backs his mate up. "One thing your victories have taught us, lord, is to see all foes as potential allies. Why compel such formidable warriors to contest us, when, incented aright, they may march at our sides? After all, it is not our object to defeat and smash all peoples simply for the sake of defeating and smashing them."

I raise a palm to shield the sun, regarding both officers. The older,

Matthias, is near thirty, as I have said, with a dense chestnut beard and eyes that call to mind the image of Diomedes in the hero shrine at Leucadia. The younger, Crow, cannot be twenty-two, beardless and lean as a whippet, but with an aspect crackling of purpose and intelligence.

I have taken to our two lieutenants. Command of the Malcontents, I tell them, shall be theirs.

"Do you understand, gentlemen, why we must cross this river? God help us, upon those ramparts yonder stands the only worthy foe this army has faced since Persia! Look at me. Do you think I don't share your dissatisfaction? Am I not as frustrated by the petty campaigns and gloryless sieges we have been compelled to fight since the fall of Darius? There look, across the river . . . Raj Porus and his princes. I love him! He has brought me back to life! And he will reinspirit this corps too, and your company with it, when we face him, again as soldiers and as an army."

Four

TELAMON

WHEN I WAS A BOY I HAD TWO TUTORS. Aristotle taught me to reason. Telamon taught me to act. He was thirty-three; I was seven. No one appointed Telamon over me; rather I fell in love with him and refused to be driven from his side. He seemed to me then, and does to this day, the perfect incarnation of the soldier. I used to trek the drill field in his train, aping his gait. The men pissed themselves laughing. But I intended no disrespect. I wished only to walk like him, stand like him, ride like him. He is from Arcadia in southern Greece. My mother wished me to speak pure Attic. "Listen to the boy! He drawls like an Arcadian!" Telamon was a sergeant then; he is a general now. Still I cannot bring him in from the field to the staff tent; he will not come. His idea of a good breakfast is a night march, and of a good dinner, a light breakfast.

When I was ten I begged Telamon to teach me what it meant to be a soldier. He would not respond in words. Rather he packed Hephaestion and me three days into the winter mountains. We could not get him to speak. "Is this what being a soldier means, traveling in silence?" At night we nearly froze. "Is this what it means, enduring hardship?" Was he trying to teach us to hold silence? Obey orders? Follow without question?

At the third dusk we chanced upon a pack of wolves, chasing a stag onto a frozen lake. Telamon whipped onto the ice at the gallop. In the purple light we watched the pack fan out in its pursuit, turning the prey first one way, then another, always farther from the treeline and the shore. Wolf after wolf made its run at the fast-fatiguing buck. At last one caught him by the hamstring. The stag crashed to the ice; in an instant the pack was on him. Before Hephaestion and I could even draw rein, the wolves had torn his throat out and were already at their feed.

"That," Telamon declared, "is a soldier."

I remember looking on as a lad of eleven, when Telamon (serving then under my father) formed up his company prior to the first march-out against the Triballians. He ordered each trooper to unshoulder his pack and set it upright at his feet. Telamon then proceeded down the line, rifling each kit, discarding every item of excess. When he was done, the men had nothing left but a clay cup, an iron spit, and a chlamys cloak-and-blanket.

There are further items, Telamon taught, which have no place in the soldier's kit. Hope is one. Thought for future or past. Fear. Remorse. Hesitation.

On the eve of battle at Chaeronea, when I was eighteen and first commanded squadrons of Companion Cavalry, Hephaestion and I paced the lines, puzzling over this axiom of our mentor. How could a soldier perform without hope? Clearly our men's expectations were heaven-high, as were our own; in fact we had spared no measure to elevate their hopes of glory, riches, the mastery of Greece. We were laughing, as young men will, with our mates when a sergeant of the staff rode up with a secretary, taking down each man's will. Not a fellow would sign of course. "Give my globes to Antipater!" "Leave my ass to the army!" I was about to chip in my own remark, when Black Cleitus asked, "Who will get your horse, Alexander?" He meant Bucephalus, a prize worth ten lifetime's wages. The thought of parting from him sobered me. At once Telamon's axiom came clear.

A warrior must not advance to battle hopeless—that is, devoid of hope. Rather let him set aside all baggage of expectation—of riches, celebrity, even death—and spur beneath extinction's scythe lightened of all, save surrender to that outcome known only to the gods. There is no mystery to this. All soldiers do it. They must, or they could not fight at all.

This is what Telamon meant when he pared his soldiers' packs or trekked to frozen peaks to show two boys the cold kill of predation.

Another time when we were youths, Hephaestion and I asked Telamon if self-command had a place in the soldier's kit. "Indeed," he replied, continuing to stitch his overcloak, which chore our query had interrupted. "For the self-control of the warrior, which we observe and admire in his comportment, is but the outward manifestation of the inner perfection of the man. Such virtues as patience, courage, selflessness, which the soldier seems to have acquired for the purpose of defeating the foe, are in truth for use against enemies within himself—the eternal antagonists of inattention, greed, sloth, self-conceit, and so on. When each of us recognizes, as we must, that we too are engaged in this struggle, we find ourselves drawn to the warrior, as the acolyte to the seer. The true man-at-arms, in fact, can overcome his enemy without even striking a blow, simply by the example of his virtue. In fact he can not only defeat this foe but also make him his willing friend and ally, and even, if he wishes, his slave." Our mentor turned to us with a smile. "As I have done with you."

There is a clue here.

Perhaps in the simple virtues I learned as a boy lies a way back, for myself and for this army. Time is short. The men will not wait, nor will this river.

Let us retrace the route then, my young friend—I to recount and you to attend. From the start.

From Chaeronea.

Book Two

LOVE OF GLORY

Five

THE OBLIQUE ORDER

CHAERONEA IS A PLAIN NORTHWEST OF THEBES. Here, in his forty-fifth year (and my eighteenth), Philip led the army of Macedonia against the assembled corps of the Greeks. It was the last great battle of his life and the first of mine.

The plain at Chaeronea runs northwest by southeast. The ground is in lavender and fragrant herbs, perfume plants, with the fortified acropolis on the rising ground to the south and Mount Acontion opposite across the pan. An army advancing from the northwest enters the plain at its widest part, where it stretches beyond three thousand yards. You cross a stream called the Haemus. Blood River. On the left is the course called Cephisus. Upon this the Greeks anchored their right wing. Their left rested on the citadel of the city. The foe's front was something under two miles across, or about twenty-eight hundred shields.

For centuries Chaeronea has been the site of clashes at arms. It is a natural theater of war, as are the neighboring plains of Tanagra, Plataea, Leuctra, Coronea, and Erythrae. The history of Greece has been written here. Men have bled and died on these fields for a thousand years.

This day a different kind of battle will be fought. This day my father will put an end to the preeminence of the Greeks. We will be the Greeks now. We of Macedon. We whom our cousins of the south have spurned and despised, whom Demosthenes of Athens has called "suppositious bastards." Today we will wring from Greece's grasp the standard of the West. From this day, we will be civilization's champions.

The enemy force is between thirty-five and forty thousand; our own just shy of forty. The foe has sufficient strength to stack his infantry between eight and sixteen shields deep across the entire front.

The elite regiment of Greece is the Sacred Band of Thebes. Its numbers are three hundred. The unit is constituted, so the poets declare, of pairs of lovers. The notion is that each man, dreading disgrace in the eyes of his beloved, will fight like one possessed, or, if overrun, stand by his comrade to the last.

"What rubbish!" Telamon is corrosive on the subject. "If bungholing your mate was all it took to make first-rate soldiers, the sergeant's chore would be no more than 'Face about and bend over!' " My father likewise knows Thebes well, having endured three years there as a hostage in his youth. Of course the Sacred Band is not pairs of lovers. How, after the youth's first beard? What the band is, is the boldest and most athletic of Thebes's noblest families, including, this day, six Olympic champions and scores of prizewinners from Greece's lesser games. The expenses of the regiment are borne by the state, her members relieved of all civic obligation, save training for war. Theban maids fling themselves at the knights of the Band, in vain, alas, for these, as their countryman Pindar attests

> *have taken Strife as their bride,*
> *and to her are faithful unto death.*

The Sacred Band are all hoplites, heavily armored infantry. Their panoply is a helmet of bronze or iron (six pounds), bronze front-and-back cuirass (twelve pounds), shin guards (two pounds each), and a three-foot-across bowl-shaped shield, oak faced with bronze (twelve to fourteen pounds). In other words, thirty-four to thirty-six pounds of "pot and plate," not counting weapons (another ten pounds), cloak and chiton, and footgear. The Greek hoplite is the most heavily armored infantryman in the world. With shields at high port and lapped, helmet crowns and eye slits alone visible above the upper rims, the Sacred Band presents to the foe a solid wall of bronze and iron.

The Band is three hundred on the parade ground only. In the field it is twenty-four hundred. Each hoplite is complemented by seven militia infantrymen, to make a file of eight, and has reserve companies to pack it sixteen deep, a total of forty-eight hundred. The Band has no cavalry and fears no cavalry. Horse troops are useless, the Thebans believe, against the bronze-armored, densely packed, spear-bristling phalanx.

Like all elite infantry of the southern Greeks, the Sacred Band fights in close order. The warriors' weapons are the eight-foot spear, with which they strike overhand from behind the lapped faces of their shields, and the short Spartan-style cut-and-thrust sword, which they use for the close work. The Band advances to the cadence of the flute, and has no call for retreat. Its code is Stand and Die. Its men are beyond question the finest infantry of Greece and, the ten thousand Immortals of Persia not excepted, the elite armored corps of all the world.

This day I will destroy them.

Here is how I learned the job was mine. At Pherae in Thessaly, the final staging stop before Philip's army pushed south to Chaeronea, my father commanded a full-dress run-through. The exercise was supposed to strap up at dawn, but the day had passed without orders, midnight had come and gone, and only then, well into the third watch of the night, did the word come down to bring the troops on line, in the dark, amid a cacophony of groans, gripes, and sergeants' bellowing. Of course Philip had planned it so. He wanted the men tired and hungry, half-pissed and disordered. It would more closely simulate the disarray of battle. Now at the last minute he arrived himself, with half the Companion Cavalry, a thousand Light Horse of Thessaly and three hundred Thracian lancers. The mass of horse threw the field into even greater disorder. A waxing moon stood over; the plain, freshly drenched by an unseasonable downpour, glistened slick and treacherous in a still-misting drizzle. "Plugs off! Skin 'em back!" Philip commanded via the brigade master sergeants, meaning the corps was to strip the cornel caps and oiled-fleece covers from the warheads of its eighteen-foot sarissas.

At once it felt like a fight. Honed iron emerged to the wet. Now an infantryman must take care and not jostle, for with the slightest mis-handling, these whetted edges could dice a comrade's ear or put out his eye. Philip ordered shields uncovered too. Off came the oxhide liners. Curses rustled. Now the wet would work its mischief, the bronze facings would take hours of toil for the men to reburnish. We could hear the grumbling and bitching. Horse piss sluiced; you could smell shit now, from the men and the mounts, and liquor and leather, the acrid breath of the mingled squadrons mixing with the tang off the grass and the smell of oil on iron, which evokes battle like no other.

My father had taken a post on the knoll beneath the shrine of the Aleuadae. I rode up with Hephaestion and Black Cleitus, a crack cav-alry officer who would come to command the Royal Squadron of the Companions; we reined to the left of the king, who was addressing his generals Parmenio and Antigonus One-Eye, likewise on horseback. The other brigade commanders ringed in on the right and rear. Philip recited the order of battle. One question hung unspoken: To whom would go the honor of facing the Sacred Band?

Philip passed right over it. No mention. Until Antigonus, unable to contain himself, spat in impatience across the front. "Who gets the Band, Philip?"

The king ignored him, continuing his recitation. Then, casually as shooing a fly: "The Thebans? My son will take care of them."

This was the first and only time Philip spoke in my presence on the subject, adding only (this addressed not to me but to the company as a whole) that I would have four brigades of heavy infantry, six thousand men, and all of the Companion Cavalry.

Hephaestion was furious when we left. "Your father has overarmed you."

My friend feared Philip diluted my glory by offering so stout a force.

I told him he did not know my father. "On battle's eve, he'll pull one brigade of foot and half the horse." Which he did.

My father was not mad or perverse, as many believed, but canny as a cat. He read his generals, as he put it, like a whore her steady fucks. And he knew me. He loved me, I believe, more than he knew or told. But Philip was a king, and he wished his son to be no less. Antipater has not told me so to this day, fearing my displeasure, but another has reported of that dawn, that he, Antipater, when Philip jerked half my force two hours before battle, had confronted his master: "Are you trying to kill Alexander?" To which my father had replied, "Only to try him."

Three nights later we reach Chaeronea. The enemy's main armies—Thebans, Athenians, and Corinthians—already occupy the waist of the plain, with their several corps of mercenaries and citizen troops of Megara, Euboea, Achaea, Leucas, Corcyra, and Acarnania rolling in all night. It takes our own force the whole of the next day to complete its march-up, lead units first, then the main body, finally the stragglers.

I arrive with my own squadrons immediately after the scouts and rangers. We are the lead elements, the first main-force Macedonian units on the field. It is our job to range ahead of the advancing army, to alert Philip to the enemy's dispositions and to any treachery laid in the main body's path. There is no call to worry. The Greeks are in plain sight, waiting for us to come up and crack skulls. We chase off the foe's skirmishers and seize a likely-looking camp. I order the ranger horse to fan out across the plain, stake out the line for the whole army. As each succeeding unit comes up, the quartermasters steer it into place.

My command, if such a grand term may be applied to it, is constituted in equal parts of veteran infantry officers—great Antipater, Meleager, Coenus—handpicked by my father to temper any youthful rashness on my part, and mates my own age—Hephaestion, Craterus, Perdiccas, longhaired Leonnatus, whom we call "Love Locks." These will take squadrons of Companion Cavalry. Black Cleitus commands my Bodyguard; Telamon is my master-at-arms. He points out the Sacred Band across the way. "Let's have a look."

Any evolution by the army of Thebes will be spearheaded by the

Sacred Band. Far more significant, however, will be its signature formation: the oblique order. As we ride across in the failing light, our eyes scour the terrain and the foe's configuration, seeking clues to how he will deploy.

The oblique order was invented by Thebes's legendary general, Epaminondas. Before his time, Greek wars were simple slugfests. Armies lined up across from each other, came to close quarters, and proceeded to beat one another's brains out, until one side cried quit. Often one army bolted before the other had even struck a blow. That served just as well to settle whatever issue had been in dispute.

The Spartans had made themselves masters of this type of shoving match and regularly thrashed the Thebans and all other rivals.

The oblique order ended that. Epaminondas never favored that term. He called it *systrophe*, "amassment." It worked like the fists of a boxer, who does not punch with both hands simultaneously but holds one back while striking with the other. Epaminondas lined up his army as before, on a parallel front across from the foe. But instead of clashing with equal weight along the full length of the line, he concentrated his strength on one wing, the left, and held the other wing back, or "refused" it. In battle the Spartans always placed their superior troops on the right: This was their post of honor; it was where their king fought, surrounded by his *agema*—the bodyguard of his corps of knights. By setting his power on the left—immediately opposite the Spartan king—Epaminondas took the enemy head-on. If he could make their crack companies break, he believed, all lesser elements would turn and run.

How did Epaminondas strengthen his left? First he arrayed it, not eight shields in depth, as the Spartans did, or sixteen, as Theban generals had done in the past, but thirty-, even fifty-deep. Next he put into his soldiers' fists a new weapon—the twelve-foot pike, which outreached the Spartan eight-foot spear by half. Last, Epaminondas reconfigured his countrymen's shields, scalloping recesses left and right and taking up the weight by straps around the neck and shoulder, so that his pikemen had both hands free to wield the long spear.

Epaminondas met the Spartans on the plain at Leuctra and annihilated them. This was the overthrow Greece had awaited for centuries. At one blow, long-downtrodden Thebes became the dominant land power of Hellas and he, Epaminondas, its singular hero and genius.

My father knew Epaminondas. At the height of Thebes's new power, it had taken hostages of the house of Macedon. My father was one of them. He was thirteen. His period of detention at Thebes proved three years. He was treated well, and he kept his eyes open. By the time he came home, there was no wrinkle of the Theban phalanx he had not mastered.

When he became king, Philip made over the Macedonian army in the image of the Theban. But he went Epaminondas one better. He added six feet to the two-hand pike, making it eighteen instead of twelve. This was the sarissa. Now, projecting before the army's foremost rank came a hedge of honed iron, not just of the first three ranks but of the first five. Into this no enemy, however brave or heavily armored, could hope to advance and survive. Philip did not leave it at that, however. He transformed the army of Macedon into a full-time professional force, billeted in barracks and paid in wages, month by month. He and his great generals Parmenio and Antipater drilled the phalanx until it could deploy from column to line, turn to flank, countermarch, and execute every evolution the old-fashioned hoplite could, faster, smarter, and with absolute cohesion. The world had never seen a weapon like the sarissa phalanx of Macedonia. Bring Epaminondas back from the grave and Philip's pike infantry will obliterate him.

My mates and I cross the field, now, at Chaeronea. The knights of the Sacred Band are out front of their position, oiled up and performing their gymnastics like the Spartans at Thermopylae. A better-looking bunch could not be imagined. Even their squires are handsome. Their camp is laid out square as a geometer's rule. The stacked arms dazzle in the late light.

We rein-in at half a stone's toss. I introduce myself and declare for all that Thebes and Macedon should not be fighting each other, but campaigning conjointly against the throne of Persia.

The Thebans laugh. "Then tell your father to go home!"

I indicate their camp. "Is this where your post will be tomorrow?"

"Perhaps. Where will yours be?"

Black Cleitus, it turns out, knows two of the fellows—wrestlers, brothers, from the games at Nemea. They swap tales and catch up on the news. In the midst of this, a striking-looking officer of between forty and fifty years comes out on foot toward me. "Can this indeed be Philip's son?" he inquires with a smile. He was a friend to my father, he says, introducing himself as Coroneus, son of the general and statesman Pammenes. It was in Pammenes' house that Philip passed his term as hostage at Thebes. "Your father was fourteen and I was ten," Coroneus relates. "He used to hold my head underwater and beat my buttocks."

I laugh. "He did the same to me!"

Coroneus motions a handsome lad of twenty forward. "May I present my son?" It seems overformal to remain on horseback; my mates and I dismount. Can it be that we shall be fighting these splendid fellows with the morrow's sunrise?

Coroneus's son is named Pammenes, after his grandfather; a handsome lad in impeccable armor, half a head taller than his father. Sire and heir take station beside each other, fellow knights of the Sacred Band. "This is how we stand in formation," declares the youth.

I discover myself fighting tears. The dagger at my waist is Toth steel encrusted with gems; its worth is a talent of silver. I address Coroneus. "My friend, will you accept this from me in gratitude for your care of my father?"

"Only," he returns, "if you will take this." And he gives me the lion's crest of his breastplate—of cobalt and ivory, inlaid with gold.

"What fine gentlemen," says Hephaestion as we recross the field.

Here, for your education, Itanes, I must address a question that causes all young officers consternation. I mean the experience of empathy for the foe. Never be ashamed to feel this. It is not unmanly. Indeed, I believe it the noblest demonstration of martial virtue. My father did not. One evening, succeeding the victory at Chaeronea, I chanced to speak with him of this moment with the Theban knight Coroneus. Philip attended closely. "And what, my son, did your heart say in that

hour?" He meant to tease me, I could see, not from malice, but to cor-
rect my ways, which he believed overly chivalrous. "Did you feel pity for
those whom it was your charge to slaughter? Or could you turn your
heart to flint, as men say your father does so well?"

We were home at Pella; the occasion was dinner with Philip's officers. These now fell attentively silent, turning toward me.

"I felt, Father, that since I was prepared to pay with my own life, so
was I sanctioned to take the life of the foe—and that heaven took no
exception to this bargain."

Murmurs of "Hear, hear!" approved this. "Indeed," my father observed with a laugh, "Achilles himself could not have answered more in
the ancient spirit. But tell me, my son, how will Achilles of old fare in
our modern era's corrupt and inglorious affrays?"

"He will elevate them, Father, by his virtue and by the purity of his
purpose. And where he stands, even in this degraded latter day, shall be
a noble world and uncorrupted."

This I said, and meant it. What I did not offer aloud was something
other. In that moment, as my father made trial of me before his officers,
I felt my daimon, my inhering genius. It entered as a ghost enters a
room. The sensation was clarity and unshakable conviction. I perceived, as never I had before, that my gift exceeded my father's by orders of magnitude. I seemed to look straight through him. He saw it. So
did Parmenio at his shoulder, and Hephaestion and Craterus at mine. It
was a moment between generations, one declining, the other in ascent.

What did my daimon offer in that instant of exchange of gifts with
the knight Coroneus? He showed a sword with double edges: the first of
empathy, communion, even love; the second of stern Necessity. "They
are slain already"—so spoke my genius—"these gallant corpsmen of
Thebes. In taking their lives, Alexander, you enact only that dance or-
dained before earth's foundation. Enact it well."

All next day the armies jigger and rejigger. At dawn the Sacred
Band is posted as a unit at the Thebans' extreme right. Six hours later I
ride out; the Three Hundred are now distributed as a fore rank across
the foe's center and left. This game is far from idle, for where the Sacred

Band takes station will give away, as much as such posting can, the foe's overall scheme. My regiments rehearse countermoves, covering every contingency. Still no dispatch from my father. He has not yet sent the courier, stripping me of half my force. My spies in his tent report that word will come around midnight. I instruct my commanders to exercise all mounts lightly; no animal to be overwatered or overfed. The horses are strung tight, like we are; I don't want their bellies going sour. Toward dark, our outposts take two prisoners. Black Cleitus brings them in. I should pack them straightaway to Philip, and I will, but . . .

"Let me poke these birds, Alexander. I'll lay they've got a song in 'em."

Cleitus is a true blackguard, sixteen years my senior and as arrant a rogue as my country, homeland of knaves, can produce. Later, in Afghanistan, he and Philotas (who would come to command the Companion Cavalry) were the only crown-rankers to balk at my example to crop their beards and take the clean-shaven mode I favored. Philotas refused out of vanity, Cleitus from loyalty to Philip. I could not hold it against him. Cleitus can fight. His balls are of iron. He was my father's First Page—and lover—when I was an infant. It was Cleitus's honor to bear me to my naming bath; he notes this in public every chance he gets. I find this simultaneously irritating and amusing. Cleitus is an expert with dagger and garrote; the king has enlisted his services on no few occasions. Hephaestion considers him a thug; my mother has twice tried to have him poisoned. But he is so fearless, both in debate and on the field, that I find myself not only listening but genuinely liking him. Hephaestion and I will rue the casualties we must inflict on the Sacred Band. Cleitus suffers no such delicacy. He can't wait to get in there and start hacking off heads. That the enemy are better men than he only enlarges his pleasure. He is, as the playwright Phrynichus remarked of Cleon of Athens,

a villain, but our own villain.

We interrogate the prisoners for tomorrow's posting of the Sacred Band. Both swear that the company will hold down their extreme right, against the river. I don't believe them. "What trade do you follow?" I grill the elder. He claims he's a tutor of geometry, a *mathematicos*. "Tell us, then," I say, "in a right triangle, what is the relation between the square of the hypotenuse and the sum of the squares of the other two sides?" A fit of coughing seizes the fellow. Cleitus prods him at sword point. "You wouldn't be an actor, would you, mate?" The younger man's curls look suspiciously perfect. "Give us a bit of *Medea*, you sons of whores!"

The Thebans would be mad to post the Sacred Band on their extreme right. If they do, I need only refuse my left to strand them high and dry. Can they swing across to the center from this position, leading their adjacent units like a closing gate? Not if I hold back a force of foot and horse, to take them from flank and rear when they try. I review this with Antipater, whom my father has assigned to me as mentor and adviser. "The Band will be center or left, Alexander, never right. Even the Thebans are not that thick."

We rehearse till midnight. Afterward Hephaestion and I troop the lines. Chaeronea is famous for the herbs its farmers grow for the fragrance trade. The scent perfumes the valley, stronger with the night.

"Can you feel it, Alexander?"

He means the sense of something epochal.

"Like the taste of iron on the tongue."

We are both thinking that this fragrant plain will, by tomorrow's noon, reek of blood and slaughter. I realize that my friend is weeping.

"What is wrong, Hephaestion?"

It takes him moments to reply. "It struck me just now that this hour, which is so immaculate, will never come again. All will have altered with tomorrow, ourselves most of all."

I ask why that has made him weep.

"We will be older," he says, "and crueler. We will have entered at last into events. That is a far different state from standing, as we do now, upon the threshold." He draws apart; I see he trembles. "That field of possibility," he observes, "which has opened out limitlessly before us all our lives, will by tomorrow's eve have narrowed and contracted.

Options will have closed, replaced by fact and necessity. We will not be boys tomorrow, Alexander, but men."

I quote Solon, that

He who would wake must cease to dream.

"Don't think so much, Hephaestion. Tomorrow is what we were born for. In heaven it may be different, but here, no man may gain except by losing."

"Indeed," Hephaestion concedes with gravity. "And will I lose your love?"

So this is what troubles his tender heart! Now it is I who tremble. I take his hand. "That, you can never lose, my friend. Here or in heaven."

Two hours before dawn the courier comes: All officers assemble for final orders.

Philip's tent is bedlam, crammed in the dark not only with the marshals and brigade commanders of Macedon, horse and foot, but with the captains of the allied Thessalians, Illyrians, Paeonians, Thracians, and the other half-savage tribesmen, all of them blind-sozzled, and all, despite their brass and bluster, aquake with terror. War is fear, let no man say otherwise. And even these wild boars of the north feel Death's tread about them in the dark.

Where is Philip? Tardy as ever. His campaign tent is a patchwork appropriated from the commissariat; heaven only knows where the real thing went. The night has turned chill and gusty; the flaps buffet with a concussion that unnerves the grooms and Pages. Outside, the couriers' ponies balk at their pickets. Inside, cressets gutter in the gale. The generals know they are in for the fight of their lives this day, against the Thebans, who stand at their zenith, vanquishers of the Spartans, unbeaten over thirty years. At their shoulders marshals half of Greece—Athenians, Corinthians, Achaeans, Megarians, Euboeans, Corcyrians, Acarnanians, Leucadians, braced up by five thousand mercenaries recruited from as far afield as Italy—all with the main forces of their armies and all fighting to defend sacred hearth and soil. Today will change the world. This clash will decide the fate not just of Greece but of Persia and all the East, for once Philip triumphs here, he will launch out of Europe into Asia, to overturn the order of the earth. Men and beasts shudder, taut as bowstrings. All are spooked, even colonels with half a hundred campaigns, while the younger captains chatter in the chill like colts.

At once comes the scrape of boots on the "cat step," the portal fronting the picket lines. Into the midst strides my father. It is as if a great lion has padded into the tent. The hair stands up all over my body. At one beat, the mood catapults from trepidation to absolute assurance. Its signal is a sigh, a collective expulsion of breath. Every man knows, at once and without speech, that with Philip here, we cannot lose. My glance holds riveted to my father. What is fascinating is how little he does. He does not thrust himself forward. If anything, he holds back. The eyes of the commanders, even those of the great generals, track Philip as he works his way across the warped plank floor. He is gnawing one of those jerked-meat sticks the troops call a "dogleg." As he enters, an aide hands him the briefing roll. He parks the dogleg between his teeth, wiping one hand on his cloak and the other on his beard. Parmenio and Socrates Redbeard, a colonel of the Companion Cavalry, move apart from the king's campaign chair; a Page angles it outward. My father does not advance to the head of the table and seize control of the council. Instead he drops like a sack of meal into his seat, more concerned with his greasestick, it seems, than with the fight to come. It is impossible to overstate the effect this insouciance produces. Philip glances up to Parmenio and, indicating the field plots and disposition sheets, speaks only these words: "My friend . . ."—as if to say, Forgive my tardiness, please continue.

Parmenio does. And here is another turn to note. Although the officers attend gravely upon this general's recital of the instructions of battle, his actual words matter not at all. The captains have been briefed and rebriefed; they know their assignments, buckle and strap. All that counts at this hour is the confidence in Parmenio's voice—and the silent presence of Philip at his shoulder.

As for me and my orders, these are tolled with utter nonchalance. "Alexander's squadrons," Parmenio pronounces, "will destroy the Theban heavy infantry on the left."

The briefing concludes. My father invokes neither gods nor ancestors. He simply rises, tossing his greasestick to the floor, and glances to his comrades with an air of cheerful anticipation. "Now, gentlemen," he says. "Shall we get to work?"

Six

CRATERUS

THE FOLLOWING ARE THE MEN AND UNITS under my command at Chaeronea. Six squadrons of Companion Cavalry—the Apollonian, Bottiaean, Toronean, Olynthian, Anthemiot, and Amphipolitan—twelve hundred ninety-one men; with three brigades of sarissa infantry, the Foot Companions of Pieria under Meleager, of Elimeotis under Coenus, and the Argead regiment of Pella under Antipater, who is also in overall command of our infantry. Philip has taken my fourth foot brigade, of Tymphaea under Polyperchon. Of cavalry, my father has recalled to his own use the Royal Squadron and all five squadrons of Old Macedonia, about fourteen hundred, under Philotas. He retains as well for himself on the right and Parmenio in the center the Thracians, Royal Lancers, and the Paeonian Light Horse—in other words, all of the army's light cavalry.

Each of my squadrons of horse is at full strength, two hundred twenty-eight, except that of Torone, which is understrength at one ninety-seven, and Anthemos at one-eighty-two. Not a man has gone sick or injured. I take the Apollonian for myself, keeping its colonel, Socrates Redbeard, and combining the five others into two brigades of three and two, placing Perdiccas in command of the forward, which will charge with me, and Hephaestion at the head of the wing, which will hold back, as a force of threat, to fix in place the Theban right.

(Note please that the army of Macedon stood at full strength that day. We never did again. The force I embarked with for Asia was only half that in Macedonian elements, since a nearly equal force had to be left behind to garrison Greece. This day at Chaeronea, however, Philip brought the full wash. Save two squadrons of Companion Cavalry and two brigades of sarissa infantry still at Pella, we had every bat and bumper.)

My wing is completed by six regiments of hoplite infantry, allied Greeks of the Amphictyonic League, under Nicolaus, called "Hook-Nose," to a total of nine thousand, and skirmishers to nine hundred twenty, hired archers of Crete and Naxos, free bowmen of Illyria, and, the linchpin of our forward line, three nineties of Agrianian javelineers under their king, Langarus. Our tally of horse and foot totals just under sixteen thousand, facing between nineteen and twenty thousand comprising the Theban right. Each of my officers is well known to me and has been since I was a child. I would march into hell with any. Here is a tale of my dear mate Craterus.

When I was sixteen my father left the Royal Seal in my care (with his senior general Antipater as regent) while he vacated the home country to prosecute sieges against Perinthus and Byzantium. At once I mounted a punitive expedition against the wild Maedi of Thrace, whom my father had brought into subjection four years prior but who, with their neighbors the Laeaei and Satrai, had seized upon this hour of his truancy to revolt. It was winter. I took six thousand under Antipater and Amyntas Andromenes. Craterus was twenty-seven. He had been charged with homicide, an affair of honor, and was, in fact, then in custody, due to face trial the day of our departure. From confinement he pleaded with me to take him. His family owned gold mines in the hills where I intended to march; he had spent summers there as a child and claimed to know the country. He would set his own neck willingly beneath the blade, he swore, if he failed to perform some exploit of valor.

We fought two battles, at the Ibys and the Estros, river crossings, and after a pursuit of two days and a night cornered the last forty-five hundred tribesmen, under their war chief Tissicathes in the great wooded pass between Mounts Haemus and Othotis. A savage blizzard had got up. The foe held the heights, which we must seize to overhaul his column. It was late afternoon; snow was dropping in heaps. I called Craterus to me.

"You say you know this country."

"By Hades' iron balls, I do!"

He declared there was a gorge, one range to the west. It would deliver us in the enemy's rear by morning. He would need fifty men and four surefooted mules, two loaded with oil and two with wine.

"For what?"

"The cold!"

Two hundred volunteered. Many who today command armies first won their place in my heart that night. Hephaestion, Coenus, Perdiccas, Seleucus, Love Locks, others long dead. I left Antipater and Amyntas with the main force, with instructions to assault the pass at dawn. Antipater was fifty-nine; I was sixteen. He was beside himself with concern for my safety—and of Philip's wrath if harm should befall me. I spoke to him apart, addressing him by the tenderest of Macedonian endearments. "Little old uncle, tomorrow morning nothing will stop me from being first to strike the foe. Better for all if I hit him from behind than from in front."

The foot of the gorge took till nightfall to reach. Snow was barrel-deep on the animals. I had considered, respecting Antipater, sending Telamon up in command of the party, with Craterus to guide him, while returning myself to the main force. One look ended that. The climb was all ice and scree. If a trail had ever existed, it was buried beneath chest-deep drifts. A torrent plunged, filling the cleft with sleet, spume, and thunderous din. I knew I must lead in person. No one else possessed the will.

The party started up. The depth of cold surpassed description, made more excruciating by the dark and the drenching wet. Worse, a north wind the natives call the "Rhipaean" roared down the gap all night. We followed the cataract, ascending a chimney of loose stone and shingle, ice-slick in the moonless dark. Each time the company crossed the river, all had to strip naked, holding weapons and kit overhead to keep our clothing and footgear dry; otherwise we would have frozen to death. We crossed eleven times, compelled by the twists of the gorge. Oil ran out. We had nothing to rub ourselves down with. The men's limbs lost all sensation.

Craterus was tremendous. He sang; he told jokes. Halfway up, we came to a cleft in the stone. "Know what's down there? A wintering bear!" Craterus declared this sent by heaven. Before any could speak, he had seized a brand, a lance and line, and plunged in.

The men clustered at the den's mouth, blue to the bone. A count of a hundred passed. Suddenly out hurtled Craterus, as if shot from a catapult. "What are you waiting for, lads? Pull!"

He'd got a noose around the bear's foot. Now the beast himself spilled free. Still half in torpor, the poor fellow must have thought himself in a hibernian nightmare. Craterus had him lassoed, hauling to jerk him off his feet, while a score of us plied our lances from all angles. The bear would not go down. Each time he rushed, our mob scattered like schoolboys. Finally the weight of our numbers overwhelmed him. What cold? We were sweating. Craterus gutted the beast of fat; we greased ourselves head to toe. He cut shoes from the fur, hacked off the bear's crown and wore it on his head. Crossing succeeding torrents, he was first in and last out, assisting each man across. Rebundling on the far side, Craterus jigged and rubbed the fellows down with more bear grease while offering ditties of corrosive obscenity. Gold cannot purchase such a fellow. We would have died without him.

With dawn, we attacked from the heights in the enemy's rear and routed him. The regiments under Antipater and Amyntas swarmed up the pass. Dividing the spoils, I made Craterus lord of Othotis, pardoned him of all transgressions, and paid from my own purse reparations to the clan of the aggrieved.

Such was Craterus, forever "Bear," who now in the dark before Chaeronea draws me aside to inform me that the men are suffering anxiety, in consternation over Philip's depletion of their numbers. "A word from you would mean the world, Alexander."

I am no believer in prebattle speeches, particularly before senior commanders and mates I have known all my life. But this occasion may call for a point or two.

"Brothers, we will find no wintering bears between ourselves and the enemy."

All tension dispels in laughter. Here in the fore rank are my comrades of that night, Hephaestion and Telamon, Coenus, Perdiccas, Love Locks, not excluding Antipater, who commanded the assault force that dawn, and Meleager, whose brother Polemon won honors that same day as a captain of heavy infantry. I go over again what we know we must do. It takes no time, so repeatedly have we rehearsed it.

"Let me underscore this only, my friends, in regard to the foe. It is not our place to hate these men or to take pleasure in their slaughter. We fight today not to seize their lands or lives, but their preeminence among the Greeks. With luck, they will fight at our sides when Philip turns for Asia and marches against the Persian throne.

"That said, let us hold this foremost in our minds: Defeating the Sacred Band is everything. No army ever won a battle when its elite unit was destroyed. And make no mistake: The Sacred Band's destruction is our task; it is the chore our king has set us."

My fellows murmur. All hesitancy has fled. They are like racehorses stamping for the gate.

"But we must do more, brothers, than overcome the enemy by might. We must show him that we are better men. Let no one dishonor himself in victory. I will flay the man I catch taking prizes and make a garrison unit out of that squadron that loses its head to blood slaughter."

Dawn ascends. The units move on line. Philip is no patient man. To the fore canters his standard rider.

We are away!

Seven

DRAGON'S TEETH

M Y FATHER DOES NOT BELIEVE in drums or pipers. In his army, sergeants call the cadence. Their cries are coarse but musical and they carry, even in the wind, like the keenest whistle. Each sergeant has his own style. I have seen good men passed over for want of throat, and mediocre rise because they had the knack to bawl the beat.

Philip's infantry steps off first. The king takes the right of the field. I have the left, Parmenio the center. Folds of ground block my sight line: My father's regiments are a mile and a third away; we can't see them and won't be able to until they've nearly reached the foe. They have moved out, though, or Parmenio's brigades in the center (which I can see) would not be dressing the line and elevating their sarissas, in their carrying slings, to march slope.

How brilliant the regiments look! Right and left, horses stamp and nicker. Eleven hundred yards separate us from the foe. I crane to the rear, to Hephaestion at the fore of his squadrons. His helmet is a visored iron *causia* burnished to silver, his mount a seventeen-hand chestnut, Swift, with a white blaze and four white stockings. There is not a handsomer man and horse on the field.

As always before a battle, gangs of local urchins dart in bold spirits across no-man's-land. Their dogs chase; it is great sport to them. Mounted couriers, ours and the foe's, gallop out and back, bearing messages and reports of last-minute shifts in dispositions. No rancor prevails among these fellows; they help one another remount after a spill. For reasons I have never fathomed, birds, too, favor fields of conflict. Swallows swoop now, and clouds of plovers. You will never see a woman and never see a cat.

Parmenio's regiments of the center push off now. Time for my wing to cinch up. I nod to Telamon; he signs to the brigade commanders. Infantry captains step out before their squares; their master sergeants backpedal beside them, sarissas elevated at the horizontal. "Dress the line! Stand ready!"

At the count of five hundred, my regiments step off. The field is almost two miles side to side, far too wide for any unified action. I cannot even see Philip, let alone ride to him. Our army will fight not one battle today but three: right, left, and center.

Philip's scheme divides the field accordingly. Our front advances on the oblique. The king's right will strike the foe first. Philip's infantry phalanx—six brigades, nine thousand men, plus the three regiments of Royal Guardsmen, a thousand apiece—will engage the Athenian heavy infantry at the extreme left of the enemy line (our right). Once in contact, Philip's front will feign retreat. There is a good deal of playacting in war and even such seasoned theatergoers as the Athenians can be hoodwinked in the heat of action. Athens's militiamen possess audacity, my father believes, but not courage. They are amateurs, citizen levy. It is twenty years since they took the field, and then only for a month. Their state of mind, as Philip's phalangites bear down on them, will be constituted of equal parts terror and overexcitement, which they will mistake for valor. In the flush of contact, they will lose their heads. Seeing the infantry of Macedon shrink before them, they will believe the fiction of their own supremacy and, carried away by this, bolt forward, anticipating the rout. Philip's regiments will withdraw before their rush. But Philip will not let go. His front ranks will hold the foe by the hedge of their projected sarissas, as a bullhound fastens on the muzzle of an ox. Philip will draw the Athenian line with him until the slope of the ground changes from downhill to up. There, his phalanx will check its retreat. The king will be upslope of the Athenians now; at the trumpet's call, the Foot Companions of Macedon will plant their soles and surge back upon the foe, the heat of whose blood will by now be plunging, as they enter what the Spartan general Lysander used to call "the hangover" of false courage. We will see the creases of the enemy's buttocks then, and the bowls of their shields as they sling them and bolt in terror to save their lives. That will be the battle's first stage.

Stage two will be Parmenio in the center. His brigades of foot will engage the Corinthians, Achaeans, and the Greek allies and mercenaries. His orders are to come to close quarters and hold. He has cavalry and light infantry on both seams, abutting my father's wing and my own, to keep contact and seal all breaches.

Stage three will be me.

I will charge the Theban heavy regiments and Sacred Band on the right (our left). Philip has not instructed me in how to attack, nor has he inquired of my dispositions—though Antipater, of course, has relayed every detail—other than to ask was I satisfied that I had what I needed. For this alone I account his greatness.

My father's plan is shrewd. By giving me the left of the field, he cedes me abundant scope for glory. If I succeed, Macedon gains a fighting prince and Philip a true heir and deputy; should I miscarry or be slain, the king knows he can still produce victory out of his own triumph on the right (he has kept six squadrons of Companion Cavalry to finish the job) and Parmenio's in the center.

Nine hundred yards now. Enemy riders transit, just out of bowshot. I have scouts out front too, to identify the colors of the individual Theban regiments and report the position of each in the enemy front. It is the responsibility of each colonel of foot to locate his enemy counterpart, so that his men know whom to hit and where in the enemy line they are stationed. This aligning of units is called "singling up." It is performed expeditiously but with tremendous care as the front advances across the field. In each company, word is passed man to man, with the veteran sergeants of the front rank picking out the pennants of the en-

emy units that their units will duel. The closer the armies get, the nar-
rower the aim, until men can almost designate individuals of the foe and
say, "That is my man; there is the shield I will strike."

I have other scouts ahead too, keen-eyed and cool-headed, who can
read a field and report without losing their heads. Their job: Find the
Sacred Band.

At eight hundred yards the enemy begins to deploy. Companies of
his extreme right start forward (we can make out the mass but not the
individual units) without haste, holding flush against the river that protects their flank.

"Do you see, Alexander?" Black Cleitus trots at my shoulder. We
have rehearsed this move of the Thebans. We think we know what it
means.

"Yes. But can it be the Sacred Band?"

Our scouts should have returned by now.

Where are they?

Where is the Sacred Band?

Cleitus: "Want me to go?" He means ride forward.

"No, stay here."

I am about to send to the rear to Hephaestion, to be sure he has seen
and understands what his squadrons must do, when he spurs up on his
own. "Have we got their colors?" He means have we found the Sacred
Band.

"Not yet."

"Let me ride out, Alexander." Cleitus means it will take minutes to
cross the field and get back. But I need him with me.

"Wait." At my shoulder, Telamon points ahead. Our scouts. The
youngest, Adrastus, called "Towhead," gallops up in a lather.

"The Sacred Band!" Towhead reins-in, breathless. "There! At the
seam of the center."

He means the knights of the Band are not on the wing against the
river, as they feigned yesterday, but have moved inboard to where the
Theban front abuts their Greek allies in the center.

"How are they formed up?"

"As a unit."

This decides everything.

One report is not enough. Still I sign to Telamon: "Brigade commanders assemble."

A second scout, Andocides, whips back. His report confirms Towhead's.

In a body we spur forward to a rise. Andocides points. "There, by the tall cypress. See their shields?"

The Sacred Band's _aspides_ are gold and scarlet; even at this distance we can make them out.

"What's their alignment?"

"Two, seven, and one. A hundred across."

He means the Sacred Band's configuration is two knights of the Band in the first and second ranks, seven ranks of militia levy in the middle; then a file-closer of the Band.

"Who's on their right?"

"Eel-eaters." Meaning the Theban militia regiments from Lake Copais. "Ten deep, like the Sacred Band."

"Only ten? Are you sure?"

Two more scouts report, confirming this.

"What's behind the Band?"

"Laundry," says Towhead. He means the hanging lines of their tents and camp.

"Well done, gentlemen." I send them back to work with a pledge of bonuses when this day is done. Our front continues its advance.

Seven hundred yards.

From the scouts' reports, I apprehend the Theban scheme.

The foe shows us massed troops along his unturnable right flank; then he advances the rightmost of these companies visibly and aggressively. His message: You cannot penetrate me on this wing. He sets his line obliquely to ours, seeking to deflect us inboard. There he shows us the Sacred Band—not stacked in unbreachable numbers, but only ten shields deep. This is the bait. The foe knows that his opponent this day is Philip's eighteen-year-old son, a callow prince on fire for glory. This youth will not be able, the enemy believes, to resist such a target. I will throw everything I've got at the Sacred Band. The foe hopes for this. He will either reinforce this elite company at the fatal instant or he has some other surprise—pitfalls or leg-breakers concealed behind his front. No matter. The foe will permit my infantry to become engaged in a shoving match. At this point I will have taken the lure. I will be in the jaws of the trap.

The Theban general is Theagenes, a canny and experienced commander who learned his craft under captains trained by Epaminondas. When I have become engaged futilely with the Sacred Band and the regiments reinforcing it, Theagenes will launch his push from his extreme right along the river. This wing—thirty, forty, even fifty shields deep—will wheel inboard like a great gate, pivoting on the hinge that is the Sacred Band, to take our line in flank and rear.

It is a good plan. It makes the most of the Thebans' strengths and minimizes their limitations. It follows the logic of the ground. And it reckons its antagonist cannily. It is predicated upon facing a young general—rash, impetuous, impatient for glory.

But the plan depends on two things not happening. One, no Macedonian penetration of the Theban line. Two, no troops of Macedon held back across from the extremity of the Thebans' great gate, to take it from flank and rear when it tries to swing shut.

This is what I will do.

The Thebans do not understand modern warfare. They believe Philip's strength resides where theirs does, in the massed formation of heavy infantry. No. The role of the Macedonian phalanx is not to slug it out, power for power, against the foe. Its job is to fix the enemy in place, while our heavy cavalry delivers the decisive shock from the flank or rear. The Theban despises cavalry. His hoplite soul holds horse troops in contempt. He cannot believe that mounted men will willingly fling themselves upon the hedgehog's back of bristling, serried spearpoints.

But we will.

I will.

Today we will make believers of them.

All this goes through my mind in one-fiftieth the time it takes to tell. By the time my brigade commanders have rallied to my colors to receive their orders, their master sergeants, sergeants, and corporals are already reconfiguring the line and rehearsing the ranks and files in the counter we have prepared and practiced, both in Thessaly on the approach march and here, in council, at Chaeronea.

Five hundred yards. Our regiments continue to advance in the oblique. What does the foe see? Only what I want him to.

He sees three brigades of sarissa infantry, forty-five hundred men, sixteen ranks deep, covering three hundred yards of the nine-hundred-yard front. (Allied infantry covers the final six hundred to our left against the river.) The sight of the Macedonian phalanx is unlike anything in warfare, ancient or modern. Instead of the stubby eight-foot spear, which the foe is accustomed to seeing, my corps advances with the eighteen-foot pike. Our front looks like a forest of murder: one serried, immaculately ordered mass, sarissas at the upright, with their honed iron blades twenty feet in the air, shafts swaying and nodding with the cadence of the advance.

The foe sees this also: that we advance upon him in the oblique. Our right leads. In other words, our foremost brigade—Antipater's—is singled up on the Sacred Band. This tells the enemy we will strike there first. I reinforce this notion by sending my missile troops, now, to rain hell upon the Sacred Band, and only the Sacred Band.

I have told you what the foe sees. Now consider what he doesn't. He doesn't see my heavy cavalry. I have four squadrons of Companions, eight hundred eighty-one men, immediately to the rear of the phalanx and concealed by its dust and its hedge of upright sarissas—and two more squadrons, under Hephaestion, held back on the left, to assault the foe's right when it starts to pivot forward. In any event, the enemy discounts cavalry. In any event he holds it in contempt.

Four hundred yards. Our javelineers out front concentrate their fire on the Sacred Band. We can hear the concussion a quarter mile away. I want the enemy to believe this is where our assault will come; I want the Sacred Band to brace, as it has planned, for my all-out attack upon it. Nor is this missile assault a ruse or formality. Our javelineers of Agriania are not boys and old men pitching spikes (like the foe's skirmishers, whom our fellows have chased with ease from the field), but the most skilled and lethal missile troops in the world. They are mountain tribesmen, allies of the north, whose sons may not call themselves men until they have brought down with one cast a boar or a lion. Downwind, their best men can sling a dart two hundred yards; point-blank their casts routinely splinter two-inch planks.

Three fifty. Our javelineers launch their missiles from so close to the foe, they can see the irises within the sockets of his helmets of bronze. Each dart weighs three to five pounds, with a warhead of solid iron. The enemy holds. He hunkers behind his bronze and oak shields and endures.

Three hundred. The first wounded, skirmishers of the foe, come underfoot. The horses smell blood. Between my knees Bucephalus shudders like a warship coming on to ram. I don't touch the reins; his pride will not bear it. Just a shift, with my seat; he collects beneath me.

I am out front now with my Bodyguard and couriers, in the interval between our rightmost phalanx brigades, Antipater's and Coenus's. Two fifty. Our javelineers fall back in strings of ten, withdrawing between the files of the advancing infantry. We can see clearly now the scarlet and gold of the Sacred Band. The foe's captains, out before their squares, are pointing out our battle standards, singling up, just as we have.

Suddenly Telamon reins at my shoulder. "Pigstickers!" He points ahead. Reinforcements are pouring in behind the foe. It is not till after the fight that we will learn from captured colors that these units are the Heracles regiment, which had been Epaminondas's, a city brigade second only to the Sacred Band in the illustriousness of its complement, and two county regiments (meaning farmers, tough Boeotian yeomen), the Cadmus and the Electra—the same divisions that overran Sparta a generation ago. In the event, I have no idea of the identity of these companies, but I see the blades of their twelve-foot pikes as they hasten into position in the rear of the Sacred Band.

It is the moment. I feel Black Cleitus's eyes on me, and Telamon's and Redbeard's and those of all the squadrons. Can I tell you how happy I am? In moments we may all be slain. My mates accept this. So do I. Death is nothing alongside this *dynamis*, our will to fight.

One hundred fifty. I sign to Telamon: "Sarissas to the attack."

On the trumpet's blare, the first five ranks of the sixteen-deep squares lower their pikes to the horizontal. Again the theater this presents to the foe is terrifying. Because of their great length, the sarissas do not descend sharply or crisply; instead their shafts lower to the attack deliberately, almost languorously. The war cry roars from forty-five hundred throats. The foe answers; we hear his hymn and anthem. Officers of the Sacred Band withdraw to their posts in the forward ranks. They lap shields with their mates. Their front forms, solid bronze. Every man plants his soles and, calling upon heaven, strengthens his knees to withstand our assault.

Warfare is theater, I have said, and the essence of theater is artifice.

What we show, we will not do.

What we don't show, we will do.

One hundred. Again I signal the trumpet. It looks to the Sacred Band in that moment as if Antipater's brigade, our rightmost, singled up upon the Band, will charge straight at it.

But it doesn't. Instead, on the trumpet, Antipater's front comes half left. The warheads of his regiments' leveled sarissas swing on the diagonal, centering no longer on the Sacred Band, but on the militia units on the Band's right. Antipater's brigade, already advancing in the oblique, simply squares its front and launches into the attack.

The Sacred Band has braced to receive the assault. But no assault comes. Instead the foe finds himself staring at a hundred yards of empty dirt.

Now, as I launch Antipater's brigade diagonally across the Sacred Band's front, I do something else. I wheel my four squadrons of Companion Cavalry (Hephaestion holds the final two in the deep left rear) from their post behind my rightmost infantry brigades, where they have been screened from the enemy's sight by the phalanx's vertical sarissas, and gallop at their head to our right wing, behind Antipater's attacking brigade. The squadrons of horse come from line of squares to column of wedges. This is the formation called Dragon's Teeth. Each wedge is a tooth and each tooth follows the tooth before it.

Our Companion Cavalry is running "round the turning post," like racehorses in the hippodrome. When we clear Antipater's right wing, we will come left in a column of wedges and charge the foe with all the speed and violence we possess.

Do the captains of the Sacred Band see this? Indeed they do. By now they reckon my scheme completely. But they are caught between two evils. Come forward to attack Antipater's brigade (which has, by its diagonal crossing, exposed its right flank), and my cavalry will rip into them on their own exposed left. Stand fast and Antipater will eat their flanking units alive. Either way, I will pile into them at the gallop with eight hundred cavalry charging boot-to-boot.

The foe sees what is coming. But he can do nothing about it. He is all heavy infantry. His bulk is rooted to the earth. He has as much chance against us as the tree has against the axe.

As the Sacred Band comes forward (as it must, to attack Antipater's brigade in flank), our wedges of Companion Cavalry appear on their left, hurtling toward them. The foe's reinforcing companies of the Heracles, Cadmus, and Electra regiments must flood forward now, filling the breach created by the Sacred Band's charge. We can see their captains shouting and gesticulating for this, and their gallant ranks straining to obey.

Infantry is mass and immobility.

Cavalry is speed and shock.

A gap opens between the Sacred Band and its supporting units. Into this gap I charge.

Bucephalus is first to strike the foe. My horse is a prodigy. He stands seventeen hands high and weighs over twelve hundred pounds. His hooves on the earth make tracks broad as skillets; his quarters are the size of regimental kettles. I cannot imagine the terror that must have seized that initial warrior of the Sacred Band as my stallion's driving knees crashed upon him, followed by the massive bulk of his iron-armored chest. The front parted before me with a sound like rending metal. I could feel Cleitus and Telamon behind me on the left, Socrates Redbeard on the right.

A cavalry charge is nothing grander than a directed stampede. Men have believed that horses will refuse to overrun massed infantry, as they will balk at running into a wall of stone. But horses are herd animals, and in the madness of the rush, they will follow the leader headlong off a cliff. In the formation of the wedge, where the commander's horse is alone at the point, the mounts of the succeeding chevrons are not following their own eyes and senses; they're following the lead horse. And if the leader is brave enough or reckless enough, spurred on by a rider impetuous enough, the trailers must follow. The same instinct that drives a herd off a precipice will propel it into massed infantry.

The foot-knights of Thebes cannot believe the mounted foe is mad enough to hurl himself upon their elevated spear points. But here we are. The shaft of my lance snaps in two against the shield of some spectacularly valorous fellow, whose own eight-footer splinters in the same instant against the iron plate lapping Bucephalus's chest. The foe's eyes fasten on mine through the slits of our helmets; I read his fury and exasperation, matching my own, at the cursedness of our mutually rotten luck. Down he plunges beneath Bucephalus's knees; in a moment his helmet is staved. I feel revulsion at the waste of such a gallant heart and vow to myself for the thousandth time that I, come to power, will never again permit Greek to work slaughter against Greek.

Muralists depict the clash of cavalry with lances thrusting, sabers slashing. But in the crush it is the horse who does the damage, not the man. The rider in a melee is, to all purposes, out of his mind. So is his mount, and he, the rider, must use this against the foe. Hemmed by shouting, weapon-wielding men, the animal's instincts supersede all training. Bucephalus rears and plunges, as a stallion will in the wild. He kicks at anything behind him and strikes with his teeth at any flesh he can reach. When a horse senses something moving beneath his belly, he will stamp with his hooves, as at a snake or wolf. Heaven help the man, fallen beneath him in combat. All these instincts the cavalryman must employ against the foe. But the lead rider can have only one object: punch through. Keep moving. The man at the point draws the wedge behind him. If he stalls, the whole rush founders.

We are ten deep into the mass of the foe. A sea of helmets and spear points boils beneath me. I claw for my saber, but in the initial crash, the sheath has ruptured; I can't get the jammed blade out. For an instant I consider shouting to Cleitus or Telamon, "Firewood!," the cavalryman's cry when his lance shatters and he must get another. But no, it would be infamous to strip a comrade for my own need. Instead I tear off my helmet and hoist it overhead, intending to strike with it as a weapon. At once cheers erupt. A lucky star has watched over my career, and here at its inception it does not fail. The Companions take the stunt as a gesture of triumph. It is seen even by the ranks of our pikemen, at that instant crashing to grips along the Theban front. They too salute it ecstatically; I hear them surge forward and see the foe give back before their press. I reelevate the helmet and sling it with all my strength across the ranks of the foe. With a great cry, our infantry falls upon them. The enemy's reinforcements give way. Our first wedge punches through.

A highway opens before us. We are in the clear. The foe's camp is fifty yards ahead; it is already in full flight. Telamon overhauls me and tosses me his lance. The wedges re-form upon my colors. We charge from the rear. Each fifty is one tooth of the dragon, and each tooth tears off a steak from the meat of the foe.

The enemy has no chance against our attacking divisions. What infantryman with his eight-foot spear or militiaman with his twelve-foot pike can stand against the phalanx man with his eighteen-foot sarissa? And our Companion Cavalry, on fire for glory, would that day have overrun Olympus itself.

In minutes the struggle on my wing breaks down into three clashes. Against the river the foot companies of the enemy's right, which have come forward against our allied infantry, are being taken in flank and rear by Hephaestion's squadrons of horse. Our divisions under Amyntas and Nicolaus pin them from the front; they are being massacred. In the center, Coenus's brigade has locked up with the foe's militia foot; a titanic brawl rages amid storms of dust and cries of carnage. On our wing, the Sacred Band and its reinforcing regiments have been cut off. Our heavy cavalry assaults them from the rear; sarissa infantry hems them from the front. The enemy's elite corps is enveloped. Now the blood work of slaughter begins.

When a unit has been cut off from its supporting wings, its resistance becomes a matter solely of the character and courage of its components. In this, no corps I have ever dueled excelled the Sacred Band of Thebes. Their extinction was inevitable from the moment our first squadron penetrated their front. Yet the Three Hundred not only stood fast but rallied the militia troops of their own complement and the citizen regiments on their flank, compelling them by their own valor to emulation. One fought, it seemed, not warriors but champions. Timon, the Olympic boxer, slew two of our chargers, so we heard later, the second with his bare hands, breaking the animal's neck. Thootes, the pancratist, would not go down, despite three lances in his guts and half his face hacked away. The chronicle of the foe's individual gallantry filled two rolls in the dispatches. But greater yet was the way he held together. Though the penetrations of our wedges had broken up the initial four thousand into first three and then five severed companies, these units managed, by rushes upon our fronts in the breaks of our rushes upon them, to recombine and re-form into a fighting square. They fought their way out, first to the lone cypress that marked their original front, then to a low wall where their camp laundry had been hung, and after that to the kitchen camp of their servants, where they formed up again behind a row of cooking trenches. Not a man showed his back. Always our force advanced against lapped shields and thrusting spears. And if we drew breath, even for an instant, the champions of the Sacred Band rushed upon us.

It is a brutal and graceless business to finish off a compact body of men who resist bravely and will not yield. In this, the sarissa phalanx is without peer, as the foe's shorter spears cannot get within five feet of the Macedonian front, while our men can cut the enemy down at will, and, in fact, the only real problem we faced was fatigue and the efficient rotation of rested men into the line to press the slaughter. The foe's thousands became hundreds, and his hundreds scores.

You could hear voices of individual officers of the foe crying out to their comrades to sell their lives dearly. I called to them to see sense and surrender. They would not. At several points in the melee, stout fellows of the foe closed ranks into knots of bronze and iron and sought to break out through the ocean of Macedonians enveloping them. Though these individuals fought with the desperation of self-preservation, they had no hope, as our ranks were too deep and too stoutly disciplined and officered. Our fellows crowded in from all quarters, at points twenty and thirty deep, elevating their sarissas to the vertical and pushing with their elbows and shoulders upon the backs of the men in the ranks before them. The brave warriors of the foe expired amid this press, going down like drowning men in the sea.

At such point it becomes the victor's responsibility to calculate the consequence of excessive slaughter and to direct the cessation of strife. I cry cease and call out again to the foe to capitulate. He still refuses. A courier gallops up from my father, summoning me to an assembly of commanders. Hephaestion's squadrons, triumphant, have joined us now from the wing; other riders spur up in joy from Parmenio in the center. Victory in every quarter! It is over. We have won! I feel no fatigue, only elation, and a monumental sense of relief.

I set Antipater and Coenus to oversee the finish of the Sacred Band, with orders to spare as many as they can, dishonoring none. With Hephaestion I transit the hinter ground on the track of my father's courier. It is the type of field a cavalryman dreams of. We are in the enemy rear; our companies range without opposition. Everywhere the foe is in flight. I am just clasping Hephaestion's arm in congratulation, when I see Coenus's adjutant Polemarchus overhauling us from the wing. He gallops up, begrimed and breathless.

"The last of the Sacred Band, Alexander . . . some are taking their own lives. What shall we do?"

Eight

THE SACRED BAND

THE SURVIVORS OF THE SACRED BAND are about two score. They have been disarmed now by Antipater and Coenus and stripped of all means of harming themselves. It is minutes after the fight. The scene is as heartbreaking as it is ghastly. All who have survived are maimed and disabled, no few horribly, yet somehow they have managed to crawl or hobble or drag one another onto one spot, the sand bank where their corps had first taken station. The lone cypress overstands them, looking like a tree of hell.

I ride up with Hephaestion and Polemarchus. One of the foe has had both legs crushed, beneath our Companions' hooves no doubt, and been blinded, among other wounds; how many it is impossible to tell beneath the matting of blood and grime that coats his arms, face, beard, and breast. This warrior, knowing his countrymen have been vanquished and the main of his comrades slain, hauls himself onto one elbow, begging the victors for death. Around him several hundred Macedonians and allies have collected, gawking at the beaten men as if they were bears in a pound.

In a hundred battles this is the rarest sight: men who stand and fight to the death. It never happens. Even the most elite units, when they know they are beaten, will seek terms or contrive measures to extricate themselves from their predicament. Yet the Sacred Band has stood and died. The survivors make no move to bind their wounds, some even opening them, seeking to bleed their substance into the sand. They have guts, these bastards. It is a measure, further, of their hatred for us, their identification of us as aliens, non-Greeks.

Philotas rides up from the right of the field. He is Parmenio's eldest son, commander this day of Philip's Companion Cavalry, and my father's favorite. He hates the Thebans with a blood passion, which is enflamed further by the sight of their magnificent valor.

"Who do you think you are, the Spartans at Thermopylae?" He ranges before them on his tall black, Adamantine. "Do you take us for Persians, you sons of whores?"

My men are elated, as victors are always, to have survived trial of death. They gape at these knights of Thebes, of whom they had been thoroughly terrified so few moments past.

"They don't look like much now, do they?" Philotas cries. Indeed they don't. "Yet these are the same villains who sided—not once, but twice—with the barbarians against their fellow Greeks, who to this day take Asiatic gold, and save their bravery to spend against us! They would rather kneel to the Persian than take us of Macedon as mates and allies!"

I command him to cease. He glares daggers at me. I see our men would loot the foe. They want souvenirs. A sword or shield, the helmet of some valiant man.

"Cease!" I command. Philotas is thirty; I am eighteen. His jaw works. I will cleave him where he stands, regardless of all his favor with my father, and he knows it. The king must appear soon, Philotas reckons. Philip will give him his way. Philotas spits and wheels his mount, showing me his back.

Moments pass. All eyes have returned to the survivors of the Sacred Band. Then the oddest thing happens. As we stand across from these men who hate us and are hated by us, they become, by some inexplicable alchemy, not enemies, but fellows of flesh and blood, soldiers like ourselves. We have all seen zealots and fanatics, eager for death. These men are not that. They are rational men, defenders of their homes and families, who simply would not quit. We make out faces of individuals now. Their postures of devotion, each true to his mates and his corps, derive from that code to which we, too, have sworn allegiance. Not a man speaks, yet each of us of Macedon, beholding the exhaustion and soul-spentness of these warriors, understands that they have fought, this day, upon a plane that we have not. They have given more than we. They have suffered more than we. And we reckon, too, that if we aim, as we do, to cross to Asia and overturn the order of the earth, we must mount to that sphere of sacrifice that we read now upon their beaten, shattered visages. This knowledge sobers us. Our hatred is supplanted by compassion, even love.

In the dust kneels the gentle knight Coroneus, his right arm hacked away at the elbow, hovering above the corpse of his son Pammenes. I feel tears burn. Soon my father and his retinue will arrive to savor their triumph. How will Philip use these men? He will be moved by their valor, as we are. But he will hold them. With honor, yes, but to exploit their capture, to wring payment and concessions from their country-men, and to break their hearts.

"Let them go." I hear my voice, as if that of a stranger.

"Do not!" cries Philotas, incredulous.

"Restore their arms," I command. "Release them!"

"You cannot! Wait for Philip!"

My hand is on my lance; my heels punch my horse's ribs. At once Hephaestion and Telamon interpose their mounts between me and this man who would defy me. Coenus and Antipater support them with ve-hemence.

"Alexander . . ." Philotas displays empty hands, seeking to appease me. "This is your victory here. But the field belongs to Philip. You must obey the king!"

I am past speech. Only the sight of my dear mates' and senior com-manders' faces, fixed to quell my wrath, checks me from soiling my iron with this patriot's blood.

Philip approaches. His seer Aristander precedes him, with a dozen

Pages and Bodyguards; Parmenio and Antigonus One-Eye come next; then the king himself. In moments the tale of the clash between me and Philotas is wrung from captains on the ground. "I should crack your skulls," Philip says, "the pair of you."

His eye has found Coroneus. I see my father weeps. The Macedonian colonel on the ground is Eugenides, whom the men call "Payday" for the scrupulousness of his accounting.

"Has my son," Philip addresses this officer, "commanded the release of these men?"

Eugenides acknowledges.

Philip nods, confirming.

"You heard the order!" Payday barks to his complement. "Restore the enemy's arms! Let them go!"

Philip does not upbraid me then. He accepts without protest my preemption of his authority. Only next morning, when we sacrifice in thanksgiving to Heracles and Zeus Hetaireios, does he take me aside.

"You could have eaten the lion's heart, my son. But you gave it back to him. He will hate you for it, I fear. You will pay on another day for this act of misplaced chivalry." He sets his hand on my shoulder. "Still I cannot fault you for it."

Chaeronea is Philip's last victory. Twenty-one months later he is slain, struck down by an assassin in the procession preceding the games celebrating my sister's wedding.

Book Three

SELF-COMMAND

Nine

MY DAIMON

AT THE INSTANT OF PHILIP'S ASSASSINATION, in the theater at Aegae in Macedon, I had just entered the colonnade, ahead of my father in the procession, to take station awaiting him beside his throne. The bridegroom, Alexander of Epirus, walked at my side; Philip had sent us ahead to demonstrate to the multitude that he needed no bodyguard. I heard the clamor in the theater. I knew at once that something terrible had happened, so dreadful were the cries, and went racing back, with Epirote Alexander. The women of the party were shrieking; the press of bodies resisted our passage like a sea. The assassin, a young noble named Pausanias, had been overtaken and slain by Perdiccas, Love Locks, and Attalus Andromenes, serving as Bodyguards of the Royal Person. At that moment it was not clear if the king still lived. To my surprise I found myself riven with anguish, not only for Philip's sake—for despite our clashes I loved and revered him—but for our nation, bereft of his lion's strength. Then came the cry. The king was dead. I still had not reached him. I found myself immediately to the rear of Philotas, Parmenio's son (the same Philotas who had offended me so gravely at Chaeronea), just as he turned to his comrade, Coenus's brother Cleander. "This is the end of Asia," pronounced Philotas. He meant that the dream of conquering Persia had expired with Philip, as no other was capable of mounting and commanding an expedition on such a scale.

I was two paces from Philotas's shoulder. He had not seen me. At once all grief for my father fled. I felt myself enter a state of rage so monumental that I could see, as if it were transpiring in fact, my sword, clutched in both hands, hewing Philotas in two at the waist. Further I saw myself eradicating every mark of his existence, down to his infant son and every barn-brat by-blow. The fury passed, so swiftly that no one, not even those close beside me in the crowd, was aware I had felt it. This rage quelled itself, replaced by a cold determination to prove Philotas's finding not only false but inverted: that Asia would be impossible *without* Philip's death, that his extinction was necessary to make the conquest of Persia come true.

I shoved through the press. My father had been carried into the shade of the wedding pavilion and laid out on an oaken bench, which made now a table for the surgeons to operate on. The blow that had slain Philip was an underhand thrust beneath the plexus of the rib cage; my father's belly and loins were painted with blood but otherwise he looked no worse than if he were sleeping off a rough drunk. How many scars he bore on his body! The physicians had bared his torso to the knees, and now, out of modesty perhaps, or in deference to my arrival, a Page named Euctemon set his cloak over the king's privates. The state of the assembly was near delirium; great generals and commanders stood one breath from panic. Only I, it seemed, remained composed.

I felt cold, and preternaturally lucid. The surgeons were two, Philip of Acarnania and Amorges, a Thracian trained at Hippocrates' academy at Cos. I thought, These doctors will fear for their personal safety now; they will dread my anger, and the nation's, for failing to save the king. I took their hands at once to reassure them.

Philotas had worked up and was making a show of his grief. My rage at him had abated; I saw him clearly for what he was, a born fighter and cavalry commander, yes, but a vain and shallow fop, as well. And I understood the source of my fury at him.

What crime had Philotas committed?

He had doubted me.

He had doubted my daimon and doubted my destiny. For this, I could never forgive him.

Ten years later in India, the army encountered for the first time the *gymnosophists*, the so-called naked wise men. Hephaestion in particular was fascinated by these ascetics and sought to plumb their philosophy. The aim of their exertions, he reported, was to seat the center of their being not in the mortal part of their nature, as does the common run of men, but in the immortal—what they call the Atman, or Self. I know what they mean, though perhaps in a less felicitous way. My daimon was, and is, so strong that I am at times possessed by it. We have talked for hours, Hephaestion and I, and Telamon and Craterus as well, of this phenomenon. I have reported that my daimon, which was a stranger to me and which I did not understand and could not control, had seized me most powerfully in that hour succeeding my father's assassination.

"He is not me," I have said, "but a creature to whom I am bound. It is as if this thing called 'Alexander' has been twinned with me at birth, fully formed, and that I only now discover it, aspect by aspect, as I grow. This 'Alexander' is greater than I. Crueler than I. He knows rages I cannot fathom and dreams beyond what my heart can compass. He is cold and canny, brilliant and ruthless and without fear. He is inhuman. A monster indeed, not as Achilles was, or Agamemnon, both of whom were blind to their own monstrousness. No, this 'Alexander' knows what he is, and of what he is capable. He is I, more than I myself, and I am indivisible from him. I fear I must become him, or be consumed by him."

All this came clear to me beside the plank bench that made my father's bier. My anger at Philotas was not fury that I myself had been offended; rather, my heart leapt to the defense of my daimon, with an intensity I could never have mustered on my own. I stood outside myself, astonished at who I was and at the resources at my disposal. The sensation was joy, and utter certainty, of myself and of my destiny. I realized I could absolve any crime—murder, betrayal, treason—but not doubt. Not doubt of my destiny. This could never be forgiven.

In that instant, over my father's corpse, all plans for the next half year's campaign presented themselves and were ratified within the private council of my heart. I knew every move I must make, and in what order I must make them. I knew, too (though I would never show it), that Philotas from this day would be my enemy.

As to the loyalty of the army, this was never in question after Chaeronea. I did not wait for the Council of Nobles to convene. I went straight to Antipater and Antigonus One-Eye (the other senior commanders, Parmenio and Attalus, being overseas, preparing the bridgehead for the invasion of Asia). This was in the big covered passage called the East Stormway, by which carriages deliver their charges to the palace in raw weather, and where the king's couriers' mounts are kept, bridled and ready to ride. Antigonus and Antipater had repaired there, with Amyntas, Meleager, and several other brigade commanders, immediately after the assassination. I have never told this. I strode in under the stone arch with Hephaestion, Telamon, Perdiccas, and Alexander Lyncestis, who had garbed me in his own war cuirass (I had only a light ceremonial vest for the procession) as an emblem of command. Moments earlier I had cradled my father's head in my hands; his blood was still wet on my forearms. Clearly the generals had been debating what to do about me. Rally to me? Accuse me?

"Alexander . . ." Antigonus began, as if seeking to reprieve this conclave.

I cut him off. "How soon can the army move?"

Antipater declared at once that he stood with me. "But your father . . ."

"My father is dead," I said, "and report of this will fly on wings, not only to the tribes of the north but to all the cities of Greece." I meant they would rise. "How soon can we march?"

It took two months. I did not sleep six hours. I would not let my generals, even two at a time, conspire together without me present. I kept them on the drill field and in my hall. I napped with Hephaestion at one shoulder, Craterus and Telamon at the other, and a company of the Royal Guard outside my door. The throne had to be protected.

A number of measures, regrettably, must be taken. I spared my half brother. My mother had gone quite cracked. She made no attempt to conceal her joy at Philip's end, for his inattention to me and his infidelity to her. His newest bride was slain at her orders. She dispatched with her own hands the babes of this union, the youngest a boy, whose existence threatened my accession. This was not all. My mother was a master of the poisoner's art and had cultivated as well her own secret order of young nobles, who would carry out her commands, consulting no other, including me. That violence was ordered by Olympias, if not in my name, then out of love for me and to secure my succession, was a source to me not only of extreme anguish but of outrage at its insult to the authority I was struggling so mightily to found. Three times in one night, I betook myself to my mother's chamber to beg her to bring her excesses under control. I had resolved before entering to place her under house arrest, if not bundle her in a drawstring sack and cart her out of the kingdom. It was like calling upon Medea. As soon as I entered, Olympias recalled her self-command and, banishing all in attendance upon her, commenced to counsel me in a tenor both maniacal and irresistible. Which of my father's generals could I trust. Whom must I coerce, whom influence, whom put out of the way. What must I wear, how must I speak; what steps must I take in relation to the League of Corinth, to Athens, Thebes, Persia. She was raving, yet lucid as Persephone. I could take no action against her; her guidance was too valuable. Each night as I departed, she seized my hands in hers; her eyes fastened on mine as if to fuse into me by the medium of her passion both her will to triumph and her conviction in the supremacy of my destiny.

She informed me that Philip was not my father, but that on the night of my conception, Zeus had visited her in the form of a serpent. I was God's son. She, my mother, was Heaven's bride. The queen had gone mad as a magpie. To compound the singularity of this scene, Olympias seemed in that hour to have regained the beauty of her youth. Her eyes shone, her skin glowed; her jet hair glistened in the lamplight. She was spectacular. There was no woman like her in all Greece. The only real pleasure I took in those first days was sending my generals

Antipater and Antigonus One-Eye to call upon her in her chambers.
They practically pissed themselves. I don't blame them. Who could
know with what flavorings Philip's consort had laced her wafers?

Over my father's grave, the corpse of his assassin was crucified, exposed, and burned. His young sons' throats were slit on the site; also executed were the grown sons of Prince Aeropus, my cousins, convicted
by the army of conspiracy. We buried Philip's horses with him, those he
loved most, and his youngest bride, Chianna of Eordaea. Here is the eulogy I pronounced:

> *Knights and Companions, brothers of the nation in arms, Philip
> took the throne when most of you subsisted by following your herds,
> winter pasture to summer, clad in the hides of animals. When your
> savage neighbors raided, you fled to the mountains, and even there you
> could not hold the invaders off. Philip brought you down out of your
> hideouts and taught you to fight. He restored your pride. He made you
> an army.*
>
> *He settled you in cities, gave you laws, lifted you to a life beyond
> fear and squalor. He made you rulers over the Paeonians and Illyrians
> and Triballians, who had robbed and enslaved you before he came.
> What had been Thrace, he made Macedon. The ports Athens claimed,
> he brought beneath your command. He got you gold and trade. He
> made you lords over the Thessalians, before whom you used to trem-
> ble; he humbled the Phocians, and paved the broad highway for you
> into Greece.*
>
> *Athens and Thebes had raped your mothers and sisters and
> stolen your goods at their whim. Philip broke their pride, so that
> instead of paying tribute to the one and hopping at the beck of the
> other, they come now before us, suing for protection. How thorough
> is his mastery of war? I read down the roll of Greeks and Persians,
> Cyrus the Great and the elder Darius, Miltiades at Marathon,
> Leonidas at Thermopylae, Themistocles, Cimon, Pericles, Brasidas
> and Alcibiades, Lysander and Pelopidas and Epaminondas. All are
> children alongside Philip. The Greeks named him supreme com-*

mander for the coming war against Persia, not because they wished it (for they hate and despise us, as you know), but because his greatness commanded nothing less. Say "I am a Macedonian." Before Philip, men laughed in your face. Now they quake. All this he did, and brought honor not only to himself but to you, and to our country.

The army swept down to Greece and set things in order. At Corinth I was acknowledged hegemon of the League of States, succeeding to my father's place. Now the tribes beyond the Danube made their break. We went north by forced marches. The men's will to fight was unquenchable. We fought four battles in six days, crossing the mightiest river in Europe twice without ships or bridges, getting four thousand men and fifteen hundred horses to the far shore in a single day. In all this time, not a soldier was disciplined, nor a harsh command given voice.

North of the Danube, the army broke ten thousand wild Celts and Germans in a field of wheat. These savages stand a head taller than we do, massive specimens who can lift their own ponies, yet they fled like rats before this machine founded and elevated to perfection by my father and Antipater and Parmenio.

Crossing the Axius at Eidomene, trekking home victorious, I draw up just to watch the column pass. No wagons. Philip had banned them as too slow. No women, no traders. One pack animal for five men and one servant for ten. Everything the army needs it carries on its back, in wicker rucksacks (fifty pounds of kit) with a counterpack (thirty) across the chest and iron causia helmets strapped in front. Each phalangite packs his eighteen-foot sarissa in two pieces, with the bronze sleeve on his belt, and his oxhide shoes hanging by rawhide laces round his neck. Barefoot, the column takes the ford as if it were dry land. By heaven, how the men move! Where the foe expects us, we are forty miles past. Where he believes we'll be tomorrow, we are tonight; where he makes us out to be today, we have passed through yesterday.

I watch the Agrianes trek. These are my own men, hired from the north with my own purse and incorporated now into my army. For mountain fighting, javelineers are indispensable, for the enemy makes defensive stands at passes, which cannot be assaulted head-on, but the heights must be taken and, for this, heavy infantry is useless. The Agrianes travel light, with only a chlamys cloak-and-blanket like our own, and no armor or helmet. All the weight is in their weapons. Some carry as many as a dozen. The crafting of each javelin can take months, with sacrifices offered to the shaft of ash or cornel while it still grows on the tree. "Truth" is the missile weapon's supreme virtue, meaning the absolute straightness of its line, for a warped javelin will not fly true. Each dart or spike, as the Agrianians call them, is carried in a doeskin sleeve lined with beeswax. No measure is spared to protect its truth. The javelineers sleep with their spikes; I have seen men wrap them in their cloaks while they themselves shiver, to keep the snow and wet from swelling the grain. Each man's dart bears his sign and the sign of his clan; after a fight, he scours the field, retrieving his own and no other's. It is death to do so. A blooded dart receives its own name, and one which has made a kill is passed down from father to son.

The javelineer's art is taught down generations; boys train for years before being allowed to cast a man-sized spike. In the field the Agrianes fight as pairs—father and son, older brother and younger—the senior serving as hurler and his apprentice as loader and spotter. They are like hunters; they play the wind. They know how to keep their dart's head down upwind and in a crosswind to lead their cast like fowlers taking prey on the wing. A javelin is thrown by a sling and with spin. It takes tremendous skill to cast a spike so that it does not "top" or "sail." To behold the perfection of flight achieved by a master, his missile neither "pluming" nor "tailing," but "holding its head up" as it tracks in to its target—this is a thing both beautiful and terrifying, and the man who can do it is accounted of supreme consequence. I have trained a thousand hours with the javelin. It looks easy; it is impossible. The Agrianes are devastating. Their mere appearance in the field has caused valiant foes to withdraw without a fight.

I am yarning with their prince Amalpis, on horseback at the Axius crossing, when a courier gallops up from the south:

Thebes is risen on report of Alexander's death in battle.
The populace dances in the streets,
proclaiming Greece's dawn of freedom.

Patriots of Thebes, the dispatch says, have surprised our garrison and murdered its commanders. The city has revolted; the whole south threatens to follow.

Hephaestion and Craterus spur to me. I feel my daimon as I read. The sequence of experience is this: a flush of rage, succeeded immediately by a chill; then a state of pure, detached objectivity. Emotion has fled. My mind is pellucid. I am thinking the way an eagle thinks, or a lion. The route south to Thebes is lucky; from where we stand, we need not trek back through Pella, Macedon's capital, where the army's passage will be reported by spies. Instead we can cross the high country, touching no towns, making Pelinna in Thessaly before any but goatherds sight us. I will stand on the doorstep of Thebes before these bastards even learn I'm alive.

The fury I experience is not, I recognize, at the Thebans for seeking their freedom; one must admire their spirit for that. Nor am I inflamed at their joy on report of my death. The distinction is subtle.

It is that they could *believe me dead*. That they dare credit such a thing.

The affront, do you see, is to my daimon.

It is nine days to Pelinna. We make it in seven. The column drives south, impelled by anger. Our garrison commander at Thebes was a well-loved fellow, Amyntas, called Abrutes, "Eyebrows." Here is his story. His wife Cynna bore only daughters, four without a son. The man pledged his estate to the goddess if she would send a boy child. She did, but fever carried the lad off in infancy, crushing Abrutes and, of course, impoverishing him. It chanced that he had a brother and a cousin whose wives both gave birth to sons at the same time and who had other healthy boy children. Each without the other's knowledge came to this officer and offered their newborns. The men arrived at Abrutes's house within minutes of each other. All were so struck by the coincidence that they dropped to their knees, worshiping heaven. Within a year Abrutes's wife delivered triplets, all boys. So our good fellow had gone in a matter of months from a state of desolation without male issue to the father of five strapping lads. They all grew straight and strong (they were ten and eleven now) and he loved them and was proud of them, and they of him and of his post as garrison commander at Thebes. The Thebans slit his throat and hung him on a hook. His executive officer was a captain of Anthemos named Alexides. The Thebans flung him, bound, from the battlements above the Ismenian Gate and left his corpse for dogs and crows.

The army presses south at a furious pace. You can tell when men truly rage because they are silent. Reports of wider revolt reach us on the march. Insurgents exiled by Philip have returned to Acarnania and been welcomed; our garrison in Elis has been expelled; the Arcadians annul their oaths, marching to Thebes's aid; Argos, Ambracia, and Sparta make plans to rise. At Athens, we learn later, the demagogue Demosthenes has appeared garlanded in the Assembly; he has even produced an eyewitness who claims to have seen my dead body. The city boils over with jubilation.

On the trek, men sign to me, thumb across the throat. They want Athens. Antigonus One-Eye cites Athens's outrages of our country in the past—the fates of Eion, Scyros, Torone, and Scione, where all adult males were massacred and women and children sold as slaves. Athens's fleet is three hundred, Antigonus reminds me; she cries poor but, dosed with courage, could prove the dagger in our back when we march on Persia.

My daimon does not want Athens. Athens is Greece's jewel. Who razes her stands with Xerxes in infamy.

Six days past Pelinna, we strike the Boeotian frontier. Dawn fourteen, the army appears before Thebes. The city is paralyzed with terror. Our forces surround the walls, sealing off all escape from within and all reinforcement from without.

Still the Thebans will not quit. They raid our camp under cover of truce. The men of our garrison remain in their hands, trapped in the citadel Cadmea. The foe threatens to spit them over coals if I don't withdraw. Meanwhile he sneaks couriers out, calling on all Greece to rise, now, to shuck the yoke of Macedon.

I parley with the enemy, hoping for accommodation. He will not give it. Next noon Perdiccas on his own makes a rush on the Electra Gate. The Thebans resist; I must send the archers and three phalanx brigades, then follow myself at the head of the Royal Guards. The foe cracks at the Cadmea. We are in the city now. One push and Thebes will fall.

Antipater reins beside me, in the square beneath the Thebiad, with Amyntas and Antigonus One-Eye. "You are reluctant, Alexander, to order the destruction of so famous a city. You would not be remembered as the man who fired the birthplace of Heracles, native state of Oedipus and Epaminondas. That is past. Piss on it!"

I am at war not with Thebes, I see, but with my daimon.

"Show clemency," Antigonus warns, "and you lose the army!"

Hephaestion confronts him: "Command a massacre and we lose Alexander!"

I listen.

I will give the order.

I will wipe Thebes from the earth.

"Spare those citizens," I direct, "who have taken our cause. Save the house of the poet Pindar and those of his heirs, and all shrines and altars of the gods. Take no action until I have sacrificed to Heracles and received token of his assent."

Thebes is forty thousand. The roundup and slaughter take all night. The Thebans fight in the squares and the alleys. When companies become too decimated to resist as units, they break apart, each man seeking to save his own. Families bolt themselves within doors. When these are broken in, the citizens punch through the party walls with axes and make their way house to house, fleeing the Phocians and Plataeans and Orchomenians (whose cities Thebes has razed in the past) who hunt them along lanes gone to fire. From atop the walls, Hephaestion, Telamon, and I can see the dead ends where scores are trapped and butchered.

More perish by fire than sword. Within the houses, paint catches first. Roof timbers, desiccated over decades, go up like tinder. Mud bricks shatter from the heat, sending walls crashing. Plumes shoot from flues; firestorms ignite. The inferno leaps across rooftops from quarter to quarter, while the hive of tenements that is the central city funnels the blaze like a blacksmith's bellows, incinerating all in its path.

Hephaestion cannot endure the holocaust. He rides out alone onto the plain. You can see the conflagration from sixty miles and smell it from twenty. At intervals throughout the night, chiefs of the pillagers come before me. Shall we spare the tomb of Antigone? The Thebiad? The Cadmea?

Mid-second watch, I am shown the body of Coroneus, the gentle knight of Chaeronea, whose lion's crest I wear affixed to my breastplate. He has fallen leading the attack upon our garrison, one-armed, taking two of our own.

Spare nothing, I tell them.

Destroy everything.

With the dawn, Hephaestion, Telamon, and I enter the city proper. Six thousand have been slain, thirty thousand will be sold as slaves. On the Street of the Saddlers, bodies are piled as high as a man's waist. Our horses tread upon charred flesh and step over severed limbs. Women and children have been herded into the squares, awaiting the slavers' auction. Their captors have scrawled their names on them in their own blood, handier than paint, so the slave masters will know whom to pay. We pass corpses, burst by the inferno. Even Telamon is appalled. "This must have been," he says, "what Troy looked like."

I do not believe it. "This is worse."

Antipater rides up. "Well, that's that." He claps my shoulder like a father. "Now all Greece will fear you."

We have not spoken all night, Hephaestion and I, beyond commands passed through him and Telamon to the colonels manning the cordon. I have directed the slave dealers to separate no mother from her children, but to hold all families intact for sale. Now with dawn, the innocents have been herded to the Five Ways outside the Proetis Gate. The slavers are collecting the best-looking women to sell as concubines. They tear the dames' infants from their grasp, while other matrons, in compassion, take the babes among their own. "Shall I see your orders enforced?" Telamon asks.

I meet his eyes. Well-intentioned gesture seems absurd at this point. The slave masters, compelled to keep dam and pups together, will only unload the young ones out of sight down the road, or dump them dead in a ditch. At least with proxy mothers, the infants will survive.

"Let it pass," I say.

Day breaks. I peer northwest toward Chaeronea. Already packs of looters are streaming in from Phocis and Locris; they flood through the gates, mute with avarice, to pick the bones of royal Thebes. Shall I stop them? What for?

Later Hephaestion and I scrub up in the trickle of the summer Ismenus. The grime of massacre will not wash off so easily. My mate turns back toward the ruin that is Thebes. "I would not, yesterday, have thought you capable of this."

"I was not capable of it," I reply. "Yesterday."

Ten

HEPHAESTION

T HE FIRST TIME I SAW HEPHAESTION, I WAS TEN YEARS OLD. He was
eleven. He had just come down to Pella from his family's estate in
the highlands of Eordaea. Hephaestion's father, Amyntor, represented
the interests of Athens at my father's court. This was a hereditary post,
called *proxenos*, and one of great honor. However, with the abundant
friction, not to say outright warfare, between our state and the Athenians', Amyntor feared that the ire Philip sometimes felt toward him for
his advocacy of Athens's cause (though the two men had been brought
up together and remained great friends) might prejudice the king
against Amyntor's young son and thus impede the lad's career. So
Hephaestion was held apart from court life until he turned eleven. It
was only then that his father brought him to the capital, to prepare him
for the School of Royal Pages, which he would enter, as I would, at fourteen.

At that time I had a tutor named Leonidas. It was this man's habit,
as a means of "thickening my bark," to wake me an hour before dawn
and march me down to the river, where I must strip and plunge in, in
all weathers. I hated this. The Loudias at Pella is bone-numbing even in

summer; in winter its depth of cold is indescribable. I tried every trick to duck these dousings. Eventually it came to me that, rather than endure them beneath compulsion, which rendered them doubly abhorrent, I would elect to do them on my own. I began arising before my tutor, getting the chore over with while he lay yet in bed. Leonidas was much gratified by this evolution of my character, while, for my own part, the ordeal had been rendered tolerable, now that I could tell myself it was my own idea. In any event, one dawn, of a day so cold that one had to smash the ice on the river with a great stone just to get in, I was returning from my plunge, going past the Royal Riding School, when I heard hoof strikes within. I entered silently. Hephaestion was alone in the ring, mounted on a seventeen-hand chestnut, his own, named Swift, running up-and-backs, hands free, with the short lance. His teacher stood in the center of the arena, keeping up a running stream of instruction, to which Hephaestion responded with a focus that was at once keenly intense and thoroughly relaxed. I had never seen an individual, man or boy, so patient with his mount. He forced nothing, guiding the horse with legs and seat alone. He took Swift from canter to trot to canter to gallop, all the while preserving absolute straightness, even on a curved line. Advancing down the long axis of the ring, his horse was not "called to the wall" as mine was (not Bucephalus—I had not acquired him yet), and in the turns kept his legs beneath him, not lazily as my own animal, but collected, ready, with tremendous impulsion, so that when Hephaestion urged Swift to the canter and then to the gallop, the mount shot forward, dead straight and in balance, poised to respond to any command, to turn or wheel in any direction. Hephaestion himself sat the horse as if he were nailed to him. Spine erect, shoulders square, belly muscles working, he impelled the beast with a forward lean so subtle you could barely see it, and turned him with equal command, all with only his seat and legs. I flushed with shame to witness this, for it came to me, who till that moment had considered himself an accomplished rider for his age, how little of horsemanship I knew and what a complacent and ignorant brat I was. My father! Why had he set this addle-pated pedagogue Leonidas over me, to duck me in ice, when I should be learning *this*? But immediately my anger turned upon myself.

I alone am master of my life! I vowed in that instant not only to dedicate myself to the study of horses and horsemanship, to make myself without peer as cavalryman and cavalry officer, but to educate myself in all things, to become my own tutor, selecting the subjects I needed to master and seeking instruction on my own.

Hephaestion still had not seen me, nor could I summon the temerity to approach him. I thought him not only the handsomest youth I had ever seen but the handsomest person of any age. I vowed to myself, "That boy shall be my friend. When we are grown, we will ride together against the princes of Persia."

Men believe a boy's concerns to be those of a child. Nothing could be further from the fact. At ten I apprehended the world as keenly as I do today, more so, as my instincts had not yet been dulled by schooling and the stultifying superimposition of conventional thought. I knew, there, in that ring, that this boy Hephaestion would be my lifelong companion. I loved him with all my heart and knew, as well, that he would love me. Nothing in the intervening years has altered that perception.

I did not speak to him for another eighteen months. But I watched him. When a thing confounded me, I searched him out and observed him as he did it. He became aware of this. Yet he honored our tacit segregation, and I would not speak until the time was right.

By the time I was twelve, we were inseparable. And let me put this plain, for those of a depraved cast of mind: The love of young men is bound up with dreams and shared secrets and the aspiration not only for glory but for that purity of virtue that their hearts perceive as soiled or degraded among the generation senior to themselves but that they, the youth, shall reinspirit and carry through. This love is not so different from that of young girls for each other; it has its physical element, but among those of noble mind, this is far superseded by the philosophical. Like Theseus and Pirithous, Heracles and Iolaus, like Achilles and Patrocles, young men wish to capture brides for each other; they dream not of being each other's men, but each other's best men.

In my thirteenth year my father's persuasion (and his gold) brought the philosopher Aristotle to Pella, to serve as tutor to the rabble of boys, sons of the king's Companions, who cared for nothing but horses and hunting and running off to arms. Hephaestion and Ptolemy, Hector, Love Locks, Cassander, we were all in it. Aristotle's brother-in-law Euphorion was our Greek instructor. It was his job to make us spit out our horrible Macedonian and speak pure Attic stuff. Have you ever sought to master a language? There is always one boy in class who cannot get it right. Ours was Marsyas, Antigonus's son. When he tried to wrap his tongue around Athenian Greek, the rest of us blew up like puffer fish. One noon we could no longer contain ourselves. We exploded, rolling on the grass in hysterics.

Hephaestion rose and lit into us. I had never seen him so angry. Did we think this was funny? He pointed east over the sea. "That way is Persia, my numbskull friends, the lands we dream of one day conquering. The Persians know we are coming. What do they do now? As we giggle and clown, the sons of the East are hard at training. While we sleep, they toil. While we dawdle, they sweat." By now our mob was thoroughly chastened; even our tutor looked sheepish. "We will meet those youths of Persia soon enough upon the field of war. Will it suffice to prove ourselves the greater brutes? Never! We must excel the foe, not only as warriors but as men and as knights. They must say of us that we deserve their empire, for we surpass them in virtue and in self-command!"

Report of Hephaestion's tirade tore through Pella on wings. Everywhere men clapped him on the shoulder in approbation; when he entered the market, saddlers and greengrocers stood to cheer. My father summoned me in private. "This is the boy you have chosen out of all to be your friend? He seems to me a man already." Philip's highest praise. After that, it was not considered effeminate to study poetry or to labor to learn proper Greek.

This was Hephaestion who indicted me, in his way, after the holocaust of Thebes. What could I say to him? As boys we were taught, in our tutor Aristotle's phrase, that happiness consisted in "the active exercise of one's faculties in conformity with virtue." But virtue in war is written in the enemy's blood.

Regret, Telamon had taught, has no place in the soldier's kit of war.

I know this is true. But I know, as well, that no act comes without a price. All men must answer for their crimes. I shall for mine.

The razing of Thebes, however, had accomplished its purpose. It had showed Greece who held the reins. No more cities revolted; no further insurrections flared. Instead, embassies poured into Pella, tendering congratulation and lading me with effusions of praise. The Greeks had been rooting for me all along, it seemed. They couldn't do enough to help now. "Lead us, Alexander!" their ambassadors declared. "Lead us against Persia!"

Contingents of volunteers came in from Athens and all the states of the League. The army enrolled seven thousand heavy infantry and six hundred cavalry; five thousand more foot troops signed up for pay. The expeditionary force now numbered nearly forty-two thousand, counting the ten thousand foot and fifteen hundred horse already across the straits, securing the bridgehead in Asia.

The hour of the Great Embarkation approached. Pella had become an armed camp. The place boiled over with eagerness for action; anticipation had reached such a pitch that even the animals could not sleep. An act was needed. Some gesture on my part, like Brasidas's when he burned his ships at Methone, so the men would know this step was fatal, no turning back.

I called the army together at Dium for the Festival of the Muses. The coastline is spectacular there; in the distance Ossa and Olympus ascend, snow-mantled. The nation encamped across the grounds, sixty thousand men-at-arms (including those who would remain at home, under Antipater, as a garrison force), with that number twice over in wives and mistresses, grooms, squires, and the general crowd. I threw a great feast. It broke my purse and emptied the treasury. Parmenio and Antipater sat in stations of honor, with the other generals and officers ringed about.

I began giving away my lands. In Macedon the king's holdings are called *basileia cynegesia*, the Royal Hunt. These comprised at my accession about a third of the kingdom. Further, all provinces captured in war are considered "under the Crown." The result was that I held mines, farm- , pasture- , and timberlands in tens of thousands of acres. To each of Philip's generals I gave baronies, with titles and lands in perpetuity. My own estate, Lake Bluff, I presented to Parmenio, who, to his great credit, declined. Brigade commanders received princely holdings. To Hephaestion I gave the Royal Hunt of Eordaea, my father's own parkland, and estates nearly as brilliant to every officer down to the rank of captain. I gave Antigonus three valleys on the upper Strymon. To Telamon went a village overlooking Torone Bay. The more I gave away, the lighter I felt. I wished to strip my baggage to the buckle, leaving nothing but my horse and my lance. I gave fisheries away, and mines, and river and lake frontages. Down to each sergeant, men got horse properties or sheep pastures. Each man of the phalanx received a farm. I forgave all debts and granted exemptions of taxation to every man under arms. Everything that had been Philip's, and all that was mine, I conferred upon my friends. Timber tracts across the frontier, I returned to the Illyrian princes from whom I had seized them, with more parcels added, now they were our allies; wheat provinces across the Danube and pasturelands in Thrace I presented to our comrades of Thessaly, Paeonia, and Agriania. With each presentation, fresh ovations ascended. It was Perdiccas, my dear mate, when I had fixed upon him the barony of Thriassa, who asked, before all, "What will you keep for yourself, Alexander?"

I had not even considered this.

"My hopes," I replied, intending no jest. The assembly erupted into citations such as, it seemed, would never end.

Only three men remained without bounties. My brave commanders Coenus, Love Locks, and Eugenides (Payday from Chaeronea). Their names had not been called. You could see they experienced keen dismay over this. No doubt they feared they had incurred my displeasure for cause unknown, and this plunged them into desolation.

The second officer, Payday, had grounds to believe this, for he had nearly deserted on the Danube, for love of a maid of the northern tribes, and I had only spared him, he believed, out of respect for his father, who had been a *syntrophos*, a schoolmate, of Philip. In secret in the interim, however, my agents had tracked down this girl, Payday's sweetheart; she being a free woman (so we couldn't take her by force), I had petitioned her by private dispatch to accept the man's hand. She was here now in her bridal garland, concealed from her lover's sight, as were the darlings of Coenus and Love Locks, likewise in ignorance of this design.

When at last I called the trio forward and presented them with their brides, the tumult of celebration seemed to mount to heaven. We married them on the spot.

Do you know, in all the excitement, only one person thought to give a gift to me. This was Elyse, the bride of Payday. She presented me with a pair of dancing slippers, stitched by her own hand. This was the happiest I had ever been. So much so that, looking toward Mount Olympus, brilliant beneath the moon, I thought that not even the gods must know satisfaction as sweet as this.

Now the generals rose to speak. "Brothers," declared Antigonus One-Eye, "when Philip was slain, I confess I questioned in my heart if his son could fill his boots. Clearly Alexander possessed the courage, the genius, and the ambition. But could one so young command the loyalty of veterans and senior commanders? My friends, tonight we have our answer! For I see in our young king's eyes that his own selfish ends are nothing to him, but glory alone is the prize he labors for. As the Hyrcanian said of Cyrus the Great,

> *I swear to you, friends, by all the gods, he seems to me*
> *happier in doing us kindnesses than in enriching himself."*

Man after man arose to second such sentiments. Payday addressed me with tears running into the brush of his beard. "You have presented me with a bride, Alexander, my heart's darling, and more wealth than I ever dreamt of. Yet, by Zeus's hand, if you will give me leave first to seed an heir with my beloved, I wish not to idle upon these lands or to take pleasure in their bounties, but to arm and follow you wherever you lead!"

My gallant commander Coenus addressed me next. "Take us to Sardis, to Babylon, to Persepolis herself. I for one, Alexander, shall not rest until I behold you seated upon the throne of Persia itself!"

Book Four

SHAME AT FAILURE

Eleven

THE BATTLE OF THE GRANICUS

ARE YOU FOLLOWING OUR NARRATIVE, ITANES? I see you like the "bloody parts" best. Keep pace with the army, then, as it marches east out of Macedon, crosses the straits between Europe and Asia (in the opposite direction from that taken by Xerxes of Persia a hundred and fifty years earlier) and plants its lion standard on soil claimed, in our time, by Darius the Third. Where is he now, the current Lord of the East? He has not deigned to greet us, avengers of ancient wrongs, but has sent his subordinates, governors of the western provinces, with a hundred thousand horse and foot, to drive us back into the sea. His army marshals at Zeleia, in the shadow of holy Troy, blocking the so-called Asian Gates. But let us get straight to the action.

The closest I have come to being killed, so far (except at Gaza, when I was shot by a bolt from a catapult), was in this battle at the Granicus River. There the Persian knight Rhoesaces landed a blow with his saber to the fore crown of my helmet that lacked only a thumb's breadth from taking off the top of my head. Line cavalry of Persia are armed with the javelin and the *acinaces* dagger, or were at that time, before they learned from us the superiority of the lance, except the One

Thousand and the Kinsmen, whose arms are gifts of the Crown and who fight with the Damascene saber, a slashing weapon, identical to the one Cyrus the Great used. The sword is single-edged, extremely strong and heavy, with haft and blade forged of a single piece of Syrian steel.

Rhoesaces' blow sheared away the crown of my helmet at the same instant my lance entered his breast just below the right nipple. The impact of his blow took the iron foreplate of my helmet clean off, along with its crest of white kestrel feathers, not to mention opening a gash across my scalp that took, after the fight, twenty-seven stitches to sew back in place. At the time I felt nothing and was discommoded only by the blood sheeting into my eyes. There is a secret that all wounded men know, and the secret is this: When you know your wound won't kill or permanently disable you, you enjoy it. You take pride in it. At that time in the action we had already lost thirty of the bravest Companions of Socrates Redbeard's squadron, who had made the initial assault and suffered terribly beneath the fusillade of the foe, manning the bluffs above the crossing. The agony of these heroes cried out to me, whose order had sent them to their end. I wanted to bleed more, and suffer more, for their sake.

When the king of Macedon charges onto the foe at the head of his Companions, he is flanked by knights of such valor, mounted upon such superlative stock, drilled to such a pitch of prowess, and incented by such a drive for glory, as to make the force effectively irresistible. Nothing in warfare, ancient or modern, is comparable to the shock of this arm. No analogy can portray it. Black Cleitus once said he felt, at the gallop on the wing of the leading wedge, as if he were riding some spectacular warship of iron, driven before the gale. That's not bad, except it leaves out the fundamental element that gives the charge of the Companions its invincibility. I mean the heat and breath of its living, churning rush. It is not mechanical. It is visceral. At the gallop in the *embolon*'s point, I can smell the garlic on Telamon's breath to my left. My boot bangs against the shoulder of Hephaestion's mount, Swift, on my right; I feel the bronze of its breastplate and smell the turf of the divots torn up by our rush. Bucephalus beneath me is so hot that steam rises from his flesh; the jets of his nostrils scald to the touch. I feel his will, not as an extension of mine, but as a force generated by his own valiant heart. He is alive and aware not as a beast but as a warrior. His joy fires me. I feed upon it, as I feel him feed upon mine. He loves this. It is what he was born for.

As our leading wedge plunges into the shallows of the Granicus and the javelins of the foe rip past our ears with a sound like the tearing of linen, my horse and I enter a kind of ecstasy, whose essence is surrender to fate. I feel the shock of the sand and gravel bottom as Bucephalus's hooves receive it and transfer it up his forelegs. I am leaning forward to drive and direct him; I feel the impulsion of his hindquarters as his spine extends and contracts; he is collected beneath me; I ride a bolt of thunder.

We strike the foe. The smell is of stone and piss and iron. What can be prepared for, has been. What can be thought out, has. Where we are now is the sphere of pure chance. A score of missiles make us their object; a hundred hearts cry heaven's aid to bring us down. Nothing can protect us. Not our armor, not our will, not our mates at our shoulders (though in moments Black Cleitus's blade will hack off at the elbow the right arm of the Persian knight Spithridates as he poises a blow to send me to hell). Only the lord of Olympus Himself, to whom I, as all within the jaws of death, pray without ceasing.

You have asked, Itanes, if I feel fear. I answer, I may not. The soldier in the line is permitted to feel terror; the commander never. Too much depends upon him—the lives of his mates, the fate of the action. He cannot allow himself the luxury of fear. I eat mine, as a lion devours a kid. I consume it by my will to glory and my obligation to the corps.

The Granicus is a swift and shallow stream, descending from Mount Ida near the source of the Scamander, which waters the plains of Troy. Its course winds through larch and alder woods, dropping fast and cutting deep through the marine conglomerate of the seacoast; it turns round Ida's shoulder, carving a straight stony channel north toward the Propontis, across the plain of the Greek city of Adrasteia. The field is sandy but firm, good riding turf. A fine site for an army of Asia to meet and throw back an invader.

As I said, King Darius is not present. I have been sending riders forward all day, seeking sign of his chariot and distinctive armor. He is a thousand miles east, we learn, on pillows at Susa or Persepolis. I am bitterly disappointed.

The Lord of Asia believes surrogates will suffice to repel me.

Our army emerges onto the plain of the Granicus late in the day, after marching four hours from Priapus. Two hours of daylight remain. The Persians are drawn up on the far bank. Their front is all cavalry, twenty thousand, give or take (nearly four times our number), a mile and a half end to end. Their knights do not wait beside their horses, but sit them, in armor. To their rear—well behind, nearly a quarter mile— are marshaled the foe's heavy infantry, Greek mercenaries, mostly Arcadians and Peloponnesians, with some Spartans, six or seven thousand in all, a formidable force, though ours outnumbers it significantly. These foot troops are reinforced by what looks like another sixty thousand in local levy, Phrygians, Mysians, Armenians, Paphlagonians, conscripts doubtless, not even soldiers but farmers and laborers who will bolt at the first scraped knee. We are a few hundred short of forty-three thousand— sarissa infantry in six regiments of fifteen hundred each; three thousand in the Royal Guards brigades, armed as heavy infantry; with supporting divisions of Odrysian, Triballian, Illyrian, Paeonian, allied Greek, and mercenary infantry, both light- and heavy-armed, and the nearly ten-thousand-strong bridgehead force of Macedonian regulars and Thracian mercenaries, totaling another thirty thousand. Our horse are eight squadrons of Companion Cavalry under Philotas, two hundred men in each (though some are overstrength to two-fifty), except the Royal Squadron under Black Cleitus, which is three hundred. This Macedonian element is eighteen hundred total, as is the Thessalian Heavy Horse under Calas, serving beneath Parmenio, who will take the left. The Royal Lancers make another eight hundred, in four squadrons, all Macedonian; the squadron of Paeonian Light Horse adds two hundred; six hundred in allied Greek cavalry; four hundred of Thrace; five hundred Cretan archers and about the same in javelineers of Agrania. The army emerges onto the plain, about a mile from the river. "Now," I instruct Telamon, who will pass the order to form the battle line. "Smartly."

The corps deploys from order of march to line of attack. Cavalry and missile troops take the right; to their left are Nicanor's Royal Guardsmen; then, in order, filling the center, the heavy brigades of Perdiccas, Coenus, Amyntas Andromenes, Craterus, Meleager, and Philip Amyntas; the left of the line are Thracians, mercenaries, and allied Greeks, this last under Antigonus One-Eye, with the allies, hired cavalry, and Thessalians comprising the wing. I ride at the fore about an eighth of a mile, onto what passes for a hill but feels more like a pimple; we are already calling it "the Pimple." As couriers I have eleven aides-de-camp, bright, ambitious officers on fast, nimble horses with plenty of bottom. As each unit of a division has a rotation, so do these aides; they wait to my rear; their eyes never leave me. At a sign from Telamon the next courier comes forward to receive his dispatch and to speed away. I do not relay the text in person, but pass it by Hephaestion, Ptolemy, Eumenes, or Red Attalus, who, with eleven other knights, comprise my *agema*, or combat Bodyguard. The first word is the commander to whom the message is addressed. Next the text. Last, any query. "Philotas, set the line at three hundred yards back from the river, one squadron deep, in Dragon's Teeth by fifties. Stand easy. Do you need anything?" Off goes the aide at the gallop. By the time the second, third, and fourth couriers have been given their messages and have sped away, the first is back with Philotas's response.

"Rest!" The infantry looses the leather carrying slings that take the weight of their sarissas; they plunge the butt spikes of the weapons into the earth; the upright pikes look like a forest of boughless trees with one leaf of iron. The troops drop to one knee, easing the shields slung across their chests, letting the ground take the weight but keeping the strap buckled across their shoulders. Each file of sixteen has its squire and servant; these lads now scurry from man to man, passing skins of wine. The soldiers take it straight into their cupped hands. It is remarkable how much a man can suck down when fear is on him.

This past month, as we have crossed from Europe to Asia Minor, I have spent every night in conference with our forward agents and "men in place." These assemble now on horseback about my colors. I send them forward to scout the Persian front. They will tell me which units are where, commanded by whom, composed of what elements, and in what numbers.

These fellows—spies, if you like—are indispensable to any army. Some are deserters from the foe. Most are exiles, patriots of nations under the Persian heel. I have scores of them. In Greece, Philip had hundreds.

The types are interesting. One would expect villains. But you find heroes, visionaries. One must respect these fellows. They risk not career or profit, but their lives and the lives of their families. If our cause fails, they will be treated by their countrymen not as soldiers but as traitors.

How does one find such men? Easy. They find you. One man knows another, and this man brings a brother or friend. This was how my father did it. Advancing his army to threaten a state, Philip dispatched envoys to put forward his list of grievances. At the same time, he had agents in place within the foe's walls, so that when citizens of the state in question assembled to debate in public or private, there was never any deficiency of speakers disposed toward Philip, primed with arguments, lubricated with cash, and motivated by the prospect of ascendancy beneath his rule. Carrying on, Philip included in his retinue the sons of the state's leading families, either as officers, commanding their own troops, or as Royal Pages, part of his tent academy. I have no few myself in this corps. Our so-called allied Greeks, twelve thousand foot and six hundred horse, are all hostages, in fact if not in name. They cannot go home and they know it; and if they fail me, for cause false or fair, they shall receive no appeal.

If we prevail on the field today, the cities of the Aegean seaboard will topple to us like tiles. But we cannot permit chaos in this postvictory world. Liberty, order, and justice are what we must bring if we expect to secure our rear and our lines of supply and communication, and to achieve that, we must establish men in power who can be counted upon not to abuse their newly acquired stature, to run amok, or to prosecute personal vendettas. I will seek in these early campaigns to found this principle and adhere to it absolutely. Those states that take me as their friend, I shall make my friends; those that resist will be crushed without mercy.

I don't want the cities; I want Darius.

I don't care about the Aegean. I'm here for Persia.

Our spies come spurring back now. Here are my generals too. "Go now?" asks Philotas, indicating the late sun. If we're going to fight this day, he means, it must be soon or we'll lose the light.

"Is that wise?" inquires Parmenio. He is thinking that the army has marched nearly ten miles this day and that the whole mob had been blind sock-eyed the night before. It's too late in the day, he says. Why assault across a river into the teeth of the foe? He wants to flank-march by night, cross upstream or down, then fight in the morning, when the enemy has been forced to re-form and no longer has the river protecting his front.

I don't like it.

"It's good fighting weather," insists Craterus.

Perdiccas seconds this. "The men's blood is up. Let's make some widows!"

"Where's Memnon?" I want to know.

An aide spurs up, ready to ride.

"No," says Hephaestion, "I'll find him myself." And he's off at the gallop to scout the enemy lines.

Memnon is Darius's foremost general. He's a Greek from Rhodes, a mercenary. The enemy's hired Greek infantry belongs to him.

I need to know Memnon's place in the Persian line. That will influence everything.

Parmenio remarks that the foe's deployment makes no sense. "Why is his infantry back? Why is his cavalry up front?" A trick?

It's no trick; it's pride. "Persian nobles are horsemen. They want the glory of throwing us back."

It is not a field that requires long study. Just tell me where Memnon is.

I know Memnon. When I was a boy, he lived in exile for a season at my father's court at Pella. He befriended me. I learned as much of war from him as from Philip.

Memnon had fought for the Crown of Persia. His forces reconquered Ionia for Artaxerxes when I was a child. His brother Mentor restored Egypt to the Throne. The brothers stood then on a par with kings. They could coin money and found cities. Their wives were Persian nobility, their children educated at Susa and Persepolis. (In fact, they were married to the same woman, the princess Barsine—Mentor first, then Memnon, after his brother was killed.) Revolution forced Memnon to flee. He took refuge at my father's court.

Memnon was not the first year-round professional general, but he was the first other than Philip and Mentor to elevate warcraft to the status of a science. Memnon had begun as a marine. He had held commands at sea; he understood naval warfare as well as fighting on land. He thought in campaigns, not in battles. From his lips I first heard the expression "seeing the whole field," by which he meant the political and strategic context. Memnon understood politics: He could negotiate; he knew how to cultivate men and how to motivate them. He could parley in chambers; he could address an assembly. His mastery of war was total. He could attack and he could defend; he could train men and he could command them. He fed and equipped his troops and he paid them on time. His men loved him. And he had mastered his own emotions. Anger was unknown to him; pride was, in his view, a vice. If delay would win, he would stall all season. You could not provoke him. He would use gold before force, and lies and false undertakings before either. Yet when the situation called for attack, he did not hesitate. He was fearless in action and relentless in pursuit. At the same time he was not above an accommodation. He advanced his best men and served his masters with honor. If he had a weakness, it was a legitimate one: He wished to be recognized, not so much for his brilliance or even his industry as for the radicalness of his conception and his accomplishment.

Memnon was the first field commander to use maps. In those days no one had heard of such a thing. To survey the ground was considered a debasement of the art of war. A general was supposed to know the field from his own reconnaissance or from reports of trusted officers, guides, or locals. To map it was cheating.

But Memnon went beyond surveying fields. He charted specific battlegrounds, not only those upon which armies had clashed in the past but also sites unknown to war, which might prove hospitable at some subsequent time. He kept books of roads and streams, passes and heights and defiles; he plotted the length and breadth of Asia Minor down to footpaths and mountain tracks known only to goatherds. He surveyed sites suitable for camps, then studied the ways by which each might be approached, supplied, or turned. Nor did he anticipate only victory. For each camp he discovered how many columns could withdraw how quickly over which road or track; he even charted sites for ambuscades to cover the retreat he planned for, from the camp he planned for, in case he lost the battle he planned for. He recorded dates for the turning of the seasons and the risings and settings of the sun and moon. He knew the day's and night's length at any field across all Asia west of the Halys. He knew day and date of the barley harvest in Phrygia, Lydia, Cilicia, and the site of every garner, with the names of the brokers who held them. Which rivers were in spate at what season? Could they be forded? Where? When he had completed a battle exercise from his own point of view, he ran it from the foe's. How could his brilliant dispositions be countered? What weaknesses had he left exposed?

I used to visit Memnon when I was eleven. I tormented him for hours with my interrogation. I wished to know the highways of Asia. The great general sat down and taught me. Who were Persia's princes? What kind of men were they? Memnon told me of Arsites and Rheomithres, Spithridates and Niphates and Megadates. He described them in such detail that I felt I would recognize them on sight. He was in love with Persia. The scale of the empire, the grandeur, the courtliness. And the women. I caught it from him. One might suppose, reckoning my relentless aggression against her, that I abhor Persia. On the contrary. I am captivated by it. I made Memnon's man Dorus teach me the language. I can read it still, and need no interpreter to understand it aloud. I loved the names of the places: Babylon, Susa, Persepolis. Memnon was something of an amateur chef. He made a type of hummus with thyme and sesame and baked his own bread, grinding the barley in a soldier's hand mill. I brought him hares and thrushes. We went over Xenophon's *Anabasis* line by line. How narrow are the Cilician Gates? How fast may an army cross the Pillar of Jonah? Is the Euphrates defensible? How can the Persian Gates be turned? I sounded Memnon for his philosophy of war. How would he attack a fixed position? How conduct a reconnaissance? Is defense harder than offense?

Now Hephaestion returns. He has located Memnon.

"There, where the river bends. His sons are with him. Their tails are up. He's looking to knock us stiff."

Most fords are at bends. The river is shallowest where it turns. I can see the surface absent dazzle (the late sun favors us) as it spills over the boulder-strewn bed.

To Telamon: "Get Red up here."

I mean Socrates Redbeard, who commands the squadron of Companions first in today's rotation. I will hurl him at Memnon. I dispatch a rider to Amyntas Arrhibaeus, whom I will place in command of the units supporting Redbeard, and to Black Cleitus, on the wing, commanding him to bring the Royal Squadron to me in the center.

Redbeard and Amyntas arrive at the gallop. I lay out the scheme in phrases curt as code. "It'll be raining iron, Red."

He laughs. "I'm not afraid to get wet."

To my commanders, I detail the design of attack. But my mates must know not just what and how but why. I address Parmenio, speaking for the hearing of all.

"If we delay, my friend, the foe may slip away in the night. Surely Memnon is urging this course with all his vigor. It's the smart thing to do; he knows time works for him and against us. If the enemy makes off, we shall be forced to chase him from city to fortified city, while he bleeds us of money and supplies. Only win here today and these same cities fall to us without a fight." I gesture across to the river. "Look there, where the foe awaits us. Have we not prayed for such a sight? Now the Maker of Earth and Sky has given it to us. Thank Him and take what is ours!"

I turn to Telamon. "Get them up."

He signs to the corps's sergeant major. Trumpets blare. Across two thousand yards, grooms boost riders onto chargers' backs. At once the field alters. The hair rises all over my body. A cheer ascends. To my rear, the forest of pikes springs alive as men rise from one knee; on both flanks, squadrons take their wedges. The waiting is over. Generals scatter to their divisions.

The following is the order of battle of the satraps of Darius on the plain of the Granicus River.

The enemy's front is all cavalry. His left is two thousand under Arsames, provincial governor of Cilicia, with Memnon in support with five hundred Greek mercenary horse, Ionians mostly, paid from Memnon's purse. Right of these are stationed Arsites, governor of Hellespontine Phrygia, defending his home turf and in overall command, with about a thousand Phrygian and three thousand Paphlagonian cavalry, and two thousand Hyrcanians under Spithridates, satrap of Lydia and Ionia, Arsites' cousin and son-in-law of Darius. These fight under the colors of Arsites, whose pennant is a golden crane on a field of scarlet. The Persians call these standards "serpents" for their long snaky shape and the way they writhe upon the wind. Right of Spithridates stands his brother Rhoesaces, commanding a thousand mailed cataphracts of Media, in coats of iron, formed like fish scales. We hoist one after the battle: It weighs ninety pounds. The mounts that bear this armor are Parthian chargers, massive as draft horses. The Persian center is four thousand heavy cavalry, commanded by the satraps Atizyes and Mithrobarzanes of Greater Phrygia and Cappadocia, as well as Mithridates, Darius's son-in-law, with a thousand Light Horse under his own pay, himself mounted on a sorrel stallion whose worth, men said, is twenty talents. To Mithridates' right with two thousand Bactrian cavalry is Arbupales, son of Darius and grandson of Artaxerxes, the handsomest man in Persia save his father. These Bactrians (and their comrades in arms of Parthia, Hyrcania, and Media) have not trekked from their home provinces a thousand miles east; they are local estate holders, heirs of champions who conquered under Cyrus the Great and are obligated to serve in the field whenever their king calls. The enemy right is commanded by Pharnaces, brother of Darius's wife Lysaea, with divisions of Pamphylian, Armenian, and Median mounted levy commanded by Niphates, Petenes, and Rheomithres, all adherents of the royal house, and Omares, commanding the Lydian Light Horse on the Persian far right.

Three hundred yards rearward, is marshaled, on rising ground, the Greek mercenary infantry in the pay of Darius—Memnon's men, sixty-seven hundred, in three regiments, commanded by Memnon's sons Agathon and Xenocrates, and Mentor's son Thymondas. Behind the foe's mercenary infantry awaits a motley stew of local irregulars, between sixty and seventy thousand, worthless against even an army of hares.

The Royal Squadron has reached me in the center now. My groom Evagoras trots forth from the rear, leading Bucephalus. (I have ridden my parade mount, Eos, in the approach march.) My Page Andron boosts me; I mount. The corps thunders in acclamation.

"Zeus Savior and Victory!"

Forty thousand throats echo the cry. I sign to Black Cleitus and turn Bucephalus with my knees toward the right. At the canter, the Royal Squadron transits the front.

When I was a boy, Memnon taught me two principles. Cover and uncover. Direct and misdirect.

I am misdirecting now. How soon till Memnon knows? Soon I will direct. Will he grasp it? If he does, will his Persian masters pay him heed?

I sign to Telamon: "Bang the bone."

The bone is a short beam of rowan, beaten snub at one end. This is pounded with a mallet to set the cadence. The sound booms, cutting through the wind sharper than a trumpet.

Unit sergeants bawl the cadence. The line steps off. I am crossing rightward before our front, with the colors of the Royal Squadron flying. The enemy watches. Will he let me go without responding? Memnon sees me. My move right means I'm coming after him. Will the foe watch and do nothing?

The Granicus is swift but fordable. It will strike our horses at above the knee and our infantry at about the thigh.

Massed enemy cavalry lines the bluffs on the far side. They are armed not with thrusting lances as we are, but with javelins. When we enter the river, they will unload on us. The first shock will be terrible; the second will be worse.

I keep at the canter, crossing the front, two hundred yards from the stream and parallel to it. I'm still half a mile from our far right.

My scheme is as follows:

I have set at our right extremity a formidable assault force, the whole of the Companion Cavalry, reinforced by our Cretan archers and javelineers of Agriania. Memnon sees this clearly. It is directly across from him. And he sees me transiting toward it, bringing the Royal Squadron. This is misdirection.

What I'm hoping he doesn't see (direction) is another force, inboard of this wing, concealed as part of the broader battle line. This force consists of Socrates Redbeard's squadron of Companions, reinforced by two companies of light infantry under Ptolemy, son of Philip (called "Stinger" because at home he keeps bees). Stinger's is a picked outfit of two hundred, all volunteers, receiving double pay and made up of the youngest and fastest troops of the army. They have been trained to operate on foot with cavalry, against cavalry. They wear no armor, depending for protection on speed, their light but strong *pelta* shields, and their array within the ranks of attacking horsemen. Their weapons are the twelve-foot lance and the long thrusting sword. I have never used this company except in the mountains against wild tribes. They can keep pace with cavalry for a short distance, as here at the Granicus, and will work tremendous execution, I believe, within the melee that is certain to develop in the riverbed and on the bluffs beyond. In addition to Redbeard's Companions and Ptolemy Philip's light-armed, the attack group will have the superb infantry of the Royal Brigade of Guardsmen, under Attalus, Ptolemy's brother, the Paeonian Light Horse under Ariston, and the Royal Lancers in four squadrons under Amyntas Arrhibaeus, commanding the overall.

My design is to draw the enemy's eye, by the extravagance of my movement, farther and farther onto the wing. I want him to gird for an attack by me. I want him to pull out from his center more and more squadrons to mirror my lateral transit. But the initial attack will not come from me. It will come from Redbeard.

Direct and misdirect is a fancy name for a feint. Will Memnon see it? Will he be able to convince his Persian masters? Give me thirty seconds of indecision and it will be too late for him.

I keep transiting. Past Redbeard. Before the Companions. Onto the

wing. The foe responds now. Companies pull out of his center, tracking
with us to the right.

"Send Red now."

Telamon signs. Redbeard's colors stand forward. They're behind me;
the Royal and I have already transited past him. Next come Red's captains on the wing. Now Red himself on his stallion Rapacious. The line
bucks forward.

A cry goes up from all the Companions.

Red's squadron comes out into the clear. It is in four wedges.
Stinger's special infantry surge with it. Down the slope the commingled
companies advance. Red seems to hold his trot forever. Every man in
the line is shouting. The wedges come to a canter. The foot troops are
running now. I quicken my own squadron's pace. Right. Farther right.
Almost beyond the enemy's flank . . .

Here is the fix Memnon is in: If he breaks off the squadrons tracking me and uses them to meet Redbeard, I will keep transiting and get
round his flank. If he doesn't break off, Redbeard may burst through.
Now come the Lancers and the Royal Brigade. Now the Paeonians.
Cavalry and infantry to two and a half thousand.

"There goes Red!"

With a whoop, Redbeard's wedges charge.

What will happen? The Persians await us, massed on horseback,
atop the bluffs overstanding the river. Their arms are javelins and slashing sabers. They will not meet our charge with a counterrush of their
own. To do so would negate their advantage. No, they will hold their
post and launch their missiles upon us from above. The first fusillade
will be furious. Men and horses will fall; the foe will respond with jubilation. Exulting, he slings his second salvo, and his third. Our men
struggle beneath him in the current. Their footing is unstable on the
stone; their lances cannot reach the foe atop the bluffs, and they have
no missile weapons.

The enemy smells blood. He cannot contain his fever. He draws
sabers and charges. Down the face of the bluff, the foe's ranks spur. In
the river, his front compacts against our mixed horse and foot, throwing
both into disorder. A melee ensues.

Into this I will charge.

The Royal Squadron will strike the foe in six wedges of fifty. We will hit him at the seams created by his downslope rush, wherever gaps open and breaches appear. Behind us will gallop the remaining six squadrons of Companions, twenty-four more fifties. This force will mount out of the river. We will carry the bluff top and press on, seeking to break through the Persian line.

By now, the full length of our mile-and-a-half front will be moving. The regiments of sarissa infantry will be entering the river on the oblique, Nicanor's Royal Guardsmen first on the right, then Perdiccas's brigade, Coenus's next, and the other four in order. If the enemy's center stands, the Companion Cavalry will tear him up on our right. If he pulls more companies out to aid this wing, the phalanx will mount out of the river behind the spear points of its sarissas. When the foe cracks at one point, every other element will break and run.

This is how I see it; this is how it unfolds. The fight plays out exactly as I have envisioned, save one magnificent and nearly decisive shock: the spectacular valor of the Persian knights.

The fight at the ford becomes a series of rushes upon my person. This continues throughout the struggle in the river, up onto the bluffs, and well across the hinter ground.

When a champion of Persia charges, he cries out his name and his matronymic. This is so that if he achieves glory, his fellows know whom to honor, and if he falls, whom to mourn. We do not learn this till afterward from prisoners. We believe the Persians are simply mad, as each one yells something different as he plows into us. In Macedon, boys are taught to fight not as individuals but as pairs and triples; we are schooled to form against an enemy's rush into "swallowtails," inverted wedges with the leader at the base and two wingmen at the fore. The wings feed an attacker into the jaws, then fall upon him from the flanks. The effect of this is terrific against such foes as the horse tribesmen of Thrace, upon whom our cavalry learned and practiced it, who know only to fight as solitary champions. Against the Persians, who compound their vulnerability by dueling not with the lance, as we do to tremendous effect, but with the javelin and the saber, the effect is doubly devastating. Further, our heavy cavalry are protected by a front-and-back bronze corselet, while the enemy employs a breastplate only, with no protection for his back—and many disdaining a helmet as well. This concession to pride costs the foe terribly, for against the penetrating power of our lances, not even the plate of their chest armor is sufficient, whereas our fore-and-afters, and especially our iron helmets, prove of outstanding utility against the slashing saber. In combat of this type, it is no shame to strap plate across your back, as men are trying to hack you to pieces (your own, in the confusion, as well as the foe) from every quarter.

At the ford of the Granicus not only two armies clash but two opposed concepts of warfare. The Persians duel in the grand and ancient manner; the Macedonians in the modern. The proud hearts of the Crown Kinsmen of Persia cannot endure the prospect of being rolled over by a phalanx of common foot troops. Where the king and champions of Macedon fight, there the knights of the East must duel. So they bolt their stations in the line. Impelled by pride, champion after champion turns his division over to subordinates and spurs in person, with his honor guard of knights, to that wing of the field where a brilliant charge and a noble death await. The most telling observation of the day is this: that, though the Persian champions take station originally at the head of their contingents across the entire two-mile front, by battle's end their corpses are collected all at one spot, the river ford, where I cross.

Craterus slays Arbupales. Hephaestion takes down Omares with a single thrust and would have served the same to Arsames, whom his rush has unhorsed, if the Persian's squire did not spur in (the grooms of the East ride to battle alongside their masters) and catch him up by the arm. My lance slays Mithridates when he rushes before his escort, crying my name, and moments later fells Rhoesaces as his saber nearly shears off my scalp. Cleitus cuts down Spithridates, saving my life. (Arsites escapes to Phrygia, only to hang himself for shame.) Philotas kills Petenes. Socrates Redbeard slays Pharnaces. Mithrobarzanes and Niphates, each rushing alone, are taken down by swallowtails of Companions. The latter two transit more than a mile of front to fall at this site.

In other words, every prominent noble of the foe has abandoned his division and crossed the field to come after me.

When the fight is over, both shoulder pieces of my corselet have been sheared away; the facing of my breastplate, with its Gorgon's head and the Hours bossed in silver, is so battered, one cannot identify a single emblem. My gorget, which I had almost left behind because of its weight, has been torn so by a saber slash that three fingers can be thrust through the perforation. The fabric of my tunic is so saturated with blood and sweat that I cannot peel it off, but have to slice it away with the edge of a sword. Bucephalus's breastplate is pierced in six places; a chunk the size of a steak has been hacked out of his right hindquarter. His reins have been sheared through and his headpiece torn away. The coat of his chest and forelegs is so stiff with matted blood and sand that neither soap nor oil can clear it but the grooms have to cut it clean with a razor.

On our left, the regiments of horse and foot under Parmenio have fought their way out of the river, driving the Persian cavalry before them. When the enemy wing breaks at the ford, the whole front gives way. The foe's horsemen make their escape in a sweep of dust like a squall line crossing a bay.

The foe's Greek mercenaries remain. Sixty-seven hundred on the rising ground, who have not even got into the fight, the whole thing is over so quickly. They are foot troops; they can't ride away like their Persian masters. I order them enveloped. They compact their ranks into a defensive perimeter, projecting the spear points of their eight-footers. Night approaches. I rein, with Parmenio, Black Cleitus, Perdiccas, Coenus, Craterus, Philotas, and Hephaestion, before the enemy's bristling square.

Where is Memnon? I will spare the Greeks' lives if they spit him up. The ranking mercenary is a Spartan named Clearchus, grandson of the famous Clearchus who fought with Xenophon; when he comes forward, citing his lineage and swearing by the sons of Tyndareus that Memnon has fled, our men shower him with profanity.

The Spartan pleads for his comrades' lives. His troops are spawned of poverty, he declares; landless, serving only for pay, and bound by no loyalty to the Persian king. Gladly will they serve Alexander now.

"Serve in hell!" our men bawl.

They hate these Greeks who have spurned our cause and turned against their countrymen for gold.

The Spartan implores me. I make my heart stone. "Son of Leonidas, prepare to stand and die."

At my signal, the slaughter begins. I do not simply observe. I direct the massacre. Where it flags, I drive it forward. The Greeks are crying for their lives, pledging ransom, service, calling out the names of men I know, my father's name and my mother's. They enlist posterity's judgment of me and call upon heaven, beseeching mercy.

I give them death instead.

It is dark now. We need torches to see the men we are butchering. I do not cry cease until beyond a third have been slain and the survivors so riven with horror that their weapons fall from their fists and no command can make them pick them up again. They surrender on their knees. But I will not repatriate them, these bastard sons of Greece who took the barbarian's gold and armed to murder us if they could. I will burn their fate like a slave's brand into the brows of all who would follow them.

Eumenes, my Counsel of War, asks how the prisoners shall be handled. March them to Macedon, I tell him, as slaves, in chains. Passage by sea is too good for them. Make them tramp overland, in fetters at the ankles and the wrists; yoke their necks and stake them to the earth when they sleep. In Macedon they shall work the mines, with no officer or man, howsoever deserving, reprieved or ransomed, save those of Thebes, on whom I take pity.

"Under what conditions," Eumenes inquires, "shall they labor?"

"Work them," I instruct him, "on straw and nettle soup. So that all Greece may learn the toll paid by such traitors, who took up arms against their own brothers, in service to the barbarian."

It is over. Night checks all pursuit. In three hours, on this day in spring, an army of the West has wreaked such devastation as no lord of Asia has ever sustained.

The physicians seal my scalp with three copper "dog bites" and a handful of stitches. The wounded and dead are collected by torchlight. I go to them, clad in the same rags of war as they.

The first man I see is Hector, Parmenio's youngest son, who commanded a fifty under Socrates Redbeard. His thigh is cut up like a butchered ox; a terrific contusion empurples his breast. "Did you run into a door, my friend?"

"Indeed, with an iron warhead on it." He shows me the bronze of his breastplate, which saved his life.

Tears carve channels in the grime of my face. I weep from love for this lad and all his fellows. How brave they are!

Down the line of torn and maimed I pass. After battle, a wounded man feels abandoned and alone. He hears his unharmed mates outside the hospital tent, full of vigor, eager to go forward again. Dare he call to them? Often his comrades are loath to seek him out, lest the sight of his injuries cause them grief, or, superstitious as all soldiers are, that his bad luck will rub off on them. Often a wounded man feels he has failed. Will he return home a cripple? Will he read pity in his wife's eyes? A wounded man feels diminished and bereft, but most of all, he feels mortal. He has smelled hell's breath and felt the earth yawn beneath him.

For these reasons and to honor their valor, I leave no man forgotten. I kneel at the side of every one, taking his hand and soliciting his saga. Let's have your story, mate, and no modesty either! I command each to embroider his tale, and even lie about his heroism and the thrashing he has delivered upon the foe. To be wounded is a thing of terror, but to be honored and remembered fills a man with pride. Not one does not burn to return to the ranks as soon as he is able. When I show them my own wounds, or the places on my armor where the enemy's shafts have passed harmlessly through, the men weep and raise their arms to heaven. Again and again a fellow presses my hand to the site of his evisceration. So potent is my daimon, my countrymen believe, that not only will it preserve me but it will make them whole as well. I have no prizes to offer, so I strip articles of my kit—dagger and shin guards, even my boots—and give them away. The men beg me not to risk my life so recklessly. "For even luck as powerful as yours cannot be tempted forever."

It is midnight by the time we have all got bread and wine into our bellies, but not a soul craves sleep. I call the army together beneath cressets on the slope where the river turns.

"Brothers, we have only come fifteen miles inland from the sea, yet by today's action we have torn from Darius's hand a thousand miles of empire. The whole Aegean seaboard will now fall to us. Nothing stands between us and Syria, us and Phoenicia, us and Egypt. We will be the liberators of every Greek city along the coast. Wealth beyond our dreams will fall to us, and honor for an achievement of arms such as no nation of the West has ever claimed. This you have won, brothers. I salute you! But beyond this, your victory has brought that day closer when Darius of Persia must come forth and face us in person, and when he does, we shall wrest from his grasp such glory as will make today's triumph seem the exploit of children! You have honored me, friends, and honored my father. Let none forget Philip, who forged this instrument, our army, and who, if he could, would give all he ever owned to stand with us here in this hour. Philip!" I cry, and the army echoes it thrice, each time in lustier throat.

I should wait for the morrow to offer honors to our fallen. But the mention of our absent lord has sobered the corps; I feel the hour call. I sign to the honor guard. The corpses of our comrades are borne in upon captured battle wagons of the foe. I have them drawn up in two rows, facing the regiments. We have lost sixty-seven Macedonian dead, twenty-six Companion Cavalry, nineteen of Socrates Redbeard's squadron. Enemy slain, we will count later, are above four thousand.

All has become subdued; the men shift in place, unsettled by the proximity of death. I come forward onto the rise; those step closer, who will relay my words to the farther ranks. I have prepared no speech. I say what's in my heart.

"My friends, we are alive. The gods have granted us victory. We share it out, each to the other, and it is sweet. But these, our fallen comrades, cannot know what we have won. They cannot know what they have won for us by their blood and by their sacrifice. What is sweet for us holds only bitterness for them. We weep for their fate and for our loss. But these, our mates taken from us, have achieved that which none of us, still living, may claim. By their valor this day, they have elevated their station to a sphere far beyond our own."

I sign to the corps's sergeant major, who straightens, facing me.

"Brothers, present arms to these heroes."

I wait as the sergeant major faces about and bawls the command, which is relayed from division to regiment to battalion and carried out, smart and sure. Sabers and sarissas of the Knights and Foot Companions, lances of the Light Horse, javelins and bows of the mobile auxiliary snap to position before each man's eyes and heart. The army's tenor has grown simultaneously more somber and more exalted. I stand forward and face the dead.

"Fallen Companions, receive these honors which we, your brothers, now tender to you. For by these tokens shall each of us learn in what fashion we, too, in our hour, shall be used."

The command is given to order arms. I turn back, facing the corps.

"For these heroes, the nation shall commission monuments of bronze, life-size, one for each man, to be sculpted by Lysippus, whom alone I permit to render my own likeness, and these images shall be raised at home, at Dium, in the Garden of the Muses, where the nation can view them and render honor to them for all time. The family of each fallen champion will learn in detail of the heroism of its son and husband, which feats shall be set in writing beneath my hand and delivered to them as a beloved brother in arms whom we honor and shall never forget. To sons who survive them, the kingdom extends grants of land, shares in the spoils of battle; the state will pay for the education of these heroes' children, and exempt them from all service. We proffer this remission, friends, though you know as well as I that the kin of these champions will be the last to accept such waivers; rather, spurred by pride and honor, their sons will come out to us as soon as their years permit, sparing no exertion in our cause, that none may say that they were less than their fathers. Corps sergeant major, read the names of our honored fallen."

When the roll has been read, the army is commanded to stand easy.

"I honor, too, the foe. Let us never hate him. For he also has willingly undergone trial of death this day. Today the gods have granted us glory. Tomorrow, their mill may grind us to dust. Thank them for your lives, brothers, as I do for mine. And now go and take your rest. You have earned it."

Dascylium surrenders the next day; we enter Sardis and Ephesus within the fortnight. Magnesia and Tralles open their gates; Miletus falls after a struggle. We advance into Caria and commence the siege of Halicarnassus. The first night on-site, after Parmenio has briefed the generals on the excellent scheme he has devised, he turns to me and asks if he may speak.

What can this be? His resignation? I brace myself for something dire.

"I have underestimated you, Alexander. I beg your pardon."

Standing, my father's most illustrious commander beseeches my indulgence. It may be perhaps reprievable, he declares, for a general of past sixty years to regard with skepticism the ascent to supreme power of a youth barely out of his teens.

It takes moments before my officers and I comprehend that our senior speaks sincerely.

"Forgive me, Alexander, for the cautious and conventional counsel I have proffered. Clearly what applies to other men does not apply to you. I believed your father the greatest general who ever lived, but I acknowledge, observing you these months, that your gifts far surpass his. I have resisted serving you—you know it—and have held against you certain actions taken upon your accession." He means my ordering him to put to death for conspiracy his son-in-law Attalus, who was also his friend. "Now I put that behind me. I set aside my resentment of you, as I hope you can put away your suspicion of me, for I know you were not unaware of how I felt. I am your man, Alexander, and will serve you as I served your father, so long as you choose to repose confidence in me."

I rise. "You make me weep, Parmenio."

In tears I embrace the man. It is not lost on me that he has honored me doubly by tendering this testament publicly, in front of the others. It takes guts. It takes greatness of heart. By this act he invites all generals junior to himself, meaning all of them, to set aside any reservations to my preeminence. The generals applaud. They are as moved as I. Asander is the First Page on duty. "Get my father's Sigeian sword."

I tell Parmenio that Philip loved him. He rated him without peer as a commander. "Once," I relate, "when Philip entertained ambassadors of Athens, he tugged me aside and remarked with a laugh, 'The Athenians elect ten generals each year. What a surfeit of talent they must possess, for in all my career I have found only one.' And he nodded across the room toward you."

Now it is Parmenio who weeps. Asander brings Philip's sword. I set it in my senior general's hand. "It will be the greatest honor of my life, Parmenio, if you will accept me not just as your king and commander but as your true comrade and friend."

Two more anecdotes in the wake of the Granicus. The morning after the battle I arise early, as the king does every day, to offer sacrifice. Customarily, I emerge from my tent in darkness, accompanied by two Pages and a Guard of Honor; I meet Aristander the seer, or whoever will be conducting the rite, and we proceed alone in silence along the track to the altar.

This morning I stand forth and it seems the whole world has congregated. The square before my tent throngs with soldiers in the thousands, with fresh multitudes pressing in on all quarters. "What has happened?" I inquire of Aristander, fearing I have forgotten the date of some rite or ceremony.

"They want to see you, Alexander."

"See me for what?" I cannot imagine what plea or petition such a host would assemble to present.

"To see you," the seer repeats. "To look upon you."

Overnight, it seems, my stature has vaulted to the firmament. Hundreds line the lane, pressing so densely that my Pages must break a path simply for me to get through. "Alexander!" a man cries. At once the multitude takes it up. "Alexander! Alexander!" In such throat as I have never heard, even for Philip, my countrymen cry my name.

"Extend your arms, lord," Aristander urges. "Acknowledge the army."

I obey. Citations redouble.

For days afterward, I cannot take the air without hundreds trailing me about in extraordinary demonstrations of devotion. When I query a soldier directly as to why he and the others follow me so, he answers as if it were the most obvious thing in the world: "To be sure you are all right, sire. To make certain you lack nothing."

Telamon observes this phenomenon with interest. When I convey to him my uneasy sense that the army does not adhere to me *as myself* but as something other, he replies, "Indeed, your daimon."

It is my daimon the men see, not me. It is he who has brought them victory, he to whom their hopes have become attached, and he whom they fear to lose. I must embrace this, Telamon declares, as a consequence of triumph and celebrity. "You have ceased to be Alexander," he says, "and become 'Alexander.' "

The second anecdote is not a story really, only a moment.

Soldiers are sad after victory. I don't know why. A melancholy seems to descend in the aftercourse of success. This takes the whole army after the battle at the Granicus, but it strikes with particular force a cook of one mess named Admetus. This fellow is the most celebrated field chef of the army. His imagination rises to all occasions; he can always be counted upon, it seems, to concoct some dazzling dish out of nothing.

After the slaughter, however, Admetus loses all spirit. Images of carnage torment his slumber; he cannot bring himself even to cut up a goose. An army can go sour over such a seemingly trifling matter. I summon the fellow to my tent, intending to buck up his spirits. Before I can speak, a groan of despair breaks from his breast. "What is that sound?" he wails. "By heaven's tears, what is that horrible cry?"

I hear nothing.

"There, lord. Surely you must hear it!"

Now I do. Outside the tent: a musical chord, sorrowfully keening.

The entire company rises, Pages and Bodyguards together, and crosses to the portal to look outside. There, before the Guardsmen's square, stands a brace of stacked arms. Twenty-four sarissas arrayed in upright order for the night.

The wind piping across their shafts produces the mournful chord.

The cook Admetus stands transfixed. We all do. It seems this melancholy keening will be the blow that cracks his heart.

Observing this, one of the grooms, a lad we call "Underfoot," approaches the cook and addresses him in the tenderest tone. "The sarissas are singing," he declares.

The cook turns to the groom with an expression of wonder, as if the lad has materialized for the sole purpose of ministering to his distress. "They sing, yes," says the cook. "But why so sad?"

The groom takes his fellow's hand with exquisite solicitousness. "The sarissas know their work is war. They are sorry for this. They cry for the suffering they cause." And he sings in a pure, clear tenor:

> The sarissa's song is a sad song
> He pipes it soft and low.
> I would ply a gentler trade, says he,
> But war is all I know.

Admetus absorbs this with profound thoughtfulness. The company holds, breathless as dawn.

"Thank you," the cook addresses the groom, and then, straightening, turns to me. "I'll be all right now, sire." And back he tramps to his stock and ladle.

I am telling this story on campaign in Cappadocia—thirteen months after the battle at the Granicus—when a courier gallops up with the report that Memnon, besieging Mytilene, has fallen to a sudden fever. He is dead. I weep, not only out of respect for the brilliant Rhodian, though I feel that in abundance, but for the role of chance and luck in the affairs of men, and the knowledge of how tenuous is our hold, all of us, upon this thing we call life.

The man I have feared most is gone. His worth was armies.

This means, at last and for certain, that Darius must come forth and fight.

Book Five

Contempt for Death

Twelve

MIGHTY WORKS

IT IS THE MONTH OF *Ksatriyas* HERE IN INDIA. "Warrior's Month." I have taken a hunting party into the hills, partly for relief from the heat of the plains, but mostly just to gain a respite from the camp and her woes.

The spring monsoons have begun. The river has risen three feet, a staggering amount (we can measure by the stone steps that descend from the waterfronts of the native villages), and has burst its banks, where the levees do not contain it, adding a sixteenth of a mile to its breadth. How will I get across now? The camp has had to be reconfigured twice, the siege train and heavy baggage moved to higher ground each time. More man-hours have been spent by the army throwing up dikes and digging drainage channels than in training for the coming assault.

An outbreak of bottomland fever has hit the camp. The scourge strikes with utter randomness; no one knows what you catch it from, and no measure of medicine works against it. Its victims expire in a raving delirium. This is the kind of freak calamity that turns already-superstitious troops into chattering twits and drives otherwise-brave men to cluster in knots, gloomy and prey to every portent and prodigy.

We have deserters now (so far, only of the mercenaries and foreign troops) but in numbers sufficient that I dare not fall-in the corps in its entirety, lest the men see how many are the gaps in formation. Can you grasp, Itanes, from what I have told you of Chaeronea and the Granicus, how unthinkable such a state would have been in this army a few years ago?

But the gravest threat has come, again, from the company of Malcontents.

Their numbers, as I have said, are about three hundred, mostly veterans of the phalanx, with a few disaffected Royal Guardsmen. I have segregated these grumblers as a physician quarantines the contagious. Now they approach me, requesting discharge as a unit. Their petition, presented through their new officers Matthias and Crow (who have been unable to squelch it), is proffered respectfully and according to custom. It cites the unit's and individuals' years of honorable service, their innumerable citations, and the losses they have sustained without complaint. Nor is it without precedent. I have released a number of allied and hired outfits by just this process. No Macedonian company has been let go, but only because none has asked. This is no joke. If a home-grown unit revolts, it will be the end of the army. I cannot sleep for fear of this, and my generals are in a state.

Aggravating the case is a quirk in the corps's configuration. My table of organization permits no staff officers at brigade level or lower. I want all my commanders to be fighting officers; I don't want anyone the men don't respect. The system makes each captain and colonel do double duty, handling administrative chores as well as training his unit and leading it in action. This has worked till now. As I am in my officers' company constantly, at meals and in the field, the result is, I know everything that goes on in the army—what man has gotten a local girl pregnant; who feels neglected and passed over—and I can act upon this knowledge. But in recent campaigns, since Afghanistan, to be precise, an unwholesome change has come about. My officers now keep things from me. They withhold unsettling information, in fear for themselves of my fits of anger (which have gotten worse, I know, and for which I have myself alone to blame) and to protect the men under them. They dare not report a seditious outburst or an instance of disgruntlement, dreading my wrath.

Hephaestion's presence has until recently provided an avenue of reparation. An officer with a petition, although reluctant to approach me personally, has always known he could speak with Hephaestion aside, and that he, at the proper moment, would relay the man's concern to me. Now this channel has failed as well, as Hephaestion has been promoted to Parmenio's post of Number Two and now appears, to the men, too exalted to approach. So I have lost my ears.

There used to be no surprises in the army; I was on top of everything. Now irruptions burst forth fully blown. By the time I learn of trouble, it can be dealt with only by extreme measures.

This hunt in the hills, thank heaven, has cleared our heads. The generals' party is composed of Hephaestion and Craterus, Perdiccas and Ptolemy. About sixty attend them. Telamon and Eumenes head the private party, what we call "the King's List." We're after black leopard. Several have been spotted outside the perimeter, driven down from the hills by the rains. The beaters' party has scoured the mountain all day, without stumbling upon so much as a cross-eyed hare. A riotous chase breaks out just before sunset, involving a band of wild asses, which ends with several spills and a couple of cracked skulls, no harm done. We get nothing, the beasts being far too fleet on their home barrens, but the run has blown the croup out of our gorges and the fog out of our heads. Now, in grand fettle, we lounge around fires over a stew of bustard, shot by the cooks' boys, with highland peas, Ismarian wine, and barley bread plucked steaming from the ground ovens.

"I have decided," I declare, "to divert the river."

Laughter greets this. My generals regard me as if I have made a felicitous jest.

"It will be an undertaking," I continue, "of monumental scale, involving every man and beast in the army." I sign to Diades, the corps's chief engineer, who built the massive siege works at Tyre and Gaza, and whom I have included this day in the King's List. He rises and crosses to my side, carrying what my companions can clearly see are rolls of engineering plans and draftsman's sketches. "My intention, gentlemen," I say, "is not merely to turn the river into the plain to expire ignobly in swamp or slough, but to redirect it via stone earthworks in such a way as to make its new course permanent, and, by the way, provide us a dry passage to attack the foe."

My mates are not laughing now. To their credit, they already begin to grasp the vision.

Diades speaks. He's a sturdy fellow, bald as a hen's egg, and, like all engineers, practical as a pensioner. He has examined the ground, he states, and believes the job can be done. "Where the river turns, above the camp, is an outrunner of impermeable shale from the Salt Range. A new channel can be excavated and carried west to the base of the hills; the land lies low there and will carry the river, or at least a substantial portion of it. As for labor, we have beyond fifty thousand in troops alone, with matching numbers of locals in service and the general crowd. The treasury holds gold without limit, to hire more strong backs. Of horses and mules, we have twenty thousand. We even have elephants."

The labor, he says, will be hard but require no special skill. It's just digging and shoring. "Once we get the river's head turned, its own force will drive the channel in the direction we have pointed it. It will do our work for us." The engineer smiles at the council's skeptical faces. "Because a thing has never been done, gentlemen, is no reason to say it cannot be. And, in my view, no reason not to try."

The idea has just enough madness to catch on.

"Hard work is good for morale," Ptolemy observes. "It'll give the men something to bitch about instead of their troubles."

"I like it," says Craterus. "It lets us attack the river, instead of the river attacking us."

Eumenes, my Counsel of War, cites a further advantage. "An army needs something grand to capture its imagination. In Pericles' phrase,

Mighty deeds and mighty works."

"And," adds Perdiccas, "it'll shut the Malcontents up." He proposes assigning this company a prominent place in the dig. "If they malinger, the army will see it and their prestige will suffer; if they work hard, their state of mind will improve."

Hephaestion suggests competition to fire the men's spirits. Assign divisions to parallel sectors; set prizes for the first to finish. "Or establish a quota for number of yards of earth moved in, say, six days. If an outfit finishes in five, it gets the extra day off."

Craterus proposes a grand prize for the overall. "Then the unit finishing six days' work in five will elect to keep working, to hold the edge over its rivals."

I tell my mates I am thinking of sending to Ecbatana for money. The central treasury is there. One hundred eighty thousand talents of gold. I want to bring up thirty thousand, for pay and prizes and just for the heat of it. What do they think?

Ptolemy embraces it. "It excites men when there's big money in a camp."

"Better than women," agrees Perdiccas.

Craterus: "Because money buys women!"

My generals approve. Massing money is like massing troops. It means power. It presages a forward push.

I see our young officer, Crow, lean forward. He is mortified at his Malcontents' petition for discharge; he will do anything to repair the confidence I have reposed in him.

"Speak up, Lieutenant. Don't be shy."

"I was thinking, sire, if you do send back for the gold, don't announce it. Keep it secret."

That, all agree, will be impossible.

"Exactly, my lord. Let the men find out by rumor. This will treble the power of publication, and will excite the fellows further, to believe that you have something bold and brilliant still to come."

"By Heracles," declares Ptolemy, "give this man a step!" Meaning promote him to captain. Everyone laughs.

I see Matthias too burns to contribute. "Anything else, gentlemen?"

The older lieutenant suggests we send for sculptors, to carve images in the stone facings of the new channel. "Labor in this heat will be hell on the men, sire. Let them look up to noble likenesses in progress, and let them know that these will outlast them and memorialize their toil.

Here men under Alexander turned this mighty river."

"And whose," I ask, "shall these likenesses be?"

"Your own, lord, of course. But more . . ."

"Yes?"

"The men. The men themselves."

A chorus of knuckle raps seconds this motion.

"Each division of the army has its own distinctive kit. Let us have them, sire: the oryx horns of Bactria, the kestrel plumes of Sogdiana, our own lions and wolves, so that a man at the end of his labor may lift his eyes and say, 'The grandchildren of my grandchildren will look one day upon what I and my mates have wrought.'"

I approve. We all do. I commend Crow and Matthias; diverting the river was their idea.

As for my own part, I say, here is what I will do. "I will strip and join in the labor. It inspires the men to see their king toiling at their shoulders. Who will not wish to boast, 'I outshoveled Alexander!' This will be better than medicine for me and the gods' own tonic for the men. When one outfit surpasses another, I will shower the victors with bonuses and praise, and this will animate all other divisions to strive for excellence."

Craterus brings up how our enemy Porus will respond. Will he counter?

I don't care. "My quarrel is not with this king of India, but with our own men. We suffer a crisis of the spirit. If the corps possessed *dynamis*, we would need none of this. We would have crossed this river a month ago and be marching now to the Shore of Ocean and the Limits of the Earth."

All night we talk of this object. How much farther can it be? Beyond the Ganges, that we know. But how distant is that? No guide can tell us. I cannot overstate how this excites me. To stand where no man of the West has stood before! To behold that which none has seen! And forever to be the first!

Do you think me vain or self-inflated? Consider: What has Almighty Zeus portioned out for man, save this earth? Heaven He has kept for Himself. But this sphere here, beneath this sky, we mortals may roam with naught to hem us but our own will and imagination. Do you know what faculty I claim in myself as preeminent beyond all rivals? Not warcraft or conquest. Certainly not politics.

Imagination.

I can see Earth's Limit. It shines before my inner eye like a city of crystal, though I know, when I reach there, it will be but a shingly strand beneath an alien sky. No matter. It is Earth's Ultimate, of which not Heracles or Perseus have dreamt, but only I.

What will I seize when at last I stand upon that shore? Nothing. I shall not even bend to pick up a stone or shell, but only clasp my mates' hands and gaze with them upon the Eastern Ocean.

That's what I want.

That's all I want.

Do you understand, Itanes? Beyond all titles and conquests, I am, in the end, just a boy, who wishes for nothing grander than to ramble with his friends and look out for what waits beyond the next hill.

But this digression has carried us apart from our story. Let us return to the Granicus and its aftercourse.

Thirteen

KILL THE KING

YOU HAVE ACCESS, ITANES, to the army daybooks for the months succeeding the battle of the Granicus. They list the cities of Asia Minor that came over or fell to us in the sequel. I gave the Greek states their freedom and exempted them from tribute. Caria is non-Greek; I restored her queen, Ada, and accepted this lady's offer to adopt me as a son; I gave the Carians back their old laws, which the Persians had proscribed, and did not claim tribute as a conqueror but as a son. Lydia I set free, and Mysia, and both Phrygias, asking only the tribute exacted by Darius before me. One hundred and sixteen cities fell to us. We had started in early summer, to take the harvest as it came in; by the next spring, all Asia Minor from the Bosporus to Pamphylia was in our hands.

After the Granicus I forbade looting. The army had crossed to Asia as a force of liberation; no act of pillage must sully its standing in this light. The spoils we took came from Darius's treasuries in the cities we set free.

The needs of the army came first, beasts before men, for without horses and asses and mules, the corps can strike no faster than we can run and bear forward nothing more than we can load on our backs. Next, gold to shore up supply lines to the rear; ships and ports; communications with Antipater's garrison force in Greece and Macedonia; depots and magazines for the coming advance; money to bribe enemies, cash to aid friends, fees for our benefactors, bribes for forward spies and men in place; gifts and remissions for new allies, games and sacrifices for old. The men must be given time and means to carouse; they have earned it. To those newly married, I grant furlough and send them home—six hundred men, including Coenus, Love Locks, Payday. Let them spend the winter months bundled beside their brides, to return in spring, knowing they have an heir on the way.

Now the army's wages and, with both hands, their bonuses. I spend more time on this than any occupation save reconnaissance and forward supply. It is imperative that spoils be distributed equitably. Let no brave man go uncited and no coward unscourged. Letters of commendation. At Sardis in Lydia, where the army lays over to consolidate its initial advance, I employ no fewer than forty secretaries, toiling in shifts, to whom I dictate correspondence. It is my object to know the name and exploits of every man in the army. I can't of course, but I will put names to thirty and forty new faces a day. Buckets of treasure come in, golden cups and goblets of silver; I turn them at once to him who has bled in our country's cause. If I can, I set the gift in the man's hand myself; if not, it comes with my compliments in writing, something the man can send home with pride to father and mother, or hold in safekeeping for his wife and child. The wine is superb along the Aegean coast; when a batch pleases me, I save out a portion and send it to an officer I wish to honor, with a note saying Alexander has enjoyed this wine with his friends and wishes him to share it with his own.

I never let the men see me sleep. I rise before they wake and remain at work when they go to their slumber. When they drink, I drink with them; when they dance, I dance too. If I remain late at wine, I rise on steady legs and let my officers see it. When the sun blazes, I endure its heat without complaint; I sleep on the ground on campaign and on a plain cot in camp, and when we move across open country I train as we go, racing on foot and on horseback. Of treasure, let my countrymen see

I take none for myself, save articles of honor—a horse or a fine piece of armor—but set all at their service and the service of our goal.

Darius.

The Lord of Asia remains in Babylon, eight hundred miles east. Shall we go after him or let him come to us? Where shall we meet? When? With what forces?

In my country we have a game called Kill the King. It is played by two sides of boys on horseback, on a field with a goal line at each end. The lad with the ball is King. He tries to dash across the enemy's goal; his mates defend him. When the King falls, his side loses.

The grand designs for the war against Persia is no more complicated than that.

Kill the King.

Night after night as we advance down the coast, my generals and I crowd round the map table, poring over charts and reconnaissance reports, harvest projections, dispatches from forward agents and men in place. Craterus is my most aggressive commander; he wants to strike at once for the interior, for Babylon and Susa, where Darius holds his treasure and almost certainly will marshal his next army. "Get to him now," Craterus urges, "before he can raise a multitude so vast we can't hope to contest it."

Parmenio leads the Old Guard. He too fears an iron-to-iron clash against an army of millions. "Let us not tempt heaven, Alexander, but be content with the conquests Almighty Zeus has granted us. No European army has even dreamt of holding the lands we do. If Darius offers concessions, take them."

Nightly the factions clash, till the hour comes for me to set them still. I have learned from my father; I wait for an occasion, in this case Parmenio's Naming Day, which we in Macedon celebrate as Greeks do birthdays, when the senior general will feel most honored—and be most conscious of the passing years. I hold till midnight. Wine and meat have made us mellow. I make no show of royal prerogative, but speak as a soldier only, to soldiers like myself.

"Gentlemen, in campaigning against Darius we must not lose sight of this fundamental truth: Our foe rules not a nation but an empire. His allies are not friends but subject states. He rules them by might indeed, but more by a kind of myth: the fiction of his own invincibility.

"We war, my friends, not with the King but with this myth.

"Do I fear Darius's millions? Never. Let him bring half of Asia if he will. The more troops he crowds upon the field, the more he encumbers himself with superfluous arms and the greater the burden he places upon his commanders and his corps of supply. My father taught me this and I believe it: Scale of arms is worthless beyond that number of men who can march from one camp to another and arrive in one day. That is our army. Forty-odd thousand, no more. Let Darius spread his multitudes from horizon to horizon; when we strike at his heart with speed and power, the mob will flee like so many hares.

"Craterus, my friend, and you other young officers, to you I say: We will not rush into the interior, however tempting such a bold strike may appear. If we march on Babylon while Darius's myth holds intact, the city will resist; we will find ourselves besieging a fortress whose circuit walls are forty miles round and a hundred and fifty feet high. But if we defeat the king in the field, Babylon's gates will open to us on their own.

"Remember, to capture dirt means nothing while the king's myth endures.

"Nor, gentlemen, may we seek to steal Darius's realm by ruse or cunning. Let us bring his army into the field, not before it is ready, and not constituted of hastily assembled or inferior troops. Rather, let his force come in its fullest preparedness, flush with Asia's finest men. Where the king is in person, I will strike. Where his mightiest champions stand, you will attack. Then, with our victory, not only does the Lord of the East fall but also the legend that sustains him.

"No, Parmenio, we will not settle for a fingerhold at the margins of Darius's empire. We will take it all. Persepolis is only halfway. My aim is to seize every province that Persia ever held, even India, and press on to Ocean's Shore at the Ends of the Earth. I will suffer no negotiations with Darius and accept no accommodation short of unconditional surrender."

Bold business plays best, and grand aims fire men's hearts. Hephaestion is with me, as are Craterus, Ptolemy, and Perdiccas. Seleucus and

Philotas warm to the notion fast. Only those who have cut their teeth under Philip—Parmenio, Meleager, and Amyntas Andromenes (Antigonus One-Eye I have posted to Phrygia as governor)—fear such confidence is self-deceiving. I will speak to each in private. I will grant them concessions, give steps to their favorites, gift them whatever they want to bring them over, till they are with me buckle-and-strap. If they won't come, I'll get rid of them. Yes, even Parmenio.

"Have you heard, my friends, how a crocodile devours a bullock? He starts at the feet and eats his way up to the heart. This is how we shall flush Darius. We'll gulp down his empire, one state at a time. We won't rush. We'll take the seaport cities, cutting off the foe's fleet from her harbors and naval bases. We'll advance from no territory until our rear is secure and our lines of supply solid and unbroken. Let the Persian come to us. Let him stretch from his home ground, not us from ours."

For months after the battle of the Granicus, we paint-in blank spots on the map, shoring up posts and consolidating gains. We train. We rehearse. We build new roads and repair old ones. With spring, our newlyweds return from furlough. With them come thirty-two hundred reinforcements of infantry and five hundred of horse. The people at home are ecstatic at our success. I have loaded Coenus, Payday, and Love Locks with gold for recruitment bonuses; instead they have had to fight off volunteers in hundreds, so intoxicating is the prospect of riches and adventure in the East. All winter we have fought in Phrygia and Cappadocia, across the Halys and along the spine of the Taurus. The enemy are hill tribes mostly, wild free fellows who value liberty before life. I love them. What do I want from them? Only their friendship. When at last they believe this, they come in trailing gift colts and bridles of gold.

My eye remains on Darius. The king toils at Babylon, every report tells, raising and training a second army. I have set Hephaestion to run our agents and spies. He briefs me once a day, and the council every five. He gives this report at Gordium in Phrygia:

"The Persians have no standing army as such, beyond Darius's Kinsman Cavalry, six thousand, including the knights of the One Thousand Families, and the king's Household Guard, the ten thousand Immortals.

The force he is raising now to contest us must be assembled contingent by contingent from the provinces of the empire, the easternmost of which are a thousand miles from Persepolis and even farther from Babylon. It will take months for his governors to raise this levy and months more to muster it in one place. Then the multitude must be armed and trained.

"Clearly Darius will not stand pat after the debacle of the Granicus. He will rethink armament and tactics. The command will be his own. With him now, our agents report, are Arsames, Rheomithres, and Atizyes, who fought against us at the Granicus and will pass up no occasion to apprise the king of amendments and correctives. Darius has called to his court Tigranes, the most celebrated cavalry commander of Asia, and his own brother Oxathres, a great champion over six and a half feet tall, as well as the royal kinsmen Nabarzanes, Datis, Masistes, Megabates, Autophradates, Tissamenes, Phrataphernes, Datames, and Orontobates—who commanded with Memnon at Halicarnassus—all of whom are renowned for valor and horsemanship and all of whom bring, from the hereditary retainers of their provinces, powerful contingents of cavalry. Darius has also summoned to Babylon Mentor's son Thymondas, who, spies inform us, has fast-marched from the foe's naval base at Tripolis in Syria, bringing between ten and fifteen thousand Greek marines and hired infantry from the fleet. The king has with him as well Memnon's lads Agathon and Xenocrates, with eight thousand mercenaries of the Peloponnese, and the Greek captains Glaucus of Aetolia and Patron of Phocis, who are not only outstanding commanders of heavy infantry but have drawn to their colors, so all reports confirm, another ten thousand hired Greeks, crack troops, the kind who can stand up to our phalanx. So: thirty to thirty-five thousand heavy infantry against our twenty.

"Among Darius's courtiers are also numerous renegades of Greece and our own country, who work for the overthrow of Macedon and are intimately familiar with our arms and tactics. Darius too has agents, down to tent whores and laundry urchins, who track and infiltrate our camp; we may be sure that every word, even those uttered in sleep, finds its way to the ears of the foe."

When will Darius move? Where? With how many?

I offer his weight in silver to the man who brings this intelligence. When report comes, at Ancyra on the edge of the Salt Desert, it arrives not from spies or deserters but from Darius himself, in the form of a command requisition, captured by our scouts from a courier on the Royal Road. The instrument is addressed to Barzanes, governor of Mesopotamian Syria; it commands him to have waiting for the Army of the Empire, when it arrives in six months (meaning this fall), two hundred thousand amphorae of wine, fifty thousand sheep, forty thousand bushels of barley, with matching quantities of wheat, sesame, and millet, and enough water and forage, dry and green, to supply the needs of sixty thousand horses, asses, and camels. The letter specifies that a sufficient number of *muker* ovens, the round-bellied clay type, be either on-site or ready for fabrication, as well as four hundred thousand feet of rope for tents and pickets, a hundred thousand palisade stakes, and six thousand hoes and mattocks for the ditching of the camp, the raising of ramparts, and the excavation of latrines. For the royal precinct, the letter commands a site on rising ground, shaded by trees and watered by a stream from whose upper course no cup has been dipped before the king's; the area of the camp to be eight acres, raked and groomed, with an adjacent eleven for a baggage park and for picketing the animals. Darius also wishes from the governor eleven thousand pack animals, with their muleteers, dispatched at once to Babylon.

What convinces me of the dispatch's authenticity are the accommodations commanded for the royal party.

When the Persian king travels to war, he is accompanied by a baggage train a mile and a half long. That's not for the army; that's for him. His own personal stuff. He brings his wives and mother. His hairdresser accompanies him, and his cosmetician. The king brings everything that is dear to him, including his pet panther and his talking macaw; he brings busts of his ancestors, favorite pillows and books; he has flautists and timbrel players, pipers and kitharists. His entire household accompanies him, including seers and magi, physicians and scribes, porters, bakers, cooks, cupbearers, bathroom attendants, butlers, waiters, masseurs, chamberlains. His concubines come, not all three hundred sixty-five as he keeps at home, but a field version of this harem, each mistress with her own handmaidens, attendants, and beauty doctors. The Great King has his own crown-plaiters, pot-boilers, cheese-makers, drink-mixers, wine-strainers, stewards and butlers and perfumers. He has a man to carry his looking glass and a man to tweeze his eyebrows. This does not count the host of scribes and eunuchs who are the royal administrators, paymasters, poets.

This tent in which we now sit belonged to Darius; we captured it after Issus. Its original version is absolutely enormous. I have feasted six hundred in it; in Bactria we put the flaps up and exercised horses in it. When I acquired it, it came with forty skilled men, just to set it up and take it down. We divided it in quarters after Drangiana (making over the rest for a hospital and barrack tents) and now use a quarter of a quarter. Even that fraction suffices as billet for half my Pages, their refectory and infirmary, offices of the Royal Academy, my own quarters, with space left over for the duty watch of the Guard, two map rooms, a library, the staff briefing area, and this salon, which used to be the king's seraglio, where we talk and drink.

Packing this tent, Darius and his army marched from Babylon to Syria, seeking to bring me to battle. And I, overconfident and too eager to meet him, enacted the grossest blunder of my career.

Fourteen

THE PILLAR OF JONAH

THE BAY OF ISSUS IS A NOTCH IN THE SEABOARD of Asia Minor, at the elbow in Cilicia, where the coastline turns from facing south to facing west. South over the mountains lie Syria and her capital, Damascus; then Phoenicia and Palestine, Arabia and Egypt. East by the Royal Road awaits the breadbasket of the empire—Mesopotamia, the "Land Between the Rivers," the Tigris and Euphrates, and the imperial cities of Babylon and Susa.

The seaboard plain of Cilicia is enclosed by two rugged mountain ranges, the Taurus to the north and east, the Amanus to the south and east. The passes across the Taurus out of the north are called the Cilician Gates. This is a wagon road, so steep in places that a mule's asshole will open up and whistle, so mightily must the beast strain to haul its load, and so narrow in parts, the locals say, that four men abreast who start up as strangers will reach the other side as very good friends. The Persian governor Arsames has been commanded by Darius to hold the heights, but, striking swiftly with the Royal Guardsmen and the Agrianians, I get round and above and drive him out without a fight. We descend to the sprawling and prosperous city of Tarsus, set in the midst of a gorgeous plain bounded by mountains and sea and lush with every kind of fruit, vine, and grain. We capture the ports of Soli and Magarsus, to deny haven to the enemy fleet, and seize the cities of the plain, Adana and Mallus on the Pyramus. It is at the latter that the first reliable intelligence comes in, reporting the sighting of Darius's army.

The Persian multitude is five days east, at Sochi, on the Syrian side of the Amanus mountains. Their camp is sited in the Amuq plain, a broad and flat expanse, ideal for the deployment of cavalry (in which Darius outnumbers us five to one), with abundant grain and forage and resupply from Antioch, Aleppo, and Damascus. The foe will not be prized from such a site with a lever. He won't come to us. We have to go to him.

Now you must understand something, Itanes. The narrative of a battle is invariably recounted with a clarity, particularly a geographic clarity, which is seldom present in the event. One advances, the sergeants say, by two guides: Guesswork and Rumor. We fast-march to Issus, at the pocket of the bay. The mountains loom to the east; Darius waits, just fifteen miles away, on the far side. But how to get there?

When a great army passes through a region, it draws the locals from miles. An army has money. An army brings excitement. In every country Macedonians are called "Macks." "Oyeh, Mack!" the natives bawl, grinning gap-toothed as they trot at the heels of the column. Every knave has something to peddle: live fowl, onions, firewood. "You need guide, Mack?" Every jack and jasper claims to know the shortcut to sweet water and forage. His brother-in-law serves with the Persians, he swears; he can tell us where Darius sleeps and what he had for breakfast. I do not scorn these fellows. From them we learn of the passes at Kara Kapu and Obanda, of the track via the Pillar of Jonah, and, last, the Syrian Gates below Myriandrus, which will deliver us over the Amanus onto Darius's doorstep. Our forward elements seize these, all but the final. Seeking foot-by-foot intelligence of this last ladder into Syria, I interrogate in person over a hundred locals and go over with our own scouts every goat track and runnel by which the army can get to Darius or he can get to us.

Yet not one tells me of the Lion's Pass over the Amanus.

Mark this, my young friend. Sear it into your soul with brands of iron: Never, never take anything for granted. Never believe you know, so that you cease to probe and query.

I lead the army along the shore by night march, over the pass called the Pillar of Jonah, encamping at the city of Myriandrus, from which we will cross the Amanus via the Syrian Gates and attack Darius. A terrific storm covers our advance; we halt a day to rest and dry our weapons and equipment. I am exactly where I want to be, on the very site I have raced to reach. Midnight: The column marshals for the night ascent. I take the fore, with the Royal Guardsmen, the archers, and the Agrianes, stripped of all kit save armor and weapons. Suddenly two riders gallop in from the north. One is a scout of our Paeonians whose proper name I can't recall but whose nickname is "Terrier." The other is a local lad of Trynna, a village near Issus.

They have seen Darius's army.

It is in our rear.

How can this be? I hold reconnaissance reports less than three days old, showing the army of Persia, two hundred thousand strong, encamped on the plain east of the mountains. Who can believe that a host of such scale will pack out from a field so ideal to its uses, broad and level, peerless for exploiting its strength in cavalry—a site that its commanders have doubtless reconnoitered months in advance and taken extraordinary pains to water, provision, even groom for combat? Who can credit that such a multitude, encumbered by its extravagant train, will abandon this capacious arena to hem itself within the cramped defiles of Cilicia?

But it is true. Contrary to all sense and expectation, Darius's army has decamped from Sochi and marched north, across the interior of the Amanus via the Lion's Pass (of whose existence I stand in ignorance), and round the far flank from the one we had taken. The two armies have crossed in opposing directions within fifteen miles of each other, with neither aware of the other's passage.

Darius is behind us. He has cut us off. Or, more accurately, I have cut us off by my own impatience and overhaste.

Worse news is to come. Certain that Darius is on the inland side of the Amanus, I have left our sick and wounded on the coast, at our rear camp below Issus. The enemy reaches this infirmary at about the time our main body approaches Myriandrus, twenty-five miles south. Our hospital site is defenseless. Darius's troops overwhelm it.

The king orders our fellows mutilated. Macedonians are painted with pitch and set afire; others are disemboweled. The Persians cut off noses and ears and hack off right hands. Here is butchery as only the barbarian of the East practices it. When report reaches us, I am beside myself with grief. This is my fault! My folly has produced this!

Those of our sick and wounded who can get away flee south to over-haul us; the thirty-oared galley I send north to confirm Terrier's report finds a dozen and brings them back. More arrive as day breaks, in such a state of wretchedness as cannot be described. Here appears Meleager's brother Ephialtes, castrated, borne on a cart, with his cloak wadded into a compress and held with his good hand to contain his entrails. My dear mate Marsyas has two cousins among the mutilated; one carries the other, slung over his shoulder, having bled to death from the stump of his arm. The maimed men come up from the beaching ground, some able to walk, others who must be carried; they conceal their disfigure-ments with rags torn from their clothing, ashamed to be seen in such a ghastly case, though some bare their defacement, seeking to incite their comrades to revenge. The mangled men's woe is nothing alongside that of their countrymen, who surround them now, calling upon Zeus Avenger and tearing their garments in fury and despair. Every maimed arrival relays the fate of others left behind, savaged by the foe. It seems no company is spared report of one of its dear ones, upon whom such atrocities have been worked as only the fiends of the East are capable. Walking among the mutilated, I come upon Eugenides, Payday, our gal-lant squadron commander of Bottiaea, whom we married in the great feast at Dium, whose bride, Elyse, gave me the dancing slippers. For mo-ments he maintains a gallant front, then, succumbing to anguish, drops, clutching my knees. "Alexander! How can I school my son without an arm? How can I love my bride without a face?"

At the sight of these butchered comrades, I enter a state of extrem-ity such as I have never known. Better this had been done to me! Better

I had endured such mutilation than to witness its infliction upon these, my beloved mates, whose trust in me has left them undefended against such horror. And nothing can ever set it right. No grant of gold or honor, not the righteous slaughter of those who have committed these atrocities, not the overthrow of Persia herself will ever make our comrades whole. It goes without saying that the army must turn about at once and give battle. Those of the maimed who can walk crowd about me now, pleading to be armed for the coming fight, to wield weapons with their left hands, or, failing that, to bear a shield or hold a horse. I will not permit this, fearing that their state will carry them apart from themselves, to seek death at the foe's hands, and by such mischief work harm not only to themselves but to the order and cohesion of the advance.

I feel my daimon at my shoulder. I have failed him too. Arrogance. Heedlessness. Overhaste.

> *Now taste, Alexander, the bitter fruit of greatness and ambition.*
> *To you Necessity grants victory. Here is its toll. Eat it.*
> *Choke it down.*

My command post at Myriandrus stands above a crescent-shaped inlet. Below, the mutilated are being helped toward the houses of the locals, who have poured forth to offer succor, women and children as well as men, using their own beds as litters and carrying our comrades out of the dust and wind to tend them within doors. I peer down upon this grotesque spectacle. Parmenio stands at my shoulder; Craterus and Perdiccas hasten up. I see Ptolemy and Hephaestion, on horseback, working toward me through the crush. Sergeants and private soldiers press about me, countenances contorted in rage and grief. "Lead us, Alexander!" they cry. "Lead us against these butchers!"

Fifteen

PAYDAY

AT ISSUS THE SEA IS ON OUR LEFT, foothills on the right. Setting out at dusk the night before, the column has fast-marched north along the coast road, retracing the route it took two days prior. We reach the summit of the Pillar of Jonah at midnight; I order the troops to snatch a few hours' sleep among the crags, then pack them out at "army dawn," meaning two hours before the real thing. By daybreak we're descending to the plain. I keep the infantry ahead of the cavalry so the fast units don't outrun the slow. The Royal Lancers range ahead as scouts. I have dispatched three flying platoons forward as well, comprised of the youngest and strongest troopers, mounted on the fastest horses. Their job is to get me prisoners to interrogate. In war great events turn on small moments and now one breaks in our favor. My dread all night has been that Darius has outgeneraled me; that he has learned somehow, from spies or natives, of our march south to attack him and has, with consummate speed and skill, countered by his own thrust north. Can this be true? One question I cannot answer: Why has my enemy taken his great army, which is made for fighting in open plains, and penned it here in the confines of these coastal hills?

Descending from the Pillar, I get the answer. One of our grooms'
boys, Jason by name, has been among those in hospital at Issus when the
camp was ravaged by Darius. This lad presents himself to me now,
brought by his captain and colonel, to whom he has conveyed his tale.
Amid the horror of those hours in the medical camp, the colonel reports, this child had not lost his head. He had ranged through the carnage, gathering intelligence of the Persians. How, I inquire of the lad,
did he do this?

"Just asked them, sire. Walked up to them. The sons of whores took
me for a local bumpkin. I was able to find out where they had come
from, what route they had taken, and where they were going."

"And what," I ask, "prompted you to do this?"

"I knew, my lord, that you would need this intelligence." He reports
that the Persians, in fact, had no knowledge of our army's march south.
They were as ignorant as we were; they believed our force still north at
Mallus. The foe had crossed the mountain, aiming to attack us there.
The whole thing has been a colossal double blunder, mine and Darius's.

"Child," I ask, "can you ride a horse?"

"Since before I could walk."

"Then, by Zeus, you are now a cavalryman." I command Telamon to
find him a fast mount and an outfit to report to. "You shall dine at my
shoulder, Jason, tonight when we offer thanksgiving for this victory."

Minutes later, scouts return with prisoners, who confirm our youngster's report. Still I advance with caution. The pass runs right above the
sea on the southern approach to Issus; if Darius has sent troops forward
to seize the heights, he may fall upon us while we are still in column of
march. I order all commanders to bring their units into line of battle as
soon as the widening plain permits.

I need not have worried. The Persians await us in defensive order
on the sandy littoral where the river Pinarus twines to the sea. It is just
past midday when we bring the foe in sight; the sun dazzles off the Gulf
of Issus on the left.

"Do you see him?"

At my shoulder, Hephaestion points to the center of the enemy
line. Even at a thousand yards Darius's chariot cannot be missed—tall

as a teamster's cart and centered among the matched blacks of the Royal Horse Guard. We can't make out the man—the range is too far—only his plumage. Still a thrill courses. At last my rival has taken the field! At last the Lord of Asia stands before us!

Darius of Persia.

For all his central post as King of Kings, Lord of the Lands, Ruler of the Empire from the Rising to the Setting Sun, I know less of him (as does the whole world) than of any common captain in the enemy horde. When he was a knight, before he became king, he challenged a giant of the Armenians and took him down in single combat. He is tall, men say, and by far the handsomest of all the Persian host. His brother Oxathres fights with the strength of ten, yet Darius is easily his better, on horse or afoot. All this may be fact or fable.

What I *do* know is the loyalty my enemy commands, not only of his kin and countrymen but of the foreign troops, the Greeks, in his pay. The mercenaries' leaders are first-rate men, Mentor's son Thymondas, Patron of Phocis, and Glaucus of Aetolia. I have made overtures to all of them, offering double and triple pay to come over to me. They won't budge. Darius has given them Persian brides and estates; he educates their children at court. That my rival prizes these officers shows he understands war; that he treats them with honor shows he understands men.

Parmenio reins-in at my side now. He will command our left. Darius's army is two hundred thousand, division upon division, stretching back as far as sight can carry, with another hundred thousand in local levy, noncombatants, and the general crowd. We are forty-three thousand. The foe's cavalry, in tens of myriads, blankets the near bank of the Pinarus. The host of his foot are just now being drawn up in order, in a double phalanx behind the river. To the rear, for part of a mile, the plain is flat; then the slope climbs to rocky ridges. The ground underfoot is coastal scarp, carved by numerous washes and ravines at right angles to any Persian retreat. We know the ground; we came over it four nights ago.

The field for combat is not wide. Between twenty-four and twenty-six hundred yards. Darius has cavalry to spread three times that. If he had stayed on the Syrian side of the mountains, he could have done so. Here on this cramped plain he cannot. Again my luck has held.

An excellent officer named Protomachus, whom the men call "Pan Bread" for his girth, commands the Lancers, assigned this day as scouts. He canters to my colors now, with three of his lieutenants, returning from the fore.

"What's up front, Bread?"

"A pretty party, sire."

The stream of the Pinarus is not deep (we forded it four days ago without wetting our thighs), but its banks are steep, particularly on the side the enemy holds, and studded with dense thickets of brambles. Where the bluffs are less than sheer, Protomachus reports, the foe has thrown up palisades.

"Why is his cavalry on this side of the river?"

"Covering the deployment of his foot troops, behind the river. The horse were pulling back across when we rode out."

This report is worth armies. It means Darius intends to defend; he has ceded the initiative to me.

Left is the sea. Flat turf. Cavalry ground. Right: The gully-riven foothills ascend to a half-moon spur, onto which the foe's light infantry hasten now in thousands, threatening our right. Though we stand two-thirds of a mile from the enemy front, this wing already outflanks us.

Socrates Redbeard's son Sathon spurs up from his own reconnaissance. He is seventeen and eager as a green hound; two of his father's savviest sergeants ride cover for him. "The New Persians are here, lord!" The youth points toward two spreads of battle pennants on each wing of the Persian front. "See their serpents?"

For months we have been hearing through spies and deserters of a new division, called the King's Own, which has been raised, armed, and trained specifically to face us. We know nothing of this force except that it is infantry, all Persian, and its commander is Bubaces, Darius's cousin and governor of Egypt. Now here they are. I ask their numbers and armament.

"Forty thousand," replies young Sathon without a breath of hesitation. "Spearmen, not archers. In two wings, four hundred across and fifty deep."

"Did you loiter to count each head?" I ask, teasing him.

But he is earnest as an eel. "Their armor is helmets and mail coats, lord. Wicker shields, toe to crown, like Egyptians carry." He points to the center of the enemy line. "The troops in between are hired Greeks, heavy infantry; Thymondas's men, with Patron's and Glaucus's; we saw their colors at the fore. Their front is about eight hundred yards. I could not tell their depth because of folds in the ground."

The young man reports that enemy archers, about two thousand, have crossed to the near bank, fronting the foe's left, at the seam between the New Persian spearmen and the wing cavalry and slingers on their left. "Medes," reports Socrates's boy, "in open order, three divisions deep, armed with the long cane bow."

"My friend," I tell young Sathon, "your father never gave a keener report." I send him back to his squadron, beaming.

Our corps deploys in conventional order. Darius's cavalry withdraws behind the river. These divisions transit, consolidating along the shore. They are twenty-five, thirty thousand. Their ranks extend rearward nearly a mile.

My father used to say that attacking an enemy who outnumbers you is like wrestling with a bear: You have to get your dagger into his heart before the beast crushes you with his paws.

I have set myself, since Chaeronea, to make each scheme of battle simpler than the one before. Already I see today's clash—the form, that is, that Darius wishes it to take. And I see another clash. The form into which I will compel it.

Darius's vision is this: Right, along the sea (our left), the king will send his cavalry, outnumbering ours five to one, seeking to break through and round our left, to sweep back upon our sarissa phalanx in the center, whose attack, the enemy believes, will have foundered against the banks and brambles of the river and the palisades and massed formations of the King's Own spearmen and his crack Greek mercenaries. On Darius's left, from the range of hills, his light infantry will swarm down from the half-moon spur, taking our right on its un-shielded side. No matter how hard we hit him frontally, the foe believes, we cannot break through, in such great depth are his ranks stacked, and so numerous are the regiments and divisions of his center and rear. Now, my friend, to our counters. Let us add another concept to your military vocabulary.

Cover and uncover.

A commander advances against the foe "covered"—that is, with his intentions masked, either by his configuration, his feints and misdirec-tions, or by the ground itself and the elements. At the instant of attack, he "uncovers."

The reason a static defense is always vulnerable is that it is by defi-nition uncovered. The defender by his posture reveals not only his in-tentions (as Darius does here, making it apparent that he will send his cavalry from his right, along the sea) but displays what he believes to be his strengths (his flanking left wing, the river bluffs and palisades, his massed heavy infantry).

The attacker, in contrast, uncovers nothing.

The attacker maintains the option to counter every move the de-fender has, by his dispositions, uncovered.

At Issus our right wing advances over broken ground—ravines and washes of such depth as to swallow entire divisions. The ruggedness of this terrain is why Darius has set only a handful of light cavalry to de-fend this wing; he believes the ground unridable by heavy squadrons. But these gorges will let me cover. I can dispatch units left or right, screened by this rugged ground, and Darius cannot see them. This I do now. To counter the foe's strength in horse along the sea, I send all eight squadrons of Thessalian heavy cavalry to join our mercenary and allied horse already in place on this wing. I instruct Parmenio, commanding our left, to screen the movement of this body by folds of ground and by directing it to pass behind the phalanx. The Thessalians' role will be to strike the Persian cavalry from the flank when they come round our left.

With me I keep all eight squadrons of Companion Cavalry under Philotas, the four squadrons of Royal Lancers under Protomachus, and the squadron of Paeonians under Ariston. We will attack from the right.

Out front of his left, our right, Darius has set lines of archers—the skirmishers reported by Sathon, Redbeard's son. Clearly these bowmen will loose their volleys upon any element advancing against them and the infantry massed in their rear, then withdraw through the files of these troops when they become hard-pressed.

Note the uncoveredness of this disposition and the advantage it cedes the attacker. The enemy believes this his strongest post. That is why he has not palisaded it. In fact it is his weakest and most vulnerable.

Why? Because archers in massed formation are worthless against heavy cavalry. No bow can range effectively beyond a hundred yards (here, with the wind off the sea, twenty-five is more plausible), and cavalry at the gallop can cross a hundred yards in a count of seven. How many volleys will these bowmen get off before they stampede in terror back against their own comrades, throwing them into disorder?

Now let us consider the nature of these newly commissioned Persian spearmen, the King's Own.

These troops, we know from spies, are called *Cardaces*, a term in Persian which means "cadets" or "foot knights." Clearly they are Darius's generals' attempt to remedy his gravest deficiency—lack of homegrown infantry who can stand up to our Macedonian phalanx. So far so good. I applaud the intention. But I reckon too the vanity, faction, and intrigue of courtiers surrounding the Great King. Will Darius's grandees, configuring this new corps-at-arms, consult their hired Greek commanders, who possess true expertise? Never. To do so would constitute loss of face. The lordlings of the royal seat will evolve this novel arm entirely on their own.

Close-order fighting is not a skill one masters in a day. Nor is it in the Persian national character. Asiatics are archers. The bow is their weapon, not the spear. Noble youths since before Cyrus the Great have been schooled "to draw the bow and speak the truth." The fight at close quarters is not the Easterner's style; he prefers to duel at range with missile weapons. Even the shields of the King's Own, body-length wicker flats, are archers' shields, meant to be set upright upon the earth, as mobile ramparts from behind which bowmen may launch their shafts. One cannot fight in close order with such a shield. And the foe's disposition:

Fifty deep is not a formation; it is a mob. A man in the rear is more afraid of being trampled by his own mates in flight than he is of the enemy. When the fore ranks buckle, the rear will sling their shields and run.

I will charge Darius's archers and his King's Own at the head of my Companion Cavalry. This will be the dagger, thrusting to the heart of the bear. My phalanx in the center and Parmenio's foot and horse on the left will hold off the paws.

Rear of the Persian front is Darius's camp. Another hundred thousand in sutlers, wives, whores, and the general crowd. When the foe bolts in terror, he will run onto his own men. The hills behind him are riven by ditches and ravines. Troops and horses will stampede; thousands will be trampled. Those who succeed in crossing the first range will find their flight impeded by their own baggage train. Unit cohesion will vanish. The military roads will become colossal jam-ups of men, horses, and vehicles. Our cavalry will pour onto the disordered foe. The enemy who stumbles will be lanced in the back; the man who turns will reap death from the front. Scores of thousands will end their lives here, yet only a tenth will be slain by us. The rest will kill themselves and one another. In the defiles, multitudes will expire of suffocation. Their mates will flee across a causeway of their broken bodies.

All commanders have assembled on my colors now. I issue orders of battle; brigadiers spur back to their divisions. "Old friend," I ask Parmenio, "can you hold the left?"

"The sea shall bleed Persian purple."

I like this kind of talk. I gallop along the lines one last time, not to cry speeches (who can hear with the distance and the wind?), but to align the advance and to ride to individual commanders and heroes, acclaiming their exploits and calling them to glory. Citations roll down the line like waves. Cavalrymen call a horse "high" when its state of excitement reaches such a pitch as threatens to carry it away. I see this in mounts now and feel it beneath me in Bucephalus's skimming, skittering stride. We can wait no longer. In moments I must give the order to step off.

Suddenly from our rear breaks a solitary rider. The man appears from the shore road at the gallop, splits the seam between our leftmost infantry and cavalry, and drives out front for the center of our line.

Every eye turns. The horseman is one of ours, alone, bearing a battle standard of the Companion Cavalry.

Telamon: "What the hell is this?"

The pennant is the crimson of Bottiaea.

"It's Payday!"

We see now. The rider is Eugenides, who wept in my arms at Myriandrus, only hours past, mutilated by the Persians.

The army goes rigid. Payday is three-quarters dead, barely able to hold his seat. "Get him back!" I command Philotas, who at once sends horsemen at the gallop.

How can the mutilated man have come so far? He was already gravely wounded, at Issus, before the foe worked his horror on him two days past. Since then he has trekked on foot twenty miles to Myriandrus and now doubled the same track on horseback. As our Companions approach to retrieve him, his strength returns. He bolts into the clear. A cry ascends from the army.

"Payday! Payday!"

The man's disfigured face has been concealed by his regimental scarf. Now, as our comrades close on him, he tears this garment free. The sight makes our fellows rein-in despite themselves. Payday shouts something to them. He raises his right arm, severed at the wrist, and elevates the battle standard in his left.

I order all officers to their units at the gallop. I turn, myself, to spur to my post. I hear Telamon say, "There he goes." I don't need to look. The army again cries Payday's name. Without waiting for my orders, the brigades begin to move.

Sixteen

THE BATTLE OF ISSUS

Thus commences the greatest slaughter in the history of warfare between East and West, and the most decisive victory, up to that point, of the army of Macedon over the myriads of Persia.

Three battles are fought, each on separate sectors of the field, which on their own, would constitute struggles of epochal scale and complexity. Yet the seminal scheme is simplicity itself. Here. Let us sketch it on this table. What I want you to apprehend, Itanes, is the concept of effective strength. The enemy outnumbers us nearly five to one, yet *where the action is decisive,* we, not they, possess numerical superiority.

On the wing against the sea, a desperate cavalry clash will rage for most of an hour. In the center, the brigades of our phalanx will endure terrible punishment, where the river bluffs rupture their order and Darius's superb Greek heavy infantry falls upon them as they struggle to mount out of the stream. But on the right, where I attack with the Companion Cavalry, the foe breaks at first contact. His belly splits open, in great Aeschylus's phrase, like

the parting of the flesh beneath the whetted steel.

The initial shock of my Companions is hurled at the seam between the Persian King's Own and the light cavalry and skirmishers on their immediate left. Before these, on the near side of the Pinarus, the foe has arrayed Median archers—two thousand, as young Sathon has reported—in three divisions, one behind the other. The first gets off two shots, the second one, the third none at all, as their leading ranks, taking one glance at our squadrons thundering upon them boot-to-boot, turn in terror, dump their kit, and run. The mass plunges in wild disorder back through the river and crashes into the front ranks of the spearmen of the King's Own. Before our first lance has drawn blood, the foe is in full flight.

Our lead squadron is the Royal, in Dragon's Teeth on the oblique, right leading. I take the first fifty; Cleitus the second; Philotas the fourth, meaning that wedge called "the anchor." At my left shoulder rides Hephaestion; Telamon on the right; Love Locks right of him; with the *agema* of knights, my Bodyguard, forming the first three chevrons. Behind the Royal come the other seven squadrons of Companions.

The enemy are fleeing as sheep do, in waves rolling outward from a longitudinal axis. We see nothing but backs, and shields and spears being flung. In the time it takes to count a hundred, the lead squadrons of Companion Cavalry have broken through the Persian front. We have eighteen hundred across the river now, with four squadrons of Royal Lancers—eight hundred more men—right behind, and a squadron of Paeonians in the train of that. The wedges come left behind the enemy's front and spur toward Darius in the center.

The distance to the king is seven hundred yards—a long way, nearly half a mile. I am certain that Darius does not know we have struck his line, let alone penetrated it; that he will not know until a dispatch rider reaches him, if indeed one ever does. The king's attention is concentrated upon his right and his front, the sectors in which he hopes to produce victory. He is not yet aware, I am convinced, that our blade has entered his belly.

Now, my young friend, let us consider another element of dispositions in war: the line in defense.

When divisions establish themselves in a defensive line, as those of the foe have here along the Pinarus, each must lay out not one but two positions: an initial defensive front, upon which it makes its stand, and a secondary post, to which it can withdraw in the event of being hard-pressed. The defenders cannot simply stack their reserves in infinite depth, lest panic in the front ranks be communicated immediately to the rear, with no interval of containing it. Thus the fallback position. This supplemental front must be close enough to the original—three or four hundred paces—that the division can retire to it swiftly and form up to resume the defense. At the same time, this reserve post must be far enough back that the retreating soldiers can put breathing space between themselves and their pursuers.

This formation means two things for our squadrons of Companions as they break through the foe's first defensive front and wheel left in column to dash across, behind it, toward the enemy's center. First, it provides us an avenue—the space between the foe's primary defensive front and his fallback position—down which we can charge. Second, it assures us that the ranks of the foe in deep reserve (respecting their forward fellows' defensive order) will not flood into the gap to interdict us.

Our squadrons are now, as I said, seven hundred yards from Darius. We will learn later from captured officers of the Babylonians and Medes, who manned the center of the foe's secondary line, that they have indeed observed our breakthrough but have mistaken us for Darius's own Royal Horse Guard, so unthinkable is it to them that enemy cavalry, meaning us, can have penetrated so many ranks so swiftly and in such numbers.

Only one division of the foe comes forward to contest our transit, that of Mesopotamian Syria. It does so, we will discover later, not because its commanders have apprehended the danger and responded (they, like the Babylonians and Medes, cannot believe that we have broken through their densely stacked front), but because an unrelated order, misdirected and misdelivered, has commanded an unrelated division to come forward for an unrelated reason. In other words, a complete bung-up.

Can you see the field, Itanes? Then let us add another concept to your education.

Plates and seams.

A plate is a front constituted of a unit under autonomous command. In other words, a section of the battle line—company, battalion, regiment—that is not divisible, that can move only as a unit. The larger the plate, the more unwieldy the formation.

A seam is the boundary between plates.

When our sarissa phalanx with the brigades of the Royal Guard advances on line, for example, its twelve thousand men appear to constitute a solid wall. In fact, the front is composed of nine autonomous brigades—six of the phalanx and three of the Guardsmen—each capable of independent action, and each subpartitioned into battalions, likewise competent. So that this single front contains thirty-six plates and thirty-five seams, each plate capable of acting on its own, if opportunity or peril so demands, without breaking the seam that unites it to the whole.

This is *our* order. Now consider the foe's.

The Mesopotamians intercepting us are one plate with no seams. Their numbers are ten thousand (a lucky figure in Chaldean numerology) and they are under one commander, Darius's brother-in-law Sisamenes, without captains beneath him authorized for independent action.

Ten thousand in Mesopotamia is a hundred by a hundred. Can there be a more foot-bound formation? Further, the ground between them and us is split by rifts and ravines. The foe attempts to charge forward in his cumbersome mass. But the field confounds him. In addition, the Mesopotamians are archers—troops possessed of neither the arms nor the inclination to come to close quarters. I send three fifties at them as they struggle to mount out of a ravine, and these are enough to send the mob tumbling back down the face. The enemy has recognized us now. They launch at us from the floor of the rift and from the far side, but their shafts, flung uphill and into the wind, drop in our train as lightly as pine boughs in a breeze.

Our squadrons are now three hundred yards from Darius. He is, at last, aware of our rush. So are his captains of the One Thousand and the Kinsman Cavalry, and so are the Greek officers commanding the mercenary infantry of his forward line.

At this point, perhaps ten minutes into the fight, the six infantry brigades of the Macedonian phalanx have locked up with the enemy across the full fifteen hundred yards of the center. Amid the bluffs and brambles, Darius's Greek infantry and those companies of the King's Own who have not been stampeded by our Companions' penetration (with those to the right of the Greeks) press down upon our foot regiments, producing grievous casualties among their ranks, whose order has been broken by the uneven ground, the river and palisades, and by the struggle to mount the steep, rocky bank. On the wing along the sea, twenty-five or thirty thousand superb Persian cavalry under Nabarzanes (with Arsames, Rheomithres, and Atizyes, who had fought so gallantly at the Granicus) are flinging themselves upon our allied and mercenary horse, reinforced by the eighteen hundred Thessalian heavy cavalry that I have dispatched at the last minute. Stiffening this front are our archers, Cretan and Macedonian, half the Agrianes, and all twenty thousand of our Thracian, allied Greek, and mercenary light infantry, fighting as *hamippoi*—that is, foot troops integrated with cavalry.

I can see none of this from where I ride. It is clear, however, that this will be a brawl such as never has been seen, with horse and foot clashing along two thousand yards of strand, coastal wash, drift jams, and out into the sea itself. If Parmenio cannot hold our left, the foe will break through, wheel to the center in overwhelming numbers, and take our phalanx in flank and rear. The slaughter in the river will be catastrophic. And the Persians *will* break through. They are too many and too good.

My thrust must break through first. The Companions must get to Darius in the center before Nabarzanes' cavalry penetrates Parmenio on the wing.

Hephaestion tells me later that I appear like a madman, pressing the attack on every quarter, and that my horse seems crazier than I. It does not feel that way. I feel lucid and contained. Each thrust I press has an object, and each is animated not by lust for glory, but by the knowledge that our countrymen of the left and center stand in terrible jeopardy, which can be relieved only by triumph here at the center, and by the certainty that victory—utter, spectacular victory—hangs only a lance thrust away.

Darius's post is on the rising ground behind the Pinarus, a hill shaped like an overturned shield. His royal chariot stands at its peak, its plumes and standard visible above the sea of horses' headstalls and knights' hoodlike cawls. The colors of every elite regiment cluster about him. Their numbers are a thousand five hundred. Ours are eighteen hundred.

On this lone sector of the field, the forces of Macedon have, for the moment, achieved numerical superiority.

It would make a better story to say that this stroke carries the day. In truth, the struggle around the king breaks down at once into a slugging match, within the press of which neither horsemanship nor unit tactics counts for an iron spit, but the brawl takes shape as an infantry battle on horseback, or, to draw an apter analogy, like certain naval engagements in confined straits or harbors, when the ships can gain no leeway to ram and so lock up hull-to-hull alongside the vessels of the foe, leaving it to the marines to fight it out on deck. The champions of Darius's Royal Horse dare not charge upon us from their posts about the king for fear of leaving their lord vulnerable, and yet, holding stationary, as they clearly know, they might as well be sitting horses of wood. The knights of the East form up flank-to-flank, facing outboard like warships surrounded at sea. Our Companions plunge in, like triremes ramming an encircled fleet.

Two champions of the foe stand out—Oxathres, Darius's brother, and Tigranes, descendant of the famous Tigranes who followed Cyrus the Great. Neither is a specimen of heroic stature (both tall and slim, in the Persian ideal), nor do they fight as a tandem. Rather, each, as an individual, rallies fronts of the Kinsmen and the One Thousand into bulwarks, which not even our fiercest rush can penetrate. Now men and horses begin to fall in serious numbers. As at the Granicus, the superiority of the Macedonian long lance and the fore-and-aft bronze corselet proves decisive. Our men, wielding their weapons with both hands, work terrible execution upon the foe, who has been reduced to using javelins as lances, many of which had been shivered to stub ends, or else slashing with the saber (a hopelessly ineffective blow when not powered by the momentum of the gallop), protected only by their cloaks, which they have wadded up and wound about their left forearms to fend blows, and by their light linen jerkins, without helmets, only woolen head wraps, and small targeteer shields. The foe seeks to form ramparts of horses, massed flank-to-flank, while we assault singly and in wedges, thrusting our lances into the faces of the men and horses. Bucephalus is a monster, I have said, and here the push of his massive hindquarters breaks apart seam after seam of the foe. Many of the enemy fall to wounds of the throat and neck. I myself am stabbed through the thigh. I see one knight of the foe pitch from his mount, still slashing with his saber as blood shoots in surges from his severed carotid; others fall of lance thrusts driven through their windpipes or into the sockets of their eyes. Here, Black Cleitus and Philotas distinguish themselves. Philotas slays Megadates and Pharsines, half brothers of the king, while Cleitus hacks his way, it seems, through a fifth of Darius's Royal Horse. Hephaestion, too, wins honors this day, and many are slain and disabled, horses and men, in that press where blows come at you from front, back, and both sides.

At the peak of the melee, Darius takes flight. I do not see him. The realization comes only as we mount—Hephaestion and I, Telamon, Black Cleitus, and the leading wedge of the Royal Squadron—to the promontory where the king's battle standards still stand. His chariot remains, bowled over onto one side. For a moment I fear that the king has been slain. Fury nearly fells me, that another has stolen my glory.

"Darius!" I hear my voice cry. I spur about the eminence, mates will tell me later, in a state of near frenzy, while comrades on horseback call for any man who has sighted the king, and others on foot overturn bodies of men and horses, lest Darius, fallen, be trapped or concealed beneath. Suddenly Demetrius, a knight of my Bodyguard, reins-in before me.

"The king is fled, Alexander!" He points rearward, toward the

Persian camp. "Men have seen him, on horseback, making his whip sing!"

A second wave of rage seizes me, replaced in moments by a cold, incandescent clarity. I understand the political necessity of Darius's flight. The game is Kill the King; who can fault a monarch for seeking to preserve the principal of the realm? Simultaneously I am stricken with outrage, not so much that the foe, by his flight, has robbed me of my glory, to slay or capture him, but *that he could flee at all*. Do you understand?

He is a king!

He must stand and fight!

The act of making off is, to me, such an inversion of the knightly ideal as to constitute not felony but sacrilege. By Zeus, the man's wife and mother are present in the Persian camp! His young son is here to witness his valor!

Further, by taking to his heels, Darius abandons the valiant hearts of his army, men who bleed and die even now in his name and for his honor. When these divisions learn their king has forsaken them, they will break apart and be slaughtered in the rout his act of self-preservation has rendered inevitable.

Telamon reins-in at my side. He has taken a lance thrust in the bowl of his hip; blood soaks the linen of his saddlecloth. Bucephalus has simultaneously trodden on a spike; he can barely hobble. I take Telamon's horse, ceding my own to his care. My fastest riders, I send spurring to Parmenio, whose squadrons are enduring hell on the wing by the sea.

"Shout that the king of Persia has fled. Let the foe see your joy. Even if the enemy cannot understand your words, he will take your meaning—and our own men will recover courage, knowing that victory will soon be ours."

Wounded as he is, Telamon makes to join the pursuit. "Stay here," I command him, "and don't do anything stupid."

We chase Darius five miles to the enemy camp. The fall of the empire is so close, I can feel it in my palm. The camp itself is pandemonium. My pursuit party is the Royal Squadron and half the Amphipolitan, with Hephaestion, Black Cleitus, and my *agema*—four hundred men. Around us swarm a hundred thousand of the foe. The spectacle of flight defies depiction. The few outleading tracks are mobbed already by multitudes of noncombatants, confounded with the rabble of provincial levy, who have bolted in tens of thousands from the field. Behind these surge even greater throngs of line-unit Persian troops and allies.

"Find the king!" Cleitus is shouting. "Bring Alexander his purple balls!"

It is an art on disordered fields, the seizing of prisoners and their unceremonious terrorization and interrogation. Individuals are yanked off their feet by cavalrymen at the gallop and dragged by their hair or heels (hence the slang "dragooned") until they spit up some "true trash." From a eunuch of the camp, we learn that Darius has bolted on a racing stallion, escorted by his brother Oxathres and a company of Kinsman Cavalry. The fugitives spur north now. Their start on us is a count of a thousand.

We pursue the king till two hours after dark. Fifteen miles, till the night has gone so black that the road can barely be followed on foot, and our mounts are so blown that we must rest them till an hour short of midnight before they can stand our weight to trek back. Throughout all this period, men, women, children, wagons, carts, and pack animals flee past us in the dark.

Darius has gotten away.

By midnight we have retraced our track to the hills above the Persian camp. The slaughter of the enemy surpasses the worst I had imagined. With Darius's flight, his army has broken and run. As I had feared, the ravines have proved man-killers. Thousands have expired, trampled beneath their comrades' rush. Gullies the size of small stadiums are piled with corpses. When you see such masses of dead, the cause is never hostile action; rather, the wretched fellows have been overrun by their own mates, as will happen in a mob fleeing fire in an indoor assembly, when multitudes stifle in the press.

The Persian camp is five miles north of the battlefield. When we reach it, on our dead-out horses, our men are looting it.

Despair grips me. I seize the first fellow I see, a sergeant of allied cavalry called "Gunnysack"; he has so many brass lamps stuffed in his cloak, he rattles like a tinker's ass. "What do you call this?" I demand in outrage.

"My fortune, sire!" And he jigs with glee.

I am past fury. I spur down into the camp. Burning wagons and tents afire illuminate a spectacle of pillage and rapine. The site had been protected by a ditch and palisade; these have been overwhelmed in our men's stampede for treasure. Nothing stops them. Not the sight of me, nor the shouts and orders of my officers.

"Find Parmenio. Locate every commander. Bring them to me."

The Persian camp is a storehouse of plunder. Riches in such quantities as our men have never seen—horses and women, stacked arms, suits of mail, golden vases, bags of money meant as soldiers' pay—drive our fellows to a pitch of avarice nothing can contain. Prisoners in thousands have been taken, I see, confined not in one central compound, as would constitute propriety or custom of war, but impounded individually by each man of Macedon—as many captives as he can wrangle into one pack, he and his mates, and hold for ransom or just to strip their arms and goods. Wives and mistresses of the foe are dragged, shrieking, from their tents. The strumpets of the whores' camp, a hardier breed, are not only not resisting the Macedonians but are actively recruiting their commerce, to which call my countrymen fervently comply, purchasing the wenches' favors with jeweled rings they have just ripped from the fingers of soldiers dead or in flight, then backing the bawds up against pavilion posts, bending them over axletrees, or simply hurling them to the earth and ravishing them in that posture. The victors rampage from tent to tent, draping themselves with robes and vestments, earrings, bracelets, gem-encrusted swords and daggers, so that the spectacle seems, to look upon it, as if kings and priests ran riot and not common infantry.

Hephaestion reckons my state; he moves to steady me. "What are you thinking, Alexander?"

I take in the barbarous demonstration.

"That everything I have loved and labored for is folly."

Parmenio, Craterus, and Perdiccas have reached me now. The other commanders haven't the bowels to show their faces. In the quarter of the camp beneath us, we witness a phenomenon I have never seen: men wrecking their own loot out of spite and malice. Priceless urns and vases our fellows smash apart, baying with pleasure. Busts, furniture, statuary—the victors haul these forth and bash them to splinters. I see one soldier clutch an exquisite ebony chair; Hephaestion cries to him but the man beats it apart with his shield and looks up grinning, as if to say, See, we are conquerors; we are beyond law or consequence.

When at last my generals assemble, I command them to fall-in the brigades for training.

They stare as if I have gone mad.

"March kit and weapons. Now!"

No one believes me serious. They think that fatigue and loss of blood have disordered my senses, or that I speak in jest, to command that the regiments form up for parade.

"Alexander, please"—Parmenio is the only one with the guts to speak—"the men are exhausted!"

"They were not exhausted when they disgraced Macedon's name. They were not exhausted when they shamed their colors and their country."

It takes the count of six hundred to round up the troops. I transit on horseback before their riot-disordered mass.

"This day will be acclaimed a great victory! Indeed it was. Until you fouled and polluted it!"

It is impossible in the dark to drag out the allies and the hired troops, but, beneath Parmenio, Craterus, Perdiccas, and the others, I succeed in making all six brigades of the Macedonian phalanx fall-in, along with Nicanor's regiments of the Royal Guardsmen. I will not subject the horses, who are blameless, to this scourging, but I command Philotas to stand the Companions by, in order, men in full kit, including the Royal Lancers and Paeonians, and Parmenio the Thessalians.

"Corps sergeant major, array the troops in march order."

I drill the men as if they were raw recruits. The grooms and whores of the Persians, the sutlers and best boys, even the captives form up, of their own, at the margins of the plain as our colonels and masters-at-arms, at my command, take the phalanx through. Advance at the upright. Advance at the slope. A soldier bawls a curse, anonymous in the ranks. I halt the entire army.

"Sarissas at the attack!"

I make them elevate their lances two-handed. The weapon is eighteen feet long. With blade and butt spike, it weighs seventeen pounds.

"Speak up! Which of you sons of whores has more to say to me?"

We resume. I have drilled, myself, hundreds of hours with the eighteen-footer. I know every posture that produces pain, and how to make that pain excruciating. A man falls out. I double the pace. "Let the next man drop! We will stay here all night!"

My countrymen hate me now. They would drink my blood. I sign to the colonels, who pass the command to sergeant majors and sergeants. By the left flank, march! Right flank. Left oblique. To the rear.

"Have I forbidden plunder? By Zeus, is that the first standing order of this army or not?"

Men are puking now. Snot runs from their noses. Spit froths down their beards; sweat drenches their backs. The wine they have guzzled heaves back up their gorges and foams over their stinking gums.

"Are you soldiers? I called you my brothers. Together, I believed, no force on earth could stand against us. Yet we have met that force this day. It is our own wicked and ungovernable hearts!"

When a man falls, I order his mates to carry him. Let a fellow groan, I go after him with the flat of my sword. I drill the regiments till their backs break. At last, when even the wounded gimp onto the field to aid their faltering comrades, I call it off. Sergeant majors order the troops to fall-in before me. My rage has not abated one iota.

"When I saw you fight today, my countrymen, I saw men I would lead with pride against the phalanxes of hell. I saw comrades by whose side I would lay down my life with joy. To count myself among your corps, I felt, would be renown eternal and fame everlasting. Victory! Before today, I believed it to be everything. But you have shown me my error."

I stare into faces scarlet with exhaustion and black with shame. By perdition's flare, I will bind them to me. By the rivers of hell, I will make them mine.

"You have disgraced the most glorious triumph in the history of Western arms. You have brought shame upon yourselves and upon this corps. But most of all, you have dishonored me. For a man hearing of this day will not say, 'This rape was performed by Timon,' or 'That outrage was the work of Axiochus.' No, he will say these acts were committed by *men serving under Alexander*. Your misdeeds have blackened my name, for you are me, and I am you.

"Do we march for plunder, brothers? Is gold our aim, like merchants? By Zeus, I will cut my own throat if you tell me you believe that. Is it enough to rout the foe, to prove ourselves the greater brutes? Then build my pyre. I will kindle it myself before yielding to such want of imagination and such deficit of desire.

"Fame imperishable and glory that will never die—*that* is what we march for! To light that flame that death itself cannot quench. *That* I will achieve, and by the sword of Almighty Zeus, you will work it with me, every one of you!"

Not a man moves or breathes. I hate them and love them, as they love and hate me, and both of us know it.

"Brothers, I will suffer your crimes this day out of my love for you only. But hear me now and sear these words into your hearts: That man who disgraces this army again, I will not chastise as I do this night, as a father punishes his sons with care and concern for their character, but will banish that man from me and from this company forever."

This thoroughly chastens them.

"Now get out of my sight, the lot of you, except officers and generals. To you, I have more to say."

I assemble my marshals at the rear of the camp. The scourging I visit upon them, I shall never repeat, save to note that not one would have hesitated to exchange lashes of the whip for the lacerations these words carved into his soul.

Finished, I turn my fury on myself. "Ultimate responsibility for this debacle lies with me. I have not impressed sufficiently upon you, my officers, the code of chivalry by which I expect you and this army to conduct yourselves. Therefore I shall take nothing from the spoils. That portion that would have been mine will be distributed to our wounded and mutilated comrades and donated to raise memorials for our fallen."

I dismiss my officers and retire to the shelter that has been prepared for me, instructing my Pages to admit no one. I sleep all night and all morning, rising only to sacrifice on behalf of the army and to instruct the knight Leonnatus—Love Locks—to see to the comfort and security of the ladies of the Persian royal family, including Darius's wife Stateira and the queen mother, Sisygambis, who have been captured in their pavilion of the camp.

At noon Perdiccas begs entrance to me. The men are stricken with remorse, he declares; he implores me to take pity on them. I dismiss him angrily. Telamon is sent in next, and Craterus after him. Last, Hephaestion enters, with a look to the Pages that says he will endure no measure to banish him, no matter what instructions they have received from me. He entreats me in the name of my love for him to take only one step outside. Grudgingly I assent.

There before the tent, spread over acres, lies all the loot the men have taken: golden cups, robes of purple, chariots, women, suites of furniture. My countrymen surround the site in tens of thousands. Craterus addresses me in the men's name. "This is everything, Alexander, down to the last earring and amulet. Take it all. Leave us nothing. But please, do not hide your face from us."

I turn coldly to Hephaestion. "Is this what you brought me out here for?"

I start back to the tent. My friend catches my arm. He begs me not to harden my heart to our comrades. Can't I see how much they love me?

I glance from face to face; grizzled sergeants, private soldiers, senior officers. Never have I beheld expressions of such abjection. Men are weeping. I am moved to tears myself, which I contain only by supreme effort of will. I am still furious at my countrymen. I will not let them off the hook.

At last, Socrates Redbeard comes forward—brow and limbs bound in bandages—he who, of all the army, has borne the sternest use and conducted himself with the loftiest integrity.

"Have we not been true to you, Alexander? Have we not bled for you, and died for you? Have we failed you ever, or served you with anything less than all our hearts?"

I can no longer contain my tears.

"What more do you want of us?" Redbeard's voice cracks with emotion.

"I want you to be . . . magnificent."

A sigh breaks from the army entire.

"You want us to be you," Redbeard cries.

"Yes!"

"But we cannot! We are only men!" And their misery ascends to yet more excruciating apogees.

All my fury has fled.

"Can you believe I am angry with you, Socrates? Or with you, my friends?"

I can never forgive myself for causing the mutilation of our sick and wounded. For letting Darius escape, so that we must pursue and fight him again. For rendering our triumph imperfect.

"My rage is at myself alone. I have failed you. . . ."

"No!" the army cries. "Never!"

Redbeard steps toward me. I open my arms. A sound goes up from the host, which is part moan and part cry of joy. The men sweep round me in a colossal press; we sob, together, as if our hearts would break. Not a fellow, it seems, will tear himself away until his hand has touched mine and he knows he has been received again within his king's graces.

Nine months later, in Egypt, I am hailed as Horus, divine son of Ra and Ammon. Rapturous throngs line the thoroughfares; I reign as Pharaoh and Defender of Isis and Osiris. But I am not the same man I was before this clash along the Pinarus.

The commander-at-arms manipulates the ungovernable and the unpredictable. In battle, he directs the unknowable amid the unintelligible. This has always been clear to me. But it was not until the mutilation of our comrades at Issus, not until the flight of Darius and the riot of our army, not till then that I reckoned truly how little dominion even he wields, who calls himself victor and conqueror.

Book Six

PATIENCE

Seventeen

THE SEA AND THE STORM

T HIS DAY I HAVE MET AND SPOKEN for the first time with Porus, our rival across this river of India.

You watched from shore, Itanes, with the army. The delegations met on Porus's royal barge, at midchannel. This was his idea, as was the council itself—in response, I imagined, to the rapid progress of our work of diverting the river, and, additionally, the arrival of nine hundred of our transport vessels, carted overland in sections from the Indus. I welcomed this invitation to riverborne parley. The air would be cooler on the water, and I admired the spectacle of it, although the dignity of the expedition suffered a bit of a drubbing, as you saw, when our ferry snapped a line halfway across and we went spooling downriver like the cat that fell into the vat. The craft dispatched to our rescue were manned by Indian boatmen, all over seventy years of age, honored for their seniority, so that our deputies, myself included, had to strip naked and plunge into the current to retrieve the line, then haul in, hand over hand, Macedonians at one end, Indians at the other. Both parties were drenched to the skin by the time they gained the barge, where they were welcomed with much good humor (and dry again in minutes, with the heat of the country, as were our garments spread over the rails), and, as all had been shorn of excessive dignity along with our clothes, the conference seemed off to an auspicious start.

Porus is a splendid-looking fellow, a foot taller than I. His arms are as big as my calves. His hair is jet, bound in a spotless linen tiara. It has never been cut. His skin is so black, it's blue, and his teeth, inset with gold and diamonds, dazzle when he smiles, which he does often, unlike any other potentate I have met. His tunic is bright green and yellow; he carries not a scepter but a parasol, which the Indians call a *chuttah*.

Porus is not a name, it seems, but a title, comparable to Raj or King. His real name is Amritatma, which means "boundless soul." He laughs like a lion and rises from his chair like an elephant. It is impossible not to like the fellow.

His gift to me is a teak box, inlaid with ivory and gold. For a thousand years lords of the Punjab—he explains through an interpreter—have been presented with such a casket on the morn of their accession.

"What," I ask, "does one keep in it?"

"Nothing." The box is meant, Porus declares, to remind the sovereign of man's proper portion.

My gift to him is a bridle of gold, which had been Darius's.

"Why this?" he inquires.

"Because, of all I own, it is the most beautiful."

Porus receives this answer with a brilliant smile. At this point, I confess, I find myself as nonplussed as ever in any negotiation. For, although the conventions by which the Raj and I correspond are familiar and the offices of respect unexceptional, the man himself confounds me with his easy, personable nature and his utter lack of pretense.

He speaks of Darius, whom he knew and respected. They have been friends. Porus, in fact, had dispatched a thousand of his Royal Horse and two thousand *ksatriyas*, Royal Archers, to reinforce Darius at Gaugamela.

Yes, I tell him, I remember them. His Indian cavalry broke through our double phalanx and raided our forward camp; in their fighting withdrawal, they nearly killed me. And the archers were the most formidable we had ever faced.

He, Porus, had not been at Gaugamela. But, he says—indicating two dashing-looking officers, nearly as imposing as he—his sons had. He declares he has studied my generalship of that fight, or as much as he could piece together from reports, and proclaims it inspired. I am, in his phrase, "the very incarnation of the warrior commander."

I thank him and offer my own compliments.

Now things begin to run awry.

Porus has been sitting across from me, on a couch by himself, beneath the brightly colored canopy that shades both us and the company. He has just finished inviting me to tour his lands with him; it will be illuminating for me, he says, to see with my own eyes how well ordered is his kingdom, how productive the land, how happy the people, and how much they love him. He rises and crosses to the couch on which I sit, taking the place directly beside me. It is a disarming gesture, an act not just of affability but of affection.

"Stay with me," he proposes of a sudden, gesturing to the far shore, beyond which extend his lands and kingdom. "I give you the hand of my daughter and declare you my own heir and successor. You shall be my son and inherit my kingdom"—he indicates his two splendid-looking scions—"even before these children of my own flesh."

I am struck dumb at such munificence.

Porus flashes his dazzling smile. "Study with me," he continues, setting a hand warmly upon my knee. "I will teach you how to be a king."

I have glanced to Hephaestion in the interval; at these words I see his eyes go black with anger. Craterus beside him flinches, as if stung by a lash.

I feel my daimon enter, like a lion into a parlor.

I ask the interpreter to repeat the last phrase.

" 'I will teach you,' he enunciates in excellent Attic Greek, 'how to be a king.' "

I am furious now. Telamon shoots me a glare that commands, Contain yourself. I do, barely.

"Does His Majesty believe"—I address the interpreter, not looking at Porus—"that I am not a king?"

"Of course you are not!" springs the answer from Porus, succeeded by a laugh and a genial swat of my knee. The idea that he has insulted me, I see, has not even crossed his mind. He believes not only that I share his view of my lack of kingliness but that I welcome the opportunity, proffered by him now, to set this deficit aright.

Hephaestion strides before Porus. The vein in his temple stands out like a rope. "Do you dare, sir, impute a deficiency of kingly virtue to this man? For by what measure does one identify a king, save that he rout in the field every monarch on earth?"

Porus's sons have stalked forward. Craterus's hand moves to his sword; Telamon steps into the breach, restraining.

Porus has turned to the interpreter, who is rattling off the translation as fast as his tongue can untangle. The Raj's expression is one of puzzlement, succeeded by a grand and mellifluous laugh. It is a laugh loosed among friends, whose meaning is, Oh come come, fellows, let us not be upset by trifles!

With a gesture, Porus mollifies his sons and the other princes of the Indian party. He himself resumes his seat on the couch across from me, though this time leaning forward, so that our knees nearly touch alongside the table set with pitchers and refreshments.

"Your friend springs to your defense like a panther!" Porus gifts Hephaestion with another radiant smile. My mate withdraws, suddenly sheepish.

Porus apologizes to him and to me. Perhaps, he suggests, his expression has been imprecise. He has studied my career, he affirms, with a thoroughness that might surprise me.

"What I meant, Alexander, is that you are the supreme warrior, conqueror, even liberator. But you have not yet become a king."

"Like yourself," I suggest, barely containing my wrath.

"You are a conqueror. I am a king. There is a difference."

I ask what this might be.

"The difference between the sea and the storm."

I regard him, less than edified. He explains.

"The storm is brilliant and terrifying. Godlike, it looses its bolts of power, rolling over all in its path, and passing on. The sea, in contrast, remains—profound, eternal, unfathomable. The tempest hurls its thunder and lightning; the ocean absorbs all, unmoved. Do you understand, my friend? You are the storm. I am the sea."

Again he smiles.

My jaw is clenched so tight I could not reply if I wanted to. Only one aim animates me: to get clear of this parley before I dishonor myself by shedding my host's blood.

"Still I see," the Raj continues, though somewhat less amiably, "from the umbrage you take at my words, the color that flushes your breast, and the anger that you can barely contain, that it is important to you to be a king, and that my words have offered offense, though, if your heart sets store by candor, you must confess, they sting only by their truth." This need be no cause for distress, Porus continues, when one takes into account my extreme youth. "Who is a king at thirty, or even forty? That is why I have invited you to study with me, whose years might make me your father, mentor, and guide."

Craterus's eyes have read mine. He comes forward. "With respect, sir," he says, addressing the Indian king, "this interview is over."

The party of Macedon stands.

Our boats are hailed.

Porus's smile has vanished. His jaw works and his eyes go hooded and dark.

"I have offered you the hand of my daughter and the heirship to my kingdom," he declares, "to which you have responded only with sullen and wrathful silence. Therefore I make you another offer. Return to the lands you have conquered. Make your people free and happy. Render each man lord over his own household and sovereign over his own heart, instead of the wretched slaves they are today. When you have done that, *then* come back to me, and I will set myself to study at *your* feet. You will teach *me* how to be a king. Until then—"

I have turned my back on him. Our party has boarded the barge. The boatmen shove off.

Porus looms at the rail, commanding as a fortress tower.

"How dare you advance in arms against my kingdom? By what right do you offer violence to him who has never harmed you or even spoken your name except in praise? Are you a law unto yourself? Have you no fear of heaven?"

I would strike him down now, but for the spectacle of leaping boat to boat like a pirate.

"I said you are no king, Alexander, and I repeat it. You do not rule the lands you have conquered. Neither Persia, nor Egypt, nor Greece from whence you came, which hates you and would eat you raw if she could. What offices have you established to promote your people's weal? None! You have set in power only those same dynasts who oppressed the populace before, and by the same means, while you and your army pass on, like a ship that is master only of that quadrant of ocean upon which it sails, and no more. You command not even here in your own camp, which boils over with sedition and unrest. Yes, I know! Nothing happens in my country that is not reported to me, not even within your own tent."

I stand in our boat's prow. Every man's blood is up. Along both riverbanks, the armies cry out in anger and distress.

"So we shall have war, Alexander. I see you will stand for nothing else. Perhaps you shall win. Perhaps you are invincible, as all the world attests." His dark eyes meet mine across the chasm between us. "But though you stand over my dead body and set your heel upon the throat of my realm, you will still not be a king. Not even if you march, as you intend, to the Shore of the Eastern Ocean itself. You will not be a king, and you know it."

Once, when I was fourteen and served my father as a Page, I followed Philip as he stalked in fury to his quarters after an embassy with the Athenians. Hephaestion attended then as a Page, too, as did Love Locks and Ptolemy; we were all on duty that night, assigned to stand guard over the king's sleep.

"So Athens wishes peace? I'll give her hell first." Philip slung his cloak in anger. "Peace is for women! Never permit there to be peace! The king who stands for peace is no king at all!" Then, turning to us Pages, my father launched into a monologue of such blistering ire that we lads stood there, each fixed upon his post, held spellbound by his passion. "The life of peace is fitting for a mule or an ass. I would be a lion!" Who prospers in peace, Philip demanded, save clerks and cowards? And as for the welfare of his people: "What do I care to 'rule' or 'govern'? Blast them both and all the mealy arts of amity! Glory and fame are the only pursuits worthy of a man. Happiness? I piss upon it! Was Macedon happier when our frontiers were straw, to be cast down by any foe—or now, when the wide world trembles before us? I have seen my country be the plaything of enemies. I shall never permit that state again, and neither will my son!"

We touch shore after the fiasco with Porus. I still have not spoken. My generals wish to confer at once. No. I insist on inspecting the works diverting the river. Diades, the engineer, is hailed and hastens to us. We descend to the site in a freight rig, suspended by tackle stout enough to support an ox. The works themselves are spectacular, a hundred feet deep and broad as a small city. At their head, where the floodgates will be opened to draw the river into the channel, stand two tablets of sandstone fifty feet tall. Sculptors labor on scaffolding, carving an image into the rock.

"Whose face is that?" I inquire.

Diades laughs. "The king's, of course."

"Which king?"

"Why, you, lord."

I look again. "That is not my face."

All color drains from the engineer. He glances to Hephaestion, as if appealing for aid. "But it is, sire. . . ."

"Do you tell me I lie?"

"No, my lord."

"It is my father's face. The masons carve the profile of Philip."

The engineer shoots another frightened glance, this time to Craterus.

"Who told you to engrave my father's face?"

"Please! Look, lord. . . ."

"I am looking."

"Philip wore a beard. See, the image is clean-shaven!"

The lying bastard. I punch him in the face. He shrieks like a woman and drops like a slaughtered sow.

Craterus and Telamon seize my arm. On towers and scaffolds, men are gaping by the thousands.

Hephaestion's hand presses my brow. "You have a fever." Then, loudly, for all: "The king is burning up!"

Ptolemy helps Diades to his feet. The lift has halted forty feet into the pit. "Take us up!" Hephaestion commands.

At the top, we are met by a wall of gawking faces.

"The king has swallowed river water; he has taken ill," Hephaestion declares for publication. He calls for my physicians; I am spirited clear, out of the sun.

Inside the tent, I welcome the chance to feign incapacity; I drink till I'm blind, then pass out with relief. Hephaestion will not leave; he banishes the Pages and sleeps all night in the chair. Waking, I am riven with grief and remorse. My first thought is to recompense Diades with gold or honor for the outrage I have offered. Hephaestion calls me off; he has already done it.

We trek with the seers for dawn sacrifice. My brow feels as if a spike had been driven into it. Have I lost command, not only over this army but over myself? Can I rule, at this late hour, not even my own heart? It is minutes before I can even speak.

"Do you remember, Hephaestion, what you said on the eve of Chaeronea?"

"That by battle's end, we would be different people. Older, and crueler."

A long moment passes. "It gets easier."

"What?"

"To take the action."

"Nonsense! You are tired."

"I used to be able to separate myself from my daimon. It's harder now. I can't tell, sometimes, where he leaves off and I begin."

"You are not your gift, Alexander. You employ your gift."

"Do I?"

When we started out, I say, I valued in my friends courage and wisdom, spirit and humor and audacity. Now all I ask is loyalty. "In the end, I have heard, a man cannot trust even himself. Only his gift. Only his daimon."

The day I reach that state, I will have become a monster.

"The daimon," I declare, "is not a being that can be appealed to. It is a force of nature. To call it not human is only half-exact. It is inhuman. You make a pact with it. It gifts you with omniscience. But you ally yourself with the whirlwind and make your seat upon the tiger's back."

Day's end, I return with Hephaestion to Diades' excavation site. Indeed the face carved into the stone is my own.

Next morning I convene the council. "I have decided against diverting the river. Reassemble the boats brought from the Indus. We'll cross, when we do, by waterborne assault."

Eighteen

SPOILS OF WAR

WITH THE CAPTURE OF THE PERSIAN CAMP after Issus, certain correspondence fell into my hands. These were propositions addressed to Darius from various city-states of Greece, conspiring for my overthrow. Indeed the haul included a gaggle of envoys in the flesh, of Sparta, Thebes, Corinth, Elis, and Athens, all of whom stood present in the Persian camp on missions of treachery toward me.

I am no neophyte at politics. I count myself slave to few illusions. Indeed, virtually every aspect of the Aegean campaign, from depriving the expeditionary force of half its Macedonian strength—eight brigades of sarissa infantry and five squadrons of Companion Cavalry, left behind as a garrison force with Antipater in Greece—to the tedious and costly neutralization of the seacoast; my personal clemency and attentiveness to Athens; the pardons of those working against me among the Greek cities; all this, I say, was in consideration only of propitiating home opposition, the necessity of securing my base against insurrections of the states of Greece, alone or in alliance with the king of Persia, and to check the opening of a second front in my rear. I knew the Greeks resisted me. I knew they despised my race. Still part of me must have been naive; part must have believed I could make myself loved by them; that I could, by great and noble acts performed in emulation of our common Hellenic ancestors, induce them to take to their hearts if not Macedon, then me personally.

My blood ran hot when I read these letters, whose prose, whether crafted with the unctuous sycophancy of the courtier, the incendiary malice of the provocateur, or the bald power politics of the prime minister, fairly blazed with perfidy and malevolence. I read plots in which I was to be poisoned, stabbed, stoned, hanged, shot with bolts, arrows, and darts, set afire, drowned, trampled. I was to be smothered with a carpet, garroted with a cord, weighted with stones and hurled into the sea, assassinated at sacrifice, in my sleep, while heeding nature's call. Of the lexicon of epithets applied to me, I note only "this beast" and "the Malign One" (which I confess might, with some aptness, be applied to my horse), passing on to those reserved for my father (understandable), my sister (a mystery) and, vilest of all, my mother.

"Compliments," says Craterus, dismissing these.

Ptolemy calls them "the scorn of the sedge for the oak."

"At least," observes Parmenio, "we know whom to hang."

What infuriates me beyond all else is that these Greeks, before whom I have practically genuflected soliciting their good opinion, prefer union with the Persian barbarian to alliance with me! I show the letters to Telamon, knowing he will view them from a perspective all his own. "Which item of the soldier's kit," I ask my mercenary mentor, "should I be discarding now?"

"That part," Telamon replies, "which takes offense personally."

He is right, of course.

"Does it surprise you that they hate you, Alexander, whom you have deprived of liberty?"

I laugh. "I don't know why I keep you around."

"And if you freed these Greeks," he asks, "would they love you then?"

I laugh again.

"Understand you are the earthquake, Alexander. You are fire on the mountain."

"I am a man too."

"No. You gave up that luxury when you stood before the nation in arms and accepted their call as sovereign." It is a terrible thing to be a king, Telamon observes. "You think you will be different from those who went before you. But why? Necessity doesn't change. You have enemies. You must act. You find yourself proceeding with the same brutality as kings have always, and for the same brutal reasons. One cannot be a philosopher and a warrior at the same time, as Parmenio has said. And one cannot be a man and a king."

I ask Telamon what he would do with the perfidious ambassadors.

"Execute them. And not lose a minute's sleep."

"And the states of Greece?"

"Act toward them with consideration, as before. But send gold to Antipater for two more regiments."

In the end I pardon the envoys. They are, after all, brave men and patriots. But I keep them with me, hostages for their countrymen's good behavior.

What is more natural than to crave the good opinion of our fellows? We all wish to be loved. Perhaps the conqueror wants it more, even, than other men, for he seeks the adulation not only of his contemporaries but of posterity.

When I was eighteen, after the victory of Chaeronea, my father sent me with Antipater to Athens. We brought the ashes of those Athenians fallen in the battle and proffered the return without ransom of their prisoners—a noble gesture on Philip's part, whose intent was to disarm both Athens's terror and her antipathy. It worked. I became its beneficiary. I confess the celebrity went a little to my head. Then one night at a banquet, I overheard a remark accusing me of succeeding only by birth and luck. This sent my humor spiraling. Antipater saw and drew me aside.

"It seems to me, little old nephew"—he employed the Macedonian phrase of affection—"that you have elevated these Athenians as arbiters of your virtue. When in fact they are arbiters of nothing; they are just another petty state, consulting its own advantage. In the end, Alexander, your character and works will be judged not by Athenians, however illustrious their city may once have been, or by any of your contemporaries, but by history, which is to say by impartial, objective truth."

Antipater was right.

From that day, I vowed never to squander a moment's care over the good opinion of others. May they rot in hell. You have heard of my abstemiousness in matters of food and sex. Here is why: I punished myself. If I caught my thoughts straying to another's opinion of me, I sent myself to bed without supper. As for women, I likewise permitted myself none. I missed no few meals, and no small pleasure, before I brought this vice under control—or believed I had.

Nineteen

MAXIMS OF WAR

YOU HAVE SPENT NINE MONTHS NOW, ITANES, as a Page in my service. Time to emerge from the womb, don't you think?

Yes, you shall have your commission. You shall soon lead men in battle. Don't grin so broadly! For my eye will be on you, as on every cadet who graduates from the academy of war that is my tent.

It has been your privilege, these months since your acceptance into the corps in Afghanistan, to attend upon commanders of such genius as warfare has seldom seen. The officers whose meat you carve and wine you pour—Hephaestion and Craterus, Perdiccas, Ptolemy, Seleucus, Coenus, Polyperchon, Lysimachus, not to say Parmenio, Philotas, and Nicanor, Antigonus One-Eye, and Antipater, whom you have not had the fortune of knowing—each stands in his own right with the great captains of history. Now I require of you the same fidelity I demand of them. You must incorporate the conventions and principles by which this army fights. Why? Because once battle is joined, I shall be where I can control nothing beyond the division immediately under my hand, and, in the inevitable chaos, will barely be able to direct even that. You must command on your own, my young lieutenant, but how you do so cannot be random or idiosyncratic; it must follow my thought and my will. That is why we talk here nightlong, my generals and I, and why you and the other Pages attend and listen. That is why we rehearse fundamentals over and over, until they become second nature to us all.

I have asked Eumenes, my Counsel of War, to make correspondence of mine available to you. Study these letters as if they were lessons in school, but hold this foremost in mind: The pupil may differ with his tutor, the cadet never. What I set in your hands this night is law. Follow it and no force can stand against you. Defy it and I will not need to settle with you, for the foe will already have done so.

On Philosophy of War

TO PTOLEMY, AT EPHESUS:

Always attack. Even in defense, attack. The attacking arm possesses the initiative and thus commands the action. To attack makes men brave; to defend makes them timorous. If I learn that an officer of mine has assumed a defensive posture in the field, that officer will never hold command under me again.

TO PTOLEMY, IN EGYPT:

When deliberating, think in campaigns and not battles; in wars and not campaigns; in ultimate conquest and not wars.

TO PERDICCAS, FROM TYRE:

Seek the decisive battle. What good does it do us to win ten scraps of no consequence if we lose the one that counts? I want to fight battles that decide the fate of empires.

TO SELEUCUS, IN EGYPT:

It is as important to win morally as to win militarily. By which I mean our victories must break the foe's heart and tear from him all hope of contesting us again. I do not wish to fight war upon war, but by war to produce such a peace as will admit of no insurrection.

On Strategy and Campaign

TO COENUS, IN PALESTINE:

The object of campaign is to bring about a battle that will prove decisive. We feint; we maneuver; we provoke to one end: to compel the foe to face us in the field.

What I want is a battle, one great pitched clash in which Darius comes out to us in the flower of his might. Remember, our object is to break the will to resist, not only of the king's soldiers, but of his peoples.

The subjects of the empire are the real audience of these events. They must be made to believe by the scale and decisiveness of our triumphs that no force on earth, however numerous or well generaled, can prevail against us.

TO PERDICCAS, AT GAZA:

The object of pursuit after victory is not only to prevent the enemy from re-forming in the instance (this goes without saying), but to burn such fear into his vitals that he will never think of reforming again. Therefore, pursue by all means and don't relent until hell or darkness compels you. The foe who has been a fugitive once will never be the same fighter again.

I would rather lose five hundred horses in a pursuit, if it prevents the enemy from re-forming, than to spare those horses, only to lose them—and five hundred more—in a second fight.

TO SELEUCUS, IN SYRIA:

As commanders, we must save our supreme ruthlessness for ourselves. Before we make any move in the face of the enemy, we must ask ourselves, free of vanity and self-deception, how the foe will counter. Unearth every stroke and have an answer for it. Even when you think you have thought of everything, there will be more work to do. Be merciless with yourself, for every careless act is paid for in our own blood and the blood of our countrymen.

On Generosity

TO PARMENIO, AFTER ISSUS:

Cyrus the Great sought to detach from his enemy disaffected elements of the latter's forces, or others serving under compulsion. To this end he showed the Armenians and Hyrcanians honor and spared no measure to make their condition happier under his rule than under the Assyrian's. In Cyrus's view the purpose of victory was to prove more generous in gifts than the enemy. He felt it the greatest shame to lack the means to requite the munificence of others; he always wished to give more than he received, and he amassed treasure with the understanding that he held it in trust, not for himself, but for his friends to call upon in need.

TO HEPHAESTION, ALSO AFTER ISSUS:

Make generosity our first option. If an enemy shows the least sign of accommodation, match him twice over.

Let us conduct ourselves in such a fashion that all nations wish to be our friends and all fear to be our enemies.

On Tactics, Battles, and Soldiers

No advantage in war is greater than speed. To appear suddenly in strength where the enemy least expects you overawes him and throws him into consternation.

Great multitudes are not necessary. The optimal size of a fighting corps is that number that can march from one camp to another and arrive in one day. Any more are superfluous and only slow you down.

All tactics in conventional warfare seek to produce this single result: a breakthrough in the enemy line. This is as true of naval warfare as it is of war on land.

A static defensive line is always vulnerable. Once penetrated in force at any point, every other post on the line becomes moot. Its men cannot bring their arms to bear and, in fact, can do nothing except wait in impotence to be overrun by their own comrades fleeing in panic as our penetrating force rolls them up from the flank.

Be conservative until the crucial moment. Then strike with all the violence you possess.

Remember: We need win at only one point on the field, so long as that point is decisive.

Every battle is constituted of a number of sub-battles of differing degrees of consequence. I don't care if we lose every sub-battle, so long as we win the one that counts.

We fight with a holding wing and an attacking wing. The purpose of the former is to paralyze in place, by its advance and its posture of threat, the enemy wing opposed to it. The purpose of the latter is to strike and penetrate.

We concentrate our force and hurl it with utmost violence upon one point in the enemy line.

I want to feel as if I hold a lightning bolt. By which I mean that blow, poised beneath my command, which when hurled against the enemy will break his line. As the boxer waits with patience for the moment to throw his knockout punch, the general holds his decisive strike poised, careful not to loose it too early or too late.

Don't punch; counterpunch. The purpose of an initial evolution—a feint or draw—is to provoke the enemy into committing himself prematurely. Once he moves, we countermove.

We seek to create a breach in the enemy's line, into which cavalry can charge.

The line soldier need remember only two things: Keep in ranks and never abandon his colors.

An officer must lead from the front. How can we ask our soldiers to risk death if we ourselves shrink from hazard?

War is academic only on the mapboard. In the field it is all emotion.

Leverage of position means the occupation of that site which compels the enemy to move. When we face an enemy marshaled in a defensive posture, our first thought must be: What post can we seize that will make him withdraw?

The officer's charge is to control the emotion of the men under his command, neither letting them yield to fear, which will render them cowards, nor allowing them to give themselves over to rage, which will make them brutes.

Entering any territory, capture the wine stocks and breweries first. An army without spirits is prey to disgruntlement and insurrection.

Use forced marches to cross waterless territory. This minimizes suffering for the men and animals. For a march of two days, I have found it an excellent method to rest till nightfall before setting out, march all night, rest through the heat of the next day, then march again all night. By this scheme we compress two days' marching into a day and a half, and, if we find ourselves still shy of our goal with the second day's sun, it is easier for the men and horses to push on in daylight, knowing water and rest are near.

On Cavalry

The strength of cavalry is speed and shock. A static line of cavalry is no cavalry at all.

A horse must be a bit mad to be a good cavalry mount, and its rider must be completely so.

Cohesion of ranks, paramount with infantry, is even more crucial with cavalry. An enemy on foot may stand his ground against scattered horses of any number but never against mounted squadrons attacking boot-to-boot.

Cavalry need not work execution in the assault. Just break through. We can kill the enemy at leisure once we put him to flight.

It takes five years to train a trooper and ten to train his horse.

Green cavalry is worthless.

What I want in a cavalry mount is "push," or, as the riding masters call it, "impulsion."

The skills of mounted warfare require constant practice. Even a brief furlough can put a horse and rider "off their stuff," until they regain their sharpness by a return to training.

A cavalryman's horse should be smarter than he is. But the horse must never be allowed to know this.

Book Seven

AN INSTINCT FOR THE KILL

Twenty

COUNCILS OF WAR

I T TAKES DARIUS TWENTY-THREE MONTHS to raise another army after Issus. As with the first, he marshals and trains it at Babylon. This time I will go to him. This time we will duel beyond the Euphrates.

It is three years now since our army has crossed from Europe. The expeditionary force has appended to its conquests Phoenicia, both Hollow and Mesopotamian Syria, Tyre, Sidon, Gaza, Samaria, Palestine, and Egypt. I have become Defender of Yahweh, Sword of Baal, Pharaoh of the Nile. The sun priests have anointed me Child of Ra, Boatman of Osiris, son of Ammon. I embrace all honors, but especially the religious ones. They are worth armies. The Persians were blind, when they ruled Egypt, to insult the gods of the land. There is no surer way to make yourself hated; whereas to take up the native deities wins the people's love, and at no cost. Heaven speaks with the same voice in Memphis and in Macedon; I despise the man, however learned, who does not grant this. God is God, in whatever form He chooses to appear. I worship Him as Zeus, Ammon, Jehovah, Apis, Baal; lion-limbed, jackal-headed, bearded, behorned; in the form of man, woman, sphinx, bull, and virgin. I believe in them all.

The king, my father taught me, is the people's intercessor with heaven. He invokes the Creator's blessing before the seed goes into the ground and proffers thanksgiving at harvest's bounty. Before every army marches out, every vessel sails, every enterprise originates, he presides. At every crisis he entreats God's counsel and interprets it. If the king is in favor with heaven, so is the kingdom. What miscreant is so perverse as to spurn the blessing of the Almighty?

Tyre and Gaza trusted in the strength of their fortifications and compelled me to besiege them. What a waste of blood and treasure! The lives of a hundred and ninety good men were squandered over six months in consequence of Tyrian stubbornness, and Gaza cost another thirty-six and a hundred and eleven days. The bastards nearly corked me twice, with a catapult bolt through my breast and a stone that nearly made powder of my skull. Had some malign god deprived them of their senses? Did they imagine that I would permit a state to command strategic ports in my rear, by which my enemies could assail me? Did they dream that I might pass benignly on, leaving their nation intact as an example to others that defiance of my will was the path to preservation? My envoys sought to make the leading men of Tyre and Gaza see reason; I dispatched letters beneath my own hand. I pledged to make their cities richer, freer, safer. Still they resisted. They compelled me to make examples of them.

What I abhor most about such obduracy is that it robs me of the occasion to be magnanimous. Do you understand? The enemy will not see chivalry. He obliges me to fight not as a knight but as a butcher—and for this he must pay with his own ruin.

The world we see is but a shadow, Itanes, an adumbration of the True World, the Invisible World, which resides beneath. What is this realm? Not What Is, but What Will Be. The future. Necessity is the name we give to that mechanism by which the Infinite produces its works. The manifest arising out of the unmanifest. God reigns in both worlds. But He permits only His favorites to glimpse the world to come.

I felt at home in Egypt. I could happily have been a priest. In truth I am a warrior-priest, who marches where the Deity directs, in the service of Necessity and Fate. Nor is such a notion vain or self-infatuated. Consider: Persia's time has passed. In the Invisible World, Darius's empire has already fallen. Who am I, except the agent of that end, which already exists in the Other Realm and at whose birth I assist in this one?

At Antioch in Syria I held a great feast in honor of Zeus and the Muses. Ten thousand bullocks I sacrificed to the Olympians, to Heracles, Bellerophon, and all the gods and heroes of the East, beseeching their benediction for the enterprise to come.

The campaign of Gaugamela (or what would become the campaign of Gaugamela) would be by far the most complex of the war. When I called the Macedonians and allies together at the vizier's palace in Antioch, I asked Parmenio to prepare a paper on the challenges the corps would face. I have it still. Here is the script he recited from:

"The advance into Mesopotamia will require a march of between six hundred and eight hundred miles, depending on the route, much of it across waterless desert. We will be separated from our bases on the coast and thus from resupply by sea. Everything we need, we must pack on our backs or wring from the country. Further, we advance now through 'rough territories' in which we have few agents or men in place.

"Numbers. We must see to the feeding and maintenance of forty-seven thousand combatants and all their gear, plus sixty-seven hundred primary mounts and eleven thousand remounts. Baggage animals will number above fifteen thousand. In addition, the army has acquired a multitude of dependents—wives and mistresses, children, in-laws; we pack even grandmothers these days. Drinking water will present a predicament even when we have reached the Euphrates, for I hate to trust our guts to piss driven over silt, which is what that river is. Heat and sun will be worse. In summer, all reports confirm, the plains north of Babylon are fit only for creatures born with fangs or scales. The country has swallowed armies. Yet we must fight in the heat, because of the harvest dates. Leaving the seacoast in spring, we take the early wheat and barley with us; arriving in Mesopotamia in late summer, we take the second crop, milk-ripe if we're ahead of schedule, fully headed if we dawdle. That is, if Darius has not garnered or torched it, in which case we shall fight in hell on empty bellies.

"Babylon lies above the confluence of the Tigris and Euphrates, both great rivers, unfordable at any point within a hundred miles of the city. One or both must be bridged. This will be no mean feat in the face of an army exceeding a million. The country along the Euphrates is dense with crops; canals and irrigation works will block us at every turn. The plain beyond is featureless waste. Wander a mile from camp and we'll never see you again. Darius has summoned to Babylon every fighting nation of his empire. Infantry and cavalry of those eastern provinces absent at Issus—Scythians, Areians, Parthians, Bactrians, Sogdians, Indians—have joined Darius's army now and are training at Babylon as we speak. This is the breadbasket of his empire; he will defend it with everything he's got. The plains north on which he aims to fight us are broad and treeless, ideal for old-fashioned Asiatic warfare. The enemy will employ scythe-bearing chariots, mailed cataphracts, perhaps even war elephants. And he will be recruiting from horse tribesmen of the East—Daans and Massagetae, Sacae and Afghans and Arachosians—whose limitless grasslands produce war stock without number. The provinces of Media and Hyrcania alone can bring forty thousand horse, I am told, and the steppe satrapies beyond are even richer in this resource."

Parmenio concludes his presentation and sits. The hall, which is roofed in cedar and columned in alabaster, falls tomb-silent.

"Craterus, cheer us up!"

Craterus's assignment is forward supply. He cites the cities, towns, and villages by which we must pass and what native agents have been contracted with for supplies and forage, guides, pack animals, water. Depots have been established at intervals between Damascus and Thapsacus, where we will cross the Euphrates. Beyond there, we must live off the land. Craterus brings forward exiles from Darius, traders, caravan runners, mountain tribesmen. They describe the country through which we must trek. Most of us have heard it already. But I want my officers to hear it again in one another's company. I want them to take it in as a corps.

"What about wine?" Ptolemy asks.

This is the first laugh. Love Locks has that duty. His agents have identified breweries of rice and date palm beer; estate vineyards and "pockmarks," local stills that produce a liquor made from pistachios and palm sap; vile but drinkable in a pinch. He will capture them all, Love Locks vows, and, by Zeus, suck them dry on his own, if we don't catch him first. A chorus of good-natured derision assails him.

How much cash do we have? From Damascus, twenty thousand talents of gold; from Tyre, Gaza, and Jerusalem, another fifteen thousand; Egypt, eight thousand. From the cities of the seaboard, six thousand more.

This is fifty times the pot we had when we set out, but still not a tenth of what Darius holds and will use against us.

"How hot is the Euphrates Valley?" "How swift is the Tigris?" "How many are the enemy?" Each general has his sphere of responsibility. Each has his aides and adjutants; often it is they who do the answering.

I don't believe these councils accomplish much in the instant; we've heard it all before and will hear it a hundred times more in a hundred other caucuses. But I want my officers to see one another and hear one another speak. Particularly the mercenaries and allies, who understandably feel less central to the expedition than the Macedonians.

This army, as all armies, is riven by faction and jealousy—of infantry, the Old Guard, Philip's contemporaries, who feel resentment toward the New Men, my age; the Companion Cavalry of Old Macedon, raised by Philip, mistrust those of New, favored, they fear, by me. Then the Greek infantry serving under compulsion, whom nobody trusts, and their cousins, the mercenary foot, who keep to themselves, so no one knows what they think. The allied and hired horse are suspect because, being mounted, they can bolt any time they want; next the Thracians and Odrysians who barely even speak Greek; the crack Thessalian Heavy Horse, haughty to all save the Companions, from whom they demand respect, which is not always given; the javelineers and peltasts of Thrace and Agriania; the Old Mercenaries, who came over with us from Europe, hard as horn; the young bucks, who burn for action, perhaps too brightly; the foreigners and late arrivals; Armenians and Cappadocians; Syrians and Egyptians; renegades of Cilicia and Phoenicia who have joined since Issus; the Greek mercenaries who served originally under Darius; not to mention the Paeonian and Illyrian horsemen and the new infantry of the Peloponnese. Let them hear one another. Let them look in one another's eyes. I tilt the council's tenor toward magnification of the foe; it knits our bickering camps.

Parmenio is our father; there is comfort in his encyclopedic knowledge and exhaustive preparation. Ptolemy is razor-keen; he can sell you anything. Our best soldier is Craterus, and most profane; his speeches are spare as a Spartan's. The men love him. Perdiccas's ambition is as naked as his arrogance, but he knows his game; Seleucus excels all in physical courage; Coenus in cunning; while Hephaestion is a knight out of Homer. I speak little myself. I learned this from my father.

I nod to Lysimachus, say, or Simmias, indicating that I wish him to speak to the subject at hand. I love to feature junior officers, particularly those with whom the company is unfamiliar. One Angelis, a route engineer, describes a type of pontoon bridge he and his men have been developing. It relies not on pilings or claw anchors (the first burdensome, the second unreliable) but employs wicker crates filled with stones. He has tested it at the Orontes and the Jordan, rivers with silt-bottomed channels like the Tigris and Euphrates; he believes he can span a thousand feet in a day and a night and put across not just men but horses. "Heavy pile drivers needn't be borne across country by the baggage train; we can cut planks and cables on-site of local materials, which reports confirm to be abundant, and we don't even need to carry the anchors, but they too can be cobbled together on the spot."

I call Menidas to speak, colonel of the mercenary cavalry, and Aretes of the Royal Lancers. Few know these men, though they come of noble Macedonian stock, as both are recent and untried replacements for well-loved commanders. Yet our fate will ride on their will and grit. When Menidas falters in his speech, unaccustomed to addressing so illustrious a body, I cross from my place and settle in the chair at his side.

Together we field questions; I pour wine for his parched throat. He finds his voice. Craterus names him a "dark hand," slang for a prodigy who lays low out of cunning. The tent responds with a roar. I clap Menidas's shoulder. He will be fine.

Midnight comes and goes. I call for a late supper. Confident as we are, the numbers are still staggering against us. We are fifty thousand; the foe may be a million. Of course such a figure is ludicrous, as it tallies in every trollop and laundry urchin; still, we will face conscript infantry five times our total and cavalry outnumbering us even more. As the conclave breaks, Craterus gives speech to the fear on every man's mind. "Of devices that the enemy may employ, Alexander, which concerns you most?"

I reply that I have only one dread: "That Darius will flee and not face us in battle."

The pavilion erupts.

At Marathus in Hollow Syria, a letter has arrived from Darius. In it, he offers me his empire west of the river Halys (a second letter extends this to the Euphrates) with ten thousand talents of gold; he will give me the hand of his daughter, he says, and asks that I return to him his wife and son and mother, whom we have captured after Issus.

I reply:

> Your ancestors invaded my country and worked grievous harm to Greeks and Macedonians, though we had previously done nothing to them. My father was assassinated by agents in your employ, as you yourself have boasted in correspondence published before all the world. You bribe my allies to make war on me, conspire with my friends for my murder. You started this war, not I.
>
> I have vanquished in the field first those you sent against me, then you yourself and all your army. Therefore, do not address me as invader, but as conqueror. If you want anything, come to me. Ask for your mother, your wife and children; you shall have them, and whatever else you can persuade me to give. But send to me not as an equal, but as your king, and the Lord of Asia. And if you contest this, then

stand your ground and fight and do not run away, for I will follow you wherever you go.

When I write that I will give Darius whatever he asks if he but come to me, I mean it. I feel no rancor toward the man. I respect him. I would make him my friend and ally. He can have anything but his empire. That is mine, and I will take it.

Twenty-One

THE ADVANCE INTO MESOPOTAMIA

nabasis IS A MILITARY WORD. It means a "march to the Interior." In early summer, three years after the army's crossing to Asia, our anabasis seeking Darius begins.

The corps departs Tyre on the seacoast on a raw blustery dawn, making for Thapsacus, where we intend to cross the Euphrates. I have sent Hephaestion ahead with two squadrons of Companion Cavalry, fifteen hundred allied infantry, half the archers and Agrianians, and all seven hundred of Menidas's mercenary horse. He is to seize the city and throw two spans across the river, whose breadth is eight hundred yards at that point.

Tyre to Thapsacus is two hundred fifty miles. Hephaestion will arrive by midsummer and set to work; our main body should catch up at the season's scorching peak. From Thapsacus to Babylon is another four hundred and fifty miles, by the Royal Road down the Euphrates. In the heat at that season, the corps cannot be expected to average more than fifteen miles a day. Certainly I intend to push it no harder. So: middle to late fall. We will face Darius then.

I have selected Hephaestion for the work at Thapsacus, and not

Craterus or another, on the chance of intrigue. Darius and his staff will reckon that site as my likely first objective; the king is certain to send a strong detachment north from Babylon to keep an eye on me or even to contest my crossing. There may be a chance, if we are clever, to bring the commander of this division over to our side, if not now, then later. Hephaestion will throw his bridges nine-tenths of the way across the river and hold up till our main army arrives. The Persians will shout insults from the farther bank, in Greek if their numbers include hired infantry, which they will. Who better than Hephaestion to turn this occasion to our advantage? I have authorized him to make any deal he can with the Persian commander. If none can be struck in the moment, Hephaestion is to communicate to the officer that Alexander watches him, and he is a man (meaning me) who knows how to reward an act of friendship.

Our main body's route of march, departing from the coast ten days after Hephaestion, is inland via Damascus. I have commanded the provincial governor to produce on-site every armorer and swordsmith of Hollow and Rough Syria with all their tools and wares. The army lays over five days, giving the soldiers time to refit their kit for the coming fight. Damascus's market is called the Terik, "pigeon." These birds are considered gods by the Syrians; they flock in numbers uncountable and are as self-satisfied as cats.

A prodigy occurs in the marketplace. One of our sergeants, seeking his dinner, snatches a roosting *terik* and, ignorant of local reverence, wrings its neck. The quarter erupts; in moments, hundreds mob the square, shrieking in outrage. The mart, as I said, is an arsenal of armorers' and swordsmiths' shops; our fellow and his mates find themselves hemmed by armed Damascenes, howling for their blood. A general riot looms, ready to wreck the entire expedition. Suddenly the pigeon stirs in our man's hand. It is alive! The sergeant opens his fingers; the bird wings safely away. A thousand Syrians drop onto their faces, worshiping heaven.

Damascus to Homs is a six-day trek of ninety miles. A column on the march is always prey to portent and rumor. The men are bored; they gossip like housedames. What of the incident in the marketplace? Is the pigeon Darius? Will he flutter free of Alexander's grasp? Or is the ser-geant our army, preserved from slaughter by a miracle?

A two-day march of thirty miles brings us to Hamah; then five days, seventy miles, to Aleppo. On route a message arrives from Hephaestion ahead at Thapsacus: Arimmas, my appointee as governor of Meso-potamian Syria, has failed to provide the forward magazines of grain and feed the corps will need for the advance beyond the Euphrates. My first impulse is to make an example of him, but Hephaestion, anticipating this in his dispatch, requests clemency for the fellow. The scale of the enterprise has overwhelmed Arimmas; his failing is incapacity, not treachery, for which I must share the blame, elevating him to an office beyond his gifts. I remove him and send him home. Pasturage, fortu-nately, is abundant where we camp now, in the Orontes valley; a call to Antioch for muleteers brings in seventeen hundred. I put the whole army to work. We load up and move out.

We are advancing east now, into the empire. An alteration takes place in the men's demeanor. I am riding beside Telamon, on the wing of the column, when I sense the revolution.

"Can you feel it?"

He acknowledges. "Fear."

Each mile now carries the army farther from territory we have con-quered, farther from our bases on the sea. We enter the foe's domain, his stronghold. The men glance over their shoulders despite themselves, toward the road receding behind them, thinking how far it stretches from supply and safety.

Fifteen thousand reinforcements were supposed to arrive at Tripolis on the coast. Are they vital to our success? No. But their nonappear-ance, first at Damascus, then at Homs, now at Aleppo, sends a shudder of evil luck through the column. How can the commander counter? Here is something the instructors of war do not teach: the art of con-fronting the irrational, of disarming the groundless and the unknown.

We as officers debate our routes and strategies. What we forget is that the men do the same. They are not stupid. They see the country change; they know what they're marching into. In their tents and around their cook fires, they chew over every fresh piece of intelligence.

We in the command post have our sources; the corporals and private soldiers have theirs too. Daylong they interrogate the natives tracking the column, the rabble of the towns we pass through, the whores and sutlers of the general crowd, and, of course, one another. A racehorse cannot gallop the column's length faster than the newest rumor or the freshest fear.

Two stages on, at Dura Na, the column comes upon a site where Darius's army encamped eighteen months ago, in its advance toward what became the battle of Issus. Army junk spreads everywhere; you can see the lanes and latrines and the great square entrenchment whose breastworks, studded with palisade stakes and wicker hurdles, are still being stripped by the locals for firewood. On such military highways, one comes often upon the camps of vanished armies. I make it a point never to overnight on them. It's bad luck. And, in this case, I don't want the men to be unnerved by how small our force is alongside Darius's (we will fill only a fifth of the space the foe's host encamped on).

But our fellows see it. How can they not? I feel their stride change. They mutter now. How many thousands did the Persians have in this camp? How many more when we face them next? I trot alongside the column.

"Brothers, will you give me five more miles before we camp?"

Let us stretch past the foe's fort. Let the men see how strong our pace is, so they boast that our army makes two camps where the glue-footed Persian makes three.

But fear dogs the column. In camp that night an incident occurs involving a fearsome weapon our soldiers have never seen.

In any army there are resourceful fellows who can scrounge up treasure from a hill of dung. Two of ours are sergeants of the phalanx, called by the men "Patch" and "Repatch," for their habit of forbidding their mates to throw anything away. Their prize this time: a Persian scythed chariot.

Apparently a local bandit made off with the machine during Darius's advance a year and a half ago; Patch and Repatch, nosing about, have got wind of its existence and, publishing a reward among the natives, have enticed the outlaw to bring it in.

The chariot sets off a sensation. Our fellows throng about it.

"By Zeus, how'd you like to stand up to that iron . . ."

"I'd sooner shave with it."

"Take a look, mates. You'll be hiking on your knees after that runs over you."

Wicked-looking blades extend from both axles of the chariot; others are mounted on the frame and the front of the yoke pole. The bandit claims that Darius had a hundred of these "cutters" when he marched against us eighteen months ago, but he left them here, on this side of the mountains, believing the terrain in Cilicia too rough to permit their use. That's why we didn't see them at Issus. Our fellows collect about the chariot now, conjuring the havoc five score of these machines would wreak, driven at the gallop into a massed formation. Our sergeant Patch voices the prevailing sentiment: "Let's have a few hundred of these bastards on *our* side!"

Another curiosity brought in by the locals are the "crow's feet," with which Darius had intended to sow the floor of that earlier battlefield against our cavalry—and which he no doubt will use on this coming one. These devices are made of four iron spikes yoked at a single axis. Any way you strew them, one spike always points straight up.

From Dura Na a three-day march of forty-five miles brings the army to Thapsacus on the Euphrates. The date is 2 Hecatombeion, high summer. A pall of smoke hangs above the plain beyond the river, where forward parties of Persian cavalry are scorching the earth. Darius, we learn, continues augmenting his forces at Babylon, between four and five hundred miles south. His army now totals one million two hundred thousand.

A multitude of such scale, however preposterous in fact or unworkable in action, cannot fail to strike terror into the breasts of those who believe they must face it. Crossing camp on foot, I come upon our friend Gunnysack, hunkered in the dust with a score of comrades, drawing schemes with a stick.

"Are you an artist too, Sergeant?"

He is sketching a line of over a million men. How wide a front? How deep? Can such a host be possible?

"Sire, are we really going up against so many?"

"Maybe more, if you count whores and scullery lads."

"And are you not afraid, sire?"

"I would be—if I were Darius and had to face us."

The Persian has sent two mounted brigades north ahead of his army, one of three thousand under his cousin Satropates, another of six thousand under Mazaeus, governor of Babylonia. Their assignment is to devastate the country into which we advance and to contest all river crossings. We learn this from Hephaestion, who has, as I had hoped, parleyed with Mazaeus personally.

Mazaeus is an interesting fellow. He is something of a gangster. A Persian and adherent of the royal house, he has governed provinces for thirty years—first in Cilicia alone, then as supreme satrap of Phoenicia, Cilicia, and both Syrias. He received his warrant of appointment to Babylonia not from Darius but from his predecessor, Artaxerxes Ochus. Darius wished to remove him upon his accession, so the popular account declares, but Mazaeus had in the course of his tenure insinuated himself so powerfully into that peculiar Babylonian underworld called *ashtara*, "the Code," that he could not be ousted without bringing down the entire regional economy.

Mazaeus is the richest private individual in the empire; his breeding stable contains eight hundred stallions and sixteen thousand mares. He is said to have fathered a thousand sons. But what marks him out is his openhandedness to the people. The grandest secular feast of the Babylonian year is the Mazaeid, at which its host provides meat for tens of thousands and distributes grain in such quantities that families live on the issue all year long. Mazaeus is fat. His mounts are draft horses, not cavalry ponies. And he is not above poking fun at himself. At his festival each year, it is said, he takes the choral stage dressed as a woman and warbles in such a convincing key that none can pick him out from the real thing.

Withdrawing before our force, Mazaeus has let us take several prisoners. These confirm Darius's army at one million two hundred thousand. Hephaestion throws a pontoon bridge across the last uncompleted

span; we cross in five days. I rest the army four days in the plain while
we bring up the siege train and the heavy baggage.

A decision must be made on which route to take to Babylon. Shall
we march south, directly down the Euphrates, or cross east to the Tigris
and turn south from there? I call a council.

The foe's vast numbers dominate all talk. The army prattles of nothing else, and even my generals are spooked and anxious. Old feuds surface. Tempers grow short; mates snap testily at one another.

How is one to command? By consensus of his subordinates? Listen
indeed. Weigh and evaluate. Then decide yourself. Are you stumped at
the crossroads? Pick one way and don't look back. Nothing is worse
than indecision. Be wrong, but be wrong decisively. Can you please your
constituents? Never let me hear that word! The men are never happy
with anything. The march is always too long, the way always too rough.
What works with them? Hardship. Give your men something that can't
be done, not something that can. Then place yourself at first hazard.
The Spartan commander Lysander made the distinction between boldness and courage. We must have both. The audacity to conceive the
strike and the belly to carry it out.

All that being said, how *does* one make decisions? By rationality?
My tutor Aristotle could classify the world, but couldn't find his way to
the village square. One must dive deeper than reason. The Thracians of
Bithynia trust no decision unless they make it drunk. They know something we don't. A lion never makes a bad decision. Is he guided by reason? Is an eagle "rational"?

Rationality is superstition by another name.

Go deep, my friend. Touch the daimon. Do I believe in signs and
omens? I believe in the Unseen. I believe in the Unmanifest, the Yet To
Be. Great commanders do not temper their measures to What Is; they
bring forth What May Be.

Twenty-Two

SWIFT AS AN ARROW

W E MARCH EAST TOWARD THE TIGRIS.

Sound military considerations dictate this, but in truth I have made the decision based on a dream. The god Fear appears to me in the guise of a panther. The beast is so black, he seems made of night. I track him in the dark. In the dream it seems imperative that I overhaul the panther and learn what he has to tell me. I have no torch and no weapon; I advance, gripped with dread that I will stumble into him in the dark and be torn apart. I awake trembling.

We have two Egyptian seers with the army, as well as our own diviner Aristander. I sound them separately. The Egyptians both say the panther is Darius. Both dismiss my unease as based on our present deficiency of reconnaissance; our scouts have lost contact with the Persian army. The dream indicates no more than this understandable care.

Aristander makes no interpretation of the panther. Without hesitation he asks, "In which direction did the beast's tracks lead?"

We march east.

The beast is not Darius. The beast is Fear.

It is two hundred ninety-six miles from Thapsacus to the Tigris.

Why this route? My commanders have expected the other, south down the Euphrates valley. That way is clearly the easier, straight on the Royal Road, a month or month and a half to Babylon—the same route Cyrus the Younger took when he fought his brother, Artaxerxes II, at Cunaxa. The Euphrates flows at our shoulder; forage is abundant from irrigated fields; supplies can be barged downstream from country we've already overrun.

But Darius wants me to approach this way. Otherwise why has he sent Mazaeus with so weak a force to contest me? Why have him and Satropates withdraw after such feeble passes at torching the earth?

The foe means me to take the Euphrates route. He baits me to do so. No doubt his engineers have prepared battle sites along the course, on the several plains that are ideal for his grand army. His supply base is there, at Babylon; he has prime roads and the river and canals to bring up men and gear.

I can't take that way. Down the Royal Road we pass through the hottest part of the country—an irrigated corridor between scorching deserts. The network of canals makes natural strongpoints. The enemy can flood fields to check our advance or lay ambushes to assault us from the flanks. The grain is already in; only stubble remains. To get at the harvest we'll have to besiege walled cities. Liquor? The only spirits we'll have will be those we pack. And the heat. We'll lose one man in five trekking down that griddle, not to mention the horses, and those not felled by the sun will succumb to the stinking river water. I have fifteen thousand reinforcements on the march from home; if I bolt south down the Euphrates, they won't get here till it's too late. Take another, slower route, and there's a chance they'll catch up.

But what decides all is strategic. To take the Euphrates road gives the foe no incentive to move. Darius will simply wait at Babylon, on fields he has groomed for our slaughter, strewing his crow's feet and smoothing the fairways down which his scythed chariots will thunder.

I go east instead of south. Away from Babylon, into the foothills of the Armenian Taurus. Hephaestion's cavalry chase Mazaeus's scouts off our tail. Let Darius lose sight of me. Let him wonder, Where is Alexander?

Our column follows the High Line, the old military highway. It's cooler at altitude; grass is still green, not burnt to straw as in the plains. Harvested grain is held in unwalled villages; we take it with ease. And we drink sweet water from the mountains. Can Darius cut off our rear? That's a risk. But to do so, he must detach from his main body a force powerful enough to withstand our whole army (for it may be my design to lure just such a corps north to its slaughter) and he can't take that chance, not out of contact with his base across hundreds of miles.

Let the foe fidget at Babylon, wondering where I have gone. Let him stew over which way I approach. Let his ambitious generals plague him. Let him chair councils of war, where overkeen officers urge audacious moves and aggressive pushes. Nothing is harder in war than to stand fast. Darius will not have the patience for it, not after losing and running at Issus. Nor will his restless levy of horse warriors permit him such luxury. He will leave Babylon. He will come north, seeking me. This is what I want. For every mile he puts between himself and his depot is another mile for things to go wrong and events to run queer.

Meanwhile I will take my time. Subdue my flanks and rear. Give my reinforcements the chance to catch up. I will graze my cavalry mounts on green grass and water my pack animals from mountain streams. My foragers will shear the country and my troops will drill. If it takes till winter to fight, so be it. I have to feed only fifty thousand; Darius is plagued by a million and more.

That is the plan anyway, until scouts gallop in on the twenty-first day with reports that Darius has departed Babylon. He has crossed the Tigris, our riders declare, and is pushing north, hard, with all his force, to put the river—*tigris* in Persian means "arrow," for the swiftness of its current—between him and us as a line of defense. We are over a hundred twenty miles from the nearest crossing when this intelligence arrives. I strip the march force of everything but its arms. See the daybooks for our pace. Twenty-seven miles, thirty-one, thirty, thirty-four; we strike the ford in four days and cross while Darius is still a hundred miles south. No army in history has covered so much ground so fast.

But the pace has taken the sap out of us. Fording the Tigris proves a near fiasco, as the water crests breast-high on the men, moving fast as a galloping horse. We string four lines of cavalry across the ford, two above, two below, and rope them in place, while the infantry crosses in the middle. The upper cordons break the river's rush, a little, while the lower form a living wall to catch men and weapons swept away. It takes forty-eight harrowing hours for the corps to cross. The men are beyond exhaustion and are prey, now more than ever, to rumor and fear.

Enemy cavalry is burning the country ahead of us. The earth is ash for miles; dense clouds block the sun. At night flares stud the horizon. It is the landscape of my dream.

Omens and portents abound. Every raven in the sky, every serpent in the dust is fodder for the men's superstitious conjecture. Let a fellow cry out in his sleep; half the camp is thrown into hysteria. A she-goat births a kid with three horns; this presages death, say the cook-fire prophets. Scouts seeking water find a pool, which, struck by the sun, ignites to flame. Has no one heard of naphtha? It becomes a full-time chore for our seers: concocting affirmative interpretations of crackpot prodigies.

Dread has infected us. Irrational, inexplicable, inexpungible. I double the number of forward scouts and triple their bounties. The siege train catches up, with the gear we set down to make speed. Our young engineer Angelis gets a pontoon span across the Tigris, barely, and we hurry the heavy baggage across.

Where is the enemy?

Deserters from his camp begin appearing. Scouts bring them in, bound and blindfolded—disgruntled mercenaries on stolen horses, sutlers cheated of their wares, women who have suffered outrage. Procedure mandates segregation of fugitives, lest wild rumor sweep the camp. It never works. Every fool's tale spreads like fire. The enemy is one million no longer. He is two million. Three. One runaway says he crossed the plain at Opis after Darius's cavalry had passed over; the earth steamed with horse dung for forty miles. A Baghdader claims his district was commanded to produce a thousand bullocks; Darius's troopers wolfed them at one sitting—and that was only the officers.

On the march our fellows tramp in "litters," squads of eight, so they can break down their sarissas and lash them in one bundle, which two men then carry, by turns, over their shoulders. Litters are always laughing or cursing. Now I hear silence. The men trek without larking or grumbling, each packing his own eighteen-footer, often in one piece, their eyes on the dirt. At such times, the pace of events threatens to run out of hand. The temptation is to stop thinking and yield to momentum. This must be resisted at all costs.

I hate inspections. But one must be held now, to steady the men and to make sure no item is wanting—whetstones, spare spear shafts, straps. I ream a buck sergeant who carries his helmet in his hand. "Lash it to your rucksack, damn you!" Vinegar to purify water. Tallow for the men's feet. By Heracles, if I hear of a man down with blisters, I will make him trek on his hands.

I hold councils with my generals three times a day now. I sleep two hours at noon and one at night. Bucephalus is picketed outside my tent, and my groom Evagoras keeps my war kit honed and ready. It is my public role now to infuse the men with certitude. Their eyes track me instant by instant. As I banish fear, so do they. Until two nights after the inspection, when the moon goes dark and vanishes from the heavens.

An eclipse.

"Just what we needed!" Craterus rages, watching veterans of twenty campaigns huddle in groups, gaping at the sky and muttering superstitiously. Shall we expound like schoolmasters on the astronomical correlatives of the sun and moon? "Stand forth those salt-sucking Egyptians!" Craterus bawls, meaning the seers. "By Hades' mane, they'd better cook up some tasty tale."

They do. I've forgotten what. Something about the Persians being the moon and us the sun. It quells the men's dread. For now.

"Better get them moving," says Telamon.

I do.

Sweat, speed, action—these are the antidotes to fear.

But they don't work. Not this time. Scouts have located the Persian base camp, sixty miles south at a commercial crossroads called Arbela. Darius's army has advanced twenty miles beyond that, other riders confirm, crossing a stream called the Lycus. Wolf River. A great plain is there, named Gaugamela. The Persians are preparing the ground. They have two hundred scythed chariots and fifteen Indian war elephants.

I set under house arrest the riders who have brought this report. I won't let them outdoors even to piss, to keep the rumor from flaring. It does anyway. The eclipse has spooked us. And this stinking desert. We cross a skillet, scorched to ash. Nothing is living. Are we in hell?

Gaugamela—or its local hill, Tell Gomel—means "Camel's Hump." Our troops pore over this for significance. Is the name lucky? Does it foretell doom?

I ask Telamon what he thinks the men are afraid of.

"You know," he says.

But I don't.

"Success."

How can that be?

"As well they should," my mentor continues. "For with this triumph, our force will stand where no army has in all of history. The men dread this, the unknown. And you, Alexander, you shall be acclaimed as . . ."

Black Cleitus reins-in alongside, grinning at Telamon's sober demeanor. "What wild fancy," he inquires, "is this philosopher retailing today?"

I laugh. "He foretells victory."

"An imbecile could do that!" And he hoots and spurs away.

The column treks on. Ahead and behind, the sky is black from fires set by the foe. Soot and cinders descend. The mountains east have vanished in the murk. Sound carries in this soup. We hear ghostly galloping, otherworldly voices. Even the earth gives you the jumps. A man's tread punches through the crust, throwing up a plume of alkali. The stuff gets in your nose and hair; chalk coats your face; your lips crack. The horses' hooves kick up the heavy greyish dust, which rises only as high as a man's waist. The column wades through it. Then, postnoon of the second day, the sound all commanders dread.

Panic.

Something sets the corps off. No one knows what. End to end, terror reigns. Ones and twos break from their comrades, unsheathing weapons. In moments, men will be dicing one another in terror.

"Column, halt!"

An eternity passes before the corps is brought to a stop. I command, "Ground arms." Another eon as the order is passed down the miles-long line. At last each man sets his weapon at his feet on the earth.

The army recovers.

We camp that night on a featureless plain. With dusk, fog descends from the mountains. One's sight plays tricks. Soot and ash cut off the sky. Then, in the second watch:

Another panic.

Lights in the sky have been mistaken for the enemy's fires. They look real—thousands and thousands of them. Even I am fooled. It takes hours to calm the camp.

Heaven sends a wind. The skies clear for twenty minutes. Then: a dust storm. The camp becomes chaos. We tramp all next day into the gale, muffled to our eyeballs, while grit like pumice abrades every surface and lodges in every cavity. For the first time I hear from my men the litany that plagues me to this day: We have come too far, won too much; heaven has turned on us; we're frightened, we want to go home.

Another night. The dust storm abates as abruptly as it has struck. Scouts report the real Persian fires. We're a day away. I bring the corps out of column into modified line of assault. Our front is half a mile wide now. I have cavalry out on every quarter.

Noon of the fourth day. The plain of Gaugamela lies a few miles ahead, beyond a range of low hills. Will this be the place? Is this the site that will give its name to our destiny?

I ride forward, taking Black Cleitus and the Royal Squadron, Glaucias's Apollonians (he has replaced Socrates Redbeard, who is recovering from sepsis in Damascus), and Ariston's squadron of Paeonian Scouts. Persian reconnaissance riders retreat before us. The Tigris is on the right, wider here and within sight across a dusty pan. A line of gazelle bound away into a wash. We ascend the range of hills. At the crest three of our troopers sign "Enemy" and point with their lances to the southeast.

We come over the rise and there is the foe.

"By Heracles' alabaster balls!" cries Cleitus.

The Persian front stretches three and a half miles. His depth doubles that. The supply train extends as far as sight can carry. It looks like a city. No, ten cities. Detachments of enemy scouts gallop back to his center, doubtless where Darius has taken station, to report our approach. Various troops of the foe maneuver out front of his central mass, rehearsing. The plain has been smoothed like a running track, marked in various geometric azimuths.

Hephaestion points. "There are the fairways Darius's engineers have cleared for his scythed chariots. See them? Three. One fifty cars wide, by the look of it; one a hundred; another fifty on the left."

The foe has even erected mobile towers, from which, no doubt, archers and bolt-firing catapults will loose their broadsides on us when we advance.

Black Cleitus whistles. "These bastards have brought the whole pantry."

I bring the army up into the range of hills that the locals call *Arouck*, the Crescent. We bivouac in battle order.

For the first time, our men see the enemy. The scale of the Asiatic host is staggering. Too vast to evoke fear. One's response can be only awe. We gape at the Persian myriads, even I, incapable of crediting the evidence of our senses.

Twenty-Three

THE MATERIAL OF THE HEART

Y OU ASK, How long did it take to fashion the battle plan for
  Gaugamela?

I have known it since I was seven. It has played before my eyes a
thousand times. I have seen this plain in my dreams; I have imagined
Darius's order. This battle, I have fought in imagination all my life.
Nothing remains but to live it out in flesh.

We take a day to fortify a camp and to bring up the heavy baggage.
Darius holds in place. When I ride down with three squadrons to re-
connoiter the field, he does not contest me.

Night descends. I call a council of war. This time I preside myself.

"Gentlemen, we have seen the enemy's dispositions now. This is
good. We are certain today of three things we weren't yesterday. Let us
review them."

Nothing so steadies a company confronting great odds as a sober
recitation of the facts. The more dread-inducing the reality, the more
directly it must be faced.

"First, the Persian front is almost entirely cavalry. We see the killing
zones the enemy has prepared for his scythed chariots. Clearly, Darius

plans to launch them upon our advance. This is different from Issus and the Granicus, where the enemy sought only to defend. So, first: The foe will not sit still, awaiting our attack. He will attack us."

The council is one hundred seventeen. Present is every commander of every company. It gets cold at night, even in summer, in the desert. Still I insist on rigging the tent flaps all the way up. I want the troops to see their commanders at work. In minutes, thousands ring the pavilion, sitting and standing, in a press so dense one can smell the stink of their sweat and feel the steam off their breath.

"Two, the width of the enemy front. His line will overlap ours by wide margins at both wings. This tells us how Darius will attack. He will attempt a double envelopment. He will seek to encircle us on both flanks with his cavalry wings, attacking—perhaps in succession, perhaps simultaneously—from the front, first with his scythed chariots, then with his conventional cavalry. This is the second factor we must have an answer for.

"Third, and most important, the state of mind of our own men. Enemy cavalry, by all estimates, is thirty-five thousand. Ours is seven. We can't even guess at the numbers of Persian and allied infantry. Our reinforcements have not caught up. The men are fearful. Even the Companions do not demonstrate their customary zeal."

Perdiccas: "Is that all, Alexander?"

Laughter erupts. Anxious laughter.

"I forgot," I say, "Darius's war elephants."

All levity ceases.

"These, my friends, are the issues this council must address. Have I left anything out? Has anyone anything to add?"

We begin.

The material a commander manipulates is the human heart. His art lies in producing courage in his own men and terror in the foe.

The general produces courage by discipline, training, and fitness; by fairness and order; superior pay, armament, tactics, and supply; by his dispositions in the field; and by the genius of his own presence and actions.

Sound dispositions produce valor, just as faulty formations make

cowards of even the bravest. Here is the fundamental lineup for the assault:

POINT

WING   WING

In other words, a wedge. Or, if you prefer, a diamond:

POINT

WING   WING

REAR

Wedges and diamonds promote engagement. Angles produce lines
of support; wings back up points, and rears sustain wings. Soldiers in
wedges and diamonds can't hide. Their fellows see them. Shame propels
them forward and courage drives them on.

But the soundest use of the wedge is to integrate it across an entire
line of assault, as I instruct my officers in council, now, on the eve of
Gaugamela.

POINT   POINT   POINT

WING   WING   WING   WING

Why does such a lineup produce valor? I remind my commanders,
though they have seen its worth already on two continents and a hundred fields of strife.

"The men in the point battalions feel courage because they know
they are backed up on both wings. They know they cannot be flanked
and cannot be enveloped. They know further that although it is they
who must strike the foe first and alone, still their comrades will be
right behind them into the fray. And they know that, should they be
repulsed, they have a powerful front to withdraw into. As for the battalions of the second rank, their fear as they approach the enemy is
moderated because they see their forward mates bearing the brunt of
the punishment, while they themselves, for the moment, remain safe.

But here is the crucial particular, my friends: *The valor of their comrades out front fires their hearts.* For a man is not a man but he resolve, seeing his mates hurling themselves valiantly upon the foe, 'By hell's flame, I shall prove no less worthy!' A man feels shame even to hesitate and have his company's colors show poorly alongside others'; rather, he is driven on by spirit of emulation, by pride, and by honor.

"This is an article of faith with me, brothers. I believe that a man, witnessing the selflessness of another, is compelled by his own nobler nature to emulate that virtue. No harangue can make him do this; no prize or bounty. But the sight of his fellow's gallantry cannot be resisted. This is why you officers must always be first to strike the foe. By your example, you compel the hearts of your men to follow. And their courage ignites valor in the ranks of our countrymen succeeding.

"And I believe more, my friends. I believe that heaven itself is compelled by witness of intrepidity. The gods themselves cannot stand aloof from an act of true courage, but are impelled by their own higher nature to intercede in its behalf.

"Tomorrow on this plain," I instruct my officers of the flank battalions, "the enemy front will overlap ours by half a mile on each wing. It is certain that as we advance, Darius will hurl division after division of cavalry onto us from the flanks. How can we dispose our companies to maximize our countrymen's courage?

"First, we will defend by attacking. Wing officers, as soon as you come under assault, you are to attack. Do not receive the blow, but deliver it. This is not mindless audacity, only sound fundamentals. When men know they will be attacked, they feel fear; when they know they will attack, they feel strength.

"Second, dispositions." I align the six units of both flank guards into modified diamonds. My post on the right will be immediately inboard of the Royal Lancers, with the squadrons of Companion Cavalry (with the sarissa phalanx and the main body of the corps extending for a mile and a half left of that), while Parmenio, commanding the left wing, will take station inboard of a matching diamond on that wing. Here, the flank guard on my right:

Mercenary cavalry (Menidas) 700

Royal Lancers (Aretes) 800   Paeonian Light Horse (Ariston) 250

Half Agrianian javelineers (Attalus) 500

Macedonian archers (Brison) 500

"Veteran mercenary" infantry (Cleander) 6700

A diamond is nothing but four wedges—north, south, east, west. And what is a wedge? It is one unit out front and two on the wings. Do you see how the diamond can respond to an assault from any quarter simply by facing in place?

This disposition works because of the irrational element of the heart. The unit out front will charge the foe with courage because it knows it is supported on both wings and that its comrades will be into the scrape right behind it. The supporting wings have the example before them of their fore unit's valor and will strive not to fall short of it.

"Finally, brother officers, my presence and yours. When your eye seeks my colors tomorrow, you need look only to the fore. That is where I will be. And where you will be, before your companies."

I draw up, for passion has so fired my purpose that I fear my heart will run away with itself. I glance to Parmenio at my shoulder; to Hephaestion and Craterus; Perdiccas, Coenus, Ptolemy, Seleucus, Polyperchon, Meleager; Black Cleitus, Nicanor, and Philotas; Telamon and Erigyius and Lysimachus. And to the men outside, ringing the pavilion in their thousands.

Where is my daimon in this hour? He is I, and I am he.

"You have wondered, many of you, why I sleep with a copy of Homer's *Iliad* beneath my pillow. It is because I emulate the heroes of those verses. They are not figures of lore to me, but living, breathing men. Achilles is no ancestor, nine hundred years gone. He strides here, this instant, in my heart. I hold the example of his virtue before me, not in waking hours only, but undergirding even my dreams. Do we make war for blood or treasure? Never! But to follow the path of honor, to school our hearts in the virtues of strife. To contend chivalrously against the chivalrous foe refines us, as gold in the crucible. All that is base in our natures—cupidity and greed, timorousness and irresolution, impatience, niggardliness, self-infatuation—is processed and purified. By our repeated undergoings of trial of death, we burn these impurities out, until our metal rings sound and true. Nor are we ourselves, as individuals only, purified by this ordeal, but its demands bind us to one another at such a depth of intimacy as not even husband and wife can know. When I call you brothers, it is no figure of speech. For we have become brothers in arms, you and I, and not hell itself holds the power to divide us."

I pause again, scanning the faces. Death is nothing to me compared to the love I feel for these gallant comrades.

"Do I feel fear, my friends? How can I? For to stand in ranks with you, to contend for glory at your side, is all I have ever wanted. I shall sleep tonight with the bliss of an infant, for I possess in this hour all I have ever dreamed of: a worthy foe and worthy mates to face him with."

Cries of assent check my address. In the rear, men relay my words to their fellows farther back. I am standing now. I gesture down the slope from the Crescent, toward the plain of Gaugamela.

"Brothers, the fame we wring tomorrow from that field, no man or army has ever won. Not Achilles, nor Heracles, nor any hero of our race or any other. A hundred centuries from now, men will still recite our names. Do you believe me? Will you advance with me? Will you ride at my shoulder after glory everlasting?"

Citations overwhelm the pavilion. The men roar and thunder. Such acclamation resounds as to make the tent timbers quake and the earth shudder and tremble. I glance to Hephaestion. So furious is our fellows' cry, his look says, that Darius in his camp, and all his multitude, cannot hear it but with dread.

I am the living soul of the army. As blood flows from the lion's heart to its limbs, so courage flows from me to my countrymen.

A million men stand in arms against us. I will rout them by my will alone.

Twenty-Four

CAMEL'S HUMP

I RIDE CORONA AS WE DESCEND from the range of hills called the Crescent. Bucephalus trails, led by my groom Evagoras. Bucephalus's headstall and frontlet are in place, and the light combat saddle, but Evagoras packs his leg guards and breastplate on his own back. My horse is seventeen years old. I will mount him only for the final advance.

The shoulder wings of my composite corselet remain unbattened, sticking up alongside my ears. I will not dog them down till we come onto final line. I want the army to see this. It tells them to breathe easy. Their king is so confident, he's not even dressed yet.

The slope down to the plain is a mile. We descend in order of battle. Our front is twenty-seven hundred yards. The foe's, when we measure after the fight, is forty-seven fifty. He overlaps us more than a mile.

The date is 26 Boedromion, late summer, in the archonship of Aristophanes at Athens. Here, from captured documents of that day, is the order of battle of the army of the empire of Persia:

On the foe's left wing, preceding his main line: two thousand cavalry of Scythia, savage tribesmen of the Sacae and Massagetae, armed with the lance, the Scythian bow, and the *tumak*—a type of spiked mace; one thousand special cavalry of Bactria, on mailed cataphracts, armed with the javelin and the two-handed lance; one hundred scythed chariots under Darius's son Megadates. These are the companies before the front. Behind, in double line of squadrons: four thousand Royal Indian *ksatriyas*, foot bowmen from the country west of the Indus; four thousand mounted archers of Areia under their satrap Satibarzanes; one thousand Royal Arachosian cavalry under Darius's kinsman Barsaentes. Left of these, sixteen thousand Bactrian and Daan cavalry under Darius's cousin, Bessus, who stands in overall command of the left wing; two thousand mounted bowmen of India; Persian Royal Horse mixed with infantry, five thousand, commanded by Tigranes, who fought with such valor at Issus; then Susian cavalry, one thousand; Cadusian cavalry and infantry, two thousand. Next, comprising the wing of Darius's Royal Guard, ten thousand Greek mercenary infantry under the Phocian captain Patron; one thousand Kinsman Cavalry under Darius's brother Oxathres; five thousand "Apple Bearers," the elite Persian foot guard, so named because they carry lances with a golden apple instead of a butt spike. Before these stand fifty scythed chariots and fifteen Indian war elephants with their mahouts and armored turrets and six hundred Royal Indian cavalry, their mounts trained to fight alongside elephants; these are supported by the so-called deported Carians, one thousand heavy infantry; and five hundred Mardian archers. Behind: Darius himself, shielded on the right by another thousand Persian Honor Regiment cavalry, another five thousand Apple Bearers, and five thousand more Greek mercenary infantry under Mentor's son Thymondas. This is the center of the line. To its right, extending another mile and a half: Carian infantry and cavalry, more Royal Indian Horse, more Greek mercenaries; Albanians; Sittacenians, mixed cavalry and infantry; Tapurian and Hyrcanian cavalry from south of the Caspian; mounted archers of Scythia under Mauaces; Phrataphernes' Parthian and Arachosian cavalry; Atropates' Royal Median Horse; Mazaeus's Syrian and Mesopotamian cavalry. Mazaeus commands the Persian right. Fronting this wing are fifty more scythed chariots; Ariaces' crack Cappadocian cavalry; Orontes' and Mithraustes' Armenian cavalry. Then the rear multitude of provincial levy: Oxathres' Uxians; Bupares'

Babylonians; Orontobates' Red Sea conscripts; Orxines' Sittacenians, and others in numbers uncountable.

Descending to the plain, we see clearly the three fairways, groomed by Darius's engineers for his scythed chariots. Stakes mark their margins, with pennants snapping in the blow at eye height for a man on horseback. So the charioteers can see them over the dust.

To our right, as we enter the flat, a thousand yards have been strewn with iron crow's feet. Darius wants to steer us into his cutters' path. The Persian front is twenty-one hundred yards away. A mile and a third. His scouts transit our front, past bowshot, on racing stock worth a lifetime's wages. Our fast lancers chase them. I call a halt.

Squires scurry with wine sacks. We pause to rig what's broken: soles unstrung; sarissa lanyards snapped; torn shield straps and loose keepers on grommets. "Dress the line!" "Piss where you stand!"

Brigade commanders assemble on my colors: Parmenio, Hephaestion, Craterus, Nicanor, Perdiccas, Ptolemy, Seleucus, Philotas, Black Cleitus, two dozen others. Nothing to go over that we haven't rehearsed a hundred times already.

Advance on line. Come to the oblique at my command. All ranks maintain silence until the moment of assault. Accept, obey, and pass on all orders swiftly and accurately.

Commanders scatter to their units. I sign to Evagoras. He spurs onto the flat, trailing Bucephalus. My First Page takes the bridle.

Cheers roar from the throats of fifty thousand.

I scissor from Corona's back to Bucephalus's. My lance. Helmet. A second clamor, and a third. Spear shafts clash against shields. I canter to the fore, flanked by the Royal Guard, Hephaestion, Black Cleitus, Telamon.

Dust scours the flat. Ensigns snap in a south-to-north shear. Squall lines rake the pan, kicking up dusters. The plumes on my helmet tug. I tear them off and loose them on the wind.

"Zeus, our Guide and Savior!"

Here we go.

Twenty-Five

DIAMONDS ON THE WING

A T ELEVEN HUNDRED YARDS we see the stakes set by the Persians laying out the lanes for their scythed chariots. They are poles of cane, eight feet tall, with scarlet pennants snapping atop. Our fore riders trample them, to the cheers of the corps.

We advance now onto ground prepared for our slaughter. The pan has been curried smooth; three fairways have been groomed for Darius's cutters. Two are five hundred yards wide, the other a thousand. We are still too distant to make out the chariots themselves. We think we see sun-flash off their scythes, but it may be overimagination.

Hephaestion rides at my left shoulder, commanding the *agema* of the Royal Guardsmen. If I fall, he will assume command of the right wing. Black Cleitus advances on my right; he commands the Royal Squadron of Companions. Telamon rides left of Hephaestion, with Ptolemy and Peucestas; Love Locks is at Cleitus's shoulder. They are here for their fighting skills and because I can send any one of them anywhere on the field and he will die before failing me.

Darius's engineers have sown the margins of the field with iron crow's feet to contain our cavalry's advance within the killing zone of the scythed chariots. But the foe cannot strew these spikes across the entire space between our front and his; he must leave hundreds of yards clear; otherwise his own cavalry, when they charge, will run onto the spikes themselves. My scheme is to advance within the confined corridor only until our foremost ranks reach the open space. Then our front will decline sharply to the right, getting off the killing zone as quickly as possible.

I have also, before the battle, had a pronouncement cried throughout our camp to all the civilian followers of the army: that whosoever wishes, at his own hazard, to sprint out before the corps's advance and gather up the crow's feet may keep every one he takes and sell the iron for profit. And now the men in ranks behold a spectacle marvelous indeed, as great swarms of enterprising youths—our sutler's boys and laundry urchins, teamsters' brats, muleteers' lads, not to mention cooks and merchants, even some of the trollops from the whores' camp—burst forth before the army, many barefoot, all unarmed and unarmored, to brave the volleys of the archers stationed by the foe on the flanks and even among the field of spikes to throw back just such an incursion. The bolder and more industrious of our scavengers hold their ground long enough, even, to scoop up the spent arrows of the enemy, which are of no small value in their own right. The result is the field is swept clean, or halfway so, with astonishing celerity.

The enemy's front comes visible now. Its length is twice ours; it seems to extend from horizon to horizon. The deeper we advance, the more of our flanks we expose to the Persian wings.

We progress at a walk. To my left move the eight squadrons of Companion Cavalry. Their formation is half-squadron wedges. Dragon's Teeth. I transit their front at a trot and pass down the line, leftward, monitoring the advance, calling out to men by name, letting my face and colors be seen. Couriers and aides-de-camp shuttle with reports of the foe, the wings, the closing distance.

We too have staked the plain. Fore riders post as human pennants, demarking the advance. At a thousand yards, where the unsown ground begins, I signal the trumpeters: "Corps, decline half-right!"

Color bearers pivot at forty-five degrees. Behind them captains and master sergeants center on the point and deflect as well; the brigades follow. Missile troops out front chase off the foe's skirmishers. Our track is like a man wading across a river. We aim upstream on the diagonal, and our tread is angled upstream too. We slide right . . . right . . . right.

Darius can't see this yet. A thousand yards is too far. But his scout riders see. Telamon indicates a pair on thoroughbreds, spurring back to their king. We see two more, and a fifth, all galloping away with the same report.

We incline to the right across ground incompletely cleared of iron caltrops. Our objects are two: to get off this killing ground, and to make Darius jump.

How long will the foe let us deflect?

Will he permit our right wing to outflank his left?

As our main body declines right, I transit left, across our front for most of a mile, as far as Parmenio, who commands this wing. At nearly seventy years, the general still rides like a buck lancer. We review our scheme one last time. Philotas overhauls us at a hard canter, having crossed after me a thousand yards from the right.

"You're making my bung pucker, Alexander!"

He means he wants me back on the right before serious action starts. He saws the bit on his seventeen-hand black, Adamantine.

"Don't do that—you're hurting him."

He laughs. "He can't feel a thing, and neither can I!"

"Indeed," Parmenio calls to his son, "but he's not as drunk as you are!"

I'll give Philotas this: He's a born swashbuckler. Besides, we've all downed a snootful. It burns off like air.

I acknowledge Philotas's admonition: I'll return, right behind him. "Get Balacrus's darters out front."

"Go on," says Parmenio.

My party and I canter back across the front. Balacrus is a Macedonian officer commanding a mixed corps of five hundred Agrianian javelineers and an equal number of archers and darters recruited from the mountaineers of Thrace. These have come out for gold, and they have earned it. They dash forward now, on foot, on the right, through the intervals between the squadrons of Companion Cavalry, and assume their station out front of the advance. The Thracians are tattooed, bare-legged, in fox-skin caps; the Agrianes scurry in father-son teams, with their bear hounds, great shaggy beasts, who will die shielding them if they fall.

Balacrus's job is to stop the scythed chariots. His missile troops must break the machines' rush before they rip into the squadrons of Companion Cavalry.

Here is the order of the army of Macedon, right to left, as we advance:

Preceding the right: Balacrus's archers and darters, one thousand. On the wing: mercenary cavalry under Menidas, seven hundred; Royal Lancers under Aretes, eight hundred; Paeonian Light Horse, two-fifty, under Ariston; the other half of the Agrianian darters, five hundred, under Attalus. Brison's five hundred Macedonian archers are next; then the "vet mercs" of Cleander, sixty-seven hundred, infantry armed with the long lance to work against cavalry. These units comprise the right-flank guard. Their job is to hold off whatever Darius throws at us from the flank.

Left of these advance the eight squadrons of Companion Cavalry under Philotas, overstrength at two thousand one hundred forty. Next, Hephaestion with the *agema* of the Royal Guard, three hundred; then the three Guards Brigades under Nicanor, also heavy at thirty-five hundred. Next the sarissa phalanx in six brigades of fifteen hundred each—Coenus's, Perdiccas's, Meleager's, Polyperchon's, Simmias Andromenes' (replacing his brother Amyntas, who is in Macedon recruiting), and Craterus's. Adjacent to these foot troops advance half the allied Greek horse under Erigyius, and all eight squadrons of Thessalian cavalry—the finest in the world after my own Companions—under Philip, son of Menelaus. Round Parmenio, in command of the left wing, ride the horsemen of the Pharsalian squadron, by far the bravest and most brilliant of the Thessalians.

Behind these, at an interval of five hundred paces, I have deployed a second phalanx of infantry composed of the allied Greeks; the mercenaries of Arcadia and Achaea; Illyrian, Triballian, and Odrysian light infantry; the archers and slingers of Syria, Pamphylia, Pisidia; with five hundred Peloponnesian mercenaries under the Spartan Pausanias, who has come over from Darius's service—a total of just under sixteen thousand. These I have instructed to stand ready to face about in the event of being enveloped; wing units to close up with flank guards to form a "hedgehog," a defensive rectangle bristling with spear points, if we must. In between the fore and rear phalanxes are the battle squires with the spare arms and the grooms with the remounts.

The flank guard of the left is disposed like the right in a modified diamond: four hundred allied Greek cavalry under Coeranus; fifty-nine hundred Thracian light infantry under their native commander Sitalces; three hundred fifty Odrysian plainsman cavalry under Agathon; and Cretan archers, five hundred, under Amyntas. These units, like their counterparts of the opposite flank, must endure whatever assault is thrown at them by Darius's right wing, with its crack Cappadocian, Armenian, and Syrian cavalry under Mazaeus. In front, to break the foe's rush, I have posted nine hundred mercenary horse under Andromachus, a unit of reckless dash. Parmenio commands the left overall, Craterus the infantry of that wing. The right is my own.

We continue our advance in the oblique. Already our rightmost units are off the scythed chariots' fairways. Soon the leading squadrons of Companions will have passed clear too. Darius tracks with us. He has shifted the entire left of his front, keeping pace with our deflection. He can't do this forever. He must take some action to contain our lateral advance.

"There they go."

Telamon points to the Persian wing. At seven hundred yards, Darius sends his leftmost squadrons. We can see their dust and movement as they shift to contain our right.

"More dust. From the center." Love Locks indicates the companies around Darius. Units are pulling out of the middle of the Persian line.

"How many, do you think?"

"Enough to thin out their belly."

This is the gamble I have taken. It is the reason for our rightward deflection. The more squadrons we can draw off from Darius's center, the fewer we'll have to fight through to reach him.

Kill the King.

It is a dangerous game, however, drawing the enemy upon you. Everything hangs on timing. If our flank holds long enough to let my Companions charge, the empire of Persia will fall. If it breaks, not a man of Macedon will leave this field alive.

I sign to Hephaestion; I must see to the flank. He acknowledges. He commands the advance now. If I don't come back, the army is his and Parmenio's.

Do you recall, Itanes, the scheme I sketched before?

Mercenary cavalry (Menidas) 700

Royal Lancers (Aretes) 800   Paeonian Light Horse (Ariston) 250

Half Agrianian javelineers (Attalus) 500

Macedonian archers (Brison) 500

"Veteran mercenary" infantry (Cleander) 6700

This is the wing I now cross to. I want to check their order and be sure they are ready to receive an attack. We reach Aretes' Lancers first. His horses are high. Their tails are up; froth slings from their muzzles. They are starting to bunch. A hundred yards left (to the front, in relation to the Persians) I see the rear ranks of Menidas's mercenary cavalry; the same distance to the fore trot our Paeonian Light Horse under Ariston. I spur forward to them. Their mounts are as balky as Aretes'. I think: If either of these units bolts, Menidas's mercenary cavalry will go with them; the men won't be able to hold their horses.

Ariston is the Light Horse's commander. He should be at the point of the first wedge, but when we get there, I can't find him. (By chance he has taken this moment to drop back to confer with Attalus, whose javelineers, on foot, are falling behind the Lancers' pace.) Ariston's deputy is Milon, a great-nephew of Parmenio. He has not taken the lead post vacated by Ariston, as procedure demands; he rides still in his number-two slot at the wing of the leftmost wedge. I come round the formation, purple with rage. "By Zeus, does no one command here!" Love Locks is on my left, Telamon swinging round on the right. I feel him rap me on the shoulder with the shaft of his lance.

"Alexander!"

I turn. A courier races up from Menidas. "There, sire!" He points ahead to our right flank. "Do you see them?"

Out of the dust on the wing, four furlongs distant, appears a front of horsemen half a mile across.

By Heracles, it is a sight!

"What nations? Persians?"

"Bactrians, my lord." Tribal horsemen of the eastern plains.

The courier reports that this division has ridden round from the enemy front in column and come, only moments before, into line of attack. He requests orders for his commander Menidas.

"He has his orders. Attack."

I gallop with the courier back to his division. Menidas is out front with his squadron commanders. "By Chiron's furry crease"—he points to the foe—"these villains are impatient!" Menidas is a huntsman; at home he runs two hundred superb hounds. He's as cool now as if we were coursing only after hares.

The foe are not yet at the gallop. They come at the trot. Dust ascends in ranges behind them; the squall at their backs drives it with them, so that their fore ranks appear to emerge out of sand-colored murk. The plain is crusty; its surface muffles the foe's tread, making the sound seem as if it comes from twice as far as it does.

"Take your fifties straight in. I'll bring up the Lancers to rip them from the flank."

I mean that I want Menidas to attack the foe head-on in wedges of fifty. I'll align Aretes' eight hundred Royal Lancers to tear through the foe, right behind, from the side.

I spur back to the Light Horse. Ariston, their commander, comes back from the rear at the gallop.

"Are you trying to miss the show?"

My tone lets him know I'm not angry. He reports on his dash to the rear. Attalus and the javelineers, on foot, have fallen behind; he, Ariston, has got them on the run to catch up. The archers and Cleander's vet mercs are at the double too, Ariston reports. I commend him. He is thinking and acting like a commander.

I tell him what Menidas and Aretes will do. "Drop back and cover the foot troops. Come up only if you see our wing cavalry hard-pressed."

I dispatch a rider of my own to Cleander, calling for three thousand vet merc infantry to hurry forward; the remaining thirty-seven hundred to maintain their position sealing the flank, coming to the fore only should the situation become desperate.

I spur with my suite back to the Lancers. Cheers erupt at my apparition. The foe is closer, three-fifths of a mile, and plainly visible now as Ariston's Light Horse pulls out to the rear. In few words I give Aretes the scheme. He is a wild weed, this fellow, just twenty-four years old and in awe of no one, including me. I have had him up on charges a month prior, for bringing me the head of a Persian cavalry commander instead of the living man to interrogate. Who better now?

"Don't burn up on the first rush," I instruct him and his captains. "Up and back. Keep your wedges under control. Rally when you cross past Menidas and do it again."

Aretes gives me a grin.

"Will you reprove me, Alexander, if I bring you another head?"

Here comes the foe, at the canter.

"Stay alive. I need you."

Aretes' spurs bite. The Lancers shoot forward.

Our troopers have rehearsed this evolution a thousand times and worked it in action a hundred. It goes like this. Menidas's fifties up front will hurl themselves into the mass of the charging enemy. But they will

not seek a melee; they will simply rip through, breaking up the foe's formation as much as they can, then bolting at the gallop out the far side.
It is impossible for a body of horsemen not to pursue when they see the
foe in flight. And if that foe (meaning us, meaning Menidas) flees in
disorder, or feigned disorder, the pursuers will fall at once into a matching state. Bactrians are desert nomads; the concept of unit cohesion is
alien to them, as are all tactics beyond charge, circle, and withdraw.
They are horsemen but not cavalry, warriors but not an army. Watch,
now, what happens. . . .

Menidas rushes and tears through. Half the foe keep charging; the
other half, in a whooping pack, wheel to chase Menidas. In that moment, Aretes' Lancers hit them from the flank. It is not necessary to produce casualties to stop cavalry; just break up its rush. The enemy's mass,
disordered now by our crisscrossing wedges, loses resolution. The foe sees
our companies on his flanks and rear. He reins-in. He balks. Such reflex
is primal; it cannot be prevailed over except by disciplined, impeccably
officered troops, and the tribal Bactrians are anything but that.

Now Cleander's vet mercs sprint from the rear. These are not heavy
infantry weighted down with forty pounds of shield and plate, but bareheaded peltasts and foot lancers, armed with the twelve-foot spear, a
wicked weapon against cavalry that has lost its momentum and cohesion. Our fellows swarm in contourless orders called "clouds" and
"strings." How can the foe go after them? Only one-on-one, and to do
that, the enemy must break up his ranks even further. Our men fight in
pairs and triples, inflicting casualties upon the milling horsemen by
rushing in, plying their lances, then scampering clear. The foe peels
apart and gallops away to regroup.

I cannot stay. I must get back to the Companions.

Cleander tells me later that his executive officer Myrinus kept
count of the rushes and counterrushes of the day's fight on the wing.
Nineteen times the enemy hurled his divisions upon this corps, and
nineteen times our flankers threw them back. What can be said of such
men? On parade they look second-raters. Pretty girls pass them over, favoring the dazzle of the Companion Cavalry and the dash of the Royal
Guard. But here in this most epochal of victories, these unglamorous

companies will make all else possible. The vet mercs of Arcadia and Achaea—I have known these men all my life. Telamon served first in their company. The youngest at Gaugamela was forty. I can name two hundred over sixty. No soldier is a peer for the veteran. With campaigners of a certain age, one never finds a coward; they have all run off or been killed. A seasoned man knows patience and self-command. Give me a veteran corporal and keep a captain; I'll take a mature captain over a general. Nor is the long-timer's speed or strength diminished far from the youth's. In the first rush that day, I saw a cloud of thirty Achaeans go after a pod of Bactrian horsemen. One wing headed the foe's rush, turning it into the belly of the string, while the opposite closed. The vets' long lances worked terrible execution. In moments twenty of the foe became ten, and ten five.

The second wave the foe sends from the flank are Scythians—Sacae and Massagetae—steppe raiders who fight with the bow and the battle-axe. Our Lancers and Paeonians cut concourses through them. In this way the battle whipsaws, with each side penetrating the other, putting it to flight, then retiring behind a covering screen of supporting units to regroup, re-form, rearm (pulling the dead and wounded from the field, along with every still-usable lance, axe, and javelin), then attacking again, amid the caustic grit and alkali and the crusty deadfoot ground that wears horses and men down like treading in glue.

In conventional battle, clashes on the wing are over as soon as the main advance begins. Not at Gaugamela. The fight on the right goes on as long as the entire affray, and on the left, even longer. Its front is half a mile, its depth that and more. The scale of the clash enlarges minute by minute, as each side feeds in fresh divisions. Bessus, governor of Bactria, commands Darius's left; under orders from his king he draws off from the Persian center first three thousand horse, then six, then eight. I can counter only from divisions already composing my right flank; we need every other man and mount for the primary assault. Bessus's extractions come from the troops fronting the king's own person. We can see their masses, mantled in dust, as they pull out of the line behind the screen of scythed chariots, which holds, poised, as our front advances to five hundred yards, four fifty, four.

Our main line still advances at a walk. A quarter mile separates us from Darius's front.

I have returned to the Companions from the flank. The army books show eleven aides and couriers in my rotation that day; I employ only two for the center and left; the other nine shuttle continually to the right. Every message coming in says the same: Send help. And every one going back: Hang on.

I can't spare men, so I send champions. Telamon and Love Locks, Ptolemy and Peucestas. I want to dispatch Black Cleitus but he won't go; he saved my life at the Granicus and he intends to do it again here.

We can see Darius's station now. The colors of his Guard regiments collect about him, with his own royal pennants snapping overhead. Massed foot troops front his post—Greek mercenaries and his own Royal Apple Bearer Guard. His four-horse chariot stands, though we can't see it, amid squadrons of Kinsman Cavalry, twenty or thirty ranks back from the front.

We can no longer see the fight on our right; storms of murk obscure it. We can hear it though. It sounds like an earthquake. Fronting the Companions, I have Balacrus with five hundred Agrianian javelineers and the same number of Thracian archers and darters. The companies on the wing cry for them. But I need them here. I need them to stop Darius's scythed chariots when they come.

At three hundred yards, they do.

The foe's front is a hundred cars across. The machines strain from the blocks with a tantalizing indolence. We can see but not hear the drivers' whips. Sun-dazzle flashes off the scythes as the chariots work to speed. It seems to take forever. "The cars are heavy," Cleitus remarks, "packing all that iron."

The cutters' front is two-thirds of a mile across. It makes straight for our squadrons of Companion Cavalry and, left of them, Hephaestion's and Nicanor's Royal Guardsmen and the rightmost two regiments, Perdiccas's and Coenus's, of the phalanx. Cleitus looks on with absolute calm. "Beautiful, aren't they?"

I sign to him and Philotas: Open order! Hold silence. . . .

"All captains, eyes on me!"

I look left, across two miles of field. This is the last moment when even a quarter of the fight is visible from my vantage. Darius's chariots are charging there too. Fifty toward the meat of our phalanx, fifty more into Parmenio's guard on our left. The foe's conventional cavalry will make the next wave. Twenty thousand of Armenia and Cappadocia, Syria and Mesopotamia, Media, Parthia, Tapuria, Areia, Hyrcania, and Sogdiana. Zeus help you, Craterus. Heaven preserve you, Parmenio.

I glance right, to the dust and murk. Somewhere in there, beyond the chariots' killing zone but engulfed in the battle on the wing, fight Aretes' eight hundred Royal Lancers, my best mounted shock troops, short of the Companions. The courier next in rotation is a sixteen-year-old Page named Demades. They call him "Boar" for his spiky mane. He will die delivering the message I now charge him with.

"Aretes from Alexander: Pull half your Lancers; when the scythed chariots' rush has been broken, hurl your wedges at the thinnest sector of the enemy's front. Wherever you judge that to be."

The Page's pupils are the size of bread plates.

"Say it back to me, Boar."

He does, verbatim.

"Boar, I'll drink with you in Babylon!"

He spurs into the gloom.

Out front, Balacrus's darters attack the cutters in clouds. "At the horses!" I hear Philotas shout, as if anyone can hear. "Throw at the horses!"

Scythed chariots must attack in lanes. The teams have to maintain intervals right and left, so as not to foul one another. In these gaps, our brave javelineers work their havoc. These superb troops, who can hit a foot-wide plank at fifty yards, launch their second salvos while the first is still in the air, and their third as the chariots hurtle upon them. Our archers loose broadsides point-blank. In moments, the cutters' rush breaks apart. The crusty underfooting is our ally; it mires the heavy chariots' wheels. The chalk won't let the machines get to full flying speed. I see one four-horse hurtling straight toward us as its leftmost charger takes a dart flush at the base of the neck. The animal overends in the traces, taking the whole team with him and launching the driver like a doll. The team to its left is struck by no missile; only the shock of the fusillade and the sight and sound of men racing on foot in their sight line sends the animals shying in terror; the car careers wildly right, across the lanes of its fellows. Other machines swerve to avoid its blades. In instants a sector of a dozen chariots is hurled into chaos. Into the riot pour Balacrus's missile troops. I had hoped and believed that their volleys would impede the foe's rush; in the event they rout it entirely. Scythed chariots must not only attack in lanes; they must maintain a solid front. Otherwise the enemy, ourselves, can simply open ranks and let the lone car through. But in the heat of action, the braver and faster drivers outlash the laggards, so that additional gaps develop along the axis as well as the front, leaving isolated both chariots too fast and too slow. Our archers and javelineers can assault these from the flanks without fear of the scythes.

I send my next courier with the same message I gave Boar. Go! In case Boar hasn't gotten through.

On my immediate right, the battle of the flank rages without letup. Each side's squadrons have broken through the other's so repeatedly, we will learn later, that across the field an observer might remark as many of our fellows on their side as their own, and as many of theirs on ours. The brawl is not concentrated upon any single front or post; one sees neither massed melees nor heaps of men cut down together. Rather individuals fall with a terrible randomness across the breadth of the pitch. Riders are picked off in ones and twos as their mounts are brought down or tumble or give way of exhaustion. Upon a site, momentum alternates with a grisly caprice as one horseman, striving valiantly beneath the foe's assault, is retrieved by the charge of his comrades, only to have these in turn cut off and massacred by a counterrush of those who had moments earlier fled before them. Engagements involving hundreds pass without a man suffering a scratch, while two-man skirmishes swell into routs as wings of horse or clouds of foot appear from the murk to wreathe the foe beyond escape. Blown horses cave in beneath the weight of their riders. Mounts' hearts burst from exertion. A horse pushed past his limit "ties up." His muscles seize; he breaks down. Others expire of heat and shock. Scores succumb to terror alone. When

the enemy finally turns and takes flight, horses on both sides are froth-
ing not foam but blood. Hundreds lie foundered upon the field. Those
not slain or leg-broken have been worked so to exhaustion that they
can never be used again. These are fine animals, quality stock trained
from birth and loved by their men to a depth that no one who has not
served in a mounted corps can understand. To lose a brave horse is almost as bad as to lose a man; worse in its way, for no horse understands
why he fights; he does so only for love of us. His loss is as cruel as the
death of a child. There is no solace for it.

At what stage does the battle now stand? I spoke afterward to
Onesicritus (who would become my fleet steersman in India), who remained in camp and was observing from the heights, three miles back.
The sight, he reported, gave fresh meaning to the word *pandemonium*.
Onesicritus was thoroughly familiar with our battle plan and possessed
as well an excellent conception of the Persians' order; yet, even with
these held firmly in mind, he declared, he could make no sense of the
spectacle sprawling across the plain beneath him. It seemed to him as if
the field had not only inverted but revolved upon its axis, so that what
should have been left was right and what ought to have been fore had
become aft. Compounding this chaos were the towering clouds of alka-
line dust, which rendered ghostly the movements of units and wings
and from which ascended such sounds as rendered it impossible for any
man with a bent toward philosophy, so Onesicritus attested, to declare
the race of humans anything but mad.

I credit his report. The field must have looked to him as he portrayed it. Yet from where I ride, at the fore of the Companion Cavalry,
all is in order. Powerful divisions of both sides are engaged. Battles of
monumental scale rage left, right, and center. Yet for Darius and me, the
fatal blows remain undelivered. We occupy the maelstrom's eye.

The Companions advance, still at a walk. A hundred scythed chariots drive at us from the front. In thousands, Bactrian, Scythian, Sacae,
and Massagetae horsemen charge upon us from the right. Preposterous
as it sounds, every piece is right where it should be.

The first scythed chariot bursts through Balacrus's screen. Its driver
is dead, dragged behind, entangled in the reins; three of the four horses

are shot through with darts and bolts; they gallop, driven on by terror alone. The car plunges into our ranks, which part in wild haste, driven by our grooms afoot, amid the curses of riders and the bawling of beasts. A second and third cutter hurtle toward us, only to overturn out front beneath broadsides of shafts and javelins launched by Balacrus's Thracians and Agrianes. I have never seen such rage as that directed by our fellows against these machines. They hate them. Our horses' state is so high now they can barely be contained. At the left of each charger trots its groom, his right hand clutching the cheek piece of the bridle, holding the animal in check (no rider can do this alone under such conditions) while employing the weight of his body to keep the beast from bolting, as even the most impeccably trained horse will do under such conditions.

The condition is serious. If one mount flies, the whole troop will follow. Cleitus catches my eye. "Go now?" The temptation to attack prematurely is overwhelming. How can one "direct" such chaos? The attempt is excruciating. You feed one company into the fight, dispatch another to a different sector. Based on what? The sound of the brawl? A dispatch minutes old? The ordeal of command consists in this: that one makes decisions of fatal consequence based on ludicrously inadequate intelligence.

The din of bedlam ascends on the right. Tension mounts to an apogee. Riderless horses break from the gloom and bolt through our Companions' formation. I command Cleitus to hold. More cutters rush upon us. Every man and horse is coming out of his skin.

We keep advancing at a walk. One can still see. Despite cyclones of grit, vision remains possible through rifts opened by the wind. Now these, too, begin to occlude as the fight presses closer on the flank. Arrow shafts begin lancing in. Out front the clash between chariots and missile troops mounts to an excruciating pitch. In formation, one of our horses bolts, taking groom and rider with him. Two more rear in place. Terror is unstringing the animals. Cleitus at my shoulder: "Take them to a trot."

I sign for it. We bump the pace; the horses settle. Beneath me Bucephalus is a mountain. He who on parade will stamp and plunge becomes, amid the trumpets, the soul of calm. I should steady him; it is he who steadies me.

Everything comes down to Aretes, out front somewhere with his four hundred Lancers. I send a third courier, after the one I sent succeeding Boar, and another after that. "Black!" I call Cleitus. If Aretes' squadrons can't charge, I will send the Royal. I can't pull out more; the fate of all rides on the Companions' rush at Darius.

Do I tell too much detail, Itanes? You must learn how events turn on real ground. The blindness of it, the dislocation, the luck. The foe's assault from the right presses so close now that defenders of our own flank guard, dueling the enemy lance-to-lance, break rearward across the wing of the Companions' formation. Spent arrow shafts clatter among our ranks. In moments our squadrons' cohesion will break.

Now Aretes charges.

We can't hear or see it, but we sense it from the dust and the feel of the field. "Contain your horses!" I bawl, though not even Black Cleitus at my shoulder can hear me. Aretes' orders are to find the soft belly where the Persians' drawing off of units to the flank has thinned their front—and charge into it. My Companions will follow.

But in the event (though we will not learn this till days later), when this soft spot appears, two thousand of the foe's Royal Indian Horse, recalled from the wing by Darius, emerge from the dust directly in the path upon which Aretes' four hundred have come to the gallop. I cannot see this. It is beyond my sight in the gloom, nor could I have seen it on the clearest field, so screened is my position by the collision between the scythed chariots and our archers and javelineers. Aretes recounted later that he believed in the moment that all was lost. He took his four hundred straight into the Royal Indian two thousand. He could think of no other course. He knew only, he said, that to balk would be fatal. He made the decision at the stretching gallop and communicated it to his men, neither by sound nor sign, but only by the direction in which he himself plunged.

For this act I awarded him, when we took Persepolis, five hundred talents of gold, a sum equal to half the yearly tribute of Athens's empire at its pinnacle of power.

Luck is no small part of war, and here, at this instant, another stroke breaks our way. As Black Cleitus draws the Royal Squadron rightward, to charge in Aretes' stead, should he fail, I come up on the right of his leading wedge. The formation I have ordered is what we call a "side and one"—that is, a wedge heavied up on one wing, in this case the right, because the Royal Squadron's role, replacing Aretes', is to break a lane through for the main body of the Companions, who will follow, and to shield this body's critical flank (its right as it wheels left and pushes behind the Persian front toward Darius) against the mass of the foe.

Fortune conspires to place me here, beside Cleitus, when his second in command, named Alexander, spurs out of the murk at stretching speed.

"Aretes is engaged!" Alexander shouts. It turns out that Cleitus, outstanding officer that he is, has sent scouts forward on his own the moment I called the Royal to the wing, and these riders have observed the appearance of the two thousand Indian cavalry—and seen Aretes hurl his Lancers into them. Where? Alexander points into the soup. We can hear the clash, ongoing, some points to the right.

The soft spot will be there.

I make two changes. I return the Royal Squadron to the fore of the Companions (I will ride, with Cleitus, at its point). And I bring up an additional squadron, the Bottiaean, into the position we call "fist"— that is, immediately to the rear of the Royal. I want power to penetrate.

Does it sound mad, Itanes, that I, with one-twentieth of Darius's force, lay designs to break through at his threshold and wring his royal neck?

I know what I have and haven't.

I know what he has and hasn't.

I hurl myself and my Companions into the murk. Great prizes are won only at great hazard.

Twenty-Six

THE BIG WEDGE

THE THRUST AT DARIUS COMES IN ONE GREAT WEDGE. The Royal and Bottiaean squadrons comprise the point, with the Toronean, Anthemiot, and Amphipolitan making the right; the remaining Companion Cavalry squadrons compose the left, with the foot brigades of Royal Guardsmen extending this wing as they advance at the double beside the leftmost squadron of Companions; the Guardsmen yoke the cavalry to the two phalanx brigades, Coenus's and Perdiccas's, which make up the leftmost extremity of the Big Wedge.

This is one battle.

On the right, Cleander, Menidas, Aretes, Ariston, Attalus, and Brison fight another; the central phalanx fights a third; while on the left wing, Parmenio and Craterus duel the foe in a fourth. One may add a fifth and sixth. Our secondary phalanx clashes with elements of enemy horse and foot on the rear and left wing, while two miles back, in our forward camp, our disabled and noncombatants are being overrun by Royal Indian and Parthian cavalry seeking to rescue the queen and queen mother of Persia (who are not there, in fact, but in the main base camp, five miles to the rear).

No one of these struggles is visible from any other, nor is the breadth of any one discernible even to those within its sphere, so dense is the storm of grit and murk flung up by the feet and hooves of the contending multitudes.

From my post with the Companions, I can see nothing. I initiate the charge on sound alone—the clash of Aretes' Lancers against the Royal Indian Horse, which we can hear (or imagine we do) some points to the right and about three hundred yards forward.

What one unacquainted with battle does not understand is its terrible freight of fatigue. The weight of armor and weapons alone, just to bear on the parade ground, will break a man's back in an hour. And our soldier is not on the parade ground. He is in the field. He has marched under full kit, in all likelihood, half a day just to reach the ground of conflict. Has he got food in his belly? When did he last sleep? Is he sick or injured? Now add fear. Add excitement, add anticipation. There is a type of exhaustion called by the Greeks *apantlesis*. It is that enervation produced not by physical fatigue alone but also by strain on the nerves. An officer or soldier in this state is prey to make bad decisions, to fail to take actions clearly called for, to misapprehend obvious situations, and in general to become deaf, blind, and stupid. Worse, this state comes upon one with the suddenness of night and the power of a punch in the teeth. One minute a man is able; the next he is an imbecile.

This strain that a man experiences, a horse feels doubly—and a highly strung cavalry mount doubles that again. Horses cannot comprehend delay, or conservation of effort. The moment is all that exists for them, and in that moment they know only the command that you and I communicate. Is it any wonder they become so "high"? Their nerves are excruciatingly attuned to ours; they take on our fear and our excitement, and the fear and excitement of the other horses. Horses are herd animals: Dread is communicated from beast to beast instantaneously. And horses are flight animals: Their first impulse is to run. What holds them? Only their bond with us. For each horse is twinned with his rider, whose will to fight, and the union of trust he has forged over years with his animal, contains the beast and checks him from reverting to instinct. Remember, our horses have come up with us from foals. For many, we were present in their stalls at the hour of their births; our breath into their nostrils is the earliest sensation they have known. We have fed them and groomed them, curried and combed them, sat up nights when they were ill or hurt; thousands of hours we have trained together, in the ring and on the field. Not our wives or children, not Zeus Himself knows us as our horses do, or has labored in our company so many hours. Yet the truest mount will bolt; the bravest will fly. It is a wonder they remain at all, to such an unendurable pitch are their nerves wound in ranks awaiting action. Look in your charger's eye. He is wild still, for all your decade of labor, and poised so precariously between fidelity to you and the instincts of flight and fury, that one knows he can contain him no more than quicksilver or summer lightning.

I must strike fast. I must get to grips with Darius before the heart goes out of my horses and the heat bleeds away from my men.

We failed at Issus because our rush bogged down. The masses of enemy interposed between us and the king broke our momentum and gave Darius time to get away. We went too shallow. We didn't have enough push.

My object here at Gaugamela, in yoking to the Companions three brigades of fast infantry and two of heavy infantry, is to break through the Persian front *with enough force to keep going*—three hundred, four hundred yards into the foe's rear. I want to get behind Darius in force. I must be where I can cut him off if he runs.

The nonsoldier believes you can see on a battlefield. See what? The trooper on the ground is blind as a post, and even the cavalryman, from his mounted elevation, sees only smoke and dust. Our lead squadrons have barely spurred into the murk before we are stumbling over enemy infantry, themselves stampeding headlong for their lives; we dodge wrecks of scythed chariots with splendid horses dead and dying in their traces. Then, at once, a wall of enemy horse materializes as if spawned by the earth. The foe are Daans, mounted tribesmen of the eastern provinces; we can tell by their ponies, small and sturdy, and their *kurqans*—baggy trousers bloused at the knee. The Daans are about five hundred and are just then pulling out of the line, apparently to reinforce the units on their left, where Aretes is attacking. When our squadrons burst from the broth, the foe's ranks are faced away from us. They're more startled than we are. We are at the gallop, in a wedge a quarter mile across. The Daans' ranks tear open like a curtain and go up like a wall of flame.

I am at the point of the lead wedge of the Royal Squadron. The weight of all eight squadrons thunders behind me. Our mounted force is now at the identical point it was at Issus, when we broke through the archers and the King's Own. We have penetrated the enemy line, some quarter to half mile from its center, and are poised to wheel in column and launch ourselves at this post.

Where is Darius?

Between him and us stand four fronts of defenders: four thousand Persian, Susian, and Cadusian cavalry mixed with Persian, Mardian, and Carian archers; Patron's brigades of Greek heavy infantry; the five thousand spearmen of the Persian Apple Bearer Guard; and Tigranes with the regiments of Kinsman Cavalry, Darius's Royal Horse.

The wind, which gusts powerfully at Gaugamela between the plain and mountains, blows right to left across Darius's front. This means it is obscuring that sector into which we must turn and charge. Cleitus urges me to strike left at once, before the field becomes an ocean of murk. I may err, keeping on too long. But I cannot leave Darius an avenue of escape. I will not let him cheat me a second time. So I hold our track undeflected into the Persian rear. When at last I come left—four hundred yards deep—great thunderheads of chalk have been thrown up by the passage of our two thousand horses and these, piled before the wind, drift in a thick bank across the field.

We will come left and take Darius from behind. But suddenly in the blinding chalk, we run upon Patron's Greek mercenaries. These are five thousand of the enemy's crack heavy infantry, the foot guard stationed immediately on Darius's left. How can they be here now—in the king's rear, half a mile from the front? Have they witnessed the debacle of the scythed chariots and seen their Persian cohorts on both wings put to flight? Have their officers kept their heads? Have they pulled out of the line and dashed rearward at the double to take up a blocking position, defending their master from the direction in which he now faces the gravest peril? No matter: Here they are, square in our path, and forming up fast to take us on.

We simply run around them.

This is how cavalry works at its best. It does not squander its precious capital of men and horses in picturesque but wasteful melees and slugging matches. Instead it uses speed and mobility to cut off divisions of the foe, bypass them, and leave them in the dust. In moments Patron's foot troops are hundreds of yards in our rear.

Where is Darius?

He must be close, or Patron's troops would not have formed up on this site. He must be left, or they wouldn't have faced their defensive posture shielding that quarter.

I rein the Companions, sending scouts into the murk. The adventure-eager youth, afire to run off and join the cavalry, imagines battle as one grand and glorious rush at the gallop. What would such a hotblood think, to observe my commanders and me, at the epicenter of this monumental clash, halting our squadrons in place and, without haste, taking the time to dress and align our fighting front, to cover our flanks and rear, and even to recinch our kit and wipe the sweat and grime from our faces? Patience. Though I can hear the mayhem on all quarters, amplified grotesquely by the murk, and though I know that, even as I loiter, my countrymen are bleeding and dying for want of my thrust into the enemy's vitals, still I cannot prematurely sound the charge; I cannot plunge blindly into the soup. The moment is excruciating. Nor do our scouts come thundering punctually out of the gloom with certain word of the foe's position. In the event, they have become disoriented themselves, on this featureless field, and are only reacquired by a flock of our grooms, fanning out on foot into the billowing chalk.

Kill the King.

We must find Darius.

At last our riders return. Their leader is Sathon, Socrates Redbeard's son. The enemy is a quarter mile forward, he reports. The foe knows we have galloped round him; his companies have faced about, in order, to receive our assault.

"Where is Darius?"

"In the center."

"Are you certain?"

"I saw his colors, sire."

We charge.

But our scout has left out one thing, which he could not know—namely, that the knight Carmanes, captain of Darius's Household Guard, has ordered the royal standards to be displayed in the center of the line (where kings of Persia always fight) while withdrawing the monarch himself to the wing.

He fools me.

The Guards Captain fools me.

When our wedges strike the foe, Darius is already outside our right. I don't know this. None of us do. I spur Bucephalus straight for the king's colors. The melee is horse and foot commingled. The foe, recognizing my armor, hurls every champion at me, while my countrymen cry our antagonist's name and strain to locate him above the forest of spears and helmet crowns.

The Persian Royal Horse are commanded by Tigranes, champion of Issus and the most celebrated equestrian of Asia; his charger Bellacris, "Meteor," is a gift from Darius, said to be worth twenty talents of gold. Around Tigranes fight the peerless knights Ariobates, Autophradates, Gobarzanes, Massages, Tissamenes, Bagoas, and Gobryas.

A champion strikes for me. It is Tigranes. I recognize him by the brilliance of his kit and the spectacular specimen of horseflesh he rides. Ariobates spurs at his shoulder. This man is unknown to me, but clearly he is a champion of exalted station. Black Cleitus rides at my side. (Telamon and Ptolemy remain on the right of the field, aiding Cleander, as do Love Locks and Peucestas; Hephaestion commands the *agema* of the Royal Guard.) Three Pages, none over nineteen, form my Bodyguard. Tigranes leads a matching line of Kinsman Cavalry. We crash together like waves.

"Iskander!"

Tigranes cries my name in Persian, claiming me as his own. His

Meteor plows into Bucephalus like a trireme on the ram. The press swallows all. The heat sucks the breath out of you. The animals' necks, straining against each other, burn like surfaces of flame. Meteor's jaw is so close to my face that my cheek piece catches against his bit chain. His eye is wild as a monster in the sea. The horses lock up chest-to-chest, fighting their own equine war, while my antagonist and I clash like fencers, shaft against shaft, dueling for an opening. Tigranes could plunge his lance into Bucephalus's gorge as easily as I can sever Meteor's windpipe with my own. But he will not, nor will I.

"I am Tigranes!" my rival cries in Greek. I love the man. Here is a warrior! Here is a champion! I would strike at him sidearm from my right, seeking the vital flesh below the lip of his breastplate, but so densely pressed are the men and horses that I can neither incline to that side nor even move my right leg, which is pinned against Bucephalus's flank by the mass of another horse, my Page Andron's, though I cannot draw breath even to look. I strike across Bucephalus's neck, two-handed, seeking Tigranes' throat. But with the jousting horses, the warhead misses the mark, deflecting off the temple of his helmet, which is the conical type with ear guards and gorget, all gold. The killing point plunges over Tigranes' shoulder. He seizes the lance with his left hand, so far up the shaft that his fist touches mine, and thrusts his spear at me, uppercutting, with his right. The weapon is a seven-footer, cornel wood with a four-square iron point. The warhead takes me just outside the left nipple, tears through the composite of my corselet, and passes between my ribs and the inside of my left arm. I clamp tight to pin the weapon. Am I wounded? I can't tell if the lance has opened me up or missed me entirely. I know only that if I am to die, I will drag this man to hell at my side. I heave forward, atop Bucephalus's neck, as far as I can go with my right leg pinned by the horse beside me, pressing my lance with all my weight behind it, seeking either to wrench its shaft from my antagonist's grip or, if he will not let go, then to wrest him off balance. I will come clean off my horse if I have to and tear his throat out with my bare hands. But as the pair of us grapple, each clutching the shaft between us, the blow of a Persian mace takes me full force on the left shoulder, bowling me sidelong into Andron on my right, while a Macedonian lance, driven from the rear by Cleitus, though I cannot see in the press, plunges past Tigranes' carotid, catches the earpiece of his helmet, and wrenches him, headfirst, nearly from his seat. I see the strap rip and the helmet, propelled by the point of Cleitus's lance, tear free. Tigranes should spill, or his neck snap, but instead he recovers, so swiftly that he actually catches his helmet as it is tearing loose and turns, in the saddle, to sling it in fury at Cleitus.

Philotas duels Ariobates on Tigranes' left; he has slipped his rival's rush and aims a blow upon Tigranes. By now, Companions and Kinsmen have flung themselves into such a concentration on the site that the object of this tumult—Darius himself—has been all but forgotten in the frenzy.

Seeking him, I am carried apart from Tigranes. We battle through rank after rank. Cleitus shouts, pointing ahead. We can see Darius now. The king is less than fifty feet away, atop his chariot, wielding the *askara*, the two-handed lance, with furious valor against troopers of our Bottiaean squadron, the rightmost as we rushed, who have broken through the crush somehow and now hurl their horses and themselves upon the royal car. The thought that another will slay my rival nearly severs me from my reason. Only three ranks of enemy horsemen separate us from the king. I can see Carmanes, captain of the Household Guard, rally a company to break Darius's chariot clear. I drive Bucephalus forward, half-mad with fury and frustration. Suddenly from our rear appears a front of enemy heavy infantry. Patron's mercenaries, whom we ran around in our attack. Some must have slipped clear of our Big Wedge; now here they are. They break through our Bottiaeans. Their armor forms a defensive ring around the king. They will save him. I cry to heaven for wings, for strength, for anything that will get me across this press and onto my foe. My legs are so spent, I feel nothing below the waist. I drive again into the ruck. The ranks of defenders must buckle as their numbers drop and they see their king marshaling for flight. But this knowledge, when it comes, only summons the champions of Persia to more superhuman exertions. At the point of penetration, the defenders redouble their efforts, believing, one must imagine, that every moment they buy with their blood is another to speed their king clear. The foe retreats before us, always in order, always resisting. They are fresh. We are exhausted. Our line has already fought, through eight and ten ranks. Our horses have covered miles since descending to the battleground and have labored in a state of extremity for what feels like hours. I clash with a champion in iron mail, a left-hander, two ranks from the king. His lance misses the socket of my right arm by a whisker. I drive my saber into his gorge, thrusting with all my strength to propel the man from my path, but even in death, this knight interposes his person between me and his king; he pitches forward, onto my blade, to check me, by the weight of his failing flesh, from penetrating to Darius. By now I have lost all sensation in both arms. I am deaf from the din; blood frenzy makes my eyesight pulse.

I see the mercenary Patron, rallying his cohort around Darius. Carmanes' Household Guard clears a lane of flight. Their voices cry, but no sound carries; their whips crack, but no sensation reaches my ears. It is a nightmare. I am mired in tar. A double rank of defenders still shields the king; we hurl ourselves on them—Cleitus and I and the knights of the Royal Squadron—but our blows fall as if dealt underwater. I can't feel my hands. My saber lifts like a ton of lead.

"He flies!" Philotas bawls. Down the line, a hundred Macedonian throats take up the cry.

The fight goes on another two hours. My squadrons cannot break away to pursue Darius, so desperate is the struggle on both our wings, Parmenio's and Craterus's divisions on the left, Menidas's, Aretes', Cleander's, and Ariston's on the right, to whom succor must be brought at all costs, and in that interval I myself am nearly slain half a dozen times, while scores of my commanders—Hephaestion speared through the arm; Telamon shot through both legs; Craterus, Coenus, Perdiccas, and Menidas, riddled, all four, with arrow shafts—suffer desperate wounds. Of two thousand prime battle mounts, the Companions lose half to wounds or exhaustion, and the mercenaries and allies even more.

By nightfall I am on my ninth horse of the day, twenty miles southeast of the battlefield. The pursuit party is half the Royal Squadron, two quarter squadrons of Aretes' Lancers, and a patched troop of Ariston's Paeonians.

Darius has not fled south to his treasure cities of Babylon or Susa, as one might expect (apparently he has abandoned hope of holding them) but south and east to his camp at Arbela. He reaches this about midnight, we learn later from captives, leaving the bridge intact so his army in flight can cross, while he and his party flee east across the mountains, along the caravan route to Media. I chase his track till dark, rest horses and men till midnight, then press on to Arbela, reaching it next morning. Darius is hours ahead. The highway is an ocean of fugitives. We can't get through.

Aretes, who has wrung a lifetime's glory from this day's strife, reins-in beside me. His mount's flanks are caked solid with alkali; his own face, including his teeth, is black with blood and grime. "Let Darius go, Alexander. He is finished. He will never raise an army again."

I will hear no call for cessation. We press on over the foothills. Tens of thousands flee before us; we can see parties stumbling into blind canyons, guideless as we are. One of Aretes' captains spies a muleteer on a track apart from the others. We dragoon him. I will make him a rich man, I swear, if he guides us across these mountains, or cut his throat if he plays us false.

For two hours our pursuit party snakes along a trace no broader than the stream of an ox's piss. Stone chasms yawn. Each time Cleitus applies his quirt to our guide's back, claiming the track smells, the man takes his oath by all of heaven's sages. "The trail is good, lord! Good!" He leads us up a final ascent, vowing that we'll see from the summit the caravan road by which Darius has fled. But when we come off the last pitch, the trace terminates in a blind spur.

The muleteer bolts. Our fellows run him down. The man is brought before me. I am not angry; I admire his resource and his guts. "You have preserved your king's life," I tell him, "but forfeited your own."

Trekking back, my mates give themselves over to elation. Nothing stands between us and Babylon and Susa. We shall pluck brides from Asia's harems and dine on plates of gold!

"The empire is yours, Alexander. Hail, Lord of Asia!"

My daimon looks on. He knows that with Darius's flight, I have vanquished one adversary, perhaps, only to have two more take his place. First Persia's empire, whose rule now becomes my burden. And my own army, who, fattening on plunder, will dream of ease and comfort and return grudgingly, if at all, to the road to glory.

I am inconsolable. Darius has gotten away again.

Book Eight

LOVE FOR ONE'S COMRADES

Twenty-Seven

KITES

BABYLON MEANS "GATE OF GOD." Its walls are a hundred and fifty feet high and forty miles in circumference, erected, so the story goes, by Nebuchadnezzar himself. The citadel, where the Ishtar Gate ascends above the Euphrates, is five hundred feet tall, of burnt brick and bitumen. The city is sited on a blistering, magnificently ordered plain, whose canals and irrigation works are a wonder of the world, second only to the corps of tax collectors and agricultural administrators under whose supervision the land produces three harvests a year of sesame, millet, barley, wheat, and rye. The plain of Babylon is surely the most manicured tract of dirt on earth. Not a flower blooms that has not been seeded by the hand of man and does not flourish by his care and cultivation. Date palms grow in ordered ranks, in forests as dense as the pine woods of Thrace. These produce timber that will not rot underwater and, from their fruit, a type of beer that tastes pulpy (and so thick with lees, it must be sucked through a straw) but produces a keen and brilliant intoxication that does not leave a headache.

When Cyrus the Great took Babylon over two hundred years ago, he did it by diverting the Euphrates, which flows through the city, and attacking at night along the dry channel.

We have it easier. Before Gaugamela, scouts of our Paeonian Light Horse capture a number of Persians, including an extremely keen young captain named Boas, who speaks Greek and serves as an aide-de-camp to Mazaeus, commander of the Persian right and provincial governor of Babylonia. This excellent young officer has permitted himself to be taken, I am certain, on instructions of his superior. I order him released, to bear this message to Mazaeus: that, although I cannot as a gentleman urge him to betray his king in the coming fight, yet, should the affair turn out in my favor, I shall harbor no ill will to brave foes, but will look with kindness upon him who will accept my friendship. Mazaeus and his young captain fight with exemplary valor at Gaugamela, yet once Darius has fled, all allegiances are off. I send again to Mazaeus, extending my offer of accord. "You will find your answer," the governor replies, "on the wind."

When Babylon celebrates, she flies kites. In summer a hot dry wind beats across the plain, in currents that ascend powerfully at known places, such that the walls and irrigation stations fly great rafts of banners, the noble houses are made gay by snapping standards, and each dwelling, however humble, has its wind-borne jack and bunting. The kite masters of Babylon craft their creations of pressed flax dyed to brilliant colors, in every shape conceivable—swallows and butterflies, crickets and ravens, carp and perch—and soar them to unimaginable heights. The loftier a man's station, the grander his kites.

Kites sail in thousands as the army approaches Babylon. Our fellows whoop and cheer; children pave their path with petals and candies. Our host Mazaeus awaits us with his wives and children on a barge in the Royal Canal. A great entertainment has been prepared. For five miles above the town Mazaeus has had the road strewn with palm fronds and, within a mile, with wreaths and garlands. Ecstatic multitudes line the thoroughfares; silver altars burn frankincense in mounds big as handbarrows. Everything is ours. Herds of horses and cattle, cartloads of fragrances and spice; nothing is missing, down to talking crows and tigers in cages.

I have drawn up the army in battle order, to show the populace its new masters. Thessalian horse first, led by the Pharsalian squadron in burnished armor; Agrianes and Macedonian archers next; Balacrus's Thracian darters; then half the allied Greek and mercenary cavalry, Aretes' men, and Menidas's and Ariston's, the Lancers and Mounted Scouts. Those wounded, or who cannot walk or ride, remain in hospital camp north of the city, though I will bring them in as expeditiously as appearances permit. After the Lancers come Hephaestion's Royal Guard, Nicanor's Guards brigades, both in crimson cloaks with regimental sashes; then Cretan archers; allied Greek and mercenary infantry, led by Cleander's vet mercs. Behind these come the siege train and combat engineers, Diades' divisions, flanked by Andromachus's mercenary cavalry, and the other half of the allied Greek horse. The field baggage passes, to show the foe how little we need, and then, in the carriages in which we have captured them, the queen and queen mother of the empire and their retinue; Darius's young son Ochus I have mounted upon my own parade horse, Corona; he rides at my side. The ladies I have screened from sight within their carriages, which bear their royal serpents, fluttering on the air. Behind the baggage train advance in armor, sarissas at the upright, the six regiments of the phalanx, in order as they triumphed at Gaugamela—Coenus's, Perdiccas's, Meleager's, Polyperchon's, Amyntas's (under his brother Simmias), and Craterus's. Last, Sitalces' Thracians; Andromachus's mercenaries; the Greek cavalry under Erigyius; allied cavalry under Coeranus; Odrysians under Agathon; and the Achaean and Peloponnesian infantry under their home commanders.

On the second day I enter the city and sacrifice to Baal, chief deity of Babylonia, with Mazaeus and the Chaldean priests in attendance according to the holy law. Those rites of the ancient religion, which Darius has proscribed, I restore. I command that the Great Temple of Esagila, razed by Xerxes, be rebuilt. I do not permit the ladies of Darius's court to return to their apartments in the city but have them encamped, with the army on the plain of Ashai, east of the city, while I send detachments to occupy the citadels and disarm the royal guard.

On the third morning I enter Babylon to stay. The region that we know today as the province of Mesopotamia of the empire of Persia has been, centuries past, the empires of Chaldea, Assyria, and Babylonia, and the kingdoms of Ur, Sumer, and Akkad. Over these realms have ruled Semiramis, Sargon, Sennacherib, Hammurabi, Nebuchadnezzar, Ashurbanipal. Scyths and Kassites have invaded, and Hittites and Medes and Lydians and Elamites. Cyrus the Great brought these lands under Persian rule two centuries ago, as now we of Macedon and Greece subdue his heirs and make his kingdoms subject to our might.

Where is Darius?

I call a council in the great Banquet Hall. Hephaestion commands our forward intelligence. He presides with his arm cinched in a sling, wounded from a spear thrust at Gaugamela. "Spies and deserters place the king in flight east toward Persepolis, capital of the empire, or north, on the track to Ecbatana in Media."

The floor of the hall is a vast map of the empire. Hephaestion paces off the march from the site indicating Babylon, in the center, to Susa, east, then on to the other cities, while our generals observe with victors' satisfaction from their places at a great ebony table. We feast on the foe's meat and wine; business is interrupted again and again by toasts and cheers, which I cannot quell and do not wish to. "Both Persepolis and Ecbatana are a month and more of hard trek from here, and both are fronted by rugged, defensible mountains. Reports say Darius has thirty thousand men still with him. We will not overhaul him till midwinter, even if we start today, and this cannot be asked, if you want my opinion, of infantry who have just borne the sternest casualties of the campaign, or of cavalry whose men and horses have suffered even more severely."

"Besides," cries Ptolemy, "we have won!"

Perdiccas: "The men need gold—and time to spend it."

"By Heracles," adds Cleitus, "so do I!"

A chorus acclaims this.

"Indeed," I agree, "diversion is the men's due. They have earned it."

We will winter in Babylon. I need the time, in any event, to refit the army. In addition to severe casualties in men, we have suffered even graver losses in horses—over a thousand highly trained primary mounts and twice that in remounts. It will take months to acquire proper replacement stock and bring them to even minimal serviceability.

Our forces themselves need reconfiguring. The next push will be into the eastern empire. We'll be fighting not on open plains but in deserts, badlands, and mountains. We'll need lighter and faster units and, perhaps, a whole new manner of war.

"Will you hunt Darius this winter?" Parmenio inquires.

There is a difference, I suggest, between pursuit and hot pursuit. The king may flee, but he will not get away. And I indicate, on the mosaic floor, the site of Babylon. "For now, gentlemen, let us set this stable in order."

We begin.

Our conquests have schooled us in the art of taking over a country. My commanders have learned from Egypt, Palestine, Gaza, and Syria. And the process seems to go smoothly here as well, save one incident, which at the time appears trivial but in retrospect takes on the odor of an ill omen. It has to do with Philotas.

After Gaugamela, I have assigned him to bring to Babylon the spoils of Darius's battlefield suite. This he does, including the horses, chariots, and apparatus used in the celebrated rite called the Procession of the Sun. This practice of the Persian monarchy requires a train of celebrants half a mile long—company upon company of priests and magi, crownbearers and praise-singers, as well as the entire division of ten thousand Apple Bearers in full armor, with the king at the fore in his Chariot of the Sun.

Philotas gets it into his head to convene a mock procession and march it down the central thoroughfare of Babylon, both to gratify our conquerors' conceit and to show up, for the sport of it, the excess and extravagance of the empire we have overthrown. Philotas does this without informing me, so that I learn of the parade while at work in the palace, only by hearing from the street the barrages of scorn being heaped by our countrymen, and by the rabble of locals lining the Processional Way, upon the captives compelled by their participation in this spectacle to put on a show for their amusement. I stand out onto the gallery with Parmenio, Hephaestion, Craterus, and others, just as

Philotas draws the pageant up beneath this stand. "Look here, Alexander!" he crows from horseback. "What do you think of this?"

Among the captives stand the remnants of Darius's royal guard, the Apple Bearers. The deficit of this noble corps, decimated by casualties from Gaugamela and stripped further by those loyal spearmen who have remained with Darius in his flight, has been made up, I note, by thugs and ruffians off the streets. The fabled Chariot of the Sun has had its gold sheathing stripped to the bare frame, while of the emperor's one thousand white stallions, so few remain that the deficiency has been restored by plugs and jades, and even asses. My eye lights upon one captain of the Apple Bearer Guard, a man of about fifty years, with a noble bearing and numerous wounds of battle. The binding of his boot, with splints laced tight to midcalf, is that which a physician applies for a broken lower leg.

"What do I think, Philotas? I think that these are good and worthy men whom you have shamed. And I command you to disband this spectacle at once and present yourself within doors before me."

This is not, to put it mildly, the response Philotas has expected. I see him flush with outrage; he spurs toward the gallery on which I stand.

"And what do you accomplish by such reprobation, Alexander," he calls up, loudly enough for all to hear, "save to humiliate other good men, myself not least among them, by whose blood and toil you have reaped these treasures?" A stir of the throng fuels his courage. "Whose side are you on?" he demands of me, leaving off all address of courtesy and respect.

I take one stride toward the platform's edge. "Plead pardon of your king!" Parmenio commands his son, moving instantly to my shoulder. Hephaestion and Craterus hold poised at my side. One glance from me and they will cut Philotas down where he stands.

"Give thanks to heaven," I tell him, "that you have bled on the field of battle so few days past, or, for such insolence, you would bleed here now."

Afterward in private, Craterus takes stern issue with me. "What can you have been thinking, Alexander? To humble your commander of

Companion Cavalry in public, before the defeated foe? We don't need these Persians' love, but their fear!"

He is right of course. I am chastened.

But in my heart something has changed. I can no longer see the knights of Persia as enemies, nor their commons as chattel to be mal-treated and misused.

With Hephaestion I tour the barley fields along the Royal Canal. It is lunchtime and two of Mazaeus's soldiers have snatched up a live goose. A farmer is beating at them with his rake and they are laughing. Our arrival breaks up the fracas. The soldiers point me out to the planter, expecting this to shut him up. But the old man displays no awe for his conqueror. "It's all the same to me," he declares, "which of you villains seizes my crops and steals my goods. I remain poor either way."

I am taken by the fellow's boldness and stop to talk. I tell him I in-tend to maintain order and let him farm in peace. "Yes," he replies, "but you will take away this land I farm from the Persian prince who owns it now and absentee-farms it, and you will award it to one of your captains or colonels, who will farm it as an absentee in the same way. How has my lot altered? I remain enslaved to the same crop agent in town be-neath whose heel I have labored all my life, who will now run the farm for a different faraway prince." I ask exactly how destitute he is. He ticks it off on his fingers. "For every ten bushels, I furnish four to the king, two to the agent for his own use—otherwise, he will put me off the land—and keep four for myself, of which I donate one to the gods, one to the priests, one to my wife's family, and the last one I bake into bread, if I'm lucky."

I ask the farmer what he would manage differently if he could. "Give me this land," he replies, "and let me keep what I grow. And send the agent from town to work for me. I will make that fat bastard sweat!"

I offer to appoint the farmer my commissioner of agriculture or, if he will not accept this, to draw for him from the treasury such wealth that he need never work again.

"Please, no!" the old man protests with genuine terror. "Leave me nothing, sire, for, by heaven, my neighbors will crack my skull if they smell so much as half a copper, and what they miss, my wife and her kin will beat out of me till nothing remains but brittle bones."

"Then what shall I leave you, my friend?"

"My misery." And he laughs.

With Hephaestion I begin to study the system in earnest. "This type of country," my companion observes, "cannot support small farms and free yeoman, as in Macedon. Everything depends on irrigation, but to dredge the canals and keep them clear—for they silt up so fast and the reeds grow back so quickly—takes mass labor. Forced labor. The land is as fertile for tyranny," Hephaestion concludes, "as for wheat and barley."

I set up in the palace and begin to hear petitions. It becomes clear at once that power lies not with the king but with those who control access to him. An industry of corruption flourishes, not only at my threshold but along all roads and highways leading to it. Mazaeus becomes my mentor, along with Boas, the bright young captain, and two eunuchs, Pharnaces and Adramates.

The eunuch chancellors, one soon grasps, are the richest men in the kingdom and the most powerful. They direct not only the daylight affairs of the realm (their legitimate commission) but constitute as well a shadow syndicate, with its own captains and consuls, and a code of secrecy as stern as that of any other enterprise in organized crime. Adramates is the crown chancellor beneath Darius in Babylon; under him, I learn, are four subministers, who oversee a network of several thousand others—tax collectors, magistrates, administrators, and scribes. They are all in league with one another, I am informed, and all as crooked as the highway to hell. The primary functionaries of this underworld are *bagomes*, "soldiers"—that is, the managers appointed by the absentee grandees to oversee their holdings. These syndicate agents are the real power in the country. They serve the king and run circles behind his back. The eunuchs' wealth is not in money (for they are forbidden to own anything beyond their personal effects) but in *arcamas*, "influence." This, of course, is the same as money. Great generals genuflect before them and mighty captains bow at their feet. The eunuchs can turn any man off his land, seize his wife and children, deprive him of wealth, liberty, life. It is in their power to ruin even the sons and brothers of the king. "How did Darius control them?" I ask Pharnaces.

"No one can rule them, sire, not even you, save by wholesale purge—and this you dare not do, or the empire will fall apart in a day."

I ask Pharnaces about civil crime—theft, homicide, felonies of the street. It does not exist, he tells me. "For a man who steals a pear forfeits his right hand, and who speaks ill of his master loses his tongue."

The third night in the city, I instruct the crown chancellor to show me the Mint. Twenty thousand talents lie in store here, a stupefying sum, all in bullion, gold and silver, except four or five thousand in darics and staters. It is not locked up. The only sentinels, beyond the watch Parmenio has set over the precinct, are two scribes, both boys, and a registrar of such antiquity he could not have secured the place against an incursion of gnats. This, one sees, is the East. On the one hand, the produce of the empire is looted routinely by those ministers appointed to watch over it, while on the other, one could park the whole of the king's exchequer in the middle of Procession Street and not a man would help himself to a jot.

When Cyrus the Great conquered Babylonia two hundred years ago, I am instructed, he divided the land into seventeen thousand plots, which he allotted to his victorious officers and soldiers. These tracts were registered either as Bow Land, Horse Land, or Chariot Land. The holder was required to pay taxes in kind each year and turn out for the king's forces one infantryman with shield, armor, and servant from Bow Land; one cavalryman with mount, equipment, and groom from Horse Land; and one charioteer with car, team, and henchman from Chariot Land. Because many of these grant holders were commanded by Cyrus to attend at court, or elected on their own to exploit their holdings either as absentees or nonworking grandees, the day-to-day operations of the land came to be given over to local agents or managers, who contracted to pay the taxes and to remit all profits to the grant holders. These tax farmers formed a *kanesis*, a "syndicate" or "family," and conspired with one another to subvert the power of the Persian nobility while aggrandizing their own. The eunuchs who served the king were privy to these intrigues and acted in concert with them, as it served their interests to enlarge their own power at the expense of the nobles. The result was you had the official tax collectors, those who served the king, operating in collusion with the gangster tax collectors, who conspired against the king, to extract from the conquering nobility the wealth that they and the king had won—and all on the backs of the peasantry.

Now here I am. I too will divide Babylon into royal grants and cede them to my countrymen as rewards for service. What else can I do? Campaign calls me on. I would seek measures to secure justice and pro-mote the well-being of the people. But how can this be managed? In the end I have no choice but to leave affairs exactly as they are, run by ex-actly the same officials. I will do as every conqueror has done before me:

I will take the money and run.

And yet to call the workings of the state corrupt would be a mis-characterization. I pass a memorable night in converse with the queen mother, Sisygambis, who has become a sort of mentor to me. "You do not understand, my son. In the East there exists no objective standard of achievement, no impartial measure by which a man may establish or advance his station. He cannot 'get ahead.' He cannot 'succeed.' It is not like the egalitarianism of your army, Alexander, which provides an unbiased arena, within which a poor man may make his fortune and a rich man prove worthy of his fame. Here no man exists, save in subor-dination to another."

Sisygambis details for me the labyrinthine protocol of power by which one sphere of society imposes its will upon another and is in turn imprisoned by that imposition. "A network of interlocking tyrannies extends from top to bottom and side to side, and in it each man is caught like a fly in a web. Here all a man thinks of is to please his mas-ter. He has no concept of what he himself wishes. Ask him. He cannot tell you. The very concept is beyond his imagination."

This is the East. On the right hand, one beholds opulence beyond imagination; on the left, destitution that beggars description. The long-suffering of the peasantry approaches the holy. Their carriage and bear-ing possess a dignity unmatched even by kings of the West. But it is the dignity of a stone, weathering centuries, not of a man, descended of heaven.

I tell the queen mother that I wish Darius were here now, with us. "For what purpose?" she asks.

"To learn how he governed such a world. And to hear the secrets of his heart upon it."

But the lady only turns aside in sorrow. "My lord, the sovereign of the East is the least free of men. His role is to be the Living Embodiment of all that is great and noble. The grandeur of his estate imbues the lives of his subjects with hope and meaning. Yet he himself is enslaved by his office. My son Darius would not wish to tell you of his life, Alexander, but to inquire, with envy, of yours."

Money. Because all wealth is inducted upward to the king, the people have evolved underground currencies to duck the tax agent. A black economy serves all, which is partly barter, but mostly *achaema*, "trust." This takes the form sometimes of a local tender, which may be marked shards in one part of the city or bullets of lead in another, good only in the immediate neighborhood; but appears more universally as a promise-to-pay guaranteed by a kind of street-corner banker, who is either a member of one of the syndicates that run the city or operates under its protection. A fuller, shall we say, owns a shop making felt. He pays his taxes in kind, but how does he pay wages? Not in coin, for there is no such thing. He pays in chits, which are secured by the *achaemist*, the street-corner exchequer. Who protects the banker? The syndicate, which is shielded by the royal chancellors. The scheme is as complex as a galaxy and as impenetrable as the mind of God. A conqueror passing through barely fazes it. I am sure that in the broad expanse of Babylon, with its four million souls, three-quarters have never heard my name, let alone that of Darius. But the system is far more pernicious for the commons than the conqueror. Yes, a man beats his taxes. But at this cost: the stultification of all original thought and innovation. For each man is immured within his own quarter. He cannot think beyond the street in which he dwells; he has no hope and no ambition. Here is why so great a city can be carried as if its walls were of tissue.

Then there is sex.

In a society where a man's spirit is crushed from birth; where hope is absent, suffering stupefying; where the diet is despair and every man a slave—in such a culture, the individual takes his pleasure when and where he can. Some joys are simple and wholesome. Most are cruel and corrupt.

The vocabulary of depravity is nowhere as encyclopedic as at Babylon. Every imaginable spirit and intoxicant lies to hand, as does every posture of carnality and every instrument of desire; oils, scents, and lubricants, aphrodisiacs, stimulants, asphyxiants, resuscitants. Women and boys are trained in the arts of passion; shops abound, purveying devices of bondage, dominance, and submission, appliances to imprison and immobilize, to inflict pain and to relieve it. They are great love poets, the Assyrians and Babylonians. I can understand this, for in this realm alone are they free. The greatest buildings of the East are not their temples or even their palaces, but their seraglios.

And yet, despite such woe, the place is a vibrant and colorful cosmos. The women are beautiful, the children dark-eyed and full of mischief. Business booms. Water taxis ply the Euphrates, selling fruit and vegetables and carrying lovers and merchants all over town with wonderful swiftness and ease. The gay colors of the riverfront, the raucous bustle of the mercantile mart, the smells of spitted meats and baking bread are nothing if not intoxicating. The great city, sweltering on the plain, lies asweat with sensation and sensuality. It is impossible not to fall in love with the place.

Here is my quandary: I have discovered affection for these slender, dark-eyed Asiatics; it breaks my heart to behold them so wretched and unfree.

Shortly after we enter Babylon, Bucephalus is stricken with sepsis. A wound from Gaugamela becomes infected; the malady advances from its source to his heart with such rapidity (he is nearly eighteen years old) that the physicians tell me he may not last the night. I rush to his side, informing those in whose care he stands that if he dies, they themselves will follow within the hour. The best men in the army are summoned, not only of veterinary but of general medicine; I put out a call to the city at large, offering his weight in gold to that tender, Greek or barbarian, who can preserve Bucephalus's life.

The equestrian world is a small one. Within hours, a messenger arrives from the Persian Tigranes, hero of Issus and Gaugamela. His home academy lies sixty miles up the Tigris at a village called Baghdad; in his service stands Phradates, the empire's master veterinary surgeon. He is on his way, Tigranes' courier declares. A horse-ambulance and a barge follow, to transport Bucephalus. I am struck dumb by this act of compassion from my enemy.

It takes two days to work upriver. Bucephalus cannot stand; his weight must be taken by a belly sling. Phradates does not leave his side, nor do I. I speak softly to my horse and stroke his ears, as I have since I was a boy and he my greatest friend.

The Persians are nothing if not connoisseurs of horseflesh. The barge barely touches dockside at Tigranes' academy before Bucephalus vanishes amid a press of worshipers—grooms and exercise boys, veterinary students, cavalrymen in training—who have been informed of his approach and now crowd about, ecstatic at the apparition of such a specimen, even in his current desperate state. Bucephalus is like me—he thrives on attention. I look in his eyes and feel my breath return. He will recover.

We stay fifteen days as guests in Tigranes' home. The establishment is a riding academy and military school. The grounds are impeccable, with timbered barns, tracks, and lunging rings, but the spirit of the place has been devastated by war and defeat. Two walls of the stadium are hung with the bridles of comrades fallen in action; other horse warriors, crippled in battle, are housed in cottages on the grounds. All are fearful and demoralized.

At once I pledge to reconstitute the place. I have never seen such splendid-looking fellows as the Persian youths in attendance about Tigranes. I call Hephaestion aside. "Here is the answer to the empire!"

I implore Tigranes to serve with me. I wish him to raise a regiment and campaign at my side. But he will not take the field in pursuit of Darius, his king and kinsman; I can have his life, Tigranes declares, but not his service. This confirms me in my opinion that I have found, at last, a breed of noble who can lift the empire from its state of desolation.

Do you know how Phradates cured Bucephalus? By the heavens. The doctor and all physicians of Persia are magi and expert cosmologists. "Stars, like men, are born and die, my lord. But no star comes into being alone. Each has its twin. When one flares or dims, the other alters with it, simultaneously, though they reside a sky apart. You and your horse are like that. Bucephalus suffers, Alexander, because your heart is sick. He is you, this prodigy, and he will not find rest so long as your soul remains untranquil."

At this I break down like a child. I know at once what the physician means. We talk all night, he and I and Tigranes and Hephaestion.

What distresses me so about the East, I declare, is the misery of her people and the supineness with which they endure it. "Is it I who am mad, who cannot bear their woe, or they, who can? Are freedom and aspiration but bubbles upon a timeless sea of suffering? I cannot tell you the state of gloom this has cast me into."

Cannot East and West be yoked, I ask. Can't we of Europe take wisdom from Asia, and she learn liberty from us?

"In hours of consternation," Tigranes says, "I have often found a clue among children and horses. Perhaps your answer, Alexander, resides with these."

I ask what he means.

"Your aim will never succeed with the standing generation. They are too bound up in their ways. But with the rising generation . . ."

I beg him to continue.

"Marry your men to our women, Alexander. Take a Persian bride yourself. You must not make whores of the daughters of Persia, but wives. It will work! In a single generation, the heirs of such unions will compose a freshly minted race, which cannot disown either of its progenitors without disowning itself."

In the meantime, Tigranes urges, I must not pursue Darius as a prize of conquest; rather, tender to him offices of reconciliation and accord. Restore him to his throne and make him my friend and ally. "Do not degrade the noble order of Persia, Alexander, but integrate her champions and commons into your corps-at-arms and from these—Persians and Macedonians alike—appoint men of integrity to administer your empire with justice."

He will raise a regiment of these Descendants, Tigranes pledges. "It will be my honor to assist at the nativity of this New World, and I swear to you, my lord, I can bring to its cause many and noble, whose despair would lift at once at such a prospect."

On the fourteenth day Parmenio arrives from Babylon. Somehow he has learned of my conversations with Tigranes. He conducts me aside like a father. Have I taken leave of my senses? The army of Macedon will not stand me treating Persians as equals. "Depart this site of folly at once, Alexander. Every hour you remain renders those who love you more anguished and distraught."

These are men of the East, Parmenio reminds me, of whom my illustrious tutor Aristotle admonished me:

> Behave to the Greeks like a leader, but to the barbarians like
> a master.

And of whom the Spartan king Agesilaus, who knew them well, declared,

> They make good slaves but poor free men.

"Dismiss this lunacy of interfusion, Alexander! These nobles of Persia, however nimbly they sit their horses, are incapable of self-rule. They are born to the courtier's life; it is all they know, and all they ever will."

How do the Macedonians feel about the Persians? They despise them. They consider them less than women, with their trousers and their lockets of gold, and they conduct themselves toward them with insolence and contempt. Returning to the city, I must issue order and edict, and take it in person down to the level of captain and even sergeant, that these men we have defeated are not dogs; they are not to be beaten, or kicked out of the public way. But idleness and excess of cash have undone the army in other ways.

On the twenty-seventh day I preside over games in honor of the fallen. Passing the Gate of Bel-Marduk in the aftercourse, I find the lane choked with soldiers, among whom I recognize the sergeant Gunnysack, who had made such a haul of treasure after Issus. He and his mates stand on line before a table manned by a street-corner banker, an achaemist.

"What are you doing there, Gunnysack?" I hail, reining-in.

"Standing in line, sire."

I tell him I can see that. "In line for what?"

"Ain't it like the cursed army, sir? Stand in line for chow, stand in line to piss, stand in line to get paid."

I see now that he is waiting to borrow from the achaemist. "Can you be out of money, Sergeant?" I recall to him that bonuses worth three years' wages have been issued just twenty days past.

"Gone, sire. All of it." Gunnysack indicates the banker. "And we're into these blackguards for half that again."

I order the sergeant and his mates to present themselves that evening for an accounting. It seems the whole army assembles, feigning nonchalance, outside my offices.

In the corps of Macedon a squad of eight is called, as I have said, a litter. These fellows are the best of mates; they march together, pack their sarissas together, bunk, eat, and fight together. "And I see you have gone broke together."

"Aye," Gunnysack confesses. His fellows, upon receiving their windfalls, took it upon themselves to "broaden their horizons."

"Spit it out, Sergeant."

"Well, sire, we wanted to see the town. So we needed a translator. You can understand that. And a guide to show us round." The litter had found both in the same fellow, declared Gunnysack, and at quite a reasonable tariff. Then someone to refurbish the outfit, worn out on campaign. So, a tailor, a bootmaker, a haberdasher, to look spruce for the ladies. "Our guide's brother-in-law was a money changer, which we needed to keep from getting fleeced—you see how these bastards are, sire. So he came too, and better still he knew the courtesans' quarter. He showed us the ropes with the flute girls and day-raters. Good girls, just a bit down on their luck. We wanted to help 'em."

In the train of these trollops appear a perfumer, a cosmetician, a hairstylist. A barber for the men, who now look more like senators than sergeants. A bathhouse and bath master. All must dine, so a cook, a cook's boy, baker, wine steward, pastry maker. Now a place to bunk. A villa on the river, a bargain, and it comes with chambermaids, a privy matron, doorman, and night porter. One cannot walk in this heat, so a carriage, and since such cabs cannot be counted upon to appear in some strange quarter at some even stranger hour, Gunnysack and his litter-mates hire the taxi full-time, with its driver and footman and a groom for the horses, who must be fed and stabled as well. Yes, they got robbed. Yes, they got looted. Yes, they bought land and livestock.

"What, no racehorses?"

"Only two, sire!"

Three of the men have gotten married.

"Don't tell me. You're supporting their families."

I cannot stay angry at my brothers and countrymen. But what can I do? I can't award them grants of land; they'll just convert them to cash from the syndicate agents and run through this second fortune as speedily as they've blown the first. The men like it here. They're getting a taste for the easy life. Many even prattle of turning back—to Syria or Egypt, where they can throw their money around, or home, to pitch their yarns and set themselves up as petty lords. I issue a proclamation that duplicate bonuses will be paid to all, drachma for drachma, making up all that our fellows have squandered—but that the paymaster will set up his tables forty miles east down the road.

In other words: We're moving on, mates.

The corps accepts this. They have heard rumors of even greater swag at Susa and Persepolis.

Departing Babylon, I retain Mazaeus in the governorship he held beneath Darius. His treasurer, Bagophanes, I leave in place, beneath a Macedonian controller, and I keep on, as well, the chancellors Pharnaces and Adramates. The city, I garrison with veterans, mercenaries, and those whose military skills no longer fit in with the faster, more mobile corps I intend to employ in the campaigns to come.

The city has come alive with our conquering army. The soldiers' share of Darius's treasure, passed by me to them and run through their hands to the population, has yielded abundance like a mighty silt-bearing river. This hoard of wealth has never seen daylight before; now the country is incandescent with it. Purses have never been so flush or times so gay. So that when, on the thirty-fourth day, our Macedonians pack up and pull out, as relieved as many of the natives are to see the occupying army decamp, so too are they made sad, as a great jolt of vitality goes out of their lives. They line the Royal Road, two million and more, hoarse with citation as the army marches out.

The time ends with another clash between me and my commanders. Day thirty-three: We hold a memorial service, in which I order the ashes of Persian officers interred beneath a mound on the same site as those of the Macedonians. This is greeted with outrage by the corps. That night, our last in the city, I throw a feast for my officers in Darius's great Banquet Hall, the one with the map of the empire on its marble and malachite floor.

What infuriates my comrades is this: When eunuchs bar my door, and mates who have fought at my side across two continents must cool their heels and wait attendance. Black Cleitus cannot endure the sight of me in converse with Tigranes or Mazaeus or any Persian, and this night, drunk on date-palm wine, he stalks to the center of the room and explodes. "Will barbarians gain access to you before ourselves, Alexander? For I swear by the black breath of hell, I will not stand to see these trouser-wearing dandies pass through your door while I am held out."

I stride forward, offering my hand. "Cleitus, my friend. That right arm of yours preserved my life at the Granicus River. Can I forget that?"

He evades my embrace, his glance shooting to others, seeking support. Clearly no few would give it, absent fear of me.

"This is the East, Alexander. Its men are slaves and always have been. You wish to understand them? The thickest sergeant can make it plain. The place is corrupt! Each man steals from the man beneath him and pays off the man above. Treasure flows uphill to the king and each hand dips in the river as it passes by. That's how it works. You will not change it. By Zeus, I would rather be a dog than one of these serfs or landsmen. And while you endeavor to turn these bootlickers into free men, passing your days sequestered with your purple-mantled servitors, those who love you and have shed their blood at your side go neglected. We are soldiers, Alexander, not courtiers. Let us be soldiers!"

I am not angry. Fury has not seized me. Yet I perceive in this moment the gravest peril to the expedition since it marched forth from Europe. I glance to Hephaestion. He sees it too, and Craterus and Telamon at his shoulder.

"Soldiers are you? On the trek to Gaugamela," I remind my officers, "your men were so stricken with dread, and such prey to mindless panic, that they crowded about me like children in the dark. Yet now in possession of victory, they—and you—grow insolent." I turn back to my accuser, who stands atop the mosaic site designating Babylon. "Have you conquered this city, Cleitus, or has it conquered you?"

He shifts, shamefaced. He knows I know, as does all the army, of his liaison with a courtesan of the palace, and of the fortune he has torn through in days, bewitched by her.

"I will tell you what I think, my impertinent friend. I think that license and fornication have robbed you of your wits. Yes, you. All of you! For you who call yourselves soldiers have forgotten the foundations of our calling. Obedience and respect! Am I your king? Will you obey me? Or have sudden riches—which have come to you by my hand—turned you brazen and insubordinate? Do you doubt my vision, brothers? Have I lost your trust?"

The hall has gone stone-silent. My tread resounds as I stalk to the mosaic's eastern end: Greece and Macedon.

"When we set out from home, not four years past, how many of you dreamed that we would conquer even this far?"

I cross the Hellespont, indicating Troy and the northern Aegean.

"Yet we won here." At the Granicus. "And here and here and here." I stride down the coast, past Miletus and Halicarnassus to Issus. "Here, you would have turned back." Tyre and Gaza. "Here you were satisfied to remain." Egypt. "Here you counseled me to advance no farther." Syria. "Do I say false? Speak up! Let him stand forward who dares refute me!"

No one breathes. Not a man budges.

I dislodge Cleitus from the mosaic site representing Babylon.

"Now we stand here—beyond our most daring dreams—and lay designs to march even farther. To here . . ." Susa. "Here." Persepolis. "And here." Ecbatana. "Is that your aim, soldiers—if so you call yourselves? Then answer: Who will lead you?"

I draw up.

"Name him! Name your man and I shall step aside. Let this new general direct your affairs, since you find my counsel unworthy."

My glare scours the ring. Chastened countenances greet me. Not a man will meet my eye.

"Will you heed me then? Dare I call myself your king? For you may as well know now—there can be no better time to tell you—that I have no intention of halting here, halfway across this floor."

I stride past Persia and Media. To Parthia, Bactria, Areia. The high plateau of Iran and the kingdoms of Afghanistan.

"Will you conquer these lands with me, brothers? Or, sated with riches, will you bed down partway and give yourselves over to whoring and gluttony?"

Murmurs of "No!" and "Never!"

I pull back. One can scourge good men only so much.

"My friends, I know I have pressed novelty too suddenly upon you. I have tried your patience. Let me beg you then, by all the good things that my counsel has brought you so far. Bear with me. Trust me, as you have always. For when we cross beyond Persia, into lands no Greek has known . . ."

I step past the Afghan kingdoms, to the Hindu Kush and India.

". . . we will need all the good men we can get. And prepare your minds further, my friends. For from these lands we bring into subjection, I shall draw more foreign troops, and they will fight at my shoulder and at yours. It must be so. How can we work it otherwise?"

For the first time I sense the men turning toward me. They understand, or begin to. And those who don't, trust my vision and my call.

"Do you imagine, friends, that we can overturn the order of the earth without altering, ourselves? The world is new, and we will make it newer. Who will follow me? Who believes? Let he who loves me clasp my hand now and pledge his allegiance. For such dreams as I hold cannot embrace the timorous or the faint of heart."

I step to India and beyond, crossing so far that I stand, at the end, in the shadows, where the lanterns of the hall barely cast their gleam: to the Shore of Ocean at the Ends of the Earth.

"Declare yourselves now, brothers, and evermore stand by your vow. If you are with me, you are with me all the way."

As one man, the hall rises. "Alexander!" my officers cry. And again: "Alexander! Alexander!"

Twenty-Eight

MONSTERS OF THE DEEP

TWENTY DAYS TAKE US TO SUSA. Here Darius's hoard is fifty thousand talents, twelve hundred tons of gold and silver—so much that we cannot carry it with us. Another forty days of fighting and forced passages bear us within striking distance of Persepolis. We are in Persia proper now. The homeland. Darius has fled north to Ecbatana, though his satrap Ariobarzanes tries on his own to strip the capital. We beat him by covering eighty miles in two days and a night. At Persepolis the king's treasury holds 120,000 talents of gold. Packing only part of this haul to Ecbatana takes five thousand camels and ten thousand pairs of asses. The train is seventeen miles long. It is wealth on such a scale that no one even thinks to steal it. Men sit round cook fires, perched on ingots of silver. They mount their horses, stepping off bags of gold.

It is nine months since Gaugamela. The army is barely recognizable. Our reinforcements have at last caught up, fifteen thousand horse and foot; already half have been corrupted by the excess they behold on every hand. At Persepolis, it seems, half the world has come out to us. Actors and acrobats have arrived from Athens; we have chefs from

Miletus and hairdressers from Halicarnassus; saddlers and tailors have flocked in from Syria and Egypt, along with dancers and jugglers, star-readers and omen-diviners; day girls and flute girls and evening girls. Our pimps, Ptolemy observes, are more numerous than our cavalry. Every day fresh caravans arrive. What had been an army has become an industry. Every veteran, it seems, packs a bride or mistress and half her kin. My father barred wagons in his army. In mine, sergeants and even corporals truck their goods. Philip permitted one servant for ten men; in my corps, the former outnumber the latter. We wear our wealth and ride it. Philotas's string of ponies would mount a squadron in my father's army; his stock of boots would shoe a division. In Persepolis he finds a man with hair exactly like his own; he hires the fellow on, just to grow fresh tresses (the men call him "the hair farm"), which Philotas has his hairdresser (yes, he packs one too) work into crowns to fill out his own thinning thatch.

I abhor such unsoldierliness, but I have gone as slack myself. Since Damascus I have taken Memnon's widow Barsine to my bed. This at Parmenio's suggestion, to keep me from Darius's harem. But his scheme has prospered too well. I have come to care for the woman and to depend upon her offices. Barsine protects me. If not for her, petitioners and grievance-pleaders would devour every minute of my day. She bars my door and lets me work. She will not permit me to drink to excess, as is my weakness, and she stands sentry over my table.

For her birthday I throw a feast. An entertainment is staged. Acrobats armed with swords (real ones, whose edges they demonstrate by dicing juggled quinces) perform a pantomime of Persia's conquest. The stunt is meant to flatter the Macedonians but, when it concludes, Tigranes, who has become a dear friend, rises, insulted. He blames Barsine for this shameless sycophancy. To the astonishment of all, Parmenio stands.

"What is your complaint, Persian?" he demands of Tigranes. "You have won the war, not us!"

I have never seen Parmenio so stinking or so animated by woe. The chamber, which is vast, falls silent. Parmenio addresses me.

"Yes, we have lost!" he declares. "We broke these Persians in the field, but they have outsmarted us in the palace. See what we wear and eat, the retinues that attend us! You have not vanquished Darius, Alexander, but become him. And as for these mentors of yours, these spider women whom I have installed with my own hands, more fool I!"

Voices seek to cry him down, fearful of my anger. "Now you will tell me," I say, "that my father would never have conducted himself in this manner."

"As he would not."

"I am not my father!"

"Yes," replies Parmenio, "we see that plain."

Another time such insolence would have set my hand seeking a sword. But this night I feel only despair.

Hephaestion defends me. "Indeed," he testifies, "Alexander is not Philip. For Philip never faced challenges on such a scale, or even dreamt of their existence! If Philip led us, we would still be in Egypt, given over to intemperance and vice—"

"And what are we now?" demands Parmenio.

"—instead of seeking to remake the world into something bold and new!"

Parmenio laughs in Hephaestion's face. The old general is past seventy. He has already given one son, Hector, to the expedition and will lose another, Nicanor, before two months are out. His flesh bears twenty wounds of honor. He remembers me as an infant, and my father as the friend of his youth, with whom he dreamed—of what? Not this, that is certain.

He addresses Hephaestion. "I cannot sleep in this bed"—meaning the bed of access to my person—"not with you in it."

My mate rises in fury. "What does that mean, you son of a whore?"

Philotas leaps to his father's defense. He's so sock-eyed, he nearly pitches onto his teeth. The Guardians, foremost Love Locks, seize him and hold him up.

"Gentlemen! Is this the synod of philosophers?"

Laughter disarms the uproar. Pages dash, each to a man, bearing cool cloths and cut wine. When the tumult subsides, Hephaestion stands to his feet. Never have I been prouder of him than in this hour, to see him serve back patience for affront and return generosity for rancor.

"Brothers," he says, "when men strive together in hardship for a great prize, they willingly suppress individual vanity while the issue remains in suspense. But when the end has been achieved, each wants his share of the bounty. Now is the most dangerous time for us. Suddenly we are all lords and grandees. Each man judges his contributions greater than his fellows' and sulks, beholding others reap that acclaim he believes belongs rightly to himself. What has happened to us, my friends? By Zeus, when we were bleeding and dying in the field, what would we not have given to find ourselves dining on pillows with the good things of the earth spread before us? Yet now we are safe and rich, we wrangle like barn cats!

"Have we become severed from our virtue? Not yet, I think. But we live now on a scale beyond that which any man has known, save kings of Persia, and we have no choice but to rise to it. We are like the snake that swallowed the elephant. We have won this prize, so great we choke upon it. It overwhelms us, even as we claim it as our own."

Hephaestion calls upon the gods for aid and summons us, his life-long mates, to common purpose.

"My friends, let us here and now renew our commitment to one another and to our king, and pledge by our most holy bond to maintain ourselves, in the face of fortune as well as adversity, as the band of brothers we have been all our lives. Will you take this oath with me, comrades? For we here are like mariners adrift in a sea, the sea of success, and no act commands our performance more than to clasp hands, that we not glide apart from one another. For in this sea swim monsters who, beneath the surface, would chew us off at the knees."

Our mates rally to Hephaestion's call; the crisis passes. We reach Ecbatana at midsummer. Darius has fled, just days before, into the eastern empire. His final guard is thirty thousand foot, including four thousand Greeks, Patron's men who got away from Gaugamela, with five thousand archers and slingers and thirty-three hundred Bactrian horse under Bessus and Nabarzanes. A third of Asia still belongs to the king, with enough men and horses to field an army as great as any we have faced.

This is not what I fear.

Darius is finished. What strikes me with dread is that his own men will turn upon him before I can catch up and save his life.

In Ecbatana a letter has been left for me by the king. His chamberlain, whom I maintain with my suite, authenticates it as dictated beneath its author's own seal.

Alexander from Darius, greetings,

I write to you man-to-man, omitting all royal title and address. Know that you have my everlasting gratitude for your restraint toward, and care of, my queen and family. If your purpose has been, by your actions as a man, to show yourself worthy of your fame as a conqueror, you have done so. I salute you. And now, my friend, if I may presume so to address you (for I cannot but feel from our long history as antagonists as well as from the burdens we share of kingly station that we understand each other, perhaps, as no two others on earth), I beg you this favor. Do not take me captive. When we meet again on the field of battle, grant me death with honor. Do not consign me, either by your charity to spare my life or by your knightly munificence to restore me to my throne, to an existence shorn of honor. Raise my son as your own. To your care I entrust my dear ones. I know you will behave toward them as if they were your own.

My heart is touched by Darius's candor and nobility. Despite his professions, I wish more than ever to preserve his life, not only as a king but as a man. I mount a fast, strong force of Companions, Lancers, and mercenary horse, with the archers, Agrianes, and all of the phalanx not left behind to guard the treasury. The column presses east at a killing pace. We are in Hyrcania now, in the corridor between the Parthian desert and the Caspian Sea.

Weather is wild and thick with portents. Eagles and ravens abound;

Fate's hand feels close above us. Thunderheads build up each day after noon. Great bolts cleave the heavens; downpours drench the column. The foe's trail, prominent as a thoroughfare in the morning, is washed out to nothing by day's close. We smell the end of empire.

On the sixth dawn a messenger arrives from Patron, the Greek captain who remains, to his credit, loyal to Darius. The king's generals make ready to betray him, Patron reports; he pleads with me to spare no exertion in pursuit, and offers his courier as guide and escort. He himself stays with Darius to protect him from his own men, he declares, but he cannot preserve the king forever without aid.

We press on at top speed, reaching the town of Rhagae, a day's march from the Caspian Gates, on the eleventh day. The main of the phalanx can't keep up; even cavalry mounts are dropping from the pace. Deserters from Darius are coming over to us now by the hundreds; others make away on their own, the fugitives report, scattering to their homes and villages.

I rest the corps five days, then resume the pursuit. The country is desert on the far side of the Caspian Gates. At a village called Ashana, we capture Darius's interpreter, left behind because he was ill, and from him learn that the king has been disarmed and taken into custody by Bessus and Nabarzanes. Bessus, who commanded Darius's left at Gaugamela, is governor of Bactria, the country toward which the fugitives now flee. All the king's cavalry belong to him; he is master of the fleeing division in fact, if not in name.

I strip our party to only the Companions, Lancers, and the youngest and strongest of the infantry, leaving Craterus in command of the troops left behind. We take our arms only and two days' rations. A fast night march brings us, next noon, to a village called Tiri. Two of Patron's men are there, left behind with wounds. The Greeks, they tell us, have bolted for the mountains, fearing their own massacre at Bessus's and Nabarzanes' hands. Darius is alone, without defenders.

How far ahead?

Sixty miles.

It takes all day and a night to cross forty, by a waterless track, so rugged is the country and so close to collapse our stock. Regaining the main trace, our scouts discover, discarded, an eagle standard, bossed in gold, with wings outspread.

Darius's battle ensign.

We rest till night's cool in a village so poor it doesn't have a name. Darius has overnighted here the evening before. As we make a meal from whatever we can find, a party emerges from their hiding place in a mud hut. Mazaeus's son, Antibelus, and Bagistanes, a Babylonian nobleman, in flight from the fugitive corps. From them we learn that Darius is still alive, twenty-five miles ahead, being carted in a closed wagon under arrest.

I strip the party even further, mounting the youngest and lightest on the last horses still fit for speed. Midmorning we spy the renegades, five miles ahead. At sight of us, the column breaks apart and flees.

Twenty-Nine

THE END OF KINGS

W E FIND DARIUS'S BODY IN A DITCH, three furlongs off the main road. His belly has been pierced, more than once, and in such a manner as would indicate his arms were held or bound. These wounds did not kill him in the instant. He suffered before he died. Telamon bends now to set in order the king's cloak, which has been wrenched askew, and to turn his corpse into a posture less wanting in dignity.

"Whoever slew him," observes the Arcadian, "at least had the decency to do it from the front."

"Yes," adds Hephaestion, "but they didn't have the guts to finish the job."

I am sick with grief at this treachery and mad with fury at this waste. I remove my cloak and set it over the body. Kill the King is the game, I know, but I would have given anything to see it end other than like this. Darius's royal tiara is missing, suggesting that his murderer has added the name of pretender to that of regicide. The wreck of the carriage that bore the king sprawls in a trench beside the track.

"They had him chained." Hephaestion indicates a shackle on the rail. "The axle must have split on the climb up this hill. Here at the summit, Bessus must have given him a horse to ride. They commanded the king to do something, and he refused."

"What?" asks Telamon. "Hand over the crown?"

"That, his betrayers had already taken. Perhaps just to keep running."

We have gawked enough. It is unseemly. I order the body bathed and wrapped; we will bear it to the queen mother, for burial at Persepolis in the Tomb of Kings. I read the question in the sergeants' eyes. "Carry him on a litter," I say, "swathed in my cloak. Treat his remains as you would my own."

Reunited with the army at Hecatompylus, I am seized with a melancholy beyond any I have known. The next challenge, clearly, will be reframing for the corps the object of the expedition. Darius dead, they'll believe the chore over. They'll want to go home. I can forestall unrest temporarily by pursuit of Bessus, who will doubtless back his pretense to the throne by raising another army farther east. But beyond that, what? How?

Still, my despair is past this. I beg the company's indulgence; I ask to be left alone, save Hephaestion, Craterus, and Telamon.

In my quarters with them, I am too stricken to speak, even to drink. I read apprehension in my friends' eyes. They fear for my state of mind. Each tries by turns to put words to my despondency, as if by defining and articulating it, they can free me from its grip.

"It's a terrible thing, the death of a king," offers Craterus. "A world ends."

Telamon: "One realizes he's just a man. He bleeds like us, and dies like us."

"And if one is a king himself," Hephaestion adds, "he cannot help but read in his fellow monarch's end his own."

No. That's not it.

My mate continues. "For one of your noble temperament, Alexander, the evil here may be not so much the fact of Darius's death as the way he met it. Murdered by his own men, in chains, on the run."

He notes further that had we taken Darius alive, the continuity of the empire could more easily have been maintained; the king could have performed such rituals and offices as would be unbecoming, enacted by a Macedonian. His perpetuation, as titular lord of Persia beneath my sway, would have taken the pressure off me and off the army.

"We have lost our enemy," Craterus assays. "The object of our exertions is gone—and we have nothing to set in his place."

A silence succeeds.

"Success," says Telamon, "is the weightiest burden of all. We are victors now. All our dreams have come true."

"That too is a death," Hephaestion agrees. "Perhaps the sternest of all."

The night trails and wanes.

"Forgive me, my friends," I say, breaking the silence at last. "Go to your rest. I am all right."

It takes minutes to convince them, and minutes more to get them out the door. When I crack the portal, I glimpse thousands, banked about the building in alarm for my state.

I catch Hephaestion's arm.

"It's him," I say. "Just that."

"I don't understand."

"Darius. I wanted to talk to him. To hear his views. He is the only man, do you see, who has occupied the pinnacle on which I now must stand."

My mate searches my eyes. Am I truly well?

"I wanted so much," I say, "to make him my friend."

Thirty

PAGES

A YEAR PASSES. Our arms continue all-victorious. Half again as much territory has been brought into subjection since Gaugamela as in all the prior campaigns. But the glory has gone out of it. The glory and the legitimacy.

I have felt it for months in my own tent, among the Royal Pages. With Darius's death, the object of our expedition has been accomplished. We have plundered Persia's capital and razed her palace, symbol of crimes committed against Greece and Macedon in the past. It is over. The king is dead.

Our force pursues the pretender Bessus now; he wears the royal tiara and calls himself Lord of Asia. We have entered the Afghan kingdoms. Half my original corps has been released with honor. Our superb Thessalian cavalry: All eight squadrons have been sent home with fortunes. Seven thousand Macedonian infantry have taken their bonuses and discharges. League allies and many of the mercenaries have been told off as well, with more treasure than they can carry. Their places are taken by volunteers of their own units, electing to stay on for pay, and by new arrivals from home and from Asia Minor. The autumn after

Darius's death, three thousand Lydian cavalry and infantry join us; in winter we pick up another thousand Syrian horse and eight thousand foot from Syria and Lycia. Eager volunteers pour in from Greece and Macedon. Why not? I've got all the money in the world. At Zadracarta in Hyrcania, the regiment trained by Tigranes comes out to us; for the first time the corps has a unit entirely Persian. We have Egyptian lancers now, and Bactrian, Parthian, and Hyrcanian cavalry. Noble Persians, abhorring the usurper Bessus, make their tokens and come in. I welcome the mercenary Patron and his fifteen hundred professionals formerly in Darius's service. The army brims with new faces and new corps-at-arms. We need them, chasing Bessus across these deserts and mountains.

The administrative staff of the empire as I now reconstitute it is nine-tenths Persian (who else can run so vast and alien an enterprise?), including Artabazus, Barsine's father (whom I first knew as a boy at Pella, when he took refuge with Memnon at my father's court), and the noble Autophradates, both of whom, having fought for Darius with ex-ceptional loyalty, have come in and been appointed by me to governors' posts. And I have attached to my School of Pages a number of youths of the Persian nobility, including Artabazus's son Cophen, two of Tigranes' lads, and three of Mazaeus's. In all, eleven of forty-nine. Another seven are Egyptian, Syrian, Median. I am not so blind as not to reckon the uproar this must incite, but, I confess, I overestimate my capacity to contain it.

What has happened is this. For each foreign Page I take on, I must exclude a Macedonian. This produces disgruntlement at home, as each spurned family takes its son's rejection as an affront to honor, and in camp, as my countrymen perceive me to favor aliens. Further, Pages take lovers. This is a fact of life. These lads, thirteen and fourteen when they come out from Macedon, are readily seduced by high-ranking offi-cers ten and twenty years their senior. Sex is the least of it. Politics is all. Pages arrive from home already acquainted with the officers who will become their mentors; this is often not only known to the lads' fa-thers but encouraged and even insisted upon by them. Such bonds yoke families. Thus boys acquire champions for their careers; as Cleitus was lover to Philip when he was a Page (which in no small measure contributed to his subsequent appointment as commander of the Royal Squadron), so he now takes a Page named Angelides as his protégé. Each Page gives his mentor a seat, so to say, within my tent.

All is well, as long as I include only Macedonians. The introduction of foreigners overturns the cart. Macedonian officers refuse to take these outlanders under their care (as the boys themselves are terrified of the Macedonians). Worse are the consequences of perceived preferential treatment. Let me show favor to a son of Tigranes; Cleitus and every other homegrown now fear their own lads have been disesteemed, and they bear this hard.

Money magnifies all ills. It is one thing to succeed, and another to succeed on the scale that we have. The fault is mine. I have failed to produce a vision for the army grand enough to replace the one lost with the death of Darius. And in pursuing the object of Persian-Macedonian amity, I have gone too far, in Macedonian eyes, in adopting customs and fashions of the foe.

To make up for this, I load my countrymen with riches. Aretes' valor at Gaugamela I reward with five hundred talents; the fortune I bestow upon Menidas would dwarf the treasury of Agamemnon. Installing Parmenio as governor at Ecbatana, I give him a bed of gold. To my mother at home I send galleys of frankincense and carnelian, cinnamon and cassia. She chides me by return post.

Alexander from Olympias, greetings.

My son, your largesse has made petty kings out of once-exemplary officers. Your gifts to your friends, however well intentioned, produce consequences that cannot help you. You are corrupting them. For now each fancies himself a lord, and his kin at home put on airs and exalt their expectations. Each general you so favor exaggerates his contributions to your victories and believes himself not only indispensable but also slighted and passed over when you honor others before him. Their skins grow thin. They pout and sulk. And their wives and kin at home aggravate this by their correspondence. The more you give, my son, the more you enflame their ambition. Ptolemy wants Egypt; Seleucus covets Babylon.

Who are these dwarves to indulge such fancies, who would be nothing without you?

From the same letter:

> *When they were starving, your officers were a corps of comrades. But now each has grown touchy and quick to take insult. They are no longer mates, but rivals. You give them so much money, you make them independent of you. Give them land, my son, or women or horses. Grant them provinces, but don't give them gold. Gold buys adherents; it turns good men arrogant and bad men ungovernable.*

I have enemies now within my own tent. Those whose charge it is to serve and protect me become spies with interests divergent from my own. It is not the Pages who hatch plots, but my own officers, as long-dormant rivalries reemerge, and each, in fear of the others, schemes to strike and preempt.

> *I know your heart, my son. It is too kind. The love you bear toward your mates blinds you to their capacity for perfidy. Success has made each jealous of his place and each fearful of the other's depredations. Your tent has become a royal court, like it or not, and your warriors flatterers and sycophants.*

One night in the Afghan kingdoms a Royal Page, in great agitation, breaks in upon me in my bath. A plot has been hatched against my life, the lad declares. His mate has reported this to Philotas some days past, expecting Philotas to carry the account to me at once. Philotas has not.

I convene the council of Macedones. Philotas is brought in, bound. His father Parmenio is six hundred miles west, in command of the treasury at Ecbatana. I command Philotas to offer his defense. The plot, he says, was too trivial to report. A joke. He did not take it seriously.

"Thou villain!" roars Craterus. "You dare play dense before the king!"

Fourteen Pages are interrogated. Nine have mentors, officers of the Companions and the Royal Guard; every boy comes from a princely family back home. They all lie through their teeth.

"Torture them," says Ptolemy. "As we would an enemy at war."

All night I meet with my core commanders, Hephaestion and Craterus, Ptolemy, Perdiccas, Coenus, Seleucus, with Eumenes, Telamon, and Love Locks. "I will not," I declare, "try these boys on the wheel."

"Then pack them home," enjoins Perdiccas. Disgrace will finish them, he means, as surely as execution.

I am in despair at the fact of treachery. "By Zeus, I wish we had never won this war! I would rather have taken a spear in the guts than live to see those I love plot against my life!"

I dread too the discovery of Philotas's guilt. "What will you do," Hephaestion asks, "about Parmenio?"

I cannot execute the son and let the father live. No king can.

And Parmenio has power. I have made him governor of Media; he commands at Ecbatana now, with twenty thousand troops, many of whom revere him, and the royal treasury, 180,000 talents.

I order Philotas racked. He cracks with the first bone. Seven are implicated. The council deliberates less than twenty minutes. All will be put to death.

What will I do about Parmenio?

Thirty-One

THE AGONY OF RULE

A LL DAY AND NIGHT SUCCEEDING THE TORTURE of Philotas, I confer with my generals in my headquarters at Phrada. Hephaestion:
true as the sun. Craterus: more mine than his own. Telamon: loyal to his
own code, but a code that sanctions no treachery. Perdiccas loves the
king; Coenus, Ptolemy, Seleucus the commander. Cleitus burns so hot,
he can blurt nothing but the truth. Beyond these, and Eumenes and
Peucestas, I trust no one.

"No man speaks the truth to a king." The hour is late and I am
drunk. "And the greater the king, the less the candor. Who dares utter,
'You err, sire'? This was always our strength, we of Macedon. Our
tongues were rough but true. A man rose before Philip and spoke his
mind. My friends, you have done so, always, with me. No longer.

"What do the men say of me? I need not hear to know. 'Alexander
has changed. Conquest has corrupted him. He is not the man we loved.'
Why? Because I lead them from triumph to triumph? Because I deliver
the wide world into their arms? Because I lade them with treasure and
send them home propped on pillows?"

I am ranting. I see it in my mates' eyes. Ptolemy is the keenest of my marshals. "Alexander, may I state the peril as I see it?"

"Please do."

I have been pacing. I take my seat.

"And, brothers"—Ptolemy turns to his fellow generals—"call me to book if I speak false, but second me if I tell true."

He turns to me.

"My friend, each of us fears you now."

I am struck, as by a blow.

"It is true, Alexander. Believe it. Every officer feels the same."

I scan my comrades' faces. "But how, my friends? Why?"

"We fear you—and one another. For now it seems you, who were once our mate and comrade, have ascended to the firmament. We dreamt as brothers all our lives to unseat the Lord of Asia. Now you have become him."

"But I am not, Ptolemy. I am who I was."

"No! How can you be?" His gesture takes in the chamber in which we convene. It has been Darius's. "By the gods, look at this place! The pillars are cedar; the vault is ivory."

"But it is still us beneath."

"No, Alexander." I see it takes all his courage to continue. "I speak with candor, hazarding your displeasure. What if you take my words ill? Tomorrow you seize my corps and give it to Seleucus. . . ."

"Can you believe me capable of such inconstancy?"

The room falls silent.

Philotas.

My countrymen are thinking of our former mate, in chains, awaiting execution. And more. His kin and comrades throughout the army: Amyntas Andromenes and his brothers Simmias, Attalus, Polemon; my own bodyguard Demetrius; thirty captains; a hundred lieutenants. Must I take all their lives? And that of Philotas's father, Parmenio, as well?

Perdiccas speaks. Next to Craterus, he is my toughest general.

"Alexander, we confer as brothers here. No blame obtains. We seek solutions. Ptolemy spoke; I envied his courage." A moment, then: "The men say this of you: that you believe yourself a god. . . ."

I make to protest. Perdiccas's urgency overrides me.

"I dismiss this," he says. "We all do. But here is the point, Alexander, and it is freighted with even graver peril: In the truest sense, you *have* become a god. You have wrought that which no man believed or even dreamed." He indicates his fellow generals. "Each of us owns pride, each knows his gifts, each believes himself capable of greatness. Yet all concur: No one could have achieved what you have. Not your father. Not one of us; not all of us together. Not any man, or men, who ever lived. Only you could have done it." He meets my eye. "We fear you, Alexander. We love and fear you, and know no longer how to act before you."

"Perdiccas," I say, "you break my heart."

"And this is not the keenest woe. That is, our fear makes us conspire. We cannot help it. I speak to Ptolemy apart. 'If they come for my head, will you take my cause?' We ask one another, Shall we act preemptively? Must we strike, before another strikes us?'"

My vision blurs. Tears sheet. "Gladly would I have perished before hearing such words."

"They are true," Craterus confirms. "We are in hell."

Once, when I was a boy, I broke in upon my father in his study as he composed a letter. His Pages sought to chase me, but Philip overrode them and called me in to his side. When he had finished writing, he handed me the roll to read. It was addressed to a certain ally and was to be delivered by one of the princes of Philip's court; beneath the valediction were these instructions: "Kill the man who brings this letter."

When I had read and absorbed this, Philip, who had risen and begun dressing for the evening's entertainment, gave me to know that he would soon be going downstairs to meet that very man, whose end this letter commanded, as well as the man's father and brother. I was appalled and asked how he would act toward the man. "I will laugh and drink with him," Philip declared, "and make him believe we are the best of mates."

Parmenio chanced to enter then, fitted out for the evening's ball. He alone of my father's generals eschewed dress armor, the lightweight stuff, for banquets and such; no matter how unmilitary the occasion, he always wore field plate. I admired him for this. He crossed now to my father; the pair embraced: I felt the love and respect between them. Then Parmenio saw that I held the letter. Clearly he was aware of its contents and reckoned now that Philip had opened it to me. He stepped before me. "Alexander," he said, and nothing more. It was an acknowledgment, I felt, of a kind of passage.

Ten years later, when Philip was assassinated and I acceded to the throne, I dispatched such a letter to Parmenio, instructing him to take into custody and put to death his son-in-law Attalus for complicity. He did.

Ten more years have passed. This time I write to Parmenio different letters, dispatching them on racing camels (to beat the news of Philotas's execution), borne by mates dear to him, so as not to excite his suspicions. While he reads these letters, his friends, at my orders, will take his life.

"To be royal," Sisygambis has said, "is to tread barefoot upon the razor's edge."

Thirty-Two

BADLANDS

THE LANGUAGE OF AFGHANISTAN IS DARI. Dari and five thousand others. Every tribe has its own tongue, and each is indecipherable alongside every other. But then you know this, Itanes. This is your country; it is here I fought your father and married your sister.

Why are we in Afghanistan? Because it commands the track to India and the Shore of Ocean. Because its warlords must be subdued before I take the army over the Hindu Kush to the Indus and the Punjab.

Examine the daybooks for this period. You will see that the corps fought for almost three years across Areia, Parthia, Drangiana, Bactria, Arachosia, and Sogdiana and could not force a single pitched battle. It was all sieges and unconventional warfare, against native fighters the troops called "wolf warriors." (Bessus had been surrendered to us by then and turned over to the Persians for their justice.) These were steppe raiders and hill tribesmen, the former mounting at one time as many as thirty thousand, the latter thrice that number, who fought both as armies and as clans. Their commander, when they had one, was the last Persian lord, Spitamenes, whom our men came to call the Grey Wolf, for the streak in his beard and his elusiveness over that stony and barren ground.

One cannot engage guerrilla forces with conventional ones. A new order must be evolved. Anticipating this after Gaugamela, I reorganized the army, making it lighter and more mobile. I chopped four feet off the sarissas. Each man dumped twenty pounds of kit. Helmets became light caps; armor we dispensed with entirely. Of cavalry, I doubled the number of Companions, integrating the Lancers and Paeonians and the best of the Persian and foreign horse. I wanted units that were fast and flexible, that could live off the land and operate independently in hostile country.

Tactics too had to adjust. Against the civilized foe, a commander has strategic targets he may seize or destroy, such as cities or supply depots, bridges or roads, the loss of which produces suffering in the foe and renders him tractable to accommodation. Against wild tribes this avails nothing. They own no property. They have nothing to lose. Indeed they care nothing even for their persons or their lives. To say one fights guerrillas is inexact. One hunts them, as he would jackals or wild boars, and he can permit himself to feel pity for them no more than for savage beasts. The tribesmen of Afghanistan were the fiercest fighters I ever faced, and their general, the Grey Wolf, the only adversary I ever feared.

The wolf warriors' religion is fatalism. They worship freedom and death. The language they understand is terror. To prevail, one must be more terrible than they. This takes some going, as these clansmen, like all rude and insular races, perceive each person outside their blood sphere not as a human being but as a beast or devil. You cannot negotiate with such foes; they are proof against all blandishment or subornation and are animated by warrior pride alone. They would rather die than submit. They are vain, greedy, cunning, vicious, mean, cowardly, gallant, generous, stubborn, and corrupt. They are capable of endurance beyond all human measure and can bear such suffering, of both flesh and spirit, as would break a block of stone.

Pursuit is the essence of wolf warfare, by which I mean pursuit until the last enemy is cornered and slain. One fights wild tribesmen best in winter. That's when the snow drives them down out of the mountains. With our reconfigured forces, we sought to go this one better. We went up after them. To defeat wolf warriors, one denies them sanctuary. When you take a village, raze it. Overhauling the foe, kill him to the last man. Leave no one. Put to death or deport the entire population. It accomplishes nothing to drive the men off; they'll just come back. Pacts or treaties? Forget them. The tribesman owns no compunction. What honor he knows is confined strictly to his own kind; to you, he cannot breathe without perjuring himself. Every oath is a sham, every promise a hoax. I have sat in tribal parleys a hundred times; if the truth was ever spoken, I never heard it.

And yet, despite their treacherousness and duplicity, one could not help but admire these fellows. I came, myself, to love them. They reminded me of our wild highlanders back home. Their women were proud and beautiful, their children bright and fearless; they knew how to laugh and how to be happy. In the end I could not tame them, so I married them. I wed your sister, the princess Roxanne, and paid your father Oxyartes more for the privilege than I hope you ever learn. It was the kind of stunt my own father would have approved of. And it has worked.

As for Spitamenes, at the finish I beat him with money. The free cavalry of Afghanistan—Parthians, Areians, Bactrians, Drangians, Arachosians, Sogdians, Daans, Massagetae—cared nothing for whom they worked. After twenty-odd months of chasing the Grey Wolf into dead ends and onto blind spurs, I saw wisdom and called up the cash. You never saw foes turn into friends so fast. Within days we had pacified four thousand square miles. I simply bought the country. If Spitamenes had had deeper coffers, he might have bested me. I could not outfight him, but I outspent him.

The Afghan will fight for money, but he won't work for it. To ask is an insult. Here is how we got round it. Say we wished to transport a hundred wine jars to Kabul. We learned to ask for *ghinnouse*, "a favor"— and to let the natives themselves turn it into work. One approaches the chief. "Would you please, as a favor to me, transport with your pack train this lamp when you trek to Kabul?" "Of course," replies the fellow, "it would be my pleasure." Then when he shows up, you have your wine jars waiting. "Hmm," observes the chief, "would you like us to take these wine jars to Kabul with this lamp?" Since no one has offered pay and no one has accepted, no one is offended. One is free to "defray expenses" by a cash contribution.

After I married into your family, I had my engineers labor an entire summer building roads into the highlands for your father, so that the army could supply him and keep him strong. Returning from campaign next spring, I saw the roads had been torn up. Rebel tribes! I went to your father to mount an action. The old man blandly announced that he had wrecked the tracks himself. I just shook my head. The clans didn't want access. They liked being isolated. It kept them free.

We fought this upside-down war for the better part of three years. To operate in such an environment, all assumptions had to be turned on their head. Whereas it is an axiom of conventional warfare never to detach from the central force a unit weaker than the whole, these tribal clashes demanded the opposite. I broke up the army into half and quarter corps, each self-contained, with its own heavy and light infantry, cavalry, archers, javelineers, engineers, and siege train. We conducted "sweeps." Two or three columns would enter a province on parallel courses. Fast couriers kept the units in contact. All commanders were instructed, upon striking the foe, to drive him toward the flanking corps. Boxing the enemy in this way was the only chance we had of drawing him into an iron-to-iron fight, and even then, the Grey Wolf slipped away more often than not.

The instrument of counterguerrilla warfare is the massacre. One must learn this art if he hopes to prevail. There is a liability to this, however. It is combat shorn of chivalry. Telamon called it "the Butcher's War," and it was. Numbers of our fellows couldn't take it. I permitted them to retire or accept discharge with honor, allotting them double and triple bonuses and making it known that no disgrace attached to their delicacy, as Craterus called it. Other men joined up, who had the stomach for such work.

You cannot fight guerrillas with ordinary forces, and you cannot fight them with ordinary men.

In this new war, certain generals came into their own. Craterus was one, Coenus another. These two had always been, with Perdiccas, my toughest and most resourceful commanders; this campaign without rules was raw meat to him. I began to operate my own corps more and more in conjunction with theirs; they were the only ones I could send into the mountains and not fear they would be ambushed and cut to pieces. Ptolemy and Perdiccas proved suited to wolf warfare as well, the former showing himself a superb siege general, the latter a spirited leader of light horse and foot.

The one commander who failed was Hephaestion. He could not kill women and children. For this, I respected him. But I could not send him into the field against a foe as formidable as the Grey Wolf; the jeopardy to his men was too great. So I brought him in to my staff. I made him my Number Two, second in command of the expeditionary force. The other generals responded with outrage. Hephaestion himself perceived this promotion as charity. Far from being gratified, he felt humiliated, and his rival marshals, who had seethed for years at his privileged station, worked now—in private, if not yet in public—to advance their own standing by producing his fall. The more I backed Hephaestion or interceded on his behalf, the more he resented me. The result was a bitter estrangement between myself and the man I needed most and depended most upon.

In Afghanistan the schism cracked open between the New Men and the Old Corps. Those veteran commanders who had cut their teeth under my father were all but gone now: Antipater and Antigonus One-Eye in garrison commands, Parmenio slain, Philotas executed; Nicanor, Meleager, Amyntas; scores more fallen in battle, passed over, or granted discharge. Only Black Cleitus remained. When I told him I planned to name him governor of Bactria, he would not even take my hand, so furious was he at what he perceived to be a sentence of exile, a posting, as he put it, to "the bunghole of the known world."

In Afghanistan too I was compelled to form that unit called the Malcontents. These, as I have said, were veterans of the Old Corps primarily, good men, many of them twenty years my senior, who remained loyal to Parmenio and bitterly resented me for the sequence of his end. These fellows were scattered across every unit of the army, sowing the contagion of disgruntlement. I quarantined them into one company, where I could keep my eye on them. But this was only a temporary answer.

Something final would have to be done with them.

The New Men now comprise the bulk of my corps. These are the young commanders, my age, thirty and under, who have made their fame with me, and owe their careers to me. But Afghanistan strains the fidelity even of this group. Guerrilla war has made my captains independent, and they have gotten a taste for it. Emboldened by autonomous command, my generals grow impatient with this backwater fray. They burn for the bright nexus of empire, for Babylon and Egypt, where the money is, and the fame and power. Worse, with administrative autonomy, the loyalty of individual soldiers has become attached to their division commanders, upon whom their advancement depends, and not to me—so that a fellow calls himself Coenus's man or Perdiccas's, and not Alexander's. Each victory these companies bring home enlarges their unit pride, not their pride in the army as a whole. And each act of barbarity committed turns them more barbarous.

Perceiving the toll this Butcher's War is taking on the army, I press the campaign even more vigorously, hoping to secure the country and move on. But one year becomes two and two three. Our divisions have depopulated entire territories. Regions thrice the size of Macedonia have been emptied of everything except dogs and crows. From a letter to my mother from Maracanda:

> My daimon is at home in this kind of fighting. I am not. My genius suffers no scruple at the decimation of villages or the dispeopling of provinces. To me such actions are unknightly. They border upon the criminal. I abhor their commission.

In Afghanistan my daimon begins to talk to me. He comes forward in resonance with the wolf warriors against whom we fight. Like them, the daimon knows no pity. Like them he owns no fear of death. You have asked, Itanes, if the daimon is properly identified with the soul. He is not. The daimon and the self are subordinate to the soul, but the daimon, should he overcome the self, may abrogate the soul. At that point a man becomes a monster.

In Maracanda, my spear took the life of Black Cleitus. I murdered him in a drunken rage. This was the most infamous act I have ever committed. More criminal than Thebes, more brutal than Tyre, far more wicked than the execution of Philotas (who earned his death by perfidy) and the elimination of Parmenio (which act was mandated by the treachery of his son).

The night had begun like every other in those years—with liquor, bragging, and contention, then more liquor and harsher contention. Coenus had just returned from a victory in the mountains, in which the two supporting columns, Ptolemy's and Perdiccas's, had shared his success. Praise for these New Men flowed with the wine.

Black Cleitus stood, defending the Old Corps.

Cleitus had a lover, a Page named Angelides; his passion for this boy knew no bounds, but the lad, a bright and ambitious fellow, could see that Cleitus's star was falling (as signalized by my appointment of him as governor of Bactria) and had come keenly to regret his choice of mentor. In secret he had made overtures to another; Cleitus knew it. He began bullying the boy, this night, commanding him to take sides.

Who were more worthy, the New Men or the Old Corps?

When Ptolemy and Perdiccas defended the former, Cleitus turned to me as arbiter. I praised both bodies, indicating by this that I wished the subject dropped.

Cleitus would not let it be. In the most brutal and invidious fashion, he reviled not only the New Men but all who had fought under me without prior service beneath Philip. When Love Locks ordered him to sober up or leave, Cleitus hurled his wine bowl in fury. "And what will you do if I don't? The same as you did to Philip?"

When my father was assassinated, Love Locks and Perdiccas were two of the three Bodyguards who overtook the killer and slew him. Many of suspicious bent had seized upon this swift and too-convenient stilling of the murderer's tongue and believed the pair complicit in his crime. As Love Locks and Perdiccas were my dear friends, the implication was that mine was the covert hand behind Philip's murder.

This was a murmur I had heard a thousand times and had dismissed as often with a rueful sigh. This night something tore inside me. I leapt from my seat, seizing the spear of Medon, the Page who stood at my shoulder. "Thou villain!" I shouted at Cleitus. "Do you dare call me parricide?"

Hephaestion intercepted me. Ptolemy and Coenus pinned my arms. A great cry filled the room. Three Pages, including Angelides, gripped Cleitus fast.

Now every long-stifled grudge spewed from the veteran's maw. He cursed me for arrogance and ingratitude, conceit and self-infatuation. Cleitus's sister Hellanice had been my nurse. Cleitus now invoked the name of this excellent matron, at whose breast I had suckled (and whose two sons had fallen gallantly in my service), and his own, whose right arm had saved my life at the Granicus.

"Yet now I and Philip are nothing to you, Alexander, but you preen in Persian purple and ordain the extinction of the same brave men without whom you would be nothing but a knave and a petty prince!"

Love Locks and Perdiccas hauled Cleitus from the chamber while I, shaking with rage, summoned every resource to maintain self-command.

Suddenly: a cry. Cleitus burst again into the hall. There was a bronze brazier in the center; Cleitus strode to it as a speaker to a stand. Before he could open his mouth, I fell upon him.

I drove the point of Medon's spear, which I still clutched, with both hands, uppercutting, into the meat of Cleitus's belly at the point below the breastbone where his cloak was bound by its regimental clasp, then thrust up and in, seeking his heart. My chest was pressed flat against his; we grappled like two rams in the mountains. I could feel the broadening wedge of the warhead as it hung up momentarily between the ribs of his dorsal spine, then punched through, with a sound like a spike cleaving a plank, and exited the flesh of his back. Cleitus was still very much alive, striking at the back of my neck with the butt of his sword. I crashed on top of him with all my weight. I felt his spine shear. For an instant there was no sensation of grief or of satisfaction. I thought only, This man will never defame me again.

The story goes that I was seized in that moment with such contrition that I sought to turn my weapon upon myself. No. That came later. Rather, I became stone-sober on the instant. Shame suffused me. I felt such mortification as I thought would part me from my reason. I was told later that I lifted Cleitus's body in my arms and, crying to heaven, pleaded for its reanimation. I shouted for the physicians—I remember that—and was only parted from the dead man's breast by the strong arms of my friends, whose expressions of horror, when I beheld them, served only to redouble my despair.

The river of Sogdiana is the Jaxartes. Across this five days later storms Spitamenes with nine thousand mounted raiders. Grief for Cleitus (and self-excoriation for my own felony) will have to wait. I marshal five flying divisions, taking the first for myself and setting in command over the others Craterus, Coenus, Perdiccas, and Hephaestion, whose pride will not endure another exclusion from action.

Here is how the Grey Wolf fights. He has grasped our tactics of pursuit by linked columns. His method is to lure us into the chase and wear us down with the country, which he knows and we don't. Then he strikes. By night upon our camps, by day from ambush on our columns. His Bactrian ponies can't outsprint our Parthians and Medians in a straight charge, but they can withdraw before us at the trot for hours, until, having run our mounts to exhaustion, he turns upon us and takes the offensive. Using these tactics, Spitamenes massacres east of Cyropolis a Macedonian column including sixty Companions, led by my brave Andromachus, who held the left wing at Gaugamela, eight hundred mercenary cavalry, and fifteen hundred hired infantry. Only three hundred and fifty escape. The rest are butchered, corpses stripped and mutilated and left for wolves.

You may imagine the state of our own divisions when report reaches us. The men's anger, frustration, and loathing for this badlands war threatens to carry them apart from themselves. They blaze to take it out on the foe, and no man owns less credibility than I to counsel restraint; nor do I wish to.

We chase Spitamenes to the Jaxartes with all five columns. At Nebdara is a ford, over which the Grey Wolf has escaped many times. He beats us there again, masses his forces on the far bank, and resists our crossing with everything he's got. Even his women shoot at us, from atop a palisade of wagons. By the time we mount a heavy assault, the marauders have fled into Scythia, vanishing onto their home sod.

I split the corps into its five columns and fan out across the steppe. Even these wild Sacae and Massagetae have villages. Even they have sites of refuge where they winter. For six days we drive north across these badlands, trailing hoof strikes and wagon traces. My column takes the left wing, with Coenus's, Hephaestion's, Craterus's, and Perdiccas's spanning right. Our front is a hundred miles. My orders are to leave nothing living.

At the seventh noon a rider gallops in from Coenus. Hephaestion's column in the center, he reports, has come upon a broad trail—the foe remarshaling. Hephaestion has not waited for help, but driven in pursuit alone.

It takes all day to cross the fifty miles to the trail. From ten we see smoke. At three we run onto foot troops of Coenus's column; they report that his fast cavalry and Craterus's have joined the clash initiated by Hephaestion. Spitamenes' Scyths are in full flight north, on their runt ponies, bolting into the dark.

"What's that smoke?"

"The Wolf's camp."

My column enters at dusk. Telamon and Love Locks ride at my shoulder. The encampment is not one village but several, strung out for half a mile along a broad sandy wash beneath chalk bluffs. Every tent and wagon has been burned. The earth is black beneath a scouring of gale-driven snow.

Entering, we can make out the site's contours. It is a fine camp, Telamon observes. "Well wooded, good water, shielded by the bluffs. The Scyths probably use it every winter."

We can see the foe's bodies now. Men of fighting age, cut down defending the camp. Their numbers are too many to count, but clearly the total is in hundreds. In the site's center, a stockade of wagons—fifty or sixty—has been hastily thrown up. Behind this the enemy's women and children have taken shelter. It requires scant imagination to reconstruct the massacre.

Hephaestion, arriving on site first and knowing that the other Macedonian commanders would be judging him when they caught up, has taken against the foe the sternest possible measures. We can see where the enemy has flung together his ring of wagons, and where Hephaestion's men have piled timber and dry brush and set it alight. The wind has done the rest. We can make out, too, places around the circle where individuals of the foe, women and children mostly, driven to desperation, have bolted clear and been cut down by our spears and javelins.

Craterus's column, right of Hephaestion's, must have arrived not long before ours. We can see Craterus himself now, on foot amid a crowd of Macedonians. He is clapping someone's back in congratulation. We can't hear his speech—we're too far away—but clearly it is something in the way of "Outstanding! That's more like it!"

The man he is acclaiming is Hephaestion.

We skirt the blackened ring of wagons. In such a conflagration, the slain are not burned to death, but asphyxiated; the holocaust sucks the wind out of their breasts, suffocating them. They are already dead by the time the flames consume their flesh. This knowledge makes no less grisly, however, the sight of infants blackened like charcoal or mothers incinerated to skeletons of ash.

I approach the circle around Hephaestion. Like Craterus, he has not yet seen me. But I see him. Upon his face sits such an expression of woe as I would give everything I own never to have seen.

He sees me now and brings himself under control. He speaks nothing of the massacre, this night or the next. But two evenings subsequent, in camp on the trek back to Maracanda, he and Craterus clash violently.

No one, since the corps marched out from Macedon, has ever applied anything but the loftiest moral purpose to our campaign. Now Hephaestion denounces this, declaring our cause "wicked" and "unholy."

Craterus replies at once and with anger. "There is no right or wrong in warfare, Hephaestion, only victor and vanquished. It is because you have no belly for this truth," he declares, "that you are not a soldier and never will be."

"If being a soldier means being like you, then I choose to be anything other."

I command them both to break off. But the rivalry between them has built up over a decade. Neither can live with it any longer.

"All actions of war are legitimate," Craterus proclaims, "if they are taken in the service of victory."

"All actions? Including massacres of women and children?"

"Such retribution," declares Craterus, "the foe brings upon himself—"

"How convenient for you!"

"—brings upon himself, I say, by his defiance of our will and his refusal to see reason. Such slaughters are committed by the foe's hand, not ours."

Hephaestion only smiles, his lips declining in articulation of despair.

"No, my friend," he says after a moment, addressing not Craterus alone but me and all the company, and himself as well. "It is *our* hands that drive the sword into their breast, and our hands, stained with their innocent blood, that can never be made clean."

We reach Maracanda on the ninth day. I inter Cleitus's corpse with what little simulacrum of honor can be mustered. It is the nadir of the war, for me and for the army.

My estrangement from Hephaestion, though more painful than ever, has evolved to that state, at least, in which he and I can address each other with absolute candor. When, again alone with me, he declares this campaign "odious," I cite great Pericles of Athens, who, speaking of his city's empire, stated that

> *it may have been wrong for us to take it, but now that we have it,*
> *it is certainly dangerous for us to let it go.*

"Ah!" my mate replies, "then you admit the possibility that this Butcher's War—and we who prosecute it—may be wicked and unjust."

I smile at his clever turn. "If we are wicked, my friend, then Almighty Zeus Himself has founded our iniquity. For He and no other has established the imperative of conquest within our hearts. Not in mine alone, or yours, but in every man in this army and in all the armies of the earth." I indicate the bronze of Zeus Hetaireios upon my writing stand. "Plead your case not to me, Hephaestion, but to Him."

That night I make up my mind. I will end this campaign of massacre, before it destroys us all, and remarshal the corps to cross into India.

We must have a good war.

We must have a war with honor.

Book Nine
🔲🔲🔲🔲🔲

LOVE FOR ONE'S ENEMY

Thirty-Three

THE NAKED WISE MEN

A SECOND MONSOON FLOOD HAS SWEPT THE CAMP. Tents have been carried off with all their tackle; every lane is mud. The site is on elevated ground and drains swiftly, but the men's state of mind remains foul and one cannot even train but every hour must be spent in repair of equipment and rehabilitation of the corps. The Indian heat remains stupefying. In the wet, the men's feet go to rot; horses' hooves swell and turn tender. The rain is warm as piss, but you cannot stand under it; it descends in volumes unimaginable. Only the bullocks and elephants can bear it, enduring with the patience of the East.

At the river's edge stand two villages, Oxila and Adaspila. These have incorporated themselves into the city which is our camp, including their women and children and their milk cows, who do, respectively, the army's laundry and supply its curds and cheese.

Also integrated into our sphere have become the gymnosophists, the "naked wise men" of India. One sees them at dawn descending to the river, where they bathe and chant. At dusk they return and set tiny lighted lamps, made of a leaf, oil, and a wick, adrift upon the current. It is a sight of great charm. Scores of these fellows tenant the camp (*infest* is Craterus's word). They are of all ages, youths to ancients, burnt black by the sun, and slender as stalks. I have feared that our fellows would prove haughty with them, kicking them out of the public way as they did the inhabitants of Babylon, but the opposite has transpired; our Macedonians have adopted these sadhus as patriarchs, and this affection has been returned by the sages, who regard our rough corps with an amused and patient beneficence.

We dine this evening, my officers and I, on a terrace of teak overlooking the river. The talk is of an incident earlier today. My party had been crossing that quadrant of the camp that abuts Oxila village. One of my Pages, a bright lad named Agathon, was striding ahead to clear the lane, when he came upon a troupe of gymnosophists taking the sun in the public way. These declined to vacate for my passage. An altercation broke out between the boy and several vendors, who took up the cudgels on the renunciants' behalf. A crowd gathered. By the time I arrived, a full-blown incident was in progress. The nut of the quarrel was this: Who was more worthy to possess the right-of-way—Alexander or the gymnosophists? As I reined-in, Agathon stood in spirited exchange with the eldest of the wise men. Indicating me, the lad declared, "This man has conquered the world! What have *you* done?" The philosopher replied without an instant's hesitation, "I have conquered the need to conquer the world."

I laughed with delight. At once our party yielded. I asked the sage what I could do for him, declaring that he could name any boon and I would grant it. "That fruit in your hand," he said. I was holding a fine ripe pear. When I gave it to him, he handed it, to eat, to a boy at his side.

Next day I hold a review of the army. Such inspections are invaluable to reinspirit demoralized troops. The fellows grumble mightily over the work to get ready, but once in formation, when they behold the scale and order of the army and the brilliance of its kit, their hearts cannot but be lifted to feel themselves part of such an illustrious corps. The sight does me good too. At home I would take three hours to complete the review, but in this heat, even a third of that will drop a man faint. So I make it quick and permit the companies to stand easy.

It is a far different army from the one that embarked from Europe eight years ago, or departed Afghanistan one season past. On the left wing, our brilliant Thessalian cavalry is gone, granted discharge at Ecbatana. In their stead we have free Afghan, Scythian, and Bactrian cohorts. Such tribesmen cannot be trained to fight like Europeans, but with their tattooed faces and panther skin–bedecked ponies, they add a dash of color and savagery. Tigranes' Successors' Cavalry, all-Persian but trained to Macedonian tactics, have joined us at Zadracarta. Andromachus's mercenary cavalry remains, though their commander has fallen, massacred by Spitamenes on the River Polytimenus. My archers are now Median and Indian, not Macedonian, and my lancers Parthian and Massagetae. The only units unaltered are Sitalces' Thracian darters (though Sitalces himself remains in Media, his son Sadocus taking his command) and the javelineers of Agriania. Replacements appear each spring like the hyacinth; I have sons, and even grandsons, of my originals, serving with distinction equal to their fathers'.

The core of the line remains the brigades of the phalanx (seven now in India, instead of six), though even these are no longer all-Macedonian; some companies are less than half homegrowns. New commanders abound—Alcetas, Antigenes, White Cleitus, Tauron, Gorgias, Peithon, Cassander, Nearchus, and others. At Zariaspa in Afghanistan, 21,600 reinforcements caught up from Greece and Macedonia. These and other units, including Patron's Greek mercenaries and six thousand Royal Syrian Lancers under Asclepiodorus, comprise the bulk of my light infantry. I have Daan horse archers now, who once fought under the Grey Wolf, and six thousand Royal Taxilean foot bowmen. Cleander's vet mercs are still with me, though Cleander himself remains at Ecbatana. Black Cleitus dead, I have taken the Royal Squadron as my own (with the Anthemiot, Amphipolitan, and Bottiaean), calling it the *agema* of the Companions. I muster the Companion Cavalry in regiments now, composed of two squadrons each, and have brought its numbers from eighteen hundred to above four thousand, including numerous Persians, Medians, Lydians, Syrians, and Cappadocians.

Is there dissension? Macedonians comprise now only two-fifths of the corps; they bitterly resent the Asiatic units I have brought in, particularly the Persians, who cannot, the Macedonians point out, even pronounce my name. I am "Iskander" to them. That I am charmed by this infuriates my countrymen, and the more senior the man, the more violent his agitation. I have twelve thousand youths of Egypt and forty thousand Persians in training with the sarissa right now in their home provinces; the Macedonians, though they never cease griping at their own pay and posting, cannot endure the thought of being replaced by foreigners.

I come now to the Malcontents. Their station in the review is as a seam unit between the Royal Guardsmen and Perdiccas's brigade of the phalanx. They look sharp, I admit. What a shame that I must stick them here, between units of unimpeachable loyalty, to hold them, if not by love, then by iron.

To inspire enthusiasm among the corps, I have formed new units, with new names and new colors. The most celebrated is the Silver Shields. This division was constituted at first only of the *agema* of the Royal Guardsmen; soon I extended it to all three Guard regiments and have enlarged it further since then to include veterans of the phalanx who have distinguished themselves in the campaign against Spitamenes. The rivets of their shields and breastplates are real silver, by weight six months' pay, though the tale is untrue that men pare shavings and spend them as specie.

New units. Native officers. These are the tricks the commander must conjure to "feed the monster," the army's never-satiated appetite for recognition, honor, and novelty. But even these are not enough. Now, on the evening terrace after the review, my officers wrangle over the feigned river crossings and sham embarkations I insist we make each night to wear out Porus's sentries by the repetition of false alarms. Thessalus, the famous actor, has come out from Athens. He is fascinated by life with the army. It's just like the theater!

"As you employ counterfeit evolutions, Alexander, to prevent the enemy from discerning your true designs, so does the dramatist. He starts his play, making much, say, of a crisis in the life of a king, seducing us by such theatrics into believing that the tale is about ambition, shall we say, or honor or greed. Only at the climax do we realize that this has all been a false front; the play's true theme is the working out of an individual's destiny beneath his own hand. And when this strikes us at the finish, it arrives with the emotional equivalent of one of your celebrated cavalry charges. The dramatist may have peopled his play with oracles and portents, prodigies and divine interventions; still, we in the audience come to see that the protagonist's choices alone have made him who he is and brought him to his end. This is tragedy. For which of us can rise above what he is? Tragedy is the arrest of a man by his own nature. He is blind to it. He cannot transcend it. If he could, it would not be tragedy. And tragedy's power derives from our own realization, commoner as well as king, that life truly is like that. We have fashioned our ruin with our own hands. All, perhaps, save these gymnosophists, who seem to seek ruin first, only to flourish in its midst!"

The party laughs and applauds. All but Hephaestion, who has become attached to these sages of India and is distressed to hear their labors dismissed with condescension. He defends them.

"These are not barbarians, Thessalus. They are not slavish, as the Babylonians, or idolatrous, as the men of Egypt. Their philosophy is ancient, profound, and subtle. It is a warrior philosophy. In my inquiries I have only scratched its surface, but it has impressed me deeply. Contrary to your assertion, my friend, I declare that these sadhus have indeed risen above who they are. For surely they were not born to the state in which we now discover them, but have arrived at it only after many trials and much labor."

Laughter and profane jibes salute this; Hephaestion bears these with good humor. It is a source of great joy to me to see him restored to grace, now that the army has moved on from Afghanistan, both in his eyes and mine, and in those of the company. Telamon looks on, as gratified as I.

"What are these yogis seeking," Hephaestion continues, "by their voluntary poverty and renunciation? They aspire, I believe, to locate their persons in God. They seek to see the world as the Deity sees it and to act toward it as He acts. They assay this not in arrogance, but humility. Don't scoff, gentlemen. Consider our friend Thessalus's analogy of the playwright. The dramatist is the god of his own play; each character is a creature of his imagination. And though the vision of these players is limited to their own self-interest, the playwright can and must 'see the whole field.' As he has empathy for all his characters, even the villains (or he could not write their parts), so must the Almighty look upon us and our world. This is the state, I believe, to which the gymnosophists aspire. Not callous indifference, but benevolent impartiality. The yogi seeks to love the wicked as well as the just, recognizing in each a brother soul on its journey through benightedness."

A chorus of knuckle raps approves this. Now Ptolemy summons Telamon to speak, recounting that he has seen the mercenary interview several of these ascetics. "In truth, our Arcadian seems more like one of these mendicants than one of us! For although he accepts pay for his labor at arms and never tires of testifying to the virtue of this, I notice he is always dead broke and gives away everything he gets as soon as he gets it." He calls Telamon to give us a speech.

"On what subject?"

"The Code of the Mercenary."

Gales of hilarity salute this. We have all heard it so often. When Telamon declines, Love Locks rises in his stead and, taking up a posture modeled impeccably on the Arcadian's, clasping his beard exactly after Telamon's fashion, mimics the mercenary's speech so exactly that the group, in delight, rains coins upon him and nearly drowns his speech with laughter.

"I do not serve money; I make money serve me. At campaign's close, I care for neither praise nor condemnation. I want money. I want to be paid. In that way, war is just work. I am not attached to it. Campaigning for money detaches me from the object of my commander's desire. I serve for the serving only, fight for the fighting only, tramp for the tramping only."

When the laughter subsides, Telamon is compelled by his mates' summons to step forward.

"Indeed, gentlemen," he acknowledges, "I have quizzed these yogis. I have learned that in their philosophy all of humanity is divided into three types: the man of ignorance, *tamas*; the man of action, *rajas*; and the man of wisdom, *sattwa*. We around this table are men of action. That is what we are. But though I have lived my own life as a man of this type, and all my previous lives—as Pythagoras would say, citing his doctrine of transmigration of the soul—I have always wished to become a man of wisdom. That is why I fight and why I have pursued the vocation of arms. Life is a battle, is it not? And how better to train for it than to be a soldier? For have you not noticed of these sages, my friends, that they are the consummate soldiers? Inured to pain, oblivious to hardship, each takes up his post at dawn and does not relinquish it for thirst, hunger, heat, cold, fatigue. He is cheerful in all weathers, self-motivated, self-governed, self-commended. Would, Alexander, that we had an army with such a will to fight! We would cross this river before the count of three hundred."

"Are you saying, Telamon," I inquire, "that your training as a soldier prepares you for the vocation of sage?"

The party responds with amusement. But I am serious. Telamon answers that he wishes he were that tough. "These men are beyond me, my friend. I must apprentice myself to them for many lifetimes."

The mercenary declares that I possess much of this quality as well.

"To your credit, Alexander, you too are not attached to your comforts or even to your life. You care nothing for the lands you have conquered or their treasure, except as they serve to further your campaigns. But there is one thing to which you are indeed attached, to your soul's detriment."

"And what is that, my friend?"

"Your victories. You remain proud of them. This is not good for you." Telamon indicates the terrace, the camp, the army. "You should be able to walk away from all this now, this night. Get up! Take nothing! Can you?"

Laughter from all. "And you think I couldn't?"

"You cannot leave your victories or your great name, and you cannot leave these comrades whom you love and who love and depend upon you. Who is master of this empire? Do you rule it, or does it rule you?"

More laughter. "You know I only endure this from you, Telamon. No one else can get away with it!"

"But, my dear friend," the Arcadian replies, not laughing, "you must be able to get up and walk away. Being a soldier is not enough. All answers are not contained within the warrior's code. I know. I have lived it many lifetimes. I am tired of it. I am ready to shuck it off, like a worn-out cloak."

Good-humored chaffing greets this. "Don't leave us!" Ptolemy cries. Others echo the sentiment profanely.

Telamon has turned toward me. "I schooled you as a boy, Alexander, to be superior to fear and to anger. You learned eagerly. You vanquished hardship and hunger and cold and fatigue. But you have not learned to master your victories. These hold you. You are their slave."

I feel anger start. Telamon sees it. He continues.

"The yogi's remark that he has 'conquered the need to conquer the world' could not have been more apt. What the sage means is that he has mastered his daimon. For what is the daimon but that will to supremacy which resides not only in all men but in beasts and even plants and is, at its heart, the essence of all aggressive life?"

This hits me like a blow.

"The daimon is inhuman," Telamon states. "The concept of limits is alien to it. Unchecked, it devours everything, including itself. Is it evil? Is the acorn, aspiring to become the oak? Is the fingerling, seeking the sea? In nature, the will to dominion is held within bounds by the limited capacity of the beast. Only in man is this instinct unrestrained and only in that man"—he addresses me with concern—"like you, my friend, whose gifts and preeminence transcend all external governance. We have all known suicides," Telamon finishes, "whose stem was this: A man must kill himself to slay his daimon."

All mirth has fled. My mates hold themselves rigid, anticipating an eruption of my wrath. On the contrary, I welcome Telamon's words. I wish to hear more, for the issues he raises are those with which I too wrestle, day and night. My mentor reads this on my face.

"Though you chaff me, Alexander, for purposing to become one day a man of wisdom, you yourself share this ambition, and have since you were a boy. It was that which drew you to me as a child, when you used to trail me around the barrack yard, marching at my heels like a shadow."

Laughter greets this, to the relief of all. Telamon continues, sober.

"Further, I declare that this quality is what makes you superior to your father. Not superior as a commander, notice I say, although you are. Or braver as a soldier, although you are. You excel your father not for these reasons, but for your moral object, because you do wish to become a man of wisdom, whereas Philip was content to fight and fuck. Your sufferings, too, are greater than his, because it pains you to fall short of that which you know yourself capable. Your father recognized this. He knew you, even as a child, as his better. This is why he both loved and feared you, Alexander. And why you, like Hephaestion and me, are drawn to these sages of India and perceive in their aspirations the sign, if not the substance, of your own."

Thirty-Four

"I HAVE COME TO HATE WAR"

AMONG THE ARMY OF THE PUNJAB, as our force now calls itself,
are a number of Indian divisions, including the Royal Horse
Guard of Taxiles, archers and infantry under Raj Sasigupta, and companies of other allied princes. It is the ancient custom of these warriors, up
to commencement of actual hostilities, to visit in person with the foe
(of whom, in this country of widespread intermarriage, many are kinsmen, mentors, and mates) and in a most fraternal spirit. Numbers of our
Indian allies paddle nightly across to Porus's lines, as no few of Porus's
men row each evening across to ours.

The Macedonians cannot conceive of such a thing. Upon first observing combatants of the foe disembarking on our shores, they arrest
them at sword point and drag them off (some not so gently) to their
commanders for interrogation. Porus's officers are outraged at this, as are
our own Indian allies. When I am made to understand the custom, I respect its chivalry. I order all captives released, their arms restored; no
more prisoners to be taken. In fact I entertain at my table numbers of
these gentlemen, sending them back across the river with gifts of honor.

There is a problem with this. It erodes the Macedonians' will to fight, as they come, with acquaintance, to admire and feel affection toward these champions of the foe. One sees these slender warriors strolling amiably about the camp, bearing their parasols and their bows of horn and ivory. When they converse, they stand on one foot like cranes, with the sole of the other set against the inside of the opposite thigh. Their hair is jet and worn in a topknot; their trousers, bloused above the knee, are of the gayest oranges and magentas. They adorn their persons with earrings of gold and possess the most brilliant smiles, and the most frequently employed. It helps to hate the enemy, I have found, or at least to consider them butchers or barbarians. The *ksatriyas* of Porus are neither, nor have they committed any crimes against the Macedonians.

Preparing for the assault, I have sent numerous scouting parties across the river. All reports portray Porus's domain as an extremely well-ordered kingdom, characterized by autonomous villages of farm small-holdings, cultivated by what would in Macedon be called a yeomanry of free, independent husbandmen, devoted to their king and regarding him with a fierce loyalty and affection. Scouts describe plots tidy and flourishing, wives hardworking and devoted, children bright and happy. In other words, the Macedonians have come to feel they are bringing war to paradise, and they like this not at all.

Worse, the monsoons approach. The river seems to toy with us maliciously. Floods surge out of the mountains without warning, the product of storms too distant to see or hear, and these carry away in moments the levees of interlaced timber, wicker, and stone, which the men have toiled for weeks in raising. Any watercraft caught on the river when these surges strike finds itself swept downstream at such a clip that rescuers along shore cannot keep it in sight even at the gallop.

Disgruntlement smolders in the faces of the army; mischief breeds in their silences. I continue preparations for the assault. Nineteen hundred boats and rafts have been constructed on-site or transported in sections from the Indus and reassembled; I have these carted under cover of the premonsoon downpours to launching points up- and downriver.

Divisions drill for waterborne assault and for action against elephants. Special boots are fitted for the horses, for fighting on marshy ground. I have sent to the rear for money and arms, to pump some spirit into the army. Two convoys are en route, from Ambhi and Regala, but with the rains and the difficult river crossings, they have not reached us. I have set a date in my mind for the attack, revealing it to no one, but delays have forced me to put it back twice, and a third time after that. Inaction demoralizes any army; it is driving this one closer to revolt and insurrection.

One evening a deputation of disaffected officers presents itself at my pavilion. Hephaestion sends the lot packing before their petition can provoke my fury. We tramp the levee afterward, Hephaestion, Craterus, and I.

"These bastards' balls are getting big," Craterus says, offering his usual profane assessment. "By the gods, I know their litany of bellyaching by heart!" And he looses a trumpetlike fart.

"Yes," I say. "But a deputation. That's a new one."

"Bung their deputation."

"They looked pretty grave." I cite by name several captains—good, serious men.

Craterus indicates the river. "Let them be good and serious about that."

In camp again, we put in a long, productive evening, until several hours past midnight, when only the Pages, yawning, and Hephaestion remain.

I ask him why he has been so quiet tonight.

"Was I? I hadn't noticed."

We have known each other too long to piss about. "Say it."

He glances to the Pages.

I sign to them: Leave us.

When they have gone, Hephaestion sits. He would take wine, I see, but will not permit himself.

"I have come," he says, "to hate war."

I should check him there. I have no need to hear the rest.

"You asked me," he says. "Shall I stop?"

A tent pillar ascends at my shoulder. I clasp it, hard, to keep my hand from trembling.

"It's not fatigue," Hephaestion explains, "or the wish to see home. It's war itself. What it is." He lifts his gaze to mine. "You feel rage now," he says. "Your daimon seizes you."

"No."

But I do. It does.

"Keep talking," I insist. "I want to hear it."

"Before, I objected to the campaign in Afghanistan but not to the wider thrust of the expedition; in fact I embraced it with a passion equal to, if not exceeding, your own. But that has changed.

"What we do is a crime, Alexander. In the end it is but butchery. For all the poets' anthems, war's object is nothing nobler than the imposition of one nation's will upon another by means of force and threat of force. The soldier's job is to kill men. We may call them enemy, but they are men like us. They love their wives and children no less than we; they are no less brave, or virtuous, or serve their country with less devotion. As for the men and others I have killed, or who have been slain at my command, I would bring them all back to life; yes, if I could, I would reanimate every one at once, no matter what the cost to me or to this expedition. I'm sorry. . . ."

He wants to stop; I won't let him.

"Till Persepolis I stood with you, Alexander. Wrongs done to Greece must be avenged. But we have slain Persia's king. We have burned her capital; we have made ourselves masters over all her lands. Now what?" He gestures east, across the river. "Shall we conquer these honest yeomen next? Why? How have they harmed us? By what right do we bring war against them? Pursuit of glory? This army stopped being glorious a long time ago. Or shall we cite Achilles and say we emulate the 'virtues of war'? Rubbish! Any virtue carried to its extreme becomes a vice. Conquest? No man can rule another. The most devoted subject will trade in an instant his wealth, earned beneath your rule, for poverty he can call his own. We had a cause. We have none now."

He rises, running his hands through his hair in distress.

"Who can stand against you, Alexander? You have become the oak that dwarfs the forest. The corps seethes with alienation and discontent. Yet one word from you will bring it to heel. Who can say no to you? Not I. Not they."

My mate regards me.

"I thought I feared the loss of your love. That's why I've kept my mouth shut. Because such a thing smacked of vanity and self-concern. But that's not what I fear. I fear the loss *of you from yourself*. Your daimon eats you alive! It devours this army! I love Alexander but fear 'Alexander.' Which are you?" He faces me with an expression of despair. "We will cross this river for you. We will get you your victory. What then?"

He finishes. His indictment is nothing I have not voiced to myself ten thousand times. But to speak it aloud, to my face . . .

"You are the bravest man I have ever known, Hephaestion."

"Only the most desperate." And he hides his face and weeps.

The clasp on his cloak is the gold lion of Macedon. He is my deputy, second in command of the expeditionary force.

"If I am killed in this fight," I ask, "will you take the army home?"

He doesn't answer.

"You should replace me," he says.

I can only smile. "With whom?"

Next day comes the elephant turd.

The sergeant called Gunnysack has been sent with one of the scouting parties across the river. He comes back with a great dried elephant splat—putty-colored, two feet high, big around as a bathtub. We have all seen the droppings of work elephants. But this, of a beast of war, is of another scale entirely. It creates a sensation in camp. Everyone has to see it. And all must speculate on the size of the creature that dropped it.

"By the gods," declares Gunnysack, "if this monster craps on you, you're a dead onion!"

The men have had contact with war elephants (we captured fifteen after Gaugamela, who didn't get into the fight) but not till now have they confronted the prospect of facing them in action. They are terrified. Now more daunting intelligence comes in: Porus, whose force of behemoths was originally fifty, has sent to his eastern princes, who have brought up three times that number, along with fresh thousands of archers, chariots, and infantry. Two hundred elephants arrayed at intervals of fifty feet, with infantry in between, make a front of nearly a mile, three ranks deep. Horses cannot endure the smell or trumpeting of these beasts; our cavalry, the soldiers fear, will neither mount out of the river in the face of such creatures nor be able to sustain a charge against them in the field. The men are appalled further by reports of the types of deaths dealt by these giants—that is, being crushed beneath their tread, gored by their tusks, even being lifted bodily by their trunks, to have one's brains dashed out upon the earth.

I check the infirmary. The sick list has tripled, flush with "accidental" woundings. Across the camp men congregate in groups; they glance up, sullen or shamefaced, when my eye lights upon them. Craterus and Perdiccas are for making examples; Ptolemy urges me to move up the assault. I want to wait (the money and equipment I have sent for will be here soon), but the mood of the camp compels me to take action. I summon the commanders of the army.

"Macedonians and allies, you are not the force you used to be. Before, when I charged the foe, I felt your fiery valor close at my shoulder. Now I glance back, afraid you will not even be in sight! Look at you. You sulk and grumble; a tub of elephant shit sets you muttering. Let us then, as my father used to say, call a spade a spade."

I address the officers outdoors, beneath the levee, so that the whole corps can gather and hear.

"I have called you together here, once and for all, either to convince you to go forward or be convinced by you to turn back. Do you find fault with me, brothers? Have our labors together proved short of profit? If that is what you believe, I have no answer for you. If, however, it is because of this toil that all of Europe and Asia is now in your hands—namely, Greece and the islands of the Aegean, Illyria, Thrace, Phrygia, Ionia, Lydia, Caria, Cilicia, Phoenicia, Egypt, Syria, Armenia, Cappadocia, Paphlagonia, Babylonia, Susiana, and the whole of the Persian Empire, not to say Parthia, Bactria, Areia, Sogdiana, Hyrcania, Arachosia, Tapuria, and half of India—then what is your complaint? Have I failed of generosity? There is not one of you I haven't made rich.

Do I keep the choicest bounty to myself? There is my bed. It is two planks and a carpet. I eat half what you do and sleep a third as long. And as for wounds, let any of you strip and display his, and I will display mine in turn. There is no part of my body, or none in front where wounds of honor are received, that has been left untorn, and no weapon whose scars I do not bear, all in your service, for your glory, and toward your enrichment!"

A shelf crosses the face of the levee, where the timbers and wickerwork conjoin. I tread this like an actor pacing a stage.

"For my part, gentlemen, I set no limit to the aspirations of a man of noble spirit, so long as these lead to feats of prowess. Yet if anyone wants to know how much farther I intend to push, let him know that the Shore of the Eastern Ocean cannot lie many leagues beyond where we stand today. There, I will quit. But not short of there.

"You are tired, my friends. Do you think I'm not? But privation and danger are the toll of deeds of glory. What is sweeter than to live bravely and to die leaving immortal renown? We convene this day as an army. Other armies will follow in ages to come. Who will equal our exploits? Look around you, brothers. Look into the faces of your comrades. You are the mightiest fighting force in history! The trials you have endured, the enemies you have overcome, the victories you have produced beggar the conquests of all who have gone before and all who will come after. Does fearful fancy precede you across this river, conjuring nations and enemies too numerous for us to face? I heard the same in Macedon. Men said we would never reach the Halys, that we should quit at the Euphrates. We could not take Babylon, timorous voices cried, or Persepolis, or Kabul. I said we could, and I have not been wrong! Yet still you doubt me.

"Perhaps we have succeeded too well. That may be our malady. This is heaven's trick on us, to sap our will, at the hour when we stand on the threshold of the ultimate. Press on with me! Brothers, give me one more push! The Shore of Ocean cannot be far. When we stand there at the Limits of the Earth—and we shall—then by heaven I will not merely satisfy you but will surpass the utmost hopes of good things that every

man has! I will send you home, or lead you there myself, while those
who remain, I shall make the envy of those who depart."

I finish. No one answers. I see the corps's terror of my wrath.

"Speak, my friends. Do not fear me. You break my heart if you do."

Silence interminable. Not one can raise his glance from the dirt.

At last, Coenus advances a pace. My heart catches with grief.
Coenus, fearless in the face of every foe, now must employ this surpass-
ing valor only to address me.

My old friend speaks:

"Seeing that you, my lord, do not desire to coerce the Macedones as
a despot, but rather to persuade them or be persuaded by them, I shall
speak not on behalf of my brother officers, whom you have laded so with
honors and treasure that we will follow you anywhere, but on behalf of
the men of the army, who have no voice save ours offered for them, and
upon whom falls most heavily the burdens of campaign."

Coenus observes that after Persepolis, many believed the army had
come too far. But in the seasons succeeding, we have come three times
farther. Our force has brought into subjection as many people and twice
as much territory as it had, even in the conquest of Persia! We have
fought twenty-four more battles and prosecuted nine more sieges. What
has become of the army?

"Surely you cannot fail to remark, Alexander, how great were the
numbers of Greeks and Macedonians who set out with you at the start
of this campaign, and how few survive intact to this day. Many you have
sent home with wealth and honors, seeing that they were worn out with
exertions, and you were right to do so. Others you established in newly
founded cities, giving them land and wives; this was well too, for you
perceived that they no longer had their hearts in the expedition. How
many others have been slain by the foe, or fallen of wounds and illness,
or been invalided from excessive toil? We have come eleven thousand
miles and fought every foot of the way! Of those who survive, few enjoy their bodily strength, and their spirit is even more impoverished.
Each man longs to see his mother and father, if they are still alive, and
his wife and children. He yearns for sight of his native land. Is this

wrong? Has he not earned it? Is this not indeed your own intention for him, when by your generosity you raise him from poverty to substance? As for my own case, you furloughed me after the Granicus, with the other newly married men, permitting me by your great kindness to over-winter at home with my bride. That was eight years ago. I have a son I have never seen. Will I perish in your service, Alexander, without once looking upon my child's face?"

Coenus urges me to take the army home in person, to look again upon my mother, settle affairs in Greece; then, if I so wish, I may mount a second expedition, with new men in place of old, fresh instead of worn. "How much more ardently will these young and eager troops follow you, Alexander, when they see that the partners in your earlier toils have been brought home by you, raised from penury to riches and from obscurity to high renown?"

My old friend finishes. He is seconded by men in their thousands, no few shedding tears and pleading with me to give hearing to his counsel.

Again I have failed to make them see. Such rage burns in my guts as I fear must split me open. It is all I can do to dismiss the assembly and retire, on fire with fury, to my tent.

Thirty-Five

SILVER SHIELDS

NOT A MAN SLEEPS THAT NIGHT. By the gods, I will grant no ease to these blue-livered bastards! At midnight I issue orders that the unit of three hundred Malcontents is to be disarmed and placed under arrest. The roundup sets the camp ablaze with rumor. Will I execute them? I command an assembly of the army for dawn, officers to fall their men in in full dress, as the law prescribes for witnessing punishment. The Malcontents will take formation barefoot and bare-headed, clad only in tunics.

Couriers arriving at nightfall report that the baggage trains with the money and equipment are only a few miles off. I send to the column commanders with secret orders. This ignites even wilder rumors.

I order a square excavated in the center of the camp, with three hundred posts erected, as for execution. The Malcontents are to be cordoned in this space. A berm is to be raised on all sides, men-at-arms posted atop.

These orders I have cried through the camp by heralds, not communicated by me, as is customary, to my generals and passed down from them through the chain of command. Let my marshals sweat too. I banish even Hephaestion, Craterus, and Telamon. Only Aristander the seer is permitted to remain. We sacrifice to Fear. One victim after another bleeds inpropitiously; I order the carcasses dumped, gutted, at the rear of the precinct. Let the army put a meaning on that!

The baggage trains arrive under torchlight three hours before dawn. I have the wagons brought up adjacent to the central square and the area sealed, not by Macedonians, whose errant tongues no one can shackle, but by Raj Ambhi's Royal Taxileans.

At dawn I am still sacrificing. I bring Hephaestion back, with Craterus, Perdiccas, Ptolemy, Coenus, and Seleucus. I command the camp bolted down tight; any man caught outside the perimeter to be executed as a spy.

I send Telamon to address the Malcontents. He directs the company to either confirm their current leaders, the young lieutenants Matthias and Crow, or elect new ones, but to be certain they are satisfied with who speaks for them, for these officers' words, come dawn, will be taken by me to be the will of all.

The sun comes up hot in India. I watch the Malcontents brought forward. Every man, it seems, has been a hero. With one glance my eye takes in Eryx, first to scale the face at Aornus; Philo, who held his shield nightlong over White Cleitus, penned by a horde of shrieking Afghans; Amompharetus, called "Half Moon" for the sword gash across his belly, who gave away three years' bonus to flood-wrecked villagers on the Oxus. Plainly, all believe this dawn will be their last. Yet not one snivels to Telamon, or so much as asks to have his name remembered to his kin at home.

I am wrong.

The fault is mine for estranging such men.

Red-eyed and red-assed, the army falls in. Already the day is blistering. The Malcontents are brought to attention within the berm. Matthias and Crow remain their commanders. Guards man the rise. Before the men stand the three hundred posts. Over each I have ordered a plain sack to be draped, muffling it from crown to base. The wrappers hang there, baggy as sleeping covers. The army stares, baffled and unnerved.

I come forward in the crimson cloak of the Companion Cavalry.

"Macedonians and allies, when I broke off the assembly last night, my gut was on fire with rage. You felt it, I know. All night in your tents, you have taken counsel among yourselves. This is as it should be, for you are not slaves fettered by the will of a tyrant, but free men. I too lay sleepless. Nightlong in my mind I heard the passions voiced on your behalf by our comrade Coenus. I heard them and I pondered them hard."

I draw up. The camp is so still, one can hear the plashing of the laundry urchins a quarter mile below along the levee.

"Brothers, do what you like. But I am going on."

From my platform I can see across the river. I gesture east toward Porus and the enemy fortifications.

"I compel no one to follow. And I give you proof, thus."

I sign to the corps's quartermaster. At his command, the chief of the baggage train advances before the army, bringing the wagons that came in last night. Some twenty of these carts disperse, briskly, as I have rehearsed them, drawing up before the allied and foreign contingents of the army. One stops before each. Tailgates drop. Teamsters pitch out sacks of riches. Gold takes up little space; in no time, fortunes mound at the feet of each division.

"Here is your pay, allies and friends. You will find, when you count it, single bonuses for infantry, double for cavalry, triple for officers. It is everything you would have received had we achieved the most complete victory. Go, then! Take your money!"

It takes moments for my speech to be translated into a score of native tongues. Murmurs commence. These mount to cries. The allies and foreign troops in the thousands roar their refusal. No! No! They will touch no treasure without earning it.

"Take it!" I advance before them. "Take it and claim you have crossed this river with Alexander and vanquished his foes. This money shall be proof to all who question your valor!"

The tumult intensifies, mounting to a pitch of warrior pride and defiance. Fiercest in their refusal are the Bactrians and Parthians; the horse tribesmen of Scythia, Sacae and Daans and Massagetae, chant their repudiation; the Royal Indians of Ambhi and Sasigupta stand silent and resolute; the mercenaries of Thrace and Greece likewise reject this recompense shorn of honor, with the Syrians, Lydians, Egyptians, and Medes concurring. Tigranes and the Persian regiments will not even deign to look.

By sign I quell the uproar.

Division commanders restore their companies to order.

I turn to the Macedonians. The corps's quartermaster drives more wagons forth. My countrymen are struck through with shame. Are they past insurrection? I will make them twist yet upon the gibbet.

"Macedonians, you have voiced your complaints and I have heard them. Here. This is what you wanted."

From the wagons, teamsters heave more sacks of gold. The bags are heavy; many rupture, striking the ground. Coins spill. In the dirt before each division, barrows of lucre ascend.

"Here are your discharges." My Pages display the rolls aloft. "You are free. Take them! I hold you no longer!"

Not a man moves. Each is stricken through with infamy.

"What keeps you, Macedonians? I release you with honor. Bend! Take your reward! Go home!"

My Pages, as I have rehearsed them, pass among the divisions, bearing the discharge warrants. Not a man will touch them.

"Transport has been arranged for you, brothers. Pack up! March home! And do not forget when you arrive to tell your wives and children how you abandoned your king alone and surrounded by enemies at the ends of the earth. Tell them, too, how allies, who could not even speak his language, remained loyal to Alexander, while you, his own kin and countrymen, took your treasure and stalked for home. Tell them this, and I am sure you will gain abundant renown. What are you gawking at? You have got what you wanted! Go, damn the lot of you. Go!"

My countrymen stand like statues. All are held by shame and suspense.

The Malcontents. Will I execute them? Will I bind them and march them to the posts to be slaughtered?

I address the Malcontents. Numbers I cite, accounting exploits of past valor. I name Eryx and Philo and Amompharetus. It is my fault, I declare, that has produced the estrangement between us.

"I have pushed you, brothers, too hard and too far. Because of your greatness, I have expected prodigies of you, and so perhaps have not sufficiently acknowledged your triumphs or shared enough in your sufferings. I have failed you, my friends. But you have failed me too. You have broken faith with me and with your countrymen. You have favored your disgruntlement over fidelity to the corps. You have sulked and cultivated your disaffection, playing the spoiled favorite and the outraged pet. Such acts are not errors of judgment; they are felonies—military crimes committed in time of war and mandating the sternest possible punishment. But as I have given our allies and countrymen a choice, so I give one to you."

I order the covers taken off the execution posts. Beneath each emerges a newly crafted shield, untouched and untarnished, set upright upon a stand and dazzling in the ascending sun. Each shield, I inform the corps, is lapped not with bronze but with silver. The rivets are silver, the facing is silver, the studs are silver. A sixth of a talent, nearly nine pounds of precious metal.

"Here are the bonuses and premiums you've been bitching for. The silver on each shield is worth three years' pay."

I sign the guards to withdraw. The company of Malcontents holds, dumbstruck. The whole army has not breathed. While they gape, I motion to the quartermaster; his men remove the post covers completely. Beside the shields stand three hundred new swords and sarissas, new shoes and tunics, helmets, cloaks, the full panoply.

The army erupts in citation. It takes the count of a hundred before order can be restored.

"This kit is for you!" I address the Malcontents. "But I do not compel you to take it. That sum, which is represented by the silver on each shield, I will give to you instead in coin, if you so elect, and release you with honor and send you home."

The Malcontents turn to Matthias and Crow. The young officers straighten to offer salute.

"Wait! Know this first before you decide!" I stride before the company of Malcontents. "Wherever the fighting is thickest, that's where I'll send you. Whatever chore shall be most hazardous, you will take the lead. Wherever the peril is greatest, I shall set you in the fore. The war elephants of Porus await us across the river. You will attack them! You will vanquish them! I will deal you no slack, who have malingered and played the army false. This last chance is yours, to reclaim your honor. Choose, brothers, but choose now!"

Matthias and Crow step to the fore first. By ones and twos, then in a body the three hundred swell forward and take up their shields. The men shed their tunics of dishonor and don new mantles of redemption and restoration. The army roars in approbation.

Beyond the river, Porus cannot fail to hear. In minutes every man he has will be fallen-in under arms.

I stand forth before the army.

"I will cross this river, brothers! Who will cross it with me?"

Thirty-Six

BATTLE OF THE HYDASPES

I NEED NOT RECOUNT THE BATTLE IN DETAIL. You were there, Itanes. You fought; you conquered. I see no need to narrate for your benefit that which you have seen with your own eyes.

Let me speak instead to the significance of the fight. What it meant to me and to the army.

It was everything we needed—a contest of heroic scale against a foe who stood his ground and dueled with honor. At conflict's end, the field was ours, indeed, but, far more important, we had preserved our antagonist Porus's life and the lives of as many of his *ksatriyas* as possible; we had been able to act toward him and them with integrity and restraint; and we had conquered not only a stubborn and manful foe but our own factious and recalcitrant selves.

Here was a brilliant victory, perhaps our greatest, because it required the most innovative tactics, the most unconventional lines of assault, the greatest coordination among disparate units—three corps, separated from each other by as many as fifteen miles, across twenty-five miles of front—on both sides of a mighty river. This battle (which was in truth an amphibious assault in coordination with a battle) presented the most

complex and demanding logistical challenge the army had ever faced—
the ferrying, via seven hundred boats and eleven hundred rafts, of forty-
seven thousand men, seventy-five hundred horses (the bulk of whom
had to be crossed at night and in a monsoon), with all their weapons,
armor, and equipment, including field catapults and stone-throwers—
and demanded the greatest flexibility and improvisation of widely scattered commanders, many of whom did not speak the same language,
across a broad and unprecedented field, against an enemy fighting not
for victory alone, but to defend home and liberty. The sheer physical ar-
duousness of the operation beggared all prior endeavors, commencing as
it did with an eighteen-mile trek upriver through the mud and thunder
of an all-night deluge (which indeed hid our movements from the foe
but which also turned the channel, already swollen from preseason
downpours, into a howling torrent), then mounting to the crossing
itself—indeed the swimming, for the last third—of a nearly mile-wide
river (all this *before* the battle, even before the marshaling, on the far
shore, for the battle); then an approach march of fifteen miles, succeeded by a clash across a two-mile front, on swampy ground, against
eighteen thousand cavalry, a hundred thousand men, and two hundred
war elephants, a force such as no Western army had ever seen, let alone
confronted and defeated. This was only the physical difficulty. The
mental and emotional strain proved of equal, if not greater, magnitude.
For the fight, as it played out, involved numerous advents and incidents
of chance, surprises, changes of front, overthrows, unexpected reverses
(the most dramatic of which was my own miscalculation at the river
crossing, when our bridgehead force of seven thousand landed on what
we took for the far shore, only to discover that the current in its furious
spate had torn out a second channel beyond, which we must now swim
or die), so that scheme after scheme had to be scrapped and new designs
improvised on the fly, not only by me, in touch with my officers, but by
dozens and scores of subordinate commanders who had lost touch with
me and with one another in the confusion, distance, and duration of the
fight. The battle lasted from before nightfall on one day, when the first
columns set forth for the crossing eighteen miles above the camp, till

sunset the next, on the far side of the river, without sleep or food, except what could be cadged on the run, for men or horses. To these challenges, officers and men rose brilliantly. The assault of our Daan mounted archers upon the enemy left, followed by my Companions' flanking charge, exceeded in shock and violence even that against Darius at Gaugamela. Hephaestion was wounded three times breaking through cavalry outnumbering his squadrons five to one. Perdiccas, Ptolemy, Peithon, and Antigenes, leading sarissa brigades, and Tauron, commanding the Median and Indian archers, against a solid mile of war elephants and infantry, broke their ranks despite terrific losses and set the great beasts milling in confusion, wreaking havoc upon their own men and one another, while Coenus's charge from the wing simply broke the enemy's back. Our foreign troops were spectacular. Scythian mounted archers threw back Porus's son's chariots at the first landing; Tigranes' Persian cavalry broke the Indian right; Raj Ambhi's Royal Taxilean Horse overwhelmed Porus's Punjabi lancers; Sadocus's Thracian darters, working with our mounted Sacae and Massagetae, routed the foe in the one counterattack that truly threatened; while Matthias's and Crow's Silver Shields, and their brothers of Neoptolemus's and Seleucus's Royal Guards (the original Silver Shields), were simply invincible in the center.

For myself, even amid the debacle of the island, I fought in a state of occupation so extreme as to constitute transport. Beneath me, Bucephalus, at twenty-one years, nearly burst his heart swimming the river; I sought to spare him and move to Corona and my other remounts for the downstream trek; he would not let me. At battle's verge again I tried to hand him off to my groom Evagoras. The fury in his eye overruled me. He would not let me from his back until the lion standard of Macedon commanded all the field.

What army could have done what we did? And, most difficult of all from a command standpoint: Up until the morning of battle, the body of the corps not only resisted even taking part in the fight but very nearly mutinied and set all our works at naught. I confess I took keener satisfaction in this triumph than in any heretofore, and I saw on the faces of my generals and comrades that they felt the same. It required no proclamation to check the army's blood lust; esteem of the foe reined it of its own.

Porus himself fought magnificently. He struggled on, atop his war elephant (a hero in its own right), after suffering numerous wounds, the toll of which was so severe that when at battle's close he at last dismounted from his bunker, he could not remount on his own, but had to be lifted, so men said, by the beast's own trunk. When I dispatched Raj Ambhi to him, seeking his surrender, Porus defied this man he considered his enemy, though by this hour he knew his own cause to be without hope, and would yield at last only to the prince Beos, his friend, whom I sent next, with pledges of clemency and honorable handling for himself and his men. "How do you wish to be treated?" I asked Porus when I had caught up in person. "Like a king," he replied, and like a king we honored him.

Most gratifying of this battle's issue was its affording of an occasion for magnanimity. A noble foe may be dealt with nobly. I was able to accept from Porus not his surrender but his undertaking of alliance and to press upon him not articles of capitulation but gifts of friendship. Prisoners were repatriated within the same day, without ransom, their arms restored to them. Further it was my pleasure, in the days succeeding the fight, to vie in munificence with my new friend. The fallen of both sides were interred with honor beneath the same mound, while the bitterness of their loss was alleviated, as much as such woe can be, by oaths exchanged, both sides pledging never to take up arms against each other again.

Finally and most significantly, the men's *dynamis*, their will to fight, had been restored. The long, degrading struggle against bandits and butchers was over. Porus's gift to the army of Macedon was itself, the reanimation of its pride and esprit.

The hour was sunset, battle's close. Rain had begun. Not the deluge of the night before, but a bright, cleansing squall that turned the sky opalescent. Astride Corona, I returned, to the shorefront opposite our camp. Surgeons and medical elements of Craterus's and Meleager's brigades, which had played the holding wing on the far side of the

Hydaspes, were just now being brought over, as all available craft had till then been required for the ferrying of troops employed in the assault. A field hospital was being set up beside a farmer's plot of leeks; wounded men, Indians as well as Macedonians, were being borne in on wagons and carts. All ill will had fled. I could see, across the field, two physicians of our corps, Marsyas of Croton and Lucas of Rhodes. They had not seen me. A boy ran up to them, delivering a message. Suddenly both burst from the tent hospital and sprinted, such as they could across the muck of the field, toward a sunken road hard by the levee. My eye followed them. A clutch of soldiers huddled in postures of exigency. Clearly someone had fallen—someone of consequence.

The hair stood up all over my body. Hephaestion? No, I'd just seen him, wounded but in no danger. Craterus, Ptolemy, Perdiccas—all accounted for. I was spurring now, at the trot and then the canter. The Indians cultivate vegetables in raised beds; the wet sucking troughs clutched at Corona's shanks. As I emerged from the plot, about fifty feet from the cluster of soldiers, several, recognizing me, stood to their feet, blanched and stricken. I saw, among the kneeling troops, my groom Evagoras.

I knew then that it was not a man they labored over.

I dismounted and crossed on foot toward the company, whose ranks parted before me, the men removing their helmets and undercaps. Bucephalus lay on his right side. I saw at once that his great heart beat no more. A thousand times in imagination I had rehearsed this hour, which I knew must come, yet the impact, in the moment, was moderated not in the slightest. I felt as if a blow had been struck with titanic execution upon the plexus of my breast. The emotion was not grief for Bucephalus, for I saw that his spirit had safely fled; rather, desolation descended for me, for my own loss, and the nation's, bereft of his soul and spirit. I sunk to one knee, clutching Evagoras's arm to keep from keeling.

One of the men cradled Bucephalus's head across his thighs. My apparition, I saw, caused him distress; he feared offering offense, should he stay or rise. I placed my hand on his shoulder. "Set his head on this," I said, but I could not shed my cloak, so without strength had my arms become. Evagoras had to remove it for me. The troopers had been ministering to Bucephalus for no short time, it was clear, struggling desperately to save him. He had expired of age and exhaustion. There was nothing they could do.

"Take the names of these gentlemen," I instructed Evagoras when sense returned. They were Odrysian cavalrymen of Menidas's squadrons, commanded in his absence by Philip, son of Amyntas. I met the eyes of each. "I shall never forget your kindness here this day."

I ordered the surgeons Marsyas and Lucas to return to their duties. Wounded men needed their care. The Odrysians, too, I released. They would not go. Like the Macedones, these knights of Thrace slay a man's horse over his grave and bury both within the same crypt; they believe the mount will bear its master again in the life to come. Here in a field of leeks, with a drizzle descending, these men now offered me their own lives, and those of their horses, to consecrate Bucephalus's tomb.

"No, my friends. But each drop of blood you proffer, I shall requite to you, made of gold. Now retire to your companies, please, and bear my gratitude with you always."

Here is the eulogy I pronounced two days later over Bucephalus's grave:

"The first time I saw this horse, he was four years old and barely broken to the bit. A dealer showed him at Pella, among other magnificent specimens. Bucephalus eclipsed them as the sun the stars, but he reared and kicked and would permit no one upon his back. My father rejected him as ungovernable. I was thirteen at the time and full of myself, as boys, and princes, are. I saw at once that who mastered such a prodigy would be worthy of the world. And I reckoned, too, that to tame a spirit like his, one must break his own heart.

"No tutor has taught me more than this horse. No campaign of war has taxed my resources as has the schooling of this beast. Days and nights in thousands have I labored, boy and man, seeking to lift myself to the plane on which his soul dwelt. He has demanded everything of me, and, receiving it, has borne me beyond myself.

"This army stands here today because of Bucephalus. It was he who broke the Sacred Band at Chaeronea; no other horse could have done it. At Issus and Gaugamela, the charges of Companions did not follow me; their mounts followed Bucephalus. Yes, he could be savage; yes, he would not be ruled. But such a spirit may not be judged by standards set for lesser beings. Why does Zeus send prodigies to earth? For the same reason He makes a comet streak across the sky. To show not what has been done, but what can be."

On this site, I pronounced, I would found a city, to be called Bucephala. May heaven bless all who make their homes within its walls.

We spaded the earth atop my dear companion's mound.

"My friends, many of you have sought to console me for this loss, citing Bucephalus's long life, his love of me and of this enterprise, his fame, his place, even, among the stars. You have recalled to me that the wide world is mine to search, and from its precincts I may select any horse I wish and train it to be a second Bucephalus. I don't believe it. In all the earth we shall not find his fellow. He was, and is no more. My own end, when it comes, is by his passing rendered less hateful to me in that hope, only, that I shall meet him again in the life to come."

Thunder broke then across the plain. Heaven's bolts cleaved the sky. The men, and I, too, wondered at the might and incidence of this sign.

"Macedonians and allies, I have tested you sorely, I know. The demands I have placed upon you would have broken any lesser company. Brothers, believe in me and in one another! This victory has brought us back. We are ourselves again. Nothing else matters. Believe in our destiny and press on. No force on earth can stop us now!"

⬓⬓⬓⬓⬓

EPILOGUE

ITANES

THESE WERE THE LAST WORDS *Alexander spoke for this record. That evening, when I presented myself, he thanked me for my witness (which had now served its purpose, he declared) and commanded me to return full-time to my post with the corps. This I did.*

After a rest of thirty days, the army continued its advance to the east. It crossed the river Acesines, another mighty torrent, and the Hydraotes, adding to Porus's dominions the kingdoms of his enemies. The southwest monsoons had begun. Seventy days the army labored on, beneath stupefying deluges, amid ungodly heat, across a quagmire of mud. Illness ravaged the column. Morale plunged. Worse, natives, when queried as to the proximity of the Eastern Ocean (which Alexander had declared "not far" when he established it as the ultimate object of the expedition), reported that thousands of miles yet remained, across territory obstructed by impassable rivers, uncrossable mountains and deserts, and defended by warriors in hosts innumerable—if in fact such Ocean existed at all. As measured by the expedition surveyors, the army had marched 11,250 miles over the past eight years. At last, on the river Hyphasis, a delegation of commanders and Companions presented themselves to the king, begging him to take pity on them. The Macedonians' endurance had reached its end. They would march east no farther.

Alexander rejected this and retired in fury to his tent. On all prior occasions this device had brought the army swiftly to heel. But the men this time had set their purpose. When Alexander realized that no word or act could turn them from their course, he made a show of taking the omens, which declared, so the diviners testified, that heaven itself accorded with the wishes of his countrymen. He would not compel them onward. The army would turn back.

He who had proved invincible to every force of man or nature yielded at last to the misery of his compatriots. When they learned of his acquiescence, they flocked about his tent in thousands, weeping for joy. They blessed and praised him, rejoicing that at last they might put a period to their trials and hope to see again dear wives and children, aged fathers and mothers, and their beloved homeland, from which they had been parted for so long.

Alexander continued his conquests on the return west, bringing into subjection numerous nations and peoples, of whom the greatest were the Oxydracae, the Mallians, Brachmanes, Agalasseis, Sydracae, the kingdoms of Musicanus, Porticanus, and Sambus, and, as well, charting heretofore-undiscovered passages to the Arabian Ocean and the Persian Sea.

At Susa he took Persian brides for the most high ranking of the Companions, ninety-two in all, in one magnificent ceremony. He himself wed Darius's eldest daughter, Stateira, selecting for Hephaestion her sister Drypetis, it being his wish that his children and Hephaestion's be cousins. He presented dowries to all the Companions and their brides, as well as a golden cup to every man of Macedon (some ten thousand, when they registered) who had taken a consort of the East.

At Ecbatana, two years after turning back, Hephaestion took fever and died. In seemed the earth itself could not contain Alexander's grief. To honor his friend, he commanded the construction of a monument two hundred feet high, at a cost of ten thousand talents. He ordered the manes of every horse and mule cropped in mourning and directed even that the battlements of the empire be broken down, every other one, so they appeared as if they wept.

I served the king then as a captain in the agema of the Companions, so that I stood in his presence between six and twelve hours a day. I may state, and you may believe, that, though he displayed without fail a cheerful and enterprising mien, yet, from the death of Hephaestion, he was never the same man.

For the first time, he began to speak of his own death and to project with apprehension the strife that must follow, predicting the succession struggles that would inevitably ensue. Roxanne was with child then. Alexander warned me to look to her safety and my own, for, when he was gone, ambitious men would discover means to discredit and disown us, if not murder us outright, to further their own ends.

Alexander returned to Babylon and turned his attention to future campaigns. He planned to bring Arabia next beneath his sway. In late spring of the eleventh year after his crossing out of Europe into Asia, he took sick. His state deteriorated rapidly over the succeeding days; no measure of the physicians availed.

The soldiers of the army, driven frantic by the rumor that their king had succumbed, and refusing to believe reassurances of their officers that he still lived, swarmed about the palace, demanding entry to him in person. This was granted. One by one, Alexander's comrades filed past his bed, dressed in their military tunics. The king could no longer speak, but he recognized each soldier and blessed him with his eyes. The following evening, his spirit departed from life among men. The date was 15 Thargelion of the Athenian calendar, 28 Daesius of the Macedonian, in the first year of the 114th Olympiad.

Alexander was thirty-two years, eight months old.

No portrayal of mine could represent the passion of lamentation that succeeded his decease, save to say that Persians and Macedonians vied in extravagance of woe, the former bewailing the loss of so mild and gracious a master, the latter the end of their brilliant and peerless king.

It is a measure of Alexander's superhuman personality and achievements that at his death the chronicle of his days did not remain as history even for an hour, but vaulted at once into the sphere of legend. Such fables of his exploits proliferated as no mortal could have accomplished. His passing left a hole at the center of the world. And yet at the same time, his presence remained so powerfully that when in succeeding seasons his generals contested one another bitterly over division of the empire, they could be made to convene civilly by one dispensation only: that they meet in Alexander's tent, before his vacant throne, upon which rested the king's crown and scepter. Men feared to offend even the shade of Alexander, lest they encounter him again beneath the earth, for surely in that world, too, none would surpass him.

And now, perhaps, it may not be out of place for this witness to speak from his own heart.

I leave to historians the reckoning of Alexander the king. Let me address only the man. Many have indicted him for the vice of self-inflation (as if these critics would have proved superior to it in his place), yet I found him the most kind and knightly of men. He treated me, a youth, as a comrade and as a soldier, never condescending, always opening his heart absent artifice.

No one was less impressed than he with the scale of his triumphs. He stated in this journal that he wished only to be a soldier. That he was. He was superior to heat and cold, hunger and fatigue, and, what is more, to greed and cupidity. Time and again, I watched him turn the choicest portions to his comrades. His bed was a camp cot; he dressed in moments, despising all adornment and superfluity. Winter and summer were the same to him; his idea of hell was absence of toil. He was more himself amid adversity and craved never ease, but hardship and danger. No man was more loved by his comrades or more feared by his enemies. He needed no speeches to fire the hearts of his fellows (though none excelled him as an orator), only to show himself before them. The sight of their king in arms rendered timid men brave and brave men prodigious. His years of campaign were not thirteen. Who has won what he has? Who shall ever again?

What Alexander said of his beloved Bucephalus may be applied to his own case: that he belonged to no one, not even himself, but only to heaven.

> Why does Zeus send prodigies to earth? For the same reason He makes a comet streak across the sky. To show not what has been done, but what can be.

I would add of Alexander that he was human, if anything too human, for his glories and excesses alike were spawned of passion and noble aspiration, never bloodless calculation. The inner plane upon which he dwelt was peopled not by his contemporaries but by Achilles and Hector, Heracles and Homer. He was not a man of his time, though no one ever shaped an epoch so powerfully, but of an era of gallantry and heroic ideals, which perhaps never existed save in his imagination, spawned by the verses of the poet. Since his death, I have not heard one man who knew him speak a word against him. His faults and crimes are eclipsed in the brilliance of his apparition, which we perceive now with terrible clarity, made bereft by its absence.

I close this document with an anecdote of India. On the river Hyphasis, when the army refused to go on, Alexander erected twelve great altars to mark for the ages the farthest limit of his conquests. I attended among numerous officers at the dedication of these monuments. The day was bright and windy, as it often is in that country in intervals between torrential downpours. As the party turned back toward camp, Telamon, the Arcadian mercenary, presented himself before the king. Apparently he and Alexander had an understanding of many years—that of all the army, Telamon alone might claim his discharge at any time, any place. This he now did.

Alexander reacted first with surprise and regret, at the prospect of being deprived of his friend's much-loved company, yet he at once recovered, offering to load the man down with treasure. What did Telamon wish? Money, women, an escort-at-arms? With a smile, the Arcadian declared that he bore on his person all he required. This, one could see, was nothing but a staff, some utensils, and a modest pack. Alexander, struck by this, asked the mercenary where he intended to go.

Telamon indicated the high road east, upon which a number of Indian pilgrims then trekked. "These fellows interest me." He wished, he said, to make himself their student.

"To learn what?" Alexander inquired.

"What comes after being a soldier."

Alexander smiled and extended his right hand.

Telamon clasped it. "Come with me," he said.

I stood directly to Alexander's left, as close to him as a man is to his own arm. It seemed to me that for a moment the king truly considered this. Then he laughed. Of course he could not go. Already aides and chancellors were calling him apart to other business. The grooms brought the party's horses. Something made me remain at Telamon's side. As Alexander prepared to mount, a sad, sweet piping caught his ear. He turned toward the sound. There, where the

Royal Lancers had made their temporary camp, a brace of cavalry sarissas stood upright, at the ready. The wind passing across their serried shafts produced the melancholy chord.

"The sarissas are singing, Telamon," said Alexander. "Tell me, will you miss their song?"

The king and the mercenary exchanged a valedictory glance; then one of Alexander's Pages boosted him onto Corona's back.

I half-recalled the tale of the sarissas' song, but could not bring back the full story. What was it? I asked the Arcadian. Telamon was about to answer, when Alexander, overhearing, turned back, in the saddle, and responded himself.

> The sarissa's song is a sad song.
> He pipes it soft and low.
> I would ply a gentler trade, says he,
> But war is all I know.

The wind rose in that moment, lifting the corner of Alexander's cloak. I saw his heel tap Corona's flank. He reined about and started for the camp, surrounded by his officers.

IN GRATITUDE

Of course to the ancient writers, Arrian, Curtius, Diodorus, Justin, Plutarch, Polybius, and others, but thanks also to the many brilliant contemporary scholars whose concepts, insights, and reimaginings of Alexander's battles I have looted shamelessly: A. B. Bosworth, P. A. Brunt, Peter Connolly, A. M. Devine, Theodore Dodge, Donald Engels, Robin Lane Fox, J. F. C. Fuller, Peter Green, G. T. Griffith, George Grote, J. R. Hamilton, N. G. L. Hammond, Victor Davis Hanson, B. H. Liddell Hart, Waldemar Heckel, D. G. Hogarth, E. W. Marsden, R. D. Milns, Sir Aurel Stein, John Warry, Benjamin Wheeler, and Ulrich Wilcken. I am indebted also to the memoirs and maxims of Caesar, Vegetius, Napoleon, Marshal Saxe, Frederick the Great, and particularly Baron de Marbot, for his swashbuckling tales of cavalry warfare. I'd also like to thank the translators and editors of the Loeb Classical Library Series; their notes and indices, interweaving all works in the series, and particularly the appendices, are tremendously helpful to any researcher, and the texts are impeccable. To my outstanding editor, Bill Thomas, for the original idea, to my in-the-trenches editor, Katie Hall, whose contributions to this manuscript have been innumerable and invaluable. To my secret weapon, author-editor Printer Bowler, and to Gene Kraay, who first sent me an article on the battle of Gaugamela and said, "This might be of interest to you." Big thanks to Erica Poseley for her expertise on equestrian matters, and to Dr. Linda Rydgig and Dr. Brad Dygert for their equine and veterinary wisdom. To Steffen White for his indefatigable creativity in supporting and promoting this project. And to Dr. Hip Kantzios, as always, for being my guru in all things Greek.

Epigraph reprinted by permission of the publishers and the Trustees of the Loeb Classical Library from XENOPHON: CYROPAEDIA, VOLUMES V and VI, Loeb Classical Library ® Volumes 51 and 52, translated by Walter Miller, pp. 9, 19, Cambridge, Mass.: Harvard University Press, 1914. The Loeb Classical Library ® is a registered trademark of the President and Fellows of Harvard College.

CHRONOLOGY B.C.

331   BATTLE OF GAUGAMELA

331/330   ALEXANDER CAPTURES BABYLON, SUSA, PERSEPOLIS,
           ECBATANA; DEATH OF DARIUS

330–327   ANTIGUERRILLA CAMPAIGN IN AFGHANISTAN

326   ALEXANDER CROSSES HINDU KUSH TO INDIA; BATTLE OF
           THE HYDASPES

326   ALEXANDER'S TROOPS REFUSE TO GO FARTHER

323   ALEXANDER RETURNS TO BABYLON

323   DEATH OF ALEXANDER AT THIRTY-TWO